THE ACCIDENT

FIONA LOWE

PRAISE FOR FIONA LOWE

"Greed, self-interest and moral drama feature in the latest novel by Fiona Lowe, the undisputed queen of Australian small-town fiction ... *The Money Club* is another enjoyable character-driven tale by Lowe that will keep you happily entertained." — *Canberra Weekly*

"A gripping tale about greed, the price paid for ill-placed trust and the lessons that come with having it and losing it all ... Ultimately, *The Money Club* is about hope." — *Weekend Australian*

"*A Family of Strangers* is an engaging, thoughtful and astute novel." — Book'd Out

"Rich, thought-provoking, and extremely absorbing, *A Home Like Ours* is yet another incredible read from the very talented Fiona Lowe."— Better Reading

"An insightful, warm and engaging story, *A Home Like Ours* is another fabulous novel from award-winning Australian author Fiona Lowe." — *Book'd Out*

ALSO BY FIONA LOWE

First Published in Australia in 2024 by
HQ Fiction an imprint of HQ Books, a subsidiary of Harper Collins Publishers Australia
Pty Ltd

This revised USA edition published in 2024 by Fiona Lowe
© 2024 by Fiona Lowe
All rights reserved.
www.fionalowe.com

To Rachael Donovan for her belief and unstinting support, and for always adding a pearl to the story line.

***

Do nothing secretly; for Time sees and hears all things and discloses all.

Sophocles

PROLOGUE

"POLICE, FIRE OR AMBULANCE?" The dispatcher spoke slowly and clearly, knowing the caller on the other end of the line was likely panicked.

"All of them!"

Yep. Freaking out. He took a deep breath. "Can you tell me what's happened?"

"An accident. Oh God! I think they're dead."

"What sort of accident?"

"It's awful! The car's upside down. I can see a man but there may be others. I can't open the door. Help me!"

"Where are you?"

"I don't know," the woman wailed. "I'm not from round here."

"Where are you traveling from?" He kept his voice calm despite the jittery sensation bubbling in his veins. These were the tough calls where logic and sleuthing fought the clock.

"Perth," she sobbed.

"And where are you heading?"

"Um ... it's ... hang on." There was the sound of papers scrunching. "Gar ... Gar-Garring-gar-up. Is that how you say it?"

"Garringarup." He brought up the map. A series of spoke roads radiated in all directions from the heritage Wheatbelt town. Coming from Perth, the woman could be on one of three roads, but it was likely the Great Southern Highway. Only he'd been doing this job for too long to depend on "likely." "Do you have GPS coordinates?"

"I don't know! How do I get them?"

He gave a moment's thought to explaining how to locate the coordinates but worried the spiraling woman may disconnect the call in the process. "Do you remember the name of the last town you drove through?"

"No."

"Do you remember anything about it?"

"It had a pub."

In small-town WA that didn't narrow it down any.

"Do you remember any signs or something like a sculpture that may give me a clue?"

There was a beat of silence. He hoped it meant she was thinking— not that they'd been disconnected.

"Um ... the ah, um ... the pub was Brook something? It's on one of those brown tourist drives."

He googled and found the Avon Valley tourist drive that ran north to south. Perth was west so he disregarded the origin of the woman's journey. "Did you come through Northam and Spencers Brook?"

"Yes!"

"And how long since you passed the tavern?"

"I don't know! Three or four songs."

"Are you still on that same road?"

There was no reply.

"Are you there?"

He swore under his breath. He logged the information he had into the computer aided-system, alerting Garringarup to the priority-one accident requiring police, ambulance and a fire truck with jaws of life. Then he typed *coordinates coming*. At least he hoped they were. Considering how patchy the cell-phone coverage was in the Wheatbelt there were no guarantees. Country life was idyllic until there was an emergency. Then the remoteness combined with a lack of service made surviving a life-threatening accident so much harder than in a city.

He rang the woman back and held his breath, hoping a tower pinged her phone.

She answered with her name, her voice breathless. "Is the ambulance coming? There's also a man and a little girl." Her voice rose to a shriek. "I found them in the ditch!"

He added *at least three seriously injured* to the log. "Juliet, are you still on the tourist road?"

"I don't know. I took the road to Garringarup."

He stared at the map. The tourist road would have led her into town so where the hell had the GPS taken her? There were at least two gravel roads she could be on. He had no choice—he was going to have to talk the distressed woman through the coordinates and hope the line didn't fall out again.

"Juliet, I need you to listen to me carefully. Can you do that?"

"There's so much blood." Her anguished cry eviscerated him. "And no one's moving."

CHAPTER ONE

THE JOLT of the Boeing 787's wheels connecting with the tarmac made Hannah Simmons grip the armrests and press her back into her seat. She didn't realize she was holding her breath until the plane slowed and the flight attendant said, "Welcome to Perth International Airport. Local time is 12:20."

Hannah glanced out the window at the ominous gray sky and shivered. Her tank top, perfect for the heat and humidity of Singapore, wouldn't be enough to keep her warm on a Perth winter's day. The moment the seatbelt sign switched off she dug her pashmina out of her backpack, then switched on her phone. A raft of pings sounded as messages downloaded. The first was from her brother, Declan, who'd driven her to Changi airport.

Hope flight was uneventful. Great to see you. Next time bring Jamie. Dx

The week in Singapore had been a mix of grief and comfort—the fourth anniversary of their parents' deaths in India early in the pandemic. Hannah appreciated Declan's gift of paying her airfare so she could spend the week with him, sharing memories and leaning on each other.

Neither of them would ever forget the phone call from the Australian Consulate giving them the shocking news. Two weeks later, after the memorial service, Declan's response to the trauma was to throw himself harder onto the international banking ladder. It was as if his life depended on early career success. Still very much single, he'd now been in Singapore for three years and Hannah tried hard not to give in to irrational feelings that her entire family had abandoned her. She was mostly successful, reminding herself that the weekly video calls with Declan were no different than when he'd lived over east. She just wished he lived a lot closer.

Hannah's reaction to their parents' deaths had been the opposite of Declan's. Floundering in everyday life, she'd been unable to make any big decisions, so instead of using her recently acquired marketing degree she'd stayed on at the call center and a part-time student job had slowly morphed into an unanticipated career. She'd risen through the ranks and gained the skills and experience to manage a large team, but she hadn't loved it. It had remained very much *just a job*. Meanwhile her friends had used the passing years to kick career goals, get married, buy houses and travel. Hannah hadn't appreciated their pity or their judgment about the fact that, unlike them, she was treading water rather than actively engaging in her life. For her own mental health, she'd eventually withdrawn from that group, socializing instead with her call-center colleagues—mostly students—who were free of judgment. But by the time she turned twenty-seven, she was very aware that she didn't fit comfortably in that group either.

It was at a New Year's Eve party a year ago, surrounded by drunk and affectionate drugged-up early twenty-somethings, that she'd decided she could at least take charge of her love life. She'd caught an Uber home, brushed up her profile on the dating apps and started scrolling. Jamie's profile had sounded great, but she'd prevaricated over his photo—he dressed like a nerd, and not a sexy one at that. But there'd been something about his eyes that called to her. That, and he was holding a border collie puppy. She was a sucker for a puppy, so she'd tapped the screen.

A couple of days of surprisingly flirty messaging had followed, along with some deeper conversations that made Hannah float on air. But the day of their first meeting, she'd walked into the café in a state of heightened anxiety. Would the intellectual chemistry that had fizzed between them in the messages be matched by physical attraction? Hannah didn't want to be shallow, but she was honest enough to know that she needed that spark or Jamie would plonk straight into the friend zone.

Her anxiety intensified when she glanced around the café, unable to see Jamie amid the throw cushions, the hanging plants and the vivid acrylic artworks. Had he stood her up?

Then, in the far corner, half-camouflaged by a stand of succulents, a bloke raised his hand and smiled. Hannah's heart lurched and her knees softened. No wonder she hadn't recognized Jamie. There was no sign of a scruffy T-shirt, glasses that needed to be binned or hair that demanded a cut. Instead, he wore a pressed pale blue Oxford shirt, sexy retro metal and tortoiseshell JFK-style glasses, and his chestnut hair was styled. He looked older than his photo suggested, but his profile had said *thirties*, which wasn't a lie although Hannah had expected just thirty rather than mid.

He must have read the surprise on her face because when she slid into the seat opposite, he gave a wry smile. "I probably should update my profile picture."

"Please don't," she blurted, then slapped her hand over her mouth as her cheeks burned.

He'd grinned then, a sexy twinkle flashing in his eyes. "I'll take that under advisement, Ms. Simmons."

As she'd already shown her hand Hannah thought she may as well keep going. "So why did you use that photo?"

He'd shrugged. "Back then I was in a different place and nowhere near ready to get back into dating. But well-meaning friends were pushing me, so to get them off my back I registered and threw up the photo. It did the job. I didn't interact with anyone and no one contacted me."

Hannah stared at him, gob smacked. "Are you saying in all that time, I'm the only person?"

"Yep. And to be honest, I'd forgotten all about the account, so the notification was a total surprise." His mouth curved up and the smile filled his eyes. "But when a gorgeous and intelligent woman randomly reaches out, I'd be nuts to say no."

The cheerleader inside Hannah had squealed and danced. He thought she was gorgeous and intelligent!

Jamie was an adult with a successful business and, compared to her, financially established. He made every other bloke she'd ever dated look like a boy. She'd soon discovered that he was thoughtful, attentive and incredibly supportive of her too. He made soothing sounds when she ranted about the job she hated and didn't roll out solutions or useless suggestions like "change jobs." He seemed to understand that of course she'd change jobs if she had a clue what else to do.

Unlike her, he'd grown up in the bush and she knew his move to Perth had been precipitated by a bad breakup. He took her to Garringarup, his hometown, for the first time on their one-month anniversary. Two months later he'd told her, "With online meetings, I only need to be in Perth three days a week so I'm moving the business back home."

The words had hit Hannah with the tingling shock of iced water, but before she could formulate a reply, Jamie had pulled her into his arms and stroked her face. "Come with me," he said.

Her brain had lurched violently from disaster to delight. Somehow, over her internal shrieks of joy, she'd managed to ask, "What would I do in a small country town?"

His answer had been simple. "Whatever you want."

Jamie was offering her a gift that she desperately wanted to accept, but her mother's voice had come back to her loud and clear: *Hannah, every woman needs her own money.*

So, she'd kissed him full on the mouth, infusing him with her thanks, then said, "As wonderful as it sounds, I don't feel comfortable about you supporting me financially. I need to pay my way."

Surprise had lit up his eyes. "Really? Wow, okay ..." He was quiet for a moment, clearly deep in thought. "How about this then? My bookkeeper's taking off around Australia in a few weeks. Why don't you do her job until you find something that floats your boat?" He'd grinned. "I pay above award rates and the rent's cheap. Even cheaper if you cook now and then."

She'd shot out her hand. "Deal."

Nine months later, she was still sharing an office with Jamie, chasing down money from clients who were slow to pay and using her marketing skills to promote his IT consultancy business. She loved working with him and knew her contributions streamlined and improved operations, freeing him up to concentrate on his areas of expertise—coding and acquiring new accounts. And whenever she heard her mother's voice reminding her that every woman needed her own income, she'd think, *I'm investing in my future, Mum.*

Hannah had been welcomed and embraced by Jamie's family and friends, and life in Garringarup, although quiet, was enjoyable. The only thing to improve it would be a sign from Jamie that they were a forever couple. In her mind they totally were, but Jamie was yet to declare it either formally or informally. Of course she wanted marriage and children, but she'd settle for a declaration of permanence and an opportunity to buy a share in Jamie's house. Mostly she wanted to divest herself of all ambiguity.

She was leery of pushing Jamie too hard too soon though. He'd been upfront with her when they'd met, telling her about his devastating breakup with his long-term girlfriend, Monique. "It rocked me," he'd said. "I was pretty useless for a couple of years."

Everyone in Garringarup wanted to tell her about Monique and did so on her first visit. It had been a relief to discover the woman had moved away and Hannah wasn't faced with a daily comparison.

"Poor Jamie, having his heart broken like that," his mother, Lydia, had said to Hannah the first time they'd met. "Thank goodness he's found you and can finally get on with his life."

But a year on, Hannah's tight grip on those heartening words was slipping.

She read the second message on her phone. *Welcome home! Call into Just Because when you can and tell me all about your trip. Freya x*

Warmth filled her and she added a heart emoji to the text. Freya and her partner, Ryan, were the serendipitous gift in Hannah's move to Garringarup. They were Jamie's long-time friends and initially Hannah had thought Freya was only being hospitable because of that, but she'd discovered Freya genuinely liked her. Their friendship had grown and now Freya was to Hannah what Ryan was to Jamie—a best friend. Freya would drop everything if Hannah needed her, and Hannah would do the same for her.

The third message was from Lydia. *In case Jamie didn't tell you, it's family dinner at the farm tomorrow night. Just bring yourselves.*

Hannah scanned the remaining messages on her phone—a reminder about her dental appointment, an overdue library book and a sale on her favorite eco-friendly cleaning system. Nothing from Jamie. Disappointment thwacked her. She'd tried calling him from Changi, but it had gone straight to voice mail, so she'd been certain she'd land to a *sorry, poss, see you soon* message.

Hannah couldn't wait to see him. While she'd been away, they'd spent more time playing phone tag than actually talking because Jamie was negotiating a new deal that had involved back-to-back meetings and a lot of after-hours entertaining. The one time they'd actually connected he'd been so unusually distracted that she'd experienced a lingering sadness for the rest of the day. She'd hated that she couldn't shake the feeling, but hated herself more for the doubts that had snuck in.

In a rare moment of perspicacity Declan had said, "Just ask him."

"Ask him what?"

"To marry you."

"I can't do that!"

He'd given her his big-brother-knows-best look. "Sure you can. He'll either say yes or no. Then you'll know exactly where you stand."

That's what terrified her. But Declan was right. Good news or bad, it would give her much-needed direction.

But first she had to get home to Garringarup.

Immigration was sluggish as three planes had landed at the same time and it took forever for Hannah's suitcase to slide onto the baggage carousel. While she waited she called Jamie. It rang out. Why wasn't he answering his cell phone?

As she entered the arrivals hall, she glanced around at the excited family groups waving *Welcome Home* banners and chauffeurs holding signs with their passengers' surnames, but she couldn't spot Jamie anywhere. She sternly told herself that Jamie wasn't the sort of boyfriend—partner—who would expect her to take a two-hour bus journey after an international flight. Then again, he spent every Monday through Wednesday working in Perth and today was Thursday. She gave herself a shake—she was being ridiculous. Jamie would have just stayed an extra night in Perth at the apartment.

She noticed people falling back to give way to what looked like a walking floral arrangement.

"Han!" A deep male voice came from behind the scarlet roses.

It sounded like Jamie, but he was the last bloke to bring one rose to the airport, let alone fifty. He showed his love in far more practical ways—filling her car with fuel, pumping up her bike tires, meeting her with coffee and a pastry.

She glanced at the man's pants and shoes—moleskins and polished RMs. "Oh my God ... Jamie?"

"Welcome back, poss." He pressed the bouquet into her arms.

"Um, ah, thank you. These are amazing."

As she struggled to hold them, she realized Jamie was no longer standing in front of her but kneeling. A murmur of anticipation shot around the arrivals hall and the volume of chatter instantly dropped. A prickle of sensation whooshed over Hannah's skin—every set of eyes in the place was trained on her.

Desperate to see Jamie's face, she lowered the flowers, resting them on the top of her suitcase. "Hi," she said, her heart suddenly thumping in the back of her throat.

He aimed his familiar and endearing smile straight at her. "Hi."

He sounded nervous, and nothing fazed Jamie McMaster. Hannah's heart skipped and her love for him surged.

"Hannah Rose." He cleared his throat. "Poss. From the moment we met you've changed my life for the better. I love waking up beside you every morning and going to sleep beside you every night. I love that you're as passionate about the success of our business as I am, and I appreciate how much time and effort you put into every aspect of our lives to make them the best they can be. I've never met anyone like you and I'm privileged that you came into my life when you did."

She was trying hard to listen, to remember his words so she could lose herself in them again and again, but excitement squealed in her mind, almost deafening her. Jamie was proposing!

His mouth drew down for a moment. "I thought I'd been in love once before, but you've shown me those feelings didn't come close. And if I hadn't realized months ago that what I feel when I'm with you is ecstatic happiness and a sense of completeness that carries me through the day, then this last week without you would have told me. I want you in my life, Hannah, by my side as we take on the future together as a team."

He flicked open a midnight-blue velvet ring box and Hannah gasped. Nestled in the folds of material was a brilliant-cut pink diamond, its clarity so dazzling she almost squinted.

Hope filled his eyes. "Will you make me the happiest man alive by marrying me?"

Her heart flipped and, as impossible as it seemed, her love for him grew. How could he entertain the slightest doubt about her answer? Like him, she wanted to live every day of their lives together. She wanted to be his wife and lover. His business partner. The mother of his children. She needed him as much as she needed air.

"Come on, love," a man with a stringy gray beard called out. "Don't leave the poor bloke hanging."

"Don't leave us hanging, you mean," someone else said.

Overwhelmed by the moment she'd long dreamed about, Hannah held her hands up around her mouth. They muffled her first yes.

Jamie swallowed. "Hannah?"

She dropped her hands and grabbed his, pulling him to his feet. "Yes! Yes, a thousand times yes!"

He grinned and, still holding the ring box, pulled her into a bear hug, picked her up and spun her around. "Thank God," he whispered into her hair as the crowd of strangers applauded and cheered.

"Put that ring on her finger," someone called out.

Laughing, Hannah pulled back and Jamie slid the engagement ring smoothly into place. She couldn't stop gazing at it, marveling at its beauty.

"It's absolutely perfect. How did you know this is exactly what I wanted?"

"Because I know you," he said simply.

The words wrapped around her with the comfort of a weighted blanket, the moment distilling everything down to its essence. He loved and respected her, and her happiness was the most important thing to him.

She rose on her toes and kissed him. "I love you so much."

"Right back at you."

He handed her the roses, grabbed the handle of her suitcase, then swung his free arm around her waist and turned her towards the exit. "Let's go plan a wedding and start the rest of our lives."

CHAPTER TWO

Freya Quayle surveyed the new display of artfully arranged baby gifts—organic cotton wraps, hand-embroidered blankets, board books, silver-plated money boxes and tiny, but decidedly cute, sheepskin baby booties. She smiled. There was something about the miniature versions of adult clothing that made even the most pragmatic person—and she included herself in that category—sigh. Not to mention the dollars they generated.

The baby section was a recent addition to her homewares and gift business, Just Because. Until recently, she'd only stocked a few items as a courtesy for older locals who didn't want to drive to Perth, but the unexpectedly healthy sales meant the section had quickly outgrown its small table. On a weekend away in York, she and Ryan had discovered an old 1950s bookcase and once it had been sanded back and painted in pastel colors it was the perfect display piece. The retro-chic look made the products shout "buy me now."

This was what Freya loved most about her business: it was constantly evolving and surprising her. When she'd announced her plans to open Just Because and focus on showcasing the talent of the Wheatbelt by stocking as many locally made products as possible, there'd been plenty of nay-sayers. She'd proved them all wrong. She was incredibly proud of what she'd achieved during six years of hard work and she was excited about the future, especially now that Garringarup was on the gourmet-food tourist route. The chic B & Bs in newly restored heritage buildings and the recent addition of a celebrity chef's paddock-to-plate restaurant were attracting Perth's Gen-Xers with their healthy disposable incomes. Freya benefitted from them popping into Just Because to buy something to remind them of their relaxing weekend away or their cheeky midweek sojourn.

Her cell phone rang and she was surprised to hear Ryan's ringtone. He was a community paramedic and almost never rang her from work —"I'm too busy saving lives," he'd always quip. Freya didn't mind; her workdays were busy too.

"Hey, what's up?" she said.

"We don't have anything on tonight, do we?"

"No." What she didn't say was, "And thank God Hannah's home so Jamie won't be dropping in for dinner."

Jamie was Ryan's best mate and Freya had always respected their friendship, but after three nights of feeding and entertaining him, she wanted Ryan to herself. "Do you have something in mind?"

"A night in, just the two of us. I've got eye fillet roasting, a bottle of cab merlot breathing and the fire's roaring."

She smiled at the thought of snuggling up with Ryan on the sofa, grateful he recognized that he and Jamie had monopolized the last few evenings with talk of plans for junior cricket, Jamie's business and tales of growing up together.

"I'm so in," she said.

"Excellent. Don't get distracted by tweaking the new baby display and be late, okay?"

She laughed. "As if. Be home in fifteen."

But she closed up the shop as soon as the call ended to make sure she didn't get caught up with ordering or display tweaking like she often did. It was rarely an issue if she did stay late at work. Ryan was just as much a workaholic as she was, both of them committed to giving one hundred and ten percent to their careers. But that didn't mean they didn't put their relationship first—their almost ten years together was testament to that.

An hour later Freya was lying on the sofa, her head on Ryan's lap, watching purple, orange and yellow flames licking and dancing around a mallee log.

"Thanks for this," she said.

Ryan stroked her hair. "Too easy. Thanks for being so accommodating with Jamie."

She breathed out so she didn't flinch. "Do you think he took on board what we said about Hannah?"

"We?" Ryan laughed. "It was pretty much all you."

She turned and looked up at him. "But you agree, right?"

"That she's the best thing that ever happened to him and she runs rings around Monique? Absolutely."

"And he needs to stop dithering and commit to her, or she may just go back to Perth."

"You also said if that happened you'd never forgive him."

"Sometimes things just need to be said."

He shot her a wry smile. "And you didn't hold back. Even if Hannah wasn't home tonight, I doubt Jamie would turn up in case he got another night of unsolicited life advice."

Freya tensed. It was a constant battle to stay impartial when it came to Ryan and Jamie's friendship. "You think I was too direct?"

The original 1915 doorbell pealed long and loud, surprising them both, and a splash of red wine from Ryan's glass landed on Freya's blouse.

"Who the hell is that?" she said.

Ryan rose to answer the door. "It won't be Jamie. He always uses the back door."

"Everyone uses the back door."

Battling unease, Freya checked her phone for messages from her mother and sister, but thankfully the only text was advertising a sale on her favorite cleaning spray. She walked into the kitchen to sponge her blouse and as she was dabbing at the stain she heard the rumble of male voices and a very familiar giggle.

"Frey," Ryan called out. "It's Hannah and Jamie. Get the champagne glasses."

She ran into the hall, hope raising her heart into her mouth. *Please, please, please.*

The moment she saw Hannah's shining eyes she knew. "Oh my God, is this what I think it is?"

Startled, Hannah looked at Jamie. "So you really didn't tell them?"

"I don't tell them everything," Jamie said, a hint of self-righteousness in his tone.

"Yeah, right," Hannah teased. "I believe you."

Ryan was slapping Jamie on the back and Hannah waved her left hand at Freya, who didn't have to feign being blinded by the sparkling pink diamond.

"It's beautiful. Congratulations." Freya hugged her friend. "I'm so happy for you." *And relieved,* but she kept that to herself.

Freya quickly put together her signature cheese platter while Ryan poured champagne, then they returned to the living room where Hannah regaled them with Jamie's proposal.

"It was so romantic. I just wish someone had filmed it so I could listen to it again."

Jamie, whose arm had been around Hannah's waist ever since they'd arrived, pulled her even closer. "It's engraved on my heart so I can do it as many times as you like."

Freya was so happy about the engagement she didn't even roll her eyes or exchange a "you've got to be kidding me" look with Ryan.

"I bet Lydia and Ian are over the moon," she said, thinking about how furious Jamie's mother had been when Monique had dumped him.

"They couldn't be happier," Jamie said. "In fact, we're getting married on the farm."

Freya glanced at Hannah for signs of disquiet, but Hannah was nodding her agreement.

"With Mum and Dad gone and Declan in Singapore, I'm not tied to Perth. This way we can get married in a few months instead of waiting for a date at a function center."

"Oh wow, that's soon," Freya said, internally cheering.

"Why wait?" Jamie said. "I'd do it tomorrow, but Mum and Dad want to throw a big wedding and Declan needs to be involved. I'm looking forward to getting to know him."

"We video called Dec from the airport," Hannah said. "Jamie asked him to be a groomsman, which was so lovely, but I want him to give me away."

"And getting married on the farm means you'll be surrounded by your new family and friends, and that's exactly what you deserve," Jamie said before looking at Ryan. "Mate, you have to be my best man."

Ryan swallowed and Freya put a reassuring hand on his thigh. She knew he hated having the spotlight turned on him, but his long friendship with Jamie was too important to him to refuse.

"Be an honor, mate."

"That deserves a toast with some of that single malt I gave you for Christmas," Jamie said.

"The one that only gets drunk when you're over?"

Jamie grinned. "That's the one. It's the perfect bevvie to discuss my bucks night."

"No eating sushi off naked women," Hannah teased.

Jamie looked askance. "I was thinking something along the lines of lawn bowling and a few beers."

Freya laughed and picked up the champagne bottle. "Come on, Han. Let's leave these two and go talk wedding plans."

Hannah followed her into the kitchen and they sat on stools at the breakfast bar.

"I'm not sure if you have a vision for the wedding," Freya said, "but we have a marquee if that helps."

Hannah looked sheepish. "I've spent the last six months daydreaming about a wedding, so I do have a vision, but before we talk about it, I want to ask you something. Will you be my maid of honor?"

Freya blinked as a rush of emotion hit her. Initially she'd reached out to the younger woman because Ryan was Jamie's best mate and the two men had asked her to help Hannah settle into Garringarup. She'd never expected them to become anything more than acquaintances, but she'd quickly realized Hannah was funny, loyal and supportive. What was originally an obligation had grown into a strong and close friendship.

"Are you absolutely sure?" Freya asked. "I mean of course I'd love to be your maid of honor but don't feel obliged just because Jamie asked Ryan. They've known each other since the sandpit. Are you sure you don't want to ask a friend from Perth?"

Hannah shook her head. "It's nothing to do with longevity and everything to do with connection. My friends in Perth slowly fell away when they didn't understand my grief for Mum and Dad. It was hard, but looking back I think we would have grown apart anyway. Our bond came from school and uni, not necessarily from having things in common. Outside of Jamie, meeting you, and Ryan, has been the best part of living in Garringarup. You get me, and not everyone in town does."

"Well, that makes two of us," Freya said. "Not everyone in town gets me either. In fact, I think I confuse the heck out of many." She raised her champagne flute to Hannah's. "Thank you. I would love to be your maid of honor and I'm happy to help in any way with the wedding. I have a big list of supply contacts through Just Because and I can wrangle some good prices out of them."

"That sounds amazing. Thanks." Hannah gave her a long look.

"What?"

Hannah's cheeks pinked. "It's nothing."

Freya laughed. "I know that look. You want to ask me something. Go on, spit it out."

Hannah took a slug of her champagne. "It's just ... you and Ryan."

"What about me and Ryan?"

"You're so happy for Jamie and me."

Freya didn't understand. "Of course we are. We're thrilled. More thrilled than I can say. After Monique, Jamie deserved to meet someone like you. The two of you belong together." Despite the slight pinch in her gut she honestly believed it.

"And you're such a tight couple so I've been wondering ..." Hannah spun her champagne flute. "Why aren't you married?"

Freya laughed, used to the question from newly engaged couples hyped up on love and tradition. "One of the many things that bond Ryan and me is that neither of us wants to get married. Ten years on and that glue's still strong."

Hannah's brow furrowed. "So, it really doesn't bother you that Ryan's never proposed?"

"Not at all. But my mother's a different story. She used to push it a lot, but since Kane walked out on Lexie she's backed right off. She knows I'll win the argument that marriage isn't a cast-iron guarantee of together forever. For me and Ryan, buying this house together was more significant than a piece of paper. What we have works for us, but that doesn't mean we're anti-marriage for other people."

"But what about when you have kids?" Hannah asked.

Freya almost said, "Kids probably aren't for us either," but tonight wasn't the time for that conversation. "Plenty of unmarried couples have children."

Hannah was gazing at her engagement ring with a dreamy look on her face. "I guess. But for me, I want to be married before we start a family."

Freya took a long slug of her champagne. "So, you and Jamie have talked about kids?"

Hannah's phone rang and she checked the screen. "Sorry, I'd better take it. It's my auntie from Melbourne."

"Use our bedroom," Freya said. When Hannah left the kitchen she plugged in the kettle, planning to offer hot drinks to everyone.

Jamie wandered in. "Where's my fiancée?"

"In the bedroom talking to her aunt." Freya expected him to go and find Hannah, but he settled on a bar stool. She almost called out to Ryan to join them, then told herself she no longer needed to do that. Jamie was engaged to Hannah and she could finally relax.

Jamie picked up a coaster and spun it in his fingers. "Thank you."

"For telling you Hannah's on the phone?"

His mouth quirked up at the corner. "For never telling Ryan about my crazy meltdown moment after Monique."

Freya's heart rate picked up. "Oh, right. *That*." The conversation she'd never been able to forget and which always sat between them like a ticking bomb.

"Yeah, *that*." He cleared his throat. "I've been doing a lot of thinking lately and, looking back, I was definitely out of my tree there for a bit. I can't thank you enough for recognizing it wasn't the real me. Seriously, Freya, I mean it. Ryan's the brother I never had and I still break out in a cold sweat when I think what I risked, not just with him, but with you." He raised his gaze to hers—clear and sincere. "I don't believe anyone else would have been quite so understanding."

"Understanding?" That wasn't quite how she remembered it. She folded her arms over her chest to stall the tremor that usually shook her whenever she thought about that night and what the fallout might have been. "I insisted you go and live in Perth."

"And thank God for that or I'd never have met Hannah." He laughed, then sobered. "Seriously, Freya, I'm bloody lucky you're the ethical, practical, kind and caring human that you are. You were right then, and you were a thousand times right the other night when you told me I should marry Hannah."

She'd thought—hoped—that her unease had vanished with the engagement announcement, but the tiny pinch in her gut bit again. "You two have talked about kids, right?"

"She's young. There's plenty of time." Jamie stretched his hand across the counter towards her. "I'm forever in your debt."

As Ryan walked into the kitchen, Jamie pulled back his hand. "What debt's that?" Ryan asked.

Jamie stood and slung an arm around Ryan's shoulders. "A debt of gratitude to both of you for telling me to stop dicking around—"

"I believe those were Freya's words, not mine," Ryan said. "And at the time you seemed more shocked than grateful."

Jamie laughed. "I appreciated their full wisdom later. You've got yourself one smart woman there, mate."

"You're not telling me anything I don't already know." Ryan crossed the kitchen and pulled Freya into a hug.

She sank into him, grateful to have weathered a storm not of her own making and to have come out the other side without Ryan having any idea about it. It was over. Jamie was engaged and after being on edge around him for so long, she could finally relax.

CHAPTER THREE

EXCITEMENT and sheer delight spun Hannah around in a twirl of joy. She pinched herself, unable to believe that her vision for her—their—wedding matched the reality in front of her.

The marquee with its chiffon-draped and fairy-light-studded ceiling looked like it had come straight from one of the many bridal magazines she'd pored over and, when white linen cloths, wooden rounds, candles and greenery graced the tables, the picture would be complete. Two hundred meters of fairy lights were strung high above the dance floor, ready to mimic the magic of the stars that would shine down on her and Jamie as they shimmied to the carefully selected tunes spun by the best DJ in the district.

Rows of white chairs faced an arbor decorated with a stunning cascade of Western Australian natives. Behind it the towering gums that lined the burbling creek at the bottom of the garden stood tall and straight, their leaves still in the torpid afternoon heat. They were the perfect backdrop for a wedding. Tomorrow, she and Jamie would be married surrounded by family and friends. She could hardly wait.

"Happy?" Freya asked.

"Ecstatic! The marquee's amazing. It's all amazing. You're so clever."

Freya smiled. "Thank you, but it's my pleasure. To be honest, Ryan and I are just glad it's getting another outing. It's been sitting in the back shed since Maeve's thirtieth."

Hannah hugged her friend. "Thank you. Not just for the marquee but for everything. I couldn't have planned a wedding in three months without you."

She couldn't believe her wedding day was almost here and she was about to marry the love of her life. Jamie was the perfect man for her in every way—attentive, kind, caring, funny ... The list of positives was almost inexhaustible. Although, if there was one tiny thing she'd change, it was their sex life. She'd put the current lackluster period down to a busy work period combined with planning a huge wedding in a very short time, but all that ended tomorrow and their honeymoon would reset everything. During the warm Tahitian tropical nights she planned to extend Jamie's sexual repertoire and show him exactly how much fun they could have. Not that she wanted anything too kinky, but she'd enjoy moving beyond missionary position.

"You've gone all starry-eyed and blush pink," Freya said. "What are you thinking about?"

Hannah laughed. "Tahiti."

Freya grinned. "A few years ago, Ryan and I had a fabulous vacation on Gili Gede. We didn't stray far from our bamboo hut right on the beach."

"That's my plan. Jamie's been working so hard he needs the rest. I wish he could have shifted today's meeting. I'll kill him if he's late."

"Jamie's never late to anything. Ryan and I on the other hand ..." Freya gave Hannah's arm a squeeze. "I promise we'll be early tomorrow."

"Thank you." Hannah's phone pinged and she sighed in relief as she read the message. "Jamie's left Perth and he's on schedule to make the rehearsal."

"Told you."

"I know. It's just he's been on edge lately." She spun her engagement ring, unable to stop doubts assailing her. "I think the wedding on top of the business's expansion is stressing him out. He never gets drunk and he came home staggering on Wednesday night after dinner at yours."

Freya's fingers tweaked a perfectly tied organza bow. "He and Ryan went to the cricket club's bachelor bash. No groom ever comes home sober from that."

"Really?"

"Really," Freya said firmly. "And because of what happened at Jake Larkin's bash, Ryan insisted it was on Wednesday and not last night. He'd never forgive himself if Jamie wasn't in one piece for the wedding." Freya pulled her hand away from the bows and looked at Hannah. "It's been a full-on three months for both of you. You've been stressed too."

Embarrassment burned as Hannah remembered her meltdown over the minor shade variation in the ribbon they'd used to decorate the mason jars. "Oh God, sorry again."

"No need." Freya was back fiddling with the organza. "But Hannah, if you're worried about marrying him then don't."

Shocked, Hannah stared at Freya. "I'm not worried about marrying him. I'm desperate to marry him."

Freya tucked her hair behind her ears. "But you *are* worried about him, so please talk to him before the rehearsal. Get all your concerns off your chest, check you're both still on the same page about the future, about hopes and dreams and kids and ..." Freya was breathing hard, concern vibrating off her. "It's better to do it before everything ramps up to warp speed. I can stall things with the celebrant if you like."

Guilt stabbed Hannah. Oh God, this was her fault! Freya was always the voice of reason but Hannah's bride stress was so out of control it was infecting the calmest person in the room. She wished her mother was here. She wouldn't be buying into Hannah's nonsense and suggesting a D&M about the marriage; she'd be telling her not to make a mountain out of a molehill.

She hugged Freya, appreciating her care and concern. "It's all good, honest. I was just having a silly wobble."

She suddenly realized that Freya didn't have a little girl clinging to her legs and fresh worries tumbled through her. "Where's Mia? She's still my flower girl, right? And what if Ryan gets called out to an emergency? It's bad enough that Declan's flight got bumped and he won't arrive until tomorrow morning. If anyone else misses the rehearsal the celebrant will have a cow."

"Breathe, Hannah," Freya said, back to being calm. "Ryan's rostered off for the next three days. He and Mia are out on a bike ride and they'll arrive five minutes before the rehearsal. You don't need an excited preschooler around any longer than necessary. It's hard enough trying to explain to her that she can't wear her dress yet."

"She's going to be so cute in all that white tulle and lace!" Hannah's excitement edged out her concerns.

"I can't guarantee her behavior will be cute all day," Freya said drily. "You have heard the saying never work with animals and children, right?"

"It's all part of the fun. Besides, you know how much I love animals and children so of course they're part of our special day."

An almost pained look crossed Freya's face.

"What?"

Freya made an odd sound then said, "I know you love them. And to be fair to Ozzie, unlike Mia, he almost always follows commands."

"As long as no one produces a ball until after the service and a rabbit doesn't cross the lawn we'll be safe." Hannah laughed. "And Ozzie will be handy for rounding up any lagging wedding guests."

"Hannah!" Jamie's mother stood on the wide veranda of the historic sandstone homestead. "I've made tea."

"Hello, Lydia," Freya called.

Lydia gave a barely polite nod and disappeared inside, the wooden screen door banging shut behind her. Hannah had never seen her so cool towards a guest.

She glanced at Freya, looking for signs of distress, but her friend looked her normal sanguine self. Even so, Hannah rushed to reassure her. "The busier Lydia is, the brusquer she gets."

Guilt immediately threaded through her. Lydia had been beyond accommodating with all of Hannah's plans for a garden wedding.

She and Freya turned towards the house and were crossing the wide expanse of lawn when a loud crack ricocheted around the garden.

"Was that a gun?" Hannah said. Now she thought she could hear a low moaning groan.

"I don't think so." Freya was looking around and suddenly she pointed. "That tree's swaying."

Hannah peered in the direction of Freya's arm. "Where? I don't see—"

"Run!"

Freya's hand tugged at Hannah's arm as a cracking, splitting, tearing sound—accompanied by the harsh warning shrieks of black cockatoos—filled the garden. The blue sky was momentarily obliterated by green leaves and sleek black and yellow feathers as the frightened birds wheeled away, their silhouettes dark against the bright blue sky.

Hannah turned in time to see an almighty gum tree drag across her vision. Time slowed as the thirty-meter trunk pounded the soft earth with a deafening thud and a thousand leaves thrashed in its wake. A tsunami of rushing air buffeted them and a cloud of dust billowed before settling over the devastating scene.

The absence of noise that followed was louder than the tree fall. Stunned, Hannah stared at what had been the marquee—now a mess of twisted poles and mangled awning buried under mounds of unwelcome greenery. Buckled tables peeked out from underneath and squashed chairs sat low to the ground, their legs driven deep into the earth.

Hannah's adrenaline-addled brain refused to grasp what her eyes were showing her. "No!" she heard herself yelling as she moved to run to the marquee.

Freya's hand held her back. "Wait. Listen. Can you hear any other trees?"

All Hannah could hear was her heart pounding in her ears. She pulled away, desperate to save her wedding. Fairy lights crunched under her feet as she grabbed at swathes of leaves and tugged uselessly at boughs, unable to move even the slenderest of them. Surrounded by the fresh crisp scent of eucalyptus, she sank onto the ground and tried not to vomit.

Arms went around her. "Thank God you're safe!" Lydia said, her breathing rapid.

"How can a tree fall when there's no wind?" Freya asked faintly, her gaze fixed on the horizontal tree.

"Gums fall on hot still days," Lydia said.

The conversation swirled around Hannah, shock rendering her numb. All she wanted was Jamie's arms around her and his voice murmuring the reassuring words, "It's okay, poss. I'm here."

Hannah pulled at her hair. "We're getting married in twenty-two hours! We'll have to delay ... except we can't delay or we'll lose thousands of dollars. Oh God, why did I let Jamie insist we get married here? We should have done it at Buckland Estate where there are no trees, only grapes." She dropped her head into her hands and rocked. "What are we going to do?"

"I'm going to have enough firewood for the next two years," Lydia said absently before clapping her hands. "Okay, let's focus. At least the ceremony site's untouched. A chainsaw and half a dozen pairs of hands will have all this cleared in a couple of hours."

"I'll make some calls and see if we can get another marquee." Freya pulled her phone out of her pocket.

"That's probably impossible on such short notice. What about the hay-shed?" Lydia suggested. "It's big enough, and we can easily create a path with tiki torches to lead people there. And there's power for the caterers."

Hannah's mind was struggling to engage beyond the overwhelming debris in front of her. "I wanted fairy lights," she sobbed. "I wanted magic."

"And you'll have it," Freya said. "I'll raid the shop, and we'll call in favors and get a team out here to turn the hay-shed into a wedding venue. We'll use all this unexpected greenery and the organza to hide the ugly bits. If Thi doesn't have enough spare flower stock, I'm sure everyone will happily donate flowers from their gardens so she can make a huge spray for the main beam. Festoon lights will magic it up better than fairy lights—we can rent them from Grogan's."

"Long trestles will suit the barn better than rounds," Lydia said. "And we can still use the original table decorations, just dot them down the center."

As Hannah listened, an image slowly formed in her mind—the silver, brown and rust-red corrugated iron shed filled with happy, laughing, dancing people. Photos of her and Jamie with the shed as a backdrop. The smell and tickle of hay—a rustic wedding rather than a garden party. An homage to Jamie's childhood on the farm and his love of the outdoors. A fizz of hope penetrated her shock. She'd embrace this enforced change by wearing her red tooled leather boots with her dress instead of the shoes she'd chosen.

"Any chance the old wagon wheels in the shed could be dusted off and hoisted up to hold lights?" she asked.

"Maybe," Freya said.

"I'll put it on the list," Lydia said. "We'll need lists upon lists if we're going to be ready by three o'clock tomorrow. Ian's on his way and the boys will be here soon to clear the gum. I'll start a phone tree. We'll need to do a snake check and remove the worst of the cobwebs before we start decorating, but it's all doable. The rehearsal dinner's now a stand-up affair to feed all the workers."

"Oh God, the celebrant's arriving at 5:00 for the rehearsal," Hannah said.

"Cancel it," Lydia said. "Rehearsals are overrated. All you have to do is walk down the aisle on your brother's arm, stand next to Jamie and the celebrant does the rest."

"Do you really think we can do it in time?" Hannah asked.

"Of course we can," Freya said. "We're resourceful, resilient country women who can deal with anything. I'll call Ryan. The more hands on deck the better." She walked away, her phone pressed to her ear.

Lydia hugged Hannah, then held her at arm's length. "Concentrate on being the bride and leave the rest to us. I promise, you and Jamie are going to have a wonderful and memorable day."

As Lydia hurried off to greet Ian, who'd just returned from town and was staring shocked and pale-faced at the tree, Freya returned. "As usual, Ryan's not answering."

Hannah couldn't understand why Freya was so accepting of this kind of behavior. She thought it had more to do with Ryan's lack of respect for Freya than his job as a paramedic. Hell, today he wasn't even on duty. It would drive her nuts if Jamie didn't text her his ETA or inform her about any change of plans. Fortunately, that had never been an issue—right from the start, Jamie had always checked in with her.

As if he'd read her thoughts her phone pinged with a message from him. *Hey, poss, bloody roadworks! Be later than I thought but will still make it in time. Can't wait to see you. Just think, in twenty-four hours we'll have rings on our fingers and I'll be the happiest man on the planet. Love you to Neptune and back. Jxo*

Hannah smiled at the love rising off the screen. There were at least three sets of roadworks between Perth and Garringarup—hopefully Jamie was stuck at the ones closest to town. She called him but the call went straight to voice mail. This wasn't unusual—although the reception was reasonable there were still places where it fell out. It meant he was probably an hour away.

She sighed and replied to his text. *Bit of drama happening. Be ready to work when you get here. Drive safely. Can't wait to see you. xxxxx*

CHAPTER FOUR

The squawking cockatoos, confused by the gap where their home had once stood tall and proud, finally settled into the surrounding trees and a thick quiet descended over the garden. Freya was aware that animals often stilled because they felt vibrations or heard sounds humans failed to detect and she glanced around. Was another tree about to fall?

Eyes peeled and ears straining, she squinted towards the creek. No creaking or groaning in the trees, no smoke on the horizon—no hint of a disturbance anywhere. A cow mooed, then a flock of corellas screeched and circled, objecting to the cockatoos in their tree. Freya let out a breath; the normal rhythm of the bush had resumed.

The ear-piercing scream of sirens split the air. Freya and Hannah automatically stared down the long tree-lined drive, despite the main road being too far away to see.

"That's police *and* ambulance," Freya said.

"How can you tell?" Hannah asked.

"Living with a first responder you learn the difference. I wonder what's happened."

As the sounds dissipated, another siren blared and Freya's heart lurched. "Shit, that's the fire truck. This must be why Ryan's not answering his phone. He'd be too busy dropping Mia off to Lexie and getting to the station. It also means Sam and Dylan are on the fire truck too."

Hannah groaned. "That's half the wedding party! I'm starting to think the universe is totally against our wedding!"

Freya crossed her fingers. "Let's hope it's just a grass fire. We need all hands on deck here."

Right then both their phones lit up, the ringtones clashing harshly in a cacophony of sound.

Freya answered her sister's call. "Hi, Lexie. Great minds—I was just about to call you. An almighty tree's crushed the marquee so the wedding rehearsal's off. Plus, I think Ryan may be on a fire call, so I guess he's dropped Mia off to you?"

"That's what I'm calling about." Lexie's voice was tense.

Freya swallowed a sigh. Since Lexie's dropkick of a husband had walked out after deciding he no longer wanted to be married or be a father, her sister—juggling single parenting and a full-time job—experienced regular meltdowns. Freya did her best to support her by giving her parenting breaks: Mia stayed over at Kitchener Street one night a week and a couple of weekends a month.

"Sorry, Lex, but none of us could have predicted a falling tree. Fortunately, no one's hurt."

"Mia's not here."

Freya suddenly remembered that Lexie, who was a clerk at the hospital, didn't finish work until 5:00. "Oh, right. Ryan probably took Mia to his mum's."

"He didn't. I just called Sally and Mia's not there. Ryan's not answering his phone and my little girl's missing! I told you I didn't want her to be a flower girl!"

Freya held her phone away from her ear. Her younger sister's area of expertise was going from zero to full-blown drama in a heartbeat. It had been this way since their mother had brought her home from the hospital, her little face puce from screaming.

"Lexie, breathe. There'll be a reasonable explanation. Maybe Ryan's not on the fire—"

"Listen to me! I'm in urgent care and I overheard the controller on the bat-phone. There's been a bad accident between a car and a bike on the new Garringarup road. Ryan was taking Mia cycling!"

Freya thought about the combination of sirens and her stomach heaved. She sucked in a breath, fighting for calm, trying hard not to follow her sister down an unsubstantiated rabbit hole. "It won't be them."

"You don't know that!"

"I know Ryan wasn't planning on riding out here."

"You know what he's like," Lexie said pointedly. "He'd see the sunshine, change his mind and it would never occur to him to tell you."

There was truth in Lexie's words. "But he hates cycling on this road because it's too narrow and there's no shoulder," Freya said. "Besides, he wouldn't have ridden beyond where he needed to."

"You're not thinking!" Lexie yelled so loudly that Freya flinched. "He takes Mia on the rail trail and it intersects with the road two kays beyond the farm."

The emergency vehicles had been heading in the direction of that intersection. Visions of Ryan and Mia, their blood-splattered bodies sprawled on the dust, assaulted Freya and her breath came in short jerky gasps. She turned abruptly, half-walking, half-running towards her car.

"I'll drive there and call you back. Ring me if you hear more," she said.

As she wrenched open the gate that separated the garden from the homestead's parking area, she heard another wail of sirens—this time returning towards town. What the hell? There hadn't been enough time for the injured to be triaged, let alone treated and loaded into the ambulance.

"Auntie Frey! Auntie Frey!"

She spun around and relief buckled her knees. Mia's pudgy hand was waving cheerily from the bike trailer and Ryan's face was wreathed in the warm and sexy smile he always reserved for her. She ran, throwing herself against him and almost knocking him off balance.

His arms locked around her waist. "Hey, gorgeous. I haven't had a hello like this since my three months over east."

Her hands gripped his upper arms, as much to reassure herself he was here and in one piece as to hold herself upright. "Did you hear the sirens?"

He nodded. "Triple threat. Must be serious."

"Yes! Lexie said it's an accident involving a car and a cyclist ... I thought ..." Her throat, still thick with anxiety, blocked further words. She rubbed her tear-stained face into his cotton-clad shoulder.

He stroked her back. "Hey, I'm here. We're fine."

"I know that now!" She tried to control her breathing, but her terror was slow to recede. "I called you! Why didn't you answer your phone?"

He gave his usual apologetic shrug. "Didn't hear it. You know the rail trail has dodgy reception."

"Yes, but I didn't know you were on the rail trail."

"Too nice a day not to ride."

"Oh, great!" She heard the shrill rise in her voice and the crack of tears. "So now on top of everything we don't have a car seat to drive Mia home."

Mia had clambered out of the trailer. "Why is Auntie Freya sad?"

"She got a fright and she needs a hug." Ryan dropped another kiss into Freya's hair.

Mia wrapped her arms around Freya's legs and kissed her knees.

Ryan dropped his voice so only Freya could hear. "What's going on? It's not like you to fall apart."

She breathed in snorty, snotty breaths as the loud whirl of a chainsaw broke around them, then pointed over the fence to the tree and the crumpled marquee. "That happened."

"Bloody hell." Ryan stared at the mess. "Is everyone okay?"

"Everyone and everything except the marquee and some tables and chairs."

His arms tightened around her. "No wonder you're no match for Lexie's catastrophizing. You're in shock."

"Maybe ... But she did say the accident was on the new Garringarup road, and you were on the rail trail so it could have been you."

"But it wasn't."

"No, thank God! You promised me we'd grow old together." She kissed him on the mouth, fusing herself to him.

It took a moment for them to realize Ryan's phone was blaring with his work ringtone.

"It must be serious if they're calling me on my day off." He stepped back and answered the call. "Ryan Gillet."

Freya squatted at Mia's height and tried to be the capable auntie the little girl knew. "Did you see any kangaroos?"

Mia nodded solemnly. "They were sleeping. Is it time for my pretty dress?"

"One more sleep." Freya was watching Ryan. His forehead was creased in deep furrows and his free hand raked through his hair.

"Shit,' he said. "How the hell did they get that so wrong? ... Right, of course, yeah ..."

Still listening to whatever was being said, Ryan nodded towards Freya's car and held his hand out for her keys. She passed them over, scooped up Mia and walked with him to the car, listening carefully but not able to glean many details.

Ryan was already seated and switching on the ignition when the call ended. "Sorry. I'll be back here as soon as I can."

Freya nodded and kissed his cheek. She knew the gig—he was needed. "Go save lives."

CHAPTER FIVE

HANNAH'S BACK ACHED. There was hay in her hair, stuck to her jeans and she swore there was some in her bra, but with a group of willing workers they'd created a safe and workable space in the hay-shed.

She took her first break in over an hour and checked her phone. There were several texts from Lydia—all updates about the new plans —but none from Jamie. Hannah had expected him to have arrived by now, and if he had, surely he'd have come straight to find her. Except if today had taught her one thing, there was no "surely" about anything. Ian had probably put him to work the moment he'd stepped out of the car.

She was about to call him when she heard the loud blast of a horn and the thrum of a diesel engine. The Garringarup party-hire truck rumbled down the rutted track.

The singlet-clad driver swung out of the cab and consulted the paperwork in his hand. "Five tables for Lydia McMaster."

"Hannah Simmons, but I'll accept the order." She pointed to the hay-shed. "Set them up in there, please."

"Hannah!" Freya yelled, her phone in her hand. "I can get a neonlight sign for the back wall. Do you want 'Better together' or 'It was always you'?"

It was a hard call but one pulled ahead. "'It was always you.' Warm lights, yeah?"

"Of course." Freya returned to her call.

Lindsay Grainger, a friend of Lydia's, stood surveying the hay-shed. "Hannah, Graeme Chin's happy to lend us oak barrels. They'd create a sense of entrance and the cake could go on one. Yes or no?"

"Um, sure." Hannah's phone rang. "Hi, Thi."

"I've rung around and sourced flowers for arrangements at the entrance of the shed, on the two main uprights and for the middle of the beam," the florist said. "But I'm only one pair of hands so I'll focus on the bouquets and the Country Women's Association will transform the shed."

"That's awesome." Hannah was breathless with thanks. "I really appreciate it."

Anticipation thrummed. It was crazy, but she had an overwhelming feeling that the new setting for the reception would eclipse the original.

"Hannah." Mia pulled at her hand. "I'm hungry."

"Are you, sweetie?" Hannah glanced around for Freya and saw her up a ladder stringing festoon lights. She smiled as an idea took hold. "Freya, Mia's hungry. Okay if I take her to the homestead for a snack?" *And to hug Jamie.*

Freya's hand paused on a beam. "I can do it."

"No, it's all good. I'll bring back food and drinks for everyone."

"Well, if you're sure. It means I can get this job finished. Mia, you go with Hannah and she'll get you a snack."

"Can Ozzie come too?" Mia asked.

"Sure thing," Hannah said. "What are you hungry for, Mia?"

The little girl's eyes widened as if she couldn't believe she was being asked the question. "Cake and chips and soda and ice-cream!"

"Party food. Why not! It's my wedding and that's a party."

Laughing, Hannah held out her hand and Mia slipped her small warm one into it, all innocence and trust. Hannah's heart swelled to bursting. If this feeling came with a child that wasn't even hers, imagine the intensity of emotions when a little chestnut-haired, brown-eyed child—a miniature Jamie—looked up at her with love in their eyes.

It was a conversation she and Jamie needed to have in Tahiti—the exact date to start baby-making. Hannah was one hundred percent ready, but the last couple of times she'd raised the topic Jamie had said, "Poss, how about we concentrate on one big event at a time, okay? Let's get through the wedding first."

Mia insisted on doing farewell waves to everyone in the hay-shed so it was another five minutes before they made it outside. The little girl eyed the newly mown grass path back to the homestead garden. "My legs are tired," she said, cadging to be picked up.

"Let's practice for tomorrow," Hannah said. She bent down and picked a few daisies and passed them to Mia. "Pretend this is your basket of flowers and you're in your pretty dress."

"Okay!" Mia clutched the drooping weeds in front of her and took three neat steps, her pink gumboots sparkling in the glow of the fast-dropping sun. "Come on, Ozzie," she instructed the dog.

Hannah smiled at the serious way Mia was walking. She wondered how much time Lexie—no, it would have been Freya—had spent teaching her how to walk down an aisle.

"And now I follow you," she said.

"Don't wave your flowers, Hannah!" Mia instructed, sounding a lot like Freya.

"I won't."

Hannah pretended she was a garden goddess, already wearing her frothy tulle Renaissance-style gown with its cascading bishop sleeves and fitted embroidered bodice. Dreaming of tomorrow, when she'd be walking this path as Hannah McMaster with her arm linked through Jamie's, she suddenly bumped into Mia.

The little girl had stopped and was pointing. "They in the way!" she said indignantly.

Hannah squinted into the setting sun and made out three

silhouettes walking towards them. It took her a moment before she recognized Lydia's height and Ian's breadth. Her heart leaped. "Jamie!"

But as his name hit the air she realized the third person wasn't her fiancé. He never wore a cap, only an Akubra. Who was it?

"Hello, Mr. Policeman!" Mia said. "I'm a flower girl."

"Oh, hi, Brett." Hannah gave him a welcoming smile. "You looking for Crystal? She's in the hay-shed doing a power of work."

The police officer removed his hat and momentarily looked away. "Actually, Hannah, I'm here on official business."

"Official wedding business?" Hannah laughed. "Thanks for picking up the programs."

He shook his head. "I mean police business. There's been an accident."

Adrenaline drenched her, raising every hair on her body then leaving her ice-cold. Her brother was flying from Singapore. Had there been a plane crash?

Somehow she forced words around the lump in her throat. "Declan? Is he okay?"

"I don't know who Declan is." Brett's fingers moved across the brim of his cap like fingers playing piano keys. "But he's not involved in this accident."

"Thank God." Relief slid over her fear. "Declan's my brother. You'll meet him tomorr—"

"Hannah." Brett's voice cracked on her name. "The accident ... it's Jamie."

A primal shriek circled Hannah—raw, agonized and terrifying. Her head jerked to the right and she saw Lydia slumped against Ian, his arm trembling as he supported her weight. Agony twisted their faces into masks of shock and devastation.

Undiluted dread poisoned every cell in Hannah's body and she gasped, remembering the sirens from earlier in the afternoon. She fought the unwanted reality—they hadn't been racing to a grass fire. They'd been rushing to Jamie.

Her hand shot out and gripped Brett's forearm. "Where is he? Is he badly hurt?" But the look on Brett's face told her it was far more than a scratch. "Are they airlifting him to Perth?"

Lydia was sobbing now, a heaving desperate wall of noise. Hannah's mind blocked the sound, her concentration fully on the police officer— Jamie's partner in his only century in cricket.

"I'm so sorry, Hannah," Brett said softly, his Adam's apple working hard. "Jamie didn't survive the crash."

Her hands were suddenly fists, striking the black flak jacket protecting Brett's chest. She could hear someone yelling, their voice taut with anguish. "No, you're wrong! You're wrong! We're getting married tomorrow!"

"I'm so sorry," Brett said again.

And then arms were turning her and holding her and she slumped into them, only to recoil because they weren't Jamie's. Only Jamie could ease this searing pain that threatened to fell her to the dirt and keep her there.

Arms flailing, head spinning, she tried to swing back to Brett. "He's not dead!" she screamed.

Then Freya was saying, "Hannah, can you hear me? Hannah, stay with me." Gentle hands stroked her hair but she didn't want to be soothed. She wanted to run. To scream. To hit and punch. Destroy everything and everyone in her path so they hurt and suffered with the same unrelenting and soul-deep devastation.

She'd visited this place once before when her parents had died. Now she was back, only this was so much worse. This was unendurable.

Her body cramped, whipping vicious and relentless pain along every limb and blackening every cell. She struggled to move air in and out of her lungs.

"Deep breaths, Han." Freya's voice was muffled. "In and out. In ..."

The edges of Hannah's mind fogged. She wasn't certain she wanted to breathe again. The darkness marched in. She willingly grabbed onto its coattails and followed.

CHAPTER SIX

IF IT HAD BEEN possible to clone herself and be in three places at once, Freya would have paid for the privilege. She'd wanted to stay with Hannah, but after Angus Cameron, one of the local doctors, had sedated her, and Lydia had said in terse, clipped tones that there was nothing Freya could do—code for "leave now"—Freya had written Hannah a note and left it on the bedside table for when she woke.

As she'd walked out of the bedroom she'd stopped in front of the wedding dress hanging in its white protective bag. Should she leave it or remove it? Which was the best option for Hannah? Which would cause her friend the least pain? Like everything connected with grief, it was impossible to know so Freya left it in the room.

Mia was too young to understand the cause of the adults' distress, but she'd witnessed Lydia and Hannah's anguished keening. She'd wrapped her arms and legs around Freya like a monkey clinging to a branch. When Freya carried her into Lexie's house, Mia hadn't wanted to transfer into her mother's arms.

"I want my pretty dress!" she'd demanded.

"Sure," Freya said. "Go put it on."

As Mia ran from the room Lexie frowned. "I'm not sure that's a good idea."

"Why not?" Freya's sigh vibrated with shock and grief. "It's not like she needs to keep it clean for tomorrow."

"God! I can't believe Jamie's dead." Lexie sounded as bewildered as everyone else when they first heard the news. "That he'll never walk into the pub again and say, 'My shout'."

Freya stared at her sister. "Really? That's what you'll remember him for?"

Lexie shrugged. "He was your friend, not mine."

"He's Ryan's best mate."

"You know what I mean. The four of you were tight. How's Hannah?"

"Imagine how gutted you think she is then triple it."

"I've got a pretty good idea. When I thought it may be Mia, I was ..." Lexie poured two glasses of wine. "Here. Drink this. You look like shit."

Freya didn't know if she wanted to laugh or cry, and the strangled sound she choked on couldn't decide either. "Thanks, but I need to get home. I need to be there when Ryan walks in."

"But he could be hours, right?"

Mia twirled into the room wearing the dress back to front, but the full handkerchief tulle skirt still rose and fell. "Look! I'm a princess!"

Lexie laughed. "You are."

Mia stopped in front of Freya. "Is it one more sleep till I'm a flower girl?"

Grief walloped Freya with the intensity of a fist to the face and silent tears rolled down her cheeks. "I'm sorry, sweetie. There's no wedding anymore."

Mia scrambled into her lap. "Don't cry, Freya. We can play weddings."

Freya looked over Mia's dark curls at Lexie. "Maybe Mummy can play. I have to go home."

"I want to come!" Mia said. "I want to see Ryan!"

"You saw Ryan today and now it's Mummy time." Freya slid Mia off her lap and walked to the door. The little girl ran after her.

Lexie handed Mia her phone to distract her, then dropped her voice. "I need you to stay."

"Lexie, please ..." Freya wished her sister could understand that as much as she loved her and Mia, tonight she could only be in one place and with one person. Ryan needed her the most.

"Fine!" Lexie snapped. "But I've been left dealing with her missing Kane and I'm not gonna deal with her disappointment over this too. Not when it was your idea for her to be flower girl! You need to come over tomorrow and play with her and—"

"Sure, okay," Freya said quickly. She had no idea what she was doing tomorrow, but right now she didn't have time for any more of Lexie's drama. "Can you give Mum a call, please."

"Why?" Lexie looked genuinely confused.

Since Kane had left, Lexie had understandably been caught up in her own issues, but surely she was aware of the twice-a-day phone calls Freya had instigated to check on their mother? Freya was positive she'd told her about them.

"They've changed her insulin and her blood sugar's all over the shop," she said. "I usually call her just to check."

"You worry too much," Lexie said.

Freya took a deep breath so she didn't say, "It's you who doesn't worry enough." She was frequently flummoxed by the things Lexie stressed over and the things she didn't. Then again, their mother had always protected Lexie and given her a sanitized version of any health crisis. But Freya didn't want to play that game anymore.

"It's easier all round if we can keep her out of the hospital and checking in is one way of doing that. Please call her."

She kissed Lexie goodbye, then dropped a kiss on Mia's head. Her niece was so engrossed in the phone she didn't notice Freya escape.

The house was dark and chilly when she arrived home, so she switched on the lights and lit the fire. Pekoe, their ginger and white cat, appeared in the kitchen and meowed. It was hard to know if it was a welcome greeting or a remonstration.

Freya picked her up and hugged her, needing the touch, but Pekoe squirmed. With a sigh, Freya released her. She'd always wanted a dog, but each time she raised the topic Ryan pointed out that as they both worked long hours it wasn't fair on an animal that craved human attention. A cat, however, was quite content with their absences.

She checked her phone again. No texts or missed calls from Ryan. She wished she'd asked Brett more questions about the accident, but he'd left soon after breaking the news and breaking Hannah's and the McMasters' hearts. All she knew was that Jamie had died on impact— his car crumpling against the solid and uncompromising trunk of a red morrel.

She texted: *I'm home. I love you xxx* and sent it to Ryan's number. Then she opened the fridge and stared at its meager contents. She hadn't restocked the fridge—they should have been dining at the long table on the McMasters' veranda, enjoying the conviviality of the rehearsal dinner.

She grabbed a packet of chips and was just pouring herself a glass of Margaret River chardonnay when she heard the back door.

Ryan walked in, his complexion gray with exhaustion, his eyes red-rimmed and filled with devastation.

"Frey—" His voice cracked on her name.

She rushed straight over, wrapping her arms around him. As he sagged against her, she staggered from his weight.

"I'm so sorry, honey," she said.

"Yeah ..."

They stood together silently, and she stroked his back until he finally lifted his head.

"Did Brett tell you?"

"He came to the farm," she said. "Hannah and Lydia both lost it, and Ian aged ten years in a heartbeat." She turned him towards the sofa. "Do you want something? Tea, hot chocolate, beer?"

"Whisky."

The choice rammed home the shattering situation—Ryan only ever drank whisky with Jamie.

Freya retrieved the bottle from the drinks cabinet. Ignoring the ice and water, Ryan poured it neat and downed two fingers in one gulp.

"It was awful, Frey. Hardest job I've ever done."

"I can't even imagine ..." She snuggled in close and tucked a blanket around them. "When did you know it was Jamie?"

"When I pulled him out."

Her heart stalled. "Oh God! Didn't you recognize the car?"

He shook his head.

"And no one warned you? How could they let you go straight in when they—"

"I arrived at the same time as everyone else." He rubbed his face. "It was a bloody shambles."

"But how? We'd heard the sirens."

"Some idiot in Perth sent them down the wrong road. They wasted twenty-five fucking minutes getting there!"

She was about to say, "How did they get it so wrong?" when Ryan added, "If they'd gone straight there, he may still be alive."

She laced her fingers into his, needing him to understand the mistake didn't affect the outcome. "Brett told me he died instantly."

"Yeah, well, Brett's not a medico, is he."

"He's seen enough accidents to know, and so have you. I know you want to blame someone for Jamie's death, but it's unlikely it was because of the dispatcher's error."

Ryan leaned forward and poured another drink. "There were other people hurt. A man and a kid a couple of years older than Mia."

"Oh God! Are they okay?"

A long sigh shuddered out of him. "They will be. We airlifted them to Perth."

Freya thought about the community that would be reeling from this tragedy. "Are they from Garringarup too?"

"Nah. They live at the ag institute."

The institute was in Muresk, north of Garringarup. "So they were on their way to Perth?" Freya said absently.

Ryan gave her a blank stare and she didn't know if his inability to comprehend was shock-induced or whisky-induced, or both.

"The man and his child," she said slowly. "They would have been driving in the opposite direction to Jamie. To Perth."

He shook his head. "They were on bikes."

"Jamie died in a car but they survived a motorbike crash?" It was hard to fathom.

"Pushbike, but yeah."

She sat up. "Hang on, what? Why would they be riding bikes so far away from Muresk?"

"They weren't. The accident was only fifteen kays from the institute."

"But that makes no sense. Jamie was coming from Perth."

"Not on that road he wasn't."

"Wait!" Freya's mind was sliding all over the map that was imprinted on her brain after living in the district for years. "Are you saying Jamie was driving on the *old* Garringarup road?" To clarify she added, "The gravel road between Muresk and here?"

"Yes! I told you. The idiot in Perth got the old and new roads mixed up. *That's* why we heard the sirens. There better be a bloody inquiry and the dickhead involved should lose his job!"

But Freya was stuck on the fact that Jamie had died on a road that ran north to south when he should have been coming from Perth, which was almost directly west of Garringarup. "What on earth was Jamie doing on that road? I mean it's not even an alternative route."

Ryan's head fell back onto the sofa. "Maybe it was something to do with the wedding."

"Like what?"

"Fuck—I can't believe he's gone, Frey. And that's nuts, because the minute I saw him, I knew."

She stroked his face. "It's not nuts. It's going to take a while for it to sink in."

"Yeah." He drained the glass and reached for the bottle.

Freya picked it up first. "You need food or you'll pass out."

"That's the plan."

On one level she understood, but she wasn't sure it was such a great idea for him to write himself off. "Come on, I'll make you an omelet."

"I'm not hungry."

"Ice-cream then?"

"Yeah. Alright." But he wrapped his arms around her.

She stayed seated, knowing he needed her more than dessert.

"The old road's a shocker," she said. "I'm surprised that bloke was attempting to cycle on it with a child."

"Nah, it's pretty along the river." Ryan's voice caught. "Jamie and I used to fish down there when we were kids."

"We can take flowers out there tomorrow," she suggested.

"Shit, no. I'm not going back."

"O-kay." His vehemence surprised her but she didn't push it. "I can't believe it's happened."

"It's all the wrong way around." Ryan's chest heaved and his tears wet her hair. "Hannah's going to his funeral instead of their wedding."

CHAPTER SEVEN

HANNAH WOKE to the low sepia glow of an unfamiliar bedside lamp and a digital clock beaming 01:01. It took her a moment to recall where she was—the homestead's guest room. She wrapped her arms around herself, pummeled her legs against the mattress and gave a silent squeal of excitement. Today was finally here—her wedding day. In fifteen hours, she'd be standing in the garden admiring how handsome Jamie was in his tux and—

The day before rushed back, images and voices assaulting her. The crash of the towering gum, the debris of the marquee, Freya up a ladder weaving festoon lighting in the hay-shed and Brett ...

There's been an accident.

She gagged and sat up fast, her breathing ragged, her throat full of sobs. It was her wedding day but Jamie was dead.

She shook her head. *No. No!* This was just a nightmare. Any second, she'd wake up and Jamie would be lying beside her, his arms around her and saying, "Relax, poss. It's gonna be great."

She tried opening her eyes but they were already open. She was wide awake and living this nightmare. Without Jamie, she couldn't face today. God—how was she going to live through all the days that followed?

She fell back, squeezed her eyes shut and pulled the covers over her head. But it didn't bring sleep. If anything, it raced her heart and turbo-charged her chaotic thoughts, hurtling them in one direction—reality.

I'm so sorry ... Jamie didn't survive the crash.

The dark and cloying warmth of the covers pressed heavily against her. She wanted to stay there in its suffocating confines, let it steal her breath, her air, her life, but her body had its own ideas. She was suddenly gasping, her chest heaving, and her arms threw back the covers.

As she sat up a piece of paper fluttered from the bedside table to the floor. She pulled on her dressing gown, then picked it up. Freya's neat script covered the yellow square.

Dear Hannah, you were sleeping so I went home but call me anytime day or night. I'll come see you tomorrow either way. All my love, Freya xxx

Hannah remembered Angus suggesting she take something to slow her mind and how she'd swallowed the little white pill and welcomed the oblivion of sleep. But the chemically induced peace had vanished and the real world was back, as bright and harsh as hunting lights.

She walked along the silent hall to the kitchen.

Lydia was sitting at the large jarrah table. At the sound of Hannah's tread she raised her head from her hands. "I'll make you a cup of tea."

"It's okay, I—"

"It gives me something to do." Lydia rose, the effort of pushing against weariness and resignation obvious, and switched on the kettle. "Whatever Angus gave us only worked for a few hours."

"I guess." Hannah's fingers shredded a tissue in her dressing-gown pocket. "When I woke up, I'd forgotten ..."

"Oh, sweetheart."

Lydia hugged her, but Hannah found she didn't want to be touched by anyone except the one person who could no longer caress, hug or kiss her. She eased away and sat at the table in the glow of Lydia's iPad. A forest of browser tabs was open.

Lydia set a mug of lemon and ginger tea in front of Hannah and pointed to the iPad. "We need to think about what we want at the funeral before we meet with Tozzi's."

Anger erupted, making Hannah shake. "I'm not meeting with a funeral director on my wedding day!"

Lydia jerked back. "No, of course not ... I'm sorry. I wasn't suggesting today ..."

"I don't want to do it tomorrow or Monday or ever!"

Ian appeared in the doorway, bleary-eyed. "Everything okay?"

"Of course it's not okay!" Hannah was screaming now, tears dripping off her nose. "How can anything be okay when Jamie's dead and my life's ruined."

Ian threw Lydia a bewildered look, then placed his hands gently on Hannah's shoulders. "Sorry, love. We're all hurting."

Hannah sucked in her lips, trying to staunch the animalistic sounds flowing out of her—sounds she'd never heard herself make. Of course Jamie's parents were hurting, but compassion was hard to find when they'd shared him for thirty-seven years. She'd barely got fifteen months instead of the promised rest of her life.

She wiped her face on the sleeve of her dressing gown and tried to steady her breathing, but all she could think about was the months spent planning the perfect wedding—a day of joy and celebration to be long remembered. Now she had to plan a funeral and every part of her balked at it. When somebody died at ninety a funeral could be a wonderful celebration of a long life lived well. But when someone died young, how could it be anything other than a lament of lost love and lost experiences?

She reached out to drop the iPad flat and hide the offending headings like *living memories, celebrating a life* and *funeral planning checklist*, when she read *unexpected death and sperm*. Pulling the device closer she reread it, checking her eyes hadn't deceived her.

"Why is there a search about sperm in the middle of all these tabs about death?' she said.

"Because it's life," Lydia said.

Hannah didn't understand. "I don't see the connection."

"Those tablets Angus gave me made me dream," Lydia said. "I kept seeing Jamie as a boy, running over the paddocks, playing under the wool table in the shearing shed, fishing by the river ..." Her voice broke. "We haven't just lost Jamie. We've lost his legacy. Your longed-for children, our beloved grandchildren."

Pain seared Hannah, stealing her breath. Now she'd never hold that chestnut-haired, brown-eyed child she'd been imagining for so long. Her heart spasmed and she lurched blindly from the table. It wasn't until she reached the home paddock fence that she realized she was outside and shoeless. Chest heaving, she tried to slow her breathing, find some calm, but Jamie's face and the image of their lost child beamed across her mind.

Tilting her head back, she looked up into the night sky, silver with shimmering stars. "Oh, Jamie. How am I going to live without you?"

Eventually, the veranda light came on and she heard the thud of Ian's footfalls before his hand found hers. She turned into his chest and sobbed. He patted her back and, when her breathing finally steadied, guided her inside.

Lydia immediately hugged her. "Hannah, darling, I didn't mean to upset you."

Hannah nodded. "It's the first time I realized that more than Jamie just died."

Lydia stroked her hair. "I know."

Hannah sat and picked up the iPad. She read the words *posthumous sperm retrieval*, but her mind couldn't absorb anything. "What does it mean?"

"Do you remember that model who had a baby using her dead husband's sperm?" Lydia said.

"Maybe." Hannah had a vague memory of it but couldn't recall any details.

"Well, she did. Apparently, sperm continue to live for some time after death and there's a technique to retrieve it." Lydia's hand gripped hers. "Hannah, if you wanted, you can still have Jamie's baby."

Numb with grief, she struggled to process the overwhelming information. "But how?"

"IVF," Lydia said.

"No, I mean Jamie's sperm." Her mind fought itself, simultaneously wanting to explore and avoid what would be involved in harvesting sperm. "How do we get it?"

"We call Angus. He'll find us an IVF fertility specialist in Perth who's happy to retrieve it. According to some of the articles, not all doctors are keen."

"And we'll call Rowan for the legal stuff," Ian said.

"What legal stuff?"

"There's laws around this sort of thing. What did you call it, Lyd?"

"Reproductive technology."

Hannah thought of the elderly family attorney the McMasters had insisted be invited to the wedding. "Rowan does farm succession planning and wills! What would he know about reproductive technology?"

"He'll know someone who knows someone," Ian said firmly. "He'll see us right."

Hope surged through Hannah. She grabbed the iPad and typed *Western Australia posthumous sperm retrieval* then scanned a legal-looking document.

"It says we have to go to the Supreme Court to get an order. Can we even afford that?"

"Don't worry about the money. That will sort itself out," Lydia said. "The important thing now is time. I wish I'd thought of it six hours ago. Ideally the sperm needs to be retrieved within twenty-four hours—"

"This article says thirty-six." Hannah realized with a jolt that she had no idea where Jamie was. Ian had identified him after she'd refused. Seeing him laid out on a silver trolley would mean he really was dead. "Is he at the hospital? Will he have to be taken to Perth?" She shuddered. "Will they have to cut him?"

Lydia tapped the iPad. "This article from New South Wales says Jamie's body will be treated with the utmost dignity and respect. I wouldn't allow anything less for my darling boy, and you wouldn't either. We'll ask Angus to explain everything, and we'll keep asking questions until we're all certain this is the right thing to do."

Lydia squeezed Hannah's hand. "I know this is a lot to dump on you, but I'd never forgive myself if I didn't tell you it was an option because it gives you choice. Unfortunately, what you don't have is the luxury of time to make the decision."

In her mind, Hannah saw that little curly-haired child again and the deep well of grief momentarily lessened. This was a way to hold onto Jamie. To keep him close. To have the baby they'd dreamed of. In the worst of times, this was a beacon of hope.

"We have to do this," she said. Then a thought sideswiped her. "Oh God, what if we can't convince the judge? I mean, Jamie and I aren't married."

"You were getting married today," Lydia said. "That's proof of commitment."

"Yes, but we weren't officially trying to get pregnant."

"Of course not. You weren't married," Lydia said emphatically, as if no unmarried couple had ever had a child. "Are you on the pill?"

The personal question made Hannah squirm. "Um, no."

"And you and Jamie were going to have children. We can all sign affidavits saying that. Maddie too. And if the court needs proof outside of the immediate family, Freya and Ryan will sign."

Hannah knew her friend would do anything for her, but she didn't know Jamie's sister very well. Jamie said that since Maddie had married a South Australian farmer and moved to the Eyre Peninsula he didn't see much of her outside of Christmas. And Jamie was a typical bloke: not great at making the effort to stay in touch when he had Lydia to keep him updated on family news. Hannah had been looking forward to getting to know Maddie, but she'd arrived soon after their lives had inexorably changed. Maddie was currently down the hall with her husband and kids. Hannah wondered how she could sleep.

As if hearing Hannah's thoughts, Maddie walked into the kitchen holding a water bottle.

"Any tea in the pot?" she asked.

"I'll pour you one, love," Ian said.

"Thanks." Maddie sat between Lydia and Hannah. "I can't sleep either."

"We don't have time for sleep." Lydia's eyes glittered. "We're racing against the clock to retrieve Jamie's sperm."

Maddie stared at them. "Is that a thing?"

"Thankfully it is."

"Oh my God! So you could have Jamie's baby?" Maddie said to Hannah.

For the first time since Brett had uttered the devastating words that had changed Hannah's life and pitched her headfirst into a terrifying black pit of despair, she glimpsed a tiny flicker of light. She was going to provide it with so much fuel it would roar into a blazing torch and illuminate her new path.

"I *will* have Jamie's baby," she said.

Maddie gripped Hannah's and Lydia's hands. "That would be amazing."

It would be more than amazing, it would be a miracle.

Hannah stood. "Let's wake up Angus and Rowan and make it happen."

CHAPTER EIGHT

FREYA WROTE Ryan a note and crept out of the house. He'd finally crashed into a deep sleep around 3:00 in the morning and she didn't want to wake him. While he slept he didn't have to face the fact that his best mate lay still and cold in the morgue—although going by Ryan's occasional thrashing of limbs she suspected there'd been moments when he'd dreamed about finding Jamie lifeless in the crumpled car.

The vermilion dawn sky gave way to the quintessential endless outback blue—a day out of the box. The sun shone and the birds shrieked and sang, chasing each other in an age-old spring dance. It was perfect wedding-day weather and if not for the shattering news of yesterday they would be rejoicing. Now the sunshine mocked their trauma.

As Freya drove through the McMasters' farm gates she tried not to flinch at the white ribbons fluttering from the she-oaks lining the driveway. Ribbons she'd tied yesterday—a lifetime ago.

She parked then picked up her cooler bag of food and one of the bouquets of flowers she'd picked from her dew-wet garden. She knew lasagna was a clichéd grief dish, but it also fed many and there would be a stream of people visiting the McMasters. She'd also made beef and ginger casserole and lemon slice.

The old homestead was eerily quiet and for a moment Freya wondered if she should have texted before driving out so early. But as she prevaricated about knocking or calling out hello, she heard the rumble of voices drifting through an open window. She knocked and walked inside.

She'd expected the air in the house to be weighted with grief, but the moment she stepped inside an unexpected, almost agitated energy whipped out to greet her. Maddie's kids rushed past into the garden and Maddie's husband, Hamish, gave Freya a quiet nod as he followed them. She heard Ian's voice and glimpsed him in the living room talking to Rowan Ferguson, Garringarup's senior lawyer. Was it about the accident? Surely it was too soon to be worrying about Jamie's will.

Freya entered the kitchen—always the heartbeat of the house—and set the food and flowers on the counter. "Hey, Hannah."

Her friend rushed across the large room and threw her arms around her. "Oh, Freya!"

Freya returned the hug. Hannah's eyes remained tear-reddened, but instead of yesterday's anguish they glittered with feverish intensity. Unease shot down Freya's spine.

"How are you?" she asked. "Did you sleep?"

"No time for sleep. And sorry, no time to talk." Hannah sounded breathless. "I have to get to Perth."

Freya blinked. "Perth? Why?"

"We've got an out-of-session court hearing at noon."

"Court hearing?" Freya knew she sounded like a parrot but none of this was making sense. The only appointments she'd expected Hannah might have today would be with Brett or with Tozzi's Funerals, and both were in town. "Hannah, what's going on?"

"I want Jamie's sperm."

Freya's mind tripped over itself. "But he's ..."

"Sperm lives up to thirty-six hours after death, but ideally retrieving it within twenty-four hours is best."

The words rushed out of Hannah's mouth and dumped themselves all over Freya. She grappled with the information. "It ... I ... That's possible? I had no idea."

"Neither did I, but thankfully Lydia remembered that model who did it. She and Ian have been amazing. Because we weren't married they've signed the papers giving their permission and Maddie's totally on board too. Angus and Rowan have gone above and beyond. Rowan even woke up a judge! Jamie's on his way to Perth, and Angus has a doctor on stand-by to do the procedure the moment we have the court order."

Freya's mind spun at the gush of words and the speed at which everything was taking place. The last time she'd seen Hannah she'd been catatonic with grief and now she was wild-eyed and hyper-excited.

Lydia walked into the kitchen. "Hannah, are you ready to—Oh, hello, Freya." Her eyes took in the flowers, the cooler bag and the basket of baked goods. "Actually, we're in a rush. Hannah, be at the car in five minutes." She left the room, calling out, "Ian, Rowan, we're leaving."

Freya was used to Lydia's coolness, but now something close to panic skittered through her. She grabbed Hannah's arm. "Are you sure about this?"

Hannah frowned and shook away Freya's hand. "Of course I'm sure. Why would you even ask?"

Because grief makes people crazy. Because Lydia suggested it.

"It just seems to be happening so fast."

"It has to, Freya. We don't have the luxury of time."

How did she tell Hannah that when it came to Jamie, Lydia was a tiger. That when Jamie was alive, Lydia had frozen out anyone who she thought might get between her and her precious son—both Freya and Monique had experienced severe frostbite. That it was possible Lydia's helpful suggestion, support and ability to move mountains was more to do with her own need to keep Jamie alive than Hannah's wellbeing. But timing was everything and right now, with all this manic energy surging around her, Freya knew if she said anything negative, Hannah wouldn't hear her.

Hannah was squeezing her own hands. "I've lost Jamie, but if I can have his baby then he'll always be close."

Agitation pumped through Freya. "I can come with you." *Be a voice of reason. Protect you.*

"Hannah!" Maddie stuck her head into the kitchen. "Come on! Every second counts."

"Thanks for the offer, you're a wonderful friend," Hannah said, "but I've got the McMasters. We'll talk tomorrow, promise." She kissed Freya on the cheek, picked up her bag and walked out.

The screen door slammed and the house fell silent, bar the tick of the clock and the buzz of the fridge. Stunned, Freya had to stop herself running outside and yelling, "Stop! Wait! Let's talk this through."

Since Hannah had arrived in Garringarup, she'd sought Freya's advice on almost every decision she'd ever made. The idea that Freya was feeling hurt by this rejection rested uneasily, but she couldn't shake the feeling that the McMasters had circled Hannah and locked everyone else out of one of her friend's most important decisions.

Sighing, she stowed the food in the fridge then left the farm.

On the drive home, Freya found herself taking a detour north to the old Garringarup road. Whenever she glanced in the rear-view mirror all she saw was a red plume of dust, but the gumtree-lined river rolled lazily on her left. Ryan was right, it was pretty.

She rounded the bend and her chest tightened when the police tape came into view. She indicated and pulled over. An unfamiliar red car, its hood concertinaed into the cabin and its door cut open like a sardine can, lay crumpled against the wide rough trunk of a towering gum. The fine white filaments of the red morrel flowers lay bright against the pearlescent paintwork as if staking a further claim. Despite the vehicle's ruinous state, the model and registration declared it was new.

Freya blinked a couple of times, but it didn't change what she saw. "What the hell, Jamie? A Porsche? On this road?"

Her heart went out to Ryan. Last night his garbled explanations hadn't made a lot of sense, but this car was the reason he hadn't known Jamie was inside it until he'd pulled him out. The luxury car was a far cry from Jamie's utilitarian four-wheel drive. She thought about what Jamie had said to her thirty-eight hours earlier—that hadn't made any sense either.

Although there was police tape, there were no police or anyone else at the site. Freya picked up the second bouquet of flowers and got out of the car to the *ek ek ek ek* call of a sacred kingfisher. She walked to the side of the tree that wasn't cordoned off and squatted to lay the flowers on the dry red earth.

"What was going on, Jamie? Why were you here?"

But the crumpled car and the silence of the bush offered no answers.

When Freya returned to Kitchener Street, Ryan was sitting at the kitchen table staring into space.

He jumped up and kissed her. "You're back."

"I am."

"I missed you."

She hugged him and wondered at the comment. So often they were ships that passed, and they'd never been one of those couples who needed to do everything together.

"I thought you needed the sleep," she said.

He rubbed his unshaven face. "Yeah, well ... Cuppa?"

"How about we go straight to lunch?" She indicated the shopping bags. "I popped into the supermarket and the bakery on the way home."

"I'm not hungry."

"Sure, but you didn't eat last night. I've got crunchy bread and all your antipasto favorites." She smiled. "I'll even make it for you."

He gave a half-hearted nod and helped her unpack the food before slicing the bread.

"How's Hannah?"

"Manic. I only saw her for a moment because they were leaving for Perth. She and the McMasters have gone to the Supreme Court to obtain permission to harvest Jamie's sperm."

The breadknife clattered to the floor. Ryan stared at her, blinking.

She picked up the knife and ran it under the faucet. "Yeah. That was pretty much my reaction too. After I left the farm I drove to the accident site."

Ryan shoved his hand through his hair. "Jeez, Freya, why? Now you can't ever unsee it."

She ripped the lids off the olives and sun-dried tomatoes. "To try and make sense of it. You never mentioned the Porsche. When did he buy it?"

"He didn't. At least I don't think he did. He wouldn't. It's so not a Jamie car." Ryan's lips twitched. "You can't put a ewe or a 'roo in the back of a Porsche and drive it across a paddock."

"So why is a red one wrapped around a tree?"

Ryan's smile flatlined. "It's the sort of thing Hannah would want for wedding photos."

Freya had lived and breathed Hannah's wedding plans and a luxury German car didn't feature. "I'm not so sure."

"Come on, she's a city girl. She probably asked Jamie for it, and you know what he's like when he's in love. He can never say no." His voice cracked. "He bloody should have."

Freya stepped around the counter and hugged him. "I know you're hurting, but even if Hannah did want a Porsche for photos, it's not her fault."

When Ryan didn't agree she said, "Have you spoken to Brett? Surely he'll have more information now about what caused the crash."

Ryan sighed. "Maybe. I'll call him Monday."

"I'm sure he'd speak to you before then if—"

"No."

"I could ask," she offered.

"Just leave it!" He slumped at her shock. "Sorry, Frey. I know you want to help, but I can't deal with how or why today. I'm still trying to wrap my head around now, and nothing changes the fact that Jamie's dead."

He plated the open sandwiches and carried them to the table. "I've extended my leave until after the funeral."

"Do we know when it is?"

He shrugged. "Probably the end of this week or early next. It depends when the coroner releases his—" He blew out a breath.

Freya tensed. Ryan was a community paramedic—a career he loved and thrived on. He didn't have difficulty saying the words "body" and "death," yet he was clearly struggling now. Usually after a traumatic event he was the one arranging counseling for his team and keeping a close eye on everyone, but this was different. Who was looking out for him?

She stalled a spurt of panic. "Should you talk to someone?"

"I've got you."

But he held onto her hand as if he feared she'd vanish on him too.

CHAPTER NINE

HANNAH WAS deaf and blind to the activity around her. All that existed was time, and even that was cloaked in a haze of dense fog that lifted momentarily only to descend again. To survive, she'd placed her trust implicitly in the McMasters, Angus and Rowan.

It had taken Angus several hours to locate a fertility specialist who was prepared to perform the sperm retrieval procedure. He'd explained that Western Australian law allowed for the collection of sperm but, nonsensically, not for the storage of it, which opened the doctor to prosecution. Even with a Supreme Court order, there were only a handful of doctors prepared to operate when they didn't know the deceased.

Instead of signing her name on the wedding register and certificate, Hannah was signing documents loaded with legalese. Applications to the coroner. Applications to the court. Even if she hadn't been laboring under mind-numbing grief she'd have struggled to fully understand the words. The only thing she was capable of was staring at the clock and willing it to slow. Willing Jamie's sperm to live.

Three o'clock. Five hours since the coroner had agreed to release the body. Three hours since Rowan had presented the affidavit and the other documents to the court. One hundred and eighty precious minutes ticking past—each one a loaded gun with a hair trigger aimed squarely at exploding any chance of sperm viability.

How long did it take for a judge to recognize her love and commitment to Jamie and their longed-for child? How long did it take for a judge to understand that in a nanosecond the accident had derailed her life, crushed all her plans, her hopes and dreams, and decimated her future? How long did it take to comprehend that she shouldn't even be in this position, let alone be dependent on people who didn't know her or Jamie, yet had the power to determine her future? It was wrong! Every part of it was utterly and inconceivably wrong.

Hannah opened her eyes and recognized the blue and red pattern of the hotel's carpet—once again her head was between her knees. It seemed to go there naturally, as if the position would defend her from the savage destruction of her life.

An unfamiliar pair of men's shoes moved into her vision. It took almost more effort than she could muster to raise her head. Suddenly she was looking into her brother's warm hazel eyes.

"Jesus, Han, I'm so sorry."

She threw herself at him and gave into tears. "I w-wish M-mum and D-dad were here."

Declan wrapped his arms around her and she welcomed his familiarity. When her tears finally eased, he handed her a packet of travel tissues and steered her away from the McMasters to a quiet spot in the lobby.

"Ian told me about your plans on the drive in from the airport," he said.

Hannah recalled the doubt on Freya's face and girded herself for unwanted criticism, but all she saw in Declan's face was wonder.

He ran his hand through his hair. "It's like something out of a sci-fi movie but in a good way, you know. I'm really glad you're going for it. Is there anything I can do to help?"

She threw her arms around his neck. "Being here is enough."

They returned to the McMasters and Hannah accepted yet another cup of tea—it was easier than saying no. She sipped it, not registering the taste, just the heat of it, then set the cup down.

Ian's phone rang and the desultory conversation circling her ceased as four sets of eyes turned his way.

"Is it Rowan?" Lydia asked.

"It has to be," Maddie said. "It's twenty-three hours."

"We have thirty-six," Lydia said doggedly.

Earlier, Angus had told them that although thirty-six hours was considered the outer limit for a successful retrieval, twenty-four hours was best.

"You need to know that if we proceed, one of Jamie's testicles will be removed. Are you okay with that?" he'd added.

"Yes," Hannah had said, her voice rolling over Lydia's.

Now Ian said, "G'day, Rowan. Any news? ... Right ... Okay, well ... Yep. Will do."

Before he'd even ended the call Lydia was saying, "Well?"

"Rowan's just delivered the court order to the morgue and the doctor's on his way."

Hannah tasted tea in the back of her throat. "The morgue? I thought they did it at the hospital in the OR."

No one voiced that OR was for the living, but it was written on their faces.

Hannah stood abruptly, clutching her bag. "I want to see him."

"Doctor Bhatt?" Ian said.

"No, Jamie. I need to see him. Talk to him."

"Han, the morgue? You sure?" Declan asked.

"Yes!"

Ian glanced at Lydia, seeking guidance.

Lydia hugged Hannah. "I think it's better to wait until Jamie's home again. After Joe Tozzi's dressed him—"

"No." An urgency had invaded Hannah and for reasons she didn't fully understand she had to see Jamie as soon as possible. "I'm seeing him today."

Maddie wrung her hands "I really don't think—"

"It's our wedding day!" Hannah's shout echoed around the hotel's lobby. Heads turned.

A suited employee appeared out of nowhere, her name badge declaring her the assistant manager. "Is there a problem I can help with?"

Hannah was sobbing now. Declan patted her back carefully as if she was an unexploded bomb.

While Ian spoke to the staff member, Lydia picked up her phone. "I'll call Angus and ask him to set it up. Perhaps Doctor Bhatt can talk to us after the procedure. Before you see Jamie."

Maddie was shoving tissues into Hannah's hands. "I'm sorry. I shouldn't have ... I didn't mean to upset you ..."

Hannah shook her head. Death was the ultimate upset. Everything else paled against it.

An hour later, Hannah arrived at the morgue accompanied by Declan and the McMasters. The unremarkable building stood behind the hospital and was surrounded by a grove of paperbarks and park seats. She shivered. Did people choose to sit here? Eat their lunch?

Declan guided her into the foyer, where a woman was waiting for them.

"I'm Tracey, one of the coronial counselors. Please follow me."

She ushered them into a private room and when the door closed behind them she said, "I'm so very sorry for your loss. Some deaths are more difficult than others to comprehend." Her gaze settled on Hannah. "I believe you were to be married today. I'm so sorry."

Hannah's anxiety spiked. "When can I see Jamie?"

"Doctor Bhatt's just finishing up so it won't be too much longer."

Hannah relaxed into a chair only to tense again when Tracey said, "Jamie's accident took place at high speed, Hannah. It was the impact that killed him and that means he doesn't look the same as when you last saw him."

"What do you mean?"

"There's extensive bruising and cuts to his face from the airbag. His jaw was broken and that means his mouth is sagging."

Despite not wanting to know, Hannah heard herself asking, "What other injuries?"

"You won't see them."

"I want to know."

Tracey consulted a notebook. "He has bruising to his torso from the seatbelt, a broken arm, pelvis and two broken legs."

"Can I touch him?"

"Of course. But he's going to feel cold, Hannah. Quite cold."

She swallowed hard, forcing away the image of Jamie lying in a refrigerated box.

"You can change your mind," Tracey said gently. "You won't be the first or the last. There's no judgment. We're here to support you in whatever you choose to do. You may prefer to see him after he's been cared for by the funeral home."

Lydia slid her hand into Hannah's. "Darling, I think that's best."

"No! The wedding should be happening and—" Hannah blinked rapidly. "It has to be now. I can't get through today without seeing him."

There was a knock at the door, then a woman walked in. "Hello, I'm Doctor Bhatt. We spoke on the phone."

Hannah stood. "I'm Hannah. Did it work?"

"I excised the contents of one of Mr. McMaster's testicles and placed it in medium. I won't be able to give you a report about the health of the sperm until it's been examined in the clinic's lab."

Disappointment thwacked her. "When will that happen?"

"I'm leaving now so give me a couple of hours. I'll call you whether the news is good or bad."

"Thank you!' Hannah threw her arms around the doctor. "Thank you."

The McMasters and Declan echoed her appreciation and Doctor Bhatt left.

Tracey's phone buzzed and she checked the screen. "Jamie's ready. How are you feeling, Hannah?"

She had no clue how to describe the writhing emotions inside her. They whipped her from the morass of devastation to blessed numbness, to fulminating anger and hopelessness, then back to despair. She didn't want to see her beloved Jamie damaged and hurt, but she couldn't not see him either.

"Now will be as bad as later," she said.

"Is that a yes?" Tracey asked.

"Yes."

"Do you want me to come with you?" Declan asked.

But even if his face hadn't screamed *please say no*, Hannah wanted to be alone with the love of her life.

She followed Tracey down the corridor to another room. She'd watched various forensic pathology television shows and was expecting a large expanse of stainless steel. This room with its cream paint, botanical pictures on the walls and a comfortable chair was unexpected. However, the sheet-covered trolley declared the room's purpose. So did the stranger standing at the back of the room.

Having been told what she would see didn't cushion the shock. Hannah's heart high-jumped into her throat, choking her, and her feet stalled at the door. She gripped the architrave to stay standing.

"Take your time."

The compassion on Tracey's face almost undid her, but she knew that if she turned and ran from the silver trolley with the black wheels and the respectful stranger in scrubs, regret would gnaw at her until she was hollow.

Forcing her legs to move was like lifting lead weights and it seemed to take an eternity to walk the length of the room—to reach Jamie.

"Are you ready?" Tracey said.

"Please stop asking me that," Hannah snapped and immediately regretted it. "I'm sorry. It's just ..." But how did she even start to explain that in the midst of the worst moment of her life, being asked to check her feelings over and over wasn't helping.

Tracey nodded at the mortuary attendant, who stepped forward. "Ms. Simmons, I'm very sorry for your loss."

"Thank you for being with him today," Hannah said. She hated the thought that Jamie had been alone last night.

"Of course." With great care, the attendant turned down the sheet.

Hannah's hand rose fast to her mouth but not soon enough to stifle the cry. *This isn't Jamie.* Her beautiful man with the twinkle in his eye and the cheeky curls falling across his forehead had never looked like this. This man's face was covered in lacerations and his hair lay flat and brushed the wrong way. She reached out and finger-combed the strands so it sat the way he'd always worn it.

"Would you like some time alone with him?" Tracey asked.

Hannah nodded.

As the attendant and counselor withdrew, Tracey indicated the button on the wall. "Press this when you're ready for us to return."

When the door closed behind them with a soft click, Hannah readied herself then touched Jamie. She flinched at the chill. His skin was always hot—a welcome heat source in their bed. His stillness could have been mistaken for sleep, but this vicious cold screamed the uncompromising and insidious truth. Hiding from it was impossible. Silent tears streamed down her cheeks.

She cupped the broken side of his face, her palm hiding the distortion of his features, and for the first time she glimpsed her Jamie. Her breath came in short gasps as she tried to form the words she'd rehearsed. The words she'd believed would steady and direct her life.

"I ... Hannah Jane Simmons take you ... Jamie Paul Raymond McMaster ... to be my husband. To have and to hold from this day forward, in—"

Sobs choked her and her legs softened. She sat down hard, dropping her head next to his. *Why? Why? Why?* The word echoed unrelentingly in her head alongside a never-ending scream. What sort of God struck down a man in his prime? What malicious pleasure could be derived from killing Jamie on the eve of their wedding? What the hell had she done to deserve this level of pain?

She raised her head and looked at Jamie through her tears. "I know you'd never willingly leave me. I know you want to be here, living the life we planned. I love you so much. I know you'll always be part of my life, and I promise you that our child will keep us connected forever."

She wished she'd thought to bring his wedding ring. She looked around the room, keen for a sign—something, anything—that told her Jamie had heard her. That his spirit was present, loving her the way he had when he'd lived.

But there was nothing. No color change in the room. No flickering light. No breeze stirring the air and no sandalwood—the scent she associated with Jamie. Just the silence of the room pressing in on her, loaded with loss.

CHAPTER TEN

When Hannah walked into Just Because late on Monday morning, Freya locked the door and put up the *Back in ten minutes* sign. Then she took Hannah into the comfortable space she'd created out the back and sat her down before making a pot of Earl Grey tea.

Asking Hannah how she was feeling was unnecessary. Exhaustion was sketched in charcoal around her eyes and mouth, and her usually clear skin was red and blotchy. Her body thrummed with restlessness—even sitting, her hands fluttered, fingers pulling at a loose thread on the sofa or picking at her nails, French shellacked for the wedding.

"When did you get back from Perth?" Freya asked when Hannah didn't speak.

"Late Saturday." Hannah stared into the fine bone china mug as if she didn't recognize her favorite tea.

"Oh, I didn't realize. If I'd known, I would have visited yesterday."

"Yesterday I couldn't get out of bed," Hannah said flatly. "Brett came."

Freya thought about the Porsche wrapped around the tree on a road that ran parallel to Perth and wondered about the police visit. "Did he have questions?"

Hannah gave her a blank look. "Questions?"

"About the accident."

"I don't think so; Ian talked to him. I wasn't up to seeing anyone." Hannah closed her eyes for a moment as if seeking strength. "He said the accident happened because Jamie swerved to miss a kid on a bike. He d-died saving a child. He was p-protecting a life and he l-lost his." Sobs racked her body.

"Oh, Hannah." Freya hugged her, wishing she could do something to lessen her pain.

Hannah pulled back and sipped her tea. "Brett told Ian that people have left flowers where it happened."

"Are you going to visit?"

Hannah shook her head violently. "Why would I want to see the place he spent his last terrifying seconds? God, I'm trying not to think about it! The only thing keeping me upright is the doctor retrieved lots and lots of healthy sperm. Enough for five or six cycles of IVF." Behind the tears, Hannah's eyes lit up. "The baby can have siblings."

Freya's hand loosened on her mug and she only just avoided dropping it. Her brain was stuck on the way Hannah had said "the baby," as if it already existed and the siblings were the ones yet to be conceived.

She knew Hannah was deep in the weeds of grief and grasping at anything that might offer her a semblance of the life she'd lost. She also knew that the strict time limitations after death to retrieve healthy sperm meant the decision to harvest was made in the thick and numbing fog of shock and grief when no one was at their best. Lydia's firm hand in the situation wouldn't have helped. Freya was so worried about Hannah that she'd done some reading. It was reassuring to discover that only a handful of women went on to use the sperm. Over time, as their grief changed, most decided against it. Which meant she could hold off voicing her concerns until Hannah was in a better emotional space.

"Are you back at home?" she asked, redirecting the conversation into safer waters.

Hannah shook her head. "Lydia suggested I wait until after the funeral."

"Are you okay with that?"

"Yes and no. I don't want to be alone in the house, but at the farm I feel Jamie's less mine."

Freya understood. Although Jamie owned a thriving IT business, he'd always stayed involved in the farm and Lydia had certainly held onto him. "I can see why it may feel that way."

"And it's not that I don't want the McMasters involved in the funeral, of course I do," Hannah said. "I mean they were so great in Perth. Without their support, no judge would have signed the retrieval order and Jamie's sperm wouldn't be frozen and waiting for me. And I don't have enough money in my account to pay for the funeral anyway. Thankfully Ian's looking after all the legal stuff—"

"Ian is?" Freya thought she must have misheard.

"Jamie was planning on making a new will—he even had an appointment with Rowan to do it—but then he had to go to Perth suddenly for work. He promised me he'd sort it after our honeymoon, put my name on the house title and we'd be each other's executors. I mean, he wasn't expecting to die!" Hannah slumped, her indignation seeming to collapse in on itself. "To be honest, I'm grateful Ian's looking after things. With the business and Jamie's personal investments, I'm sure it's a huge job and right now I'm not up to it."

Freya stopped herself from saying that if Hannah had been the executor she could have engaged an attorney to handle it all. As it was, Ian would likely ask Rowan to apply for probate.

"As his de facto wife you'll inherit his estate," she said. "I just wish all this was easier for you."

"Huh!" Hannah's strangled laugh turned into a sob. "The McMasters have a vision for the funeral but it's not what I want. It doesn't showcase the man *I* loved. Right now, it's all about Jamie the son and president of the cricket club."

"He was those things."

"I know, but he was so much more. They've completely ignored his time in Perth. If he hadn't lived there, he would never have met me! And they've chosen roses instead of natives for the flowers, and they're not even having an eco-casket. I want people to know about *my* Jamie, so I've written what I want to say, but it's going to take everything I have just to survive the service. Jamie loved you and Ryan, and I love you." She held out her hands to Freya. "Will you read it for me?"

A prickling sensation rushed over Freya's skin. "Ryan should do it."

"He's doing the eulogy and he's a pallbearer. And these are *my* words. I want a woman to read them, but not Lydia or Maddie," Hannah said, pre-empting Freya's next suggestion. "He loved you as a friend and more than anything he wanted us to be friends. And we are, best friends. It makes sense for you to do it. Please."

Standing up in church in front of half the town and reading Hannah's intimate words of love and devotion for Jamie was her worst nightmare. She'd rather stand naked in Main Street on festival weekend. But Hannah's grief was too raw for Freya to refuse her.

She squeezed Hannah's hands and allowed the lie to fall. "It would be an honor."

And when Jamie's casket was lowered into the ground, she would bury the final conversation she'd had with him and with it the risk of it ever hurting her, Ryan or Hannah.

At the funeral, Hannah barely heard Ryan delivering the eulogy. She was too busy raging at the sunshine spilling into the church and lighting the stained-glass windows to perfection. Her dearest love was dead, but the weather was immune to her pain.

She scrunched the fine cotton handkerchief in her hand and forced her gaze from the rafters to the front of the church. The claustrophobic box covered with the wrong flowers pulled everyone's attention, reminding them that Jamie lay there still and lifeless. Hannah hadn't wanted the coffin at the service—she'd wanted to listen to people talking about Jamie as if he still walked among them. Lydia had overruled her, saying that as not everyone was able to attend the viewing, the funeral was their last chance to say goodbye. She'd explained to Hannah that Jamie's friends and family needed and deserved to show their respects by carrying him to the hearse.

Now, the long rays of sunlight streaming through the rose window spun kaleidoscopes of color above Jamie's coffin as if this was a party with disco lights. It was wrong. Everything was so, so wrong. The sky should be filled with gunmetal clouds blocking the sun. Fat tears of rain should be falling while the crack and roll of thunder deafened them all. Instead, the day was infused with the vigor of spring and new life.

A sharp pain tightened Hannah's chest and she gasped.

Freya squeezed her hand. Declan's shoulder pressed gently against hers and Hannah blew out a breath, focusing on Jamie's sperm—the only part of him that still lived. Was that what the colorful whorls of sunlight were telling her? That Jamie wasn't gone forever?

Ryan cleared his throat for a third time and Hannah realized his voice was thick with emotion.

"Jamie was a bloke with eclectic tastes and talents," Ryan said. "He was as comfortable being a computer nerd as he was fencing, and none of us will ever forget his annual appearance in the Christmas panto. The year he lived in Perth was notable for a drop in the town's fundraising. He was a bloke who loved his community and he looked out for everyone. If he heard someone was doing it tough, he'd reach out with a listening ear and, if he could, give practical help. If he knew I'd attended a tough call-out, he'd suggest a beer. I've never needed him as much as I do—" Ryan's chest heaved and he swiped his hand across his face.

Freya rose and moved to stand next to him, placing her hand on his shoulder. Ryan's forehead touched it for a moment and then he recovered.

Watching the love Freya and Ryan shared flow between them rammed home exactly how much Hannah had lost. Her brittle control cracked—her head fell forward and then she was sobbing uncontrollably. Declan slung an arm around her but Hannah barely felt it.

Ryan's voice again filled the church. "Not everyone understood or appreciated Jamie's intensity—something I like to call enthusiasm—but it complemented all that we loved about him. It was never difficult being Jamie's friend, not even when he insisted on spending hours in the nets in his constant chase for a century. Not when he woke me up once a month at 3:00 in the morning saying, 'Mate, get up and look at the moon.' Or when he had a brilliant idea that involved me driving three hundred kays to pick something up for him because he'd gotten caught up with another project. He had an inexhaustible supply of energy and he liked nothing more than to pull us all along in his slipstream. And we benefitted. It was his determination and commitment that got us the new clubrooms. That gave the club the shot in the arm it needed, brought in more junior cricketers than we've seen in a decade and got us over-thirties back on the pitch and winning the Wheatbelt Cup. You can bet that he's up there now with all the other cricketing legends, bending their ears."

A ripple of appreciative murmuring circled Hannah, steadying her.

Ryan looked straight out at the crowd. "Our lives were so much richer for Jamie being part of them. I will miss him for the rest of mine."

He stepped down and on his way past the coffin pressed his palm on the glossy wooden veneer. Hannah couldn't hear what he was saying, but it looked like "Love you, mate."

Freya, who'd remained at the lectern, pulled a sheet of paper out of her clutch and adjusted the microphone. Then she dropped her head as if she was praying, before raising it and staring out across the congregation.

"Hannah's asked me to ..." She narrowed her eyes for a moment as if trying to focus, then straightened her shoulders. "Hannah's asked me to read these words she's written for Jamie. Please imagine her speaking them."

Freya smoothed the paper. "My darling Jamie, I wrote these words for our wedding, for pledging our love and our lives to each other. When I imagined that you would always be by my side, journeying with me. When the idea of one of us dying was so far away it was ridiculous to even consider. But you've been stolen from me and now I'm a shell."

Hannah's mouth moved silently in time with the words. She knew them all by heart and the familiar rush of tears came as they always did whenever she tried to say them.

"You're my every—" Freya's hands gripped the lectern, her knuckles gleaming white. "My everything. My heart ... my soul ... my sun, stars and all the planets aligned. You pulled me into your orbit, wrapped your arms around me and m-made me the c-center of your world."

Freya's ragged breathing reverberated through the microphone and Hannah willed her not to break down. The whole point of asking Freya to speak on her behalf was so she didn't fall apart. Because if that happened she feared she'd never find the strength to put the shattered pieces of herself back together.

Lydia and Maddie sobbed quietly, and there were other sounds of sniffling behind her. Everyone had loved Jamie and Hannah appreciated it, but their grief threatened to consume her. She brought her hands to her ears and silently mouthed the words she'd written. She didn't lower her hands until she knew Freya was close to finishing the speech.

"Our love will transcend this distance," Freya was saying, then she stopped and bit her lip. When she spoke again, her volume had dropped to barely audible.

Hannah couldn't hear the final words—the most important ones of all. She glanced around and saw people in the nearest pews straining to hear too. If they couldn't hear Freya, there was no way anyone in the back could.

Hannah lurched to her feet. "And so will our dreams," she said loudly, her words echoing back to her. "I promise you."

As she looked around the congregation, her gaze stalled on a brown-haired woman in an elegant hat seated at the back of the church.

Every hair on Hannah's body rose. She'd never met this woman or even seen her in person before, but she knew exactly who she was. Everyone in the church knew. Hell, the entire town knew Monique Jefferies.

CHAPTER ELEVEN

In the church hall after the service, a cup of tea was placed in Hannah's hand and replaced twice. Assorted finger foods were offered, plated and set down next to her. She was hugged, and unwanted words were spoken by people who wished they didn't have to speak at all.

"You poor thing ..."

"Such a tragedy ..."

"We don't always understand the grand plan ..."

"Take some comfort that he died a hero's death ..."

"He was one of the best ..."

As Hannah tried keeping her breathing steady while murmuring over and over "thank you for coming' to gray-faced people, her only thought was *why is Monique at Jamie's funeral?* What right did she have to come when she'd caused Jamie so much heartache and pain?

In the crush of people in the hall it was hard to single out anyone, especially as almost every woman wore a black dress and a strand of pearls. Freya was the only one whose black frock had a bright panel of swirls of green, white and purple. Hannah excused herself from the Garibaldis and walked straight to her, caught her by the arm and steered her towards the stage steps.

"Where's Monique?" she demanded.

Confusion crossed Freya's face. "Monique who?"

"Who do you think! Monique Jefferies. I saw her in the church."

"Are you sure?" Freya rose on her toes and scanned the hall. "I mean you've never met her, have you?"

"I saw photos of her on other people's Insta accounts."

Hannah shrugged away the embarrassing memory of her insecurity during her and Jamie's early days together. Back then, she couldn't understand what Jamie saw in her when she was so much younger and less worldly than him, and she'd spent far too much time looking for photos of the woman who'd broken his heart. When she found them, she saw a woman who was the polar opposite of her in every way. Monique was country born and bred, boarding-school educated and seemed to have an innate sense of her place in the world and her right to own it. The sort of woman who made Hannah feel insignificant and lacking in every way.

Of course she'd asked Jamie about Monique, but he hadn't said much, referring to her as "his lucky escape." After he and Hannah had been dating a month, he said, "She did me a favor."

"What do you mean?"

"If she hadn't left, I would never have come to Perth and met you. And that," he'd pulled her into him, "would have been a tragedy."

"I'm glad you think so."

"Oh, I do. So much so that it's time to put our exes firmly in the past where they belong. I'm only interested in looking forward."

Not wanting to spotlight their age difference, Hannah had resisted pointing out that her exes were closer to hook-ups than a real relationship. Besides, Jamie was busy showing her exactly how much he adored her and who was she to distract him from that?

"If Monique was at the funeral, the church would have been buzzing," Freya was saying. "And by now at least ten people would have told me, but no one's mentioned—" Her hand suddenly wrapped around Hannah's wrist.

Hannah followed her gaze. The crowd was falling back and Ryan was walking towards them accompanied by a tall, glamorous woman. Or was it the other way around? Ryan's face was difficult to read.

Freya swore softly. "Hannah, you don't have to talk to her."

"Why wouldn't I talk to her? Jamie was my fiancé, not hers."

"Hello, Freya." Monique kissed Freya's cheek. "It's good to see you, although not this way. I still can't believe he's—"

"None of us can," Freya said quickly. "Monique, you haven't met Hannah, have you? Hannah Simmons, Monique Jefferies."

"I'm Llewellyn-Jones now." Monique extended her hand to Hannah with a quiet smile. "I realize me being here is probably unexpected but I wanted to pay my respects to you, and of course to Lydia and Ian. David and I are so terribly sorry for your loss."

When Hannah didn't say anything, Monique glanced between Freya and Ryan, then back to her. "David's my husband, but before him, Jamie and I ... well, we—"

"Were together before I met Jamie. I know, he told me *all* about it." Hannah wanted to show Monique that she and Jamie had no secrets. Wanted to reinforce her position of holding first place in his heart. "Thank you for breaking up with him."

There was a moment's silence then Monique threw back her head and laughed. "I can see why he loved you."

The words released a pressure valve and Hannah relaxed. From what Jamie had told her, the last thing she'd expected was for Monique to be warm and kind. Then again, Monique had been the one to end the relationship and wound him. But going by the way Monique had invoked her husband's name in her words of sympathy she obviously adored David, so she understood the depth of Hannah's pain.

Hannah managed a small smile. "Thank you. I imagine your David feels grateful too. Is he here? I'd like to meet him."

"Unfortunately we couldn't get a babysitter so he's on the farm with our son."

Pain locked onto her. "You have a child?"

"Yes, a toddler. Will." Monique smiled and brought up a photo on her phone.

A little boy with a mop of chestnut hair stared back at Hannah. A little boy who looked exactly as she pictured her and Jamie's child.

Another photo filled the screen—this time the little boy sat on a tractor with his arms around the neck of a man with the same mouth and eyes.

"Will's the spitting image of David," Monique said, love clear in her voice. "But with more hair."

"He's very cute," Hannah managed as her heart threatened to tear in two.

"I think so, but then again I'm biased." Monique turned to Freya and Ryan. "Have you two finally got started on babies?"

Freya stiffened and Ryan slid his arm around her waist. Not for the first time, Hannah wondered if the reason they didn't have children was because there was a problem.

Freya was shaking her head when a shrill voice behind them cut the air.

"How dare you!"

All conversation in the hall ceased as Lydia bore down on Hannah's group, her eyes flashing. "How dare you show your face here, Monique! Masquerading as if you care!"

Monique flinched at the fulminating loathing in Lydia's voice, but her face remained calm. Hannah couldn't help but admire her composure. She was certain that if she was the object of Lydia's rage she would be quaking uncontrollably.

"Lydia, I'm so very sorry for your loss." Monique's sincerity rang through the hall as clear as a bell.

"You have no right to be here," Lydia said.

"I wanted to pay my respects to you and Ian."

"Hah! You lost that chance when you left Jamie broken and bleeding and we had to pick up the pieces. Take your fake condolences and get the hell out of here before I kick your sorry ass through the door."

Hannah couldn't stifle her shocked gasp. Lydia was always a model of decorum and manners, but right now she was unrecognizable.

"Monique." Ian stepped in next to his wife and gave a curt nod. "Be a good idea if you left. Now."

Maddie joined them, her hand on her mother's arm. "You heard my father. Get out."

Monique's gaze took in the united front of the McMasters, then landed on Hannah. "I'm sorry. I didn't come here to add to your pain."

She turned and crossed the hall to the door, her heels clacking on the hardwood boards the only sound. As myriad emotions thundered through Hannah, it was the spark of sympathy for Monique that surprised her the most.

After the formal wake, the McMasters and Hannah had returned to the farm, and a group of mostly cricket club members and partners had trooped to the pub. Freya ordered food for everyone in an attempt to soak up the booze, but with varying degrees of success. When the pub closed, she tried to make sure no one drove home.

She and Ryan walked back to Kitchener Street under a dazzling canopy of winking stars. Any other evening it would have been romantic, but tonight Freya's usual awe was replaced by the daunting reminder that human life was as fragile as a solitary snowflake.

Under the harsh scrutiny of the LED porch light, she slid her key into the lock, the action surprisingly steady since she'd consumed more alcohol in a day than she usually drank in a week. She kicked off her heels, savoring the relief of horizontal arches and the easing sting of a blister, then she made two large mugs of tea.

Ryan, tie askew and with a five o'clock shadow dark on his cheeks, lay on the sofa with his eyes closed. She'd been on guard for him today, recognizing his struggle and how difficult it was to say goodbye to his best friend. He'd drunk a lot since the service and she probably should have suggested they come home earlier, but sitting and drinking didn't require any decisions and she'd given in to that.

At the sound of mugs touching coasters on the coffee table, Ryan heaved himself up and swung his feet to the floor. "Thanks," he said wearily.

Freya sat and stroked his face. "You were amazing today."

"I thought pulling him out of that car was hard, but today ..." Ryan rubbed the back of his neck. "It should have been another forty years before I had to sit in front of his coffin."

"I know," she said softly. "But for all that, we gave him a good send-off."

"Yeah. Although who chose that last piece of music?" He shuddered at the memory. "He'd have hated it. It should have been 'Forever Young'."

"I think it was Hannah. And to be fair, Lydia probably wanted Celine Dion."

Ryan huffed out a breath—half-laugh, half-sigh. "At least he was spared that. I guess he and Hannah had a generation gap music-wise."

"They'd been together long enough for her to know what he loved, but let's face it. Not a lot of his music was funeral appropriate."

Ryan was quiet for a bit, then said, "How do you reckon he would have felt about Monique turning up?"

"It's not really about Jamie, is it?"

"What do you mean?"

"I don't know. I've never really forgiven her for what she put us— him through. And then to show up at his funeral talking about her husband, who by the way looks ridiculously similar to Jamie, and waving around photos of her kid when—"

"Hey." Ryan pulled her close and kissed her hair. "Forget her."

She snuggled in. "Yeah. Good idea."

"Cute kid but."

Freya glanced at him. "I thought we weren't talking about her."

"We're not."

His fingers played in her hair and she lay her head on his chest, loving the reassuring way it rose and fell, taking her with it. This was home. Her eyes fluttered closed.

"Frey?"

"Hmm ..."

"Marry me."

A whoosh of adrenaline tingled pinpricks all over her and her eyes flew open. "What?"

He smiled a sloppy smile. "Let's get married."

She laughed. "Yeah, right. Can you imagine?"

Ryan grinned. "I love you soooo much." He trailed kisses down her neck as his fingers unzipped her dress. "You're my everything."

"You really are wasted," she teased, unbuttoning his shirt.

He grinned. "And you love me."

And she did. But all further words and thoughts vanished under the pressure of Ryan's mouth on hers and the delicious sensations streaming through her. She sank into them, taking blessed refuge from the horrible day and the awful week.

CHAPTER TWELVE

THE FOLLOWING morning Freya and Ryan nursed epic hangovers and a few bruises from falling off the sofa. It was testament to the amount of alcohol they'd drunk that they'd thought sex was a good idea and that they were actually capable of it. She was certain both of them had fallen asleep at different times, and from what she could remember about it neither of them had come.

Sunshine and Ryan had woken her. Dressed in his work uniform, he brought her paracetamol and a large glass fizzing with a vitamin hangover cure.

"I'm giving up drinking," she mumbled, barely able to lift her thumping head off the pillow.

"Me too." He kissed her on the forehead. "Drink lots of water today, yeah?"

"You too." She suddenly remembered it was his first day back at work. Unlike her, who didn't have to make life and death decisions, he needed to be on top of his game. "Should you take today off and start tomorrow?"

He rubbed the back of his neck. "You opening Just Because?"

His question surprised her. After the accident she'd closed the shop for two days, and again yesterday for the funeral, but Ryan knew that even though the shopfront only accounted for fifty percent of her sales she didn't like disappointing her local customers or the growing tourist trade.

"Of course," she said.

"Right."

"What?"

He sighed. "No point me taking another day off if you're not here."

Considering how gutted he was by Jamie's death, Freya thought there were plenty of reasons to give himself another day. But if it was company he wanted she could compromise.

"You could work a short day and I could shut at 2:30. The weather's nice—we could have a picnic by the river."

He smiled. "I'd like that."

She added *buy picnic food* to her mental list and kissed him goodbye.

There was a constant stream of customers through the shop, although most people wanted to talk about the funeral rather than buy anything. Freya listened, sipped water and worked on a new window display. She should be ordering Christmas stock but her head wasn't up to thinking that clearly.

The last person she expected to walk into the store was Hannah, so when she did it took a moment for Freya's mind to link the vision with her. She'd assumed that after the funeral Hannah wouldn't want or be able to speak to another person today.

She greeted her with a hug. "How are you?"

Hannah shrugged. "Numb."

"Right. Yesterday was huge."

"Are you okay?" Hannah asked.

Freya almost said "a bit hungover," but stopped herself. She didn't want to imply the funeral had been a party. "All good."

"Are you sure? It's just I noticed that Monique upset you when she asked about babies." Hannah's hand reached out. "I'm sorry you're having problems."

Chrissie Lancefield swung around from the stack of throw blankets, interest keen on her face.

"Wait, what? What are you talking about?" Freya asked, utterly confused.

"I thought the reason you don't have kids yet was because you were waiting to get married," Hannah said. "But since you told me you don't believe in marriage, I've been wondering if there's a problem."

Freya's temples throbbed. What was it about women who were keen to have children wanting everyone else to have them too?

Chrissie had moved onto the water-bottle display so she was closer to Hannah. The last thing Freya needed was the gold-medalist gossip running her mouth off all around town with what many probably thought was true. She opened her own mouth, but Hannah got in first.

"It must be so hard for you. And Ryan. I wish I'd known. I'm here for you if you ever need to talk."

"Tatum Holbrook took Chinese herbs," Chrissie offered, giving up all pretense of shopping. "You should try them, Freya."

"I don't need to!" Freya saw Hannah and Chrissie exchange a look and realized she'd just yelled. "Sorry."

"That's okay. It's a stressful time." Chrissie hurried out of the shop as Hannah's brother, Declan, walked in.

"Han, you ready? We don't want to miss our flight."

"You're going somewhere?" Freya's dazed and dehydrated brain ached with conversation whiplash.

Hannah nodded. "Singapore. I'm not ready to move back into the house, but I need some time away from the farm. I just popped in to say goodbye."

Freya blinked as if that would help her understand what was going on. Yesterday Freya had offered Hannah their spare room for as long as she needed it, but Hannah had told her she wanted to stay at the farm. Less than twenty-four hours later—and only seconds after telling her "I'm here for you"—Hannah was going to Singapore?

Not that Freya needed Hannah's sympathy—she and Ryan were not struggling to conceive; hell, they weren't even trying—but some hurt landed that Hannah didn't want her support. *Stop being tired and emotional.* Of course Hannah wanted to spend time with her brother—her closest living relative. He also had the added benefits of not being part of a couple and living in a place that shared no similarities with Garringarup.

"A bit of breathing space?" Freya said and Hannah nodded. "Don't worry about the house. I'll look after the garden and water the indoor plants. What about Ozzie?"

"He's at the farm for now, but maybe you could bring him to the house now and then?"

"Sure, of course. Let us know your return flight and Ryan or I can pick you up from the airport."

"Thanks," Hannah said flatly.

They hugged goodbye and as Hannah left the shop, Freya realized it was past 2:00.

Ryan was waiting in the parking lot when she arrived at the river. He'd changed from his uniform to recently purchased smart casual clothes, which surprised her as it was just a picnic for the two of them. She hoped the choice of clothes meant he was feeling brighter in himself.

"Hey, gorgeous." He leaned in and kissed her. "I hope you brought heaps of food. I'm starving."

"I got all your faves."

Together they carried the cooler, picnic basket and blanket to a spot under a sprawling gum. As it was midweek they were the only people there, and birdsong and the burble of the creek the only noise.

Freya sat, then fell back on the blanket. "This was a bad idea."

"Why?"

"I was doing okay at work but stopping like this—I just want to sleep."

"Eat first."

Ryan unpacked the cooler and they built warm chicken and avocado rolls. Freya nibbled at hers, too busy savoring the pleasure of watching Ryan eat two before he reached for a chocolate eclair from the bakery. She loved that he was hungry—he'd hardly eaten anything in the previous week.

"What?" he asked, wiping cream from his mouth.

She smiled. "Just you eating as if you've got hollow legs. I've been worried."

"Sorry."

She wriggled forward so their knees touched. "There's nothing to be sorry about. I'm just glad you're feeling more yourself."

He caught her hand. "I couldn't have got through this last week without you."

"I'm glad you didn't have to."

"Me too. And with that in mind ..." He delved his free hand into his pocket, pulled out a ring and slid it on her finger.

She stared at the row of rubies nestled in a gold band, her thoughts as jumbled as clothes in a dryer. "What's this?"

"My grandmother's engagement ring." He gave her a curious look. "Why so surprised? I thought after last night you'd want a ring to make it official."

She tried remembering last night—most of it was hazy. *Let's get married. Yeah, right.* Her hand flew to her mouth. "Oh my God, you were serious?"

He frowned. "Of course I was serious. Weren't you?"

"We were drunk!" But the hurt in his eyes made her backpedal. "Sorry, it's just we always said we didn't want to get married. We don't believe in it. It's an anachronism and—"

He pressed a finger gently against her mouth. "I know what we said, but we never thought about dying either and that's going to happen."

"One day. But I hope it's a very long way away."

"I think we just learned it can happen at any moment."

She couldn't argue with that. "Okay, but even if it happened tomorrow, I can't see what death's got to do with us getting married?"

"Not death, life. Kids."

The noise in her head made her doubt she'd heard him properly. Surely it was her hungover brain still stuck on what Hannah had said in the shop.

"Did you just say kids?"

Ryan's gaze held a dreamy quality. "Yeah. Cute little kids."

She stared at him as if he was an alien beamed in from another planet. It had been years since they'd talked about having kids. Even then it had been in the vaguest of terms—"maybe," "possibly," "perhaps one day way in the future." Except "one day" never came because they were content with their lives the way they were.

Ryan was gripping her hands. "I want to be a dad, Frey. Jamie dying like that ... It made me realize time's finite. We've been wasting our time. Our lives."

Suddenly angry, she pulled her hands away. "We're not wasting our lives! God, we have a rich and wonderful life."

"I'm sorry." His face was one of startled contrition. "What I mean is, I've been doing a lot of thinking since Jamie died. About the meaning of life, what's important to me. Why we're here." He sighed. "I'm not explaining myself very well."

"You've never mentioned wanting children."

He frowned. "That's not true. We talked about it when we first started dating."

"That was eleven years ago!"

"So?"

"So, I didn't think you wanted them. I'm thirty-five, Ryan."

"That's not old."

"It is in baby-making terms. There no guarantees I'd get pregnant."

He gave her his special smile. "I doubt you'll have to worry. Freya was the Norse god of love and fertility. You'll romp it in."

A baby. It was such an unexpected U-turn that she couldn't organize her thoughts.

She tried picturing a baby on the picnic blanket crawling over their knees. A chubby baby with Ryan's blue eyes and her dark hair. When the image came it was as fuzzy and indistinct as the ultrasound photos several excited pregnant women had pushed into her hands. She could clearly remember her niece as a baby, so she gave herself a mental shake and tried again. This time she visualized a red-ringleted Mia. Why couldn't she picture their baby?

You're overthinking! This time it was her mother's voice. She'd said the same thing to Freya years ago when she'd drawn up a pros and cons list about moving in with Ryan.

"Listen to your heart, Freya. He loves you. Do you love him?"

"Yes."

"Has he ever hit you or threatened you?"

"No! Of course not."

"Well then." Vivian had shrugged. "You know your decision."

Her very sensible mother. The pinpricks of pain Freya got whenever she thought about Vivian's declining health jabbed her. Her mother would love a wedding and another grandchild, and Ryan clearly wanted a baby. Something deep down inside Freya ached at the thought of disappointing them.

Ryan was giving her that special smile he reserved for her and just like that Freya knew she was being ridiculous. Her inability to picture a child was everything to do with the shock and surprise of Ryan going all traditional on her. Once she wasn't hungover and her mind had time to catch up, she'd be seeing flashes of their baby every time she closed her eyes.

"Okay," she said.

"Okay to getting married and having a baby?" he checked.

She nodded, urging the excitement to come. He hugged her so hard she couldn't breathe.

CHAPTER THIRTEEN

"Mᴜᴍ?"

Freya dumped the shopping on her mother's kitchen table and sighed. There was no sign of the new placemats she'd brought from Just Because; the old ones dating back to her childhood remained, their bright colors faded by time. They'd been a wedding present and, like the rest of the house, they were stuck in a time warp. Nothing had changed since her father's death six years earlier.

A reasonable percentage of Freya's business was helping Garringarup widows redecorate their homes after a respectable mourning period. Many spoke of how they'd wanted a new look years earlier but their husbands hadn't wanted to spend the money. Vivian was the opposite: it was as if she feared that by changing anything she'd lose her memories. Freya had initially been sympathetic, but now the house needed painting, new blinds and new carpet. Despite Freya bringing carpet and blind samples and offering to organize everything, her mother was refusing to make a decision.

"Mum, it's me!"

Freya switched on the kettle and stowed the perishables in the fridge, but when she closed it her mother still hadn't appeared.

Freya checked the sunroom, the lounge and the bedroom before peering into the backyard. Towels fluttered from the line—a sure sign it was Friday—and some pots and potting mix sat on an old table, but she couldn't see her mother anywhere.

"Mum!"

She heard a groan and turned back into the house. She found her mother on the bathroom floor, propped up against the tub. "Are you okay?"

"Just a bit dizzy."

Freya noticed the beads of sweat on her mother's forehead and ran to the kitchen for some orange juice and the glucometer. Returning, she kneeled down next to the now shaking Vivian and held the glass to her lips. "Drink this."

Her mother managed to drink the full glass, then Freya checked her blood sugar. As expected, it was too low.

"Have you had breakfast?" she asked.

"Not yet. I thought I'd peg out the laundry first."

Freya leashed her frustration. "Mum, we've talked about this. The new insulin kicks in faster."

"I know that," Vivian said irritably. "And every day this week I've pinned out the laundry and then eaten breakfast."

Freya thought of the half-filled pots. "And this morning you only pinned out the laundry?"

"Stop treating me like a child!" Vivian struggled to her feet.

Used to the low blood sugar flashes of anger, Freya bit her tongue and extended her arm to help.

"What's this?" Her mother touched Ryan's grandmother's ring.

"I'll tell you over breakfast."

While her mother ate porridge, Freya told her that she and Ryan were engaged.

"Oh, darling, that's wonderful." Vivian's now-focused eyes sparkled then dimmed. "It's such a shame your father can't walk you down the aisle."

Freya didn't touch her mother's old, gnarled disappointment.

When Gerry had been diagnosed with terminal cancer, Vivian had said to her, "You owe your father a wedding." Even if Freya had considered capitulating—and she hadn't because she was busy establishing Just Because—she and Ryan had already had *the* conversation years earlier about how an archaic tradition didn't guarantee "happy ever after." The most important thing to them was their personal commitment to each other. Her father had died ten days later.

"There won't be any aisle-walking," Freya said now, checking the time.

"But St Paul's is such a pretty church and it's a family tradition. I got married there and so did your sister."

This was another reason why Freya had never wanted to get married—the fuss and the fanfare. "Mum, we don't want a big wedding."

"It doesn't have to be a big wedding. You don't have to invite the second cousins."

Freya did a quick calculation and still arrived at far more people than was comfortable. "We can talk about this later. I have to get to work so can you please check your blood sugar before I go?"

Her mother's mouth thinned. "I will do it at the same time I always do it."

Freya hesitated. It wasn't that Vivian was inexperienced with managing her diabetes, but recently things had been rockier. And with this new insulin, they were decidedly unstable.

"Anyway, that new nurse is visiting in half an hour," Vivian added. "She'll test it."

Relieved to be dodging another argument, Freya kissed her mother goodbye. "By the way, Ryan made a huge chicken curry so I put a couple of casseroles in the freezer for you."

"I'll call and thank him for finally making an honest woman of you," Vivian said. "It's way past time."

Freya walked to the car and texted Ryan. *Please can we elope?*

. . .

Lexie arrived at the store just after 10:00 dressed in her work uniform and with dark shadows under her eyes.

"I've only got a few minutes but is there something you want to tell me?" she said snippily without preamble.

Freya ushered her into the back room in case a customer walked in. "Ryan proposed."

"I know! Mum rang. When were you going to tell me?" Lexie asked accusingly.

"When you dropped Mia off tomorrow."

Lexie facepalmed. "Freya! This is huge news and you're acting like it's no big deal. When did he pop the question? Has he been planning it for ages?"

Freya recalled the drunken proposal she'd thought was a joke, followed by the reiteration over a picnic she'd organized, and decided it was unlikely to be romantic enough for her sister's sensibilities. To be honest, she didn't understand Lexie's enthusiasm for romance and weddings considering the collapse of her own marriage.

Lexie grabbed Freya's left hand and disappointment crossed her face. "He's had ten years to ask you and he does it without a ring?"

When Freya had arrived at Just Because she'd removed the ring, not ready for the town to know or to field questions about weddings. Not only did she lack answers, she hadn't even considered the questions. At home with Ryan and cocooned in their bubble of happiness, being engaged felt almost right. But outside of that coziness —like with her mother earlier and now with Lexie interrogating her— agitation popped and fizzed.

She defended Ryan. "I have a beautiful ring. It was his grandmother's."

"Well, show me!"

"It's at home," she lied. "We thought announcing it straight after the funeral was bad timing."

"Really? Death's such a downer. I know I'd want good news to help me forget."

Freya cringed. Forgetting wasn't the point. "Ryan's best friend died, Lexie."

"So why did Ryan propose now when—Oh my God! You're pregnant!"

"I'm *not* pregnant." Why was everyone from Monique to her sister suddenly assuming she had or wanted kids?

"You sure?" Lexie sounded doubtful. "Because Chrissie Lancefield told Sasha List that you're having problems and you might be on IVF. I told her she had the wrong end of the stick, but this sudden engagement's got me thinking. I mean, you've always been adamant you're never getting married and I thought you were covering your disappointment because Ryan had never asked you. But now you're engaged so—"

"It's got *nothing* to do with babies." Freya realized she'd just lied twice in quick succession. "And Chrissie's making things up as usual."

Her stomach cramped at the thought of the town hearing about the engagement from gossips instead of from her and Ryan.

"Please don't tell anyone we're engaged," she said. "Hannah's not here and I'd hate for her to hear it from anyone else. I want to be the one to tell her."

Lexie's brows rose. "Oh, like you told me?"

Freya sighed, knowing all too well how prickly and easily hurt her sister could be. "I'm sorry. I didn't actually tell Mum. I popped in with some casseroles, and thank goodness I did because she was having a hypo. Anyway, after the sugar kicked in, she noticed the ring and then I had to tell her."

Lexie looked slightly mollified. "Okay. I guess I'll forgive you."

"I'm worried about Mum."

"She sounded fine on the phone and the nurse has been, so all good." Lexie's phone buzzed and she checked the message, then swore. "God, I hate my job! I have to go or bloody Natalie will make the rest of my day hell."

When Lexie reached the door she turned back, her eyes suddenly bright. "Book a dress-hunting weekend in Perth. Ryan can mind Mia, and you and I can drink champagne and par-ty!"

Before Freya could object both their phones beeped.

Lexie called, "Looks like I'll see you tonight," then the bell rang and the door closed behind her.

Freya checked her phone. *Hey gorgeous, Mum and Dad hosting joint family engagement dinner tonight 6:30pm. Your mum and Lexie invited. Can't wait. Love ya! xx*

Reeling, Freya sat down hard on the sofa. Somehow, she'd managed to step onto a runaway train.

CHAPTER FOURTEEN

Singapore was humid, bustling and noisy—the absolute opposite of Garringarup—and sweat trickled down Hannah's back as she sipped a Tiger beer and watched the crowd inside her favorite hawkers market, the glorious Lau Pa Sat.

Today there was a family at the adjacent table with a preschooler who was wielding chopsticks like a pro and eating octopus with gusto. Would her and Jamie's child—

"Try the fried carrot cake," Declan said, pushing a plate towards her.

"Carrot cake? It looks like an omelet."

He laughed. "Right? There are no carrots in it either, just radishes and some shrimp. It's really good."

Hannah sampled it, as she had done with the satay and the nasi lemek, and agreed it was delicious despite not really tasting it. Her appetite had died with Jamie.

Anyone who didn't know her would assume she was enjoying a vacation. At breakfast each day Declan suggested a tourist destination for her to visit while he was at work, and she'd go exploring in the cool of the morning then spend the afternoon by the pool. So far she'd visited the Raffles hotel, the botanic gardens, Chinatown, Orchard Road, the Merlion, the Asian Civilizations Museum—the list went on.

Each night, unable to fall asleep, she spent hours staring at a screen, barely taking in what was streaming. Around 3:00 she'd finally fall into a fitful slumber before waking at 6:30 to the sounds of the city gearing up for a new day. She'd luxuriate in that blissful moment between waking and the rush of reality, before the memory of Jamie's death hit with the same shattering intensity as his car hurling itself against the tree.

Freya sent messages every few days with silly photos and stories of the goings-on in Garringarup. All contained the same sentiments— concern and care—and at the same time demanded nothing of her. Hannah appreciated her friend's thoughtfulness, especially when Freya was dealing with her own issues. Right now, the thought of having Jamie's baby one day in the future was the only thing keeping Hannah going. She reassured herself that she was younger than Freya so even though she would need IVF to conceive, her own experience would be far more straightforward.

"I was thinking, did you want to catch the train into Malaysia and have an explore?" Declan said. "Malacca's fascinating."

Traveling alone right now was too confronting for Hannah. "Can you come?"

Regret furrowed his brow. "Sorry, not midweek. Work's crazy."

"I think it would be too much of a rush," she said. "Anyway, I'm booked to fly home Friday." She took another slug of beer, aware that Declan was studying her.

"Are you sure you're ready to go back?" he asked.

Was she? Ian had sent a couple of brief emails—Brett had delivered a box of Jamie's personal effects from the car. Ian had also suggested sending in packers to box up the contents of the Perth apartment. *No point paying rent now it's not being used.* Hannah agreed with both points. She had no desire to return to Perth and she couldn't face packing up the apartment.

Lydia's emails were more focused on Hannah's health and

wellbeing, and she'd attached a couple of articles about grief, exercise and sleep. All emails ended with *when are you coming home?*

"I remember feeling numb for weeks after Mum and Dad died," Declan was saying. "Even the simplest decisions seemed impossible. I know with your baby plans and Jamie's business you've got some big decisions heading your way, but there's no need to rush into them. It's better to take your time. If it helps, you can stay with me as long as you need."

Singapore was a place that held no associations with Jamie, and Hannah knew part of her coping strategy was pretending this was a normal siblings-only visit. But once she was back in Garringarup, real life—a life without Jamie in it—would come rushing at her, threatening to knock her off her feet.

Her skin tingled and her breathing quickened. Declan was right: she needed more time.

"If you book a weekend in Malacca, I'll change my ticket and stay longer."

Declan smiled. "You're on."

Freya watered Hannah's pot plants while Ozzie sniffed around the house as if he was looking for Jamie and Hannah. The McMasters had gone to Perth for a few days and although the farm dogs were being cared for by the Garibaldis, Hannah had texted asking Freya if she'd look after Ozzie. Ryan was unimpressed by the freshly dug holes in their garden, but right now, in this house, Freya saw the confusion in the dog's eyes. His people's smells were in the house but both had vanished.

"One's coming back," she said under her breath. At least she hoped Hannah was coming back.

Freya could guess at some of the reasons why her friend had extended her stay in Singapore, but now it was causing her angst. Last night Ryan had stroked her ringless finger and grumbled that it had been almost a month and they still hadn't formally announced their engagement.

"Call Hannah and tell her," he said.

"What if she's by herself and she falls apart?"

"She's not alone, she's with her brother." Ryan sighed. "Look, I get it. Not a day goes by when I don't go to call or text Jamie then remember he's not in Perth for work or on vacation. But the last thing he'd want is for everyone to stop living their lives."

"We're not doing that."

"In a way we are. I want to book the function room at the pub for our engagement party and send out invitations. I can't do that until you tell Hannah."

Freya's heart rate kicked up. "We're having an engagement party?"

He laughed. "You crack me up. Of course we are, especially if you want to elope. Although I doubt your mother or Lexie would ever forgive us. After Jamie ... we need to celebrate love and life, Frey. We need it, our friends need it. Tell Hannah we're engaged, and if she doesn't want to come to the party then she has the perfect excuse by staying in Singapore."

He pulled her into his arms. "I love how caring and considerate you are, but sometimes you need to put yourself first. This is one of those times. We have no idea when she's coming back, and our parents have been herculean staying mum, but they're fit to burst. Video call her."

Ryan was easygoing but even he had his limits. Freya could tell by the look in his eyes that she was out of time.

"It's too late to call her tonight, but I'll do it tomorrow," she said. "Promise."

"Thank you." His gratitude had swum around her, part reassuring, part agitating.

Now in Hannah's kitchen, Freya ruffled Ozzie's ears and fought a wave of nausea. Telling Hannah and the town came with different challenges, and both were daunting.

"Want to see your mum?" she said, and brought up the video call app.

Her friend's pixelated face slowly came into focus along with a background of tropical palms.

"Freya, hi! Oh, and Ozzie too."

The dog raised his head, looking around for Hannah.

"I thought you'd like to see him, and ..." Freya swiveled the phone and pointed it at the plants. "Your peace lily's flowering."

Hannah peered at the screen, her bottom lip wobbling. "Jamie gave it to me soon after we met and it's never flowered. Is it a sign? It's a sign, right? From him."

Freya didn't believe in signs, and she knew peace lilies took their time to flower, but perhaps Hannah needed to believe it was connected to Jamie.

"Maybe it's time to come home," Hannah was saying. "But without Jamie, is Garringarup even home?"

"Oh, Hannah! Of course it is. You said last year you've got more friends here now than in Perth. Everyone's missing you, including Ryan and me. And Ozzie."

While Hannah talked to the dog, who now had his nose pressed to the screen, Freya's stomach rolled again. This was crazy. Ryan was right. As hard as it was for people who'd lost a loved one, or who wanted the good fortune that others had, that was life. This time she couldn't protect Hannah from hurt. All she could do was be as sensitive as possible and lead her gently towards the news. That's if she didn't throw up first.

She took a fortifying breath and leaped in. "Actually, Ryan and I have got some news—"

"Oh my God, you're pregnant!"

Bloody hell! Was this going to be everyone's reaction to their engagement? "No."

Hannah looked disappointed. "What then?"

"We're engaged."

Hannah's face froze and for a moment Freya couldn't tell if it was the internet connection or real time.

"Hannah?"

The image on the screen stayed fixed. Freya waited, hoping it would bounce back into life, but it didn't. The connection had dropped out.

Her phone buzzed. Hoping it was Hannah, she checked the notification for *Congratulations!* and a string of celebratory emojis. It wasn't that—just a calendar reminder: *Clinic appointment in ten minutes.*

If she hadn't heard from Hannah after the appointment, she'd text her.

After her cervical screening test, Freya was rearranging her clothes when Trudi, the nurse practitioner, asked, "Was there anything else you wanted today?"

"Energy," Freya quipped as she slid off the examination sofa and sat on the chair.

"It's been a rough few weeks for you on top of your normal commitments. I know you help out a lot with your mum and Mia." Trudi was peering at the computer. "It's been a while since we did all the general blood tests." She turned back. "Any chance you're pregnant?"

"Not you too!" When Trudi startled, Freya apologized. "Sorry. It's just I've been asked that question a lot lately."

"You're mid-thirties," Trudi said as if that explained everything.

"So?"

"So, from the town's perspective, you've got an established business, you're in a long-term relationship so you're way overdue for a baby. Also, unlike the town, I happen to know you're not using any contraception."

"We use condoms," Freya said curtly. "We always have."

Trudi nodded. "Right. Well, at the risk of getting my head bitten off again, you're tired, you're irritable, your breasts were tender when I examined them, and condoms can fail."

"They never have before."

"Is your period overdue?"

Freya tried to remember the date of her last period. "It was before the accid—" The glass of water she'd drunk in the waiting room surged to the back of her throat. "We had unprotected sex once," she admitted, embarrassed. "After the funeral—but it won't be that. We were both so drunk we fell asleep in the middle of it."

Trudi opened a drawer and handed her a small packet. "You better pee on a stick."

The rest of the afternoon passed in a blur. According to the computer, the in-store sales totaled fifteen. Freya could barely recall any of them or the conversations that had accompanied them. Her brain was fixed on the blue writing on the pregnancy-test stick that streamed across her mind like a stock-exchange ticker: *Pregnant 3+*

She was pregnant. How could she be pregnant?

She'd asked Trudi the same question. "But I don't understand. Ryan was so drunk he didn't come."

The nurse laughed. "There's sperm in pre-ejaculate and it only takes one."

"But I'm thirty-five! It's supposed to be hard."

Trudi shrugged. "Fertility decreases but it's still very possible. Plenty of women your age conceive."

Freya turned the open sign on the shop door to closed, then shot the lock and drove home on automatic pilot. All those years diligently using contraception and the one time they didn't, she'd got pregnant?

It's good news. Ryan will be over the moon.

He would, and making him happy gave her a buzz. She'd be happy about it too once she came out from under the shock. And at least being pregnant meant they could marry quickly and quietly without all the fuss about dresses, flowers and what sort of cake—

He'll still want the engagement party.

Freya was holding the gin bottle in her hand when the roll of nausea hit her.

Drink gin and you'll fritz my brain.

The bottle clattered onto the counter. Her body was no longer exclusively hers.

CHAPTER FIFTEEN

When Hannah walked into the arrivals hall she'd been surprised to see Lydia and Ian waiting for her instead of Freya and Ryan. Two hours later, and after a big day of travel, she'd been too weary to object when they'd driven through the farm gates instead of dropping her off at the house. She'd excused herself and fallen into bed—not that she'd slept much. She'd spent most of the night convincing herself that as she'd flown home especially to attend Freya and Ryan's engagement party, she needed to be there.

"You don't have to go," were the first words Lydia said to her at breakfast. "If Freya's the friend you believe her to be, she'll understand how hard this is for you."

The offer had tempted Hannah like cool water on a hot day. More than anything she'd wanted to sink into its easy solution, but it went against the decision to come home and face her life.

"Jamie would want me to go," she'd said. "To be there for them because he can't be."

A flicker of something indiscernible had crossed Lydia's face. "You're right. Of course he would."

Now, Hannah stood in the beautifully restored Victorian function room in the Garringarup pub with a smile fixed on her face. If there was ever an example of life moving forward while hers had slammed to a complete stop, it was this night.

The tinkle of silverware on a wineglass quieted the room and Hannah turned to see Ryan and Freya standing beside an enormous cake. Despite Freya's brightly colored dress that screamed celebration and good times, her face was pale and drawn. For a woman who should be deliriously happy, she looked almost as miserable as Hannah felt.

A beaming Ryan held a microphone in one hand and Freya's hand in the other. He addressed the crowd of family and friends. "And you lot thought we'd never do it," he joked.

"Took you long enough, bro," Dylan Langtree said.

"You're lucky you didn't lose her," Sam Dillinger said. "A few have tried."

"Yeah, right," Ryan said, but his glance at Freya was questioning.

She rolled her eyes and shook her head.

"Anyway, to be serious for a moment," Ryan said quietly, "we recently lost a good mate. Jamie's death gutted us and it put a few things in perspective."

Hannah felt the eyes of the room briefly touch her. It was a mix of sympathy, relief that they weren't her and outright curiosity about what it must be like to be her.

"The big news is we're not just getting married," Ryan continued, "we're excited to be welcoming a baby in seven months' time."

Hoots and cheers boomed around Hannah. Freya was pregnant?

Somehow Hannah managed to move her head to look at her friend who was staring at Ryan with a wide-eyed WTF look. But he was smiling at the crowd and holding up her hand as if she was the new boxing champion. Then he pulled her against him and kissed her on the mouth.

Freya, who'd told Hannah emphatically that she didn't believe in marriage, was getting married *and* having a baby. *That's supposed to be my life, not yours!* The words snarled and bit in Hannah's head.

Since Jamie's death, generalized anger at the world had not only moved in, it had unpacked and redecorated. It resided just under the surface of her skin, leaping like a flame in a breeze. It flared now. When Hannah had asked Freya straight out if she was pregnant, she'd lied to her face on video. She hadn't even had the decency to tell her the news privately. Instead, she'd left her to find out in the middle of a crowd.

As the clapping subsided, Hannah heard snippets of conversation behind her.

"I'm surprised she came back," a woman said. "It must be hard for her."

"Jamie was worth a bit though, right? She's probably making sure she gets her share," a man said.

"I heard he didn't have a will."

"Nah, he had a will, but he was keeping things tidy until he put a ring on it." The bloke laughed. "Just good business practice."

"What's the story behind the car?" someone else asked.

"Dunno. I never had him pegged as a luxury-car wanker."

The word hit Hannah like a spray of gunshot. She spun around and faced them. "I beg your pardon?"

Anthony Carbone's Adam's apple shifted up and down. "Hannah ... you're ... ah, looking good."

Rage vibrated along every tendon and bone. "Jamie was not a wanker."

"God, no." Beads of sweat broke across his forehead. "He was a great bloke, hundred percent. Sorry, Hannah."

But Hannah's fury died as fast as it had flared, leaving her light-headed and nauseated. All she wanted was to get away from people. Breathing deeply, she rushed towards the bathroom.

"Hey, Hannah."

She recognized Sam Dillinger's voice and sighed.

During her year living in Garringarup she'd noticed that, unlike their city counterparts, the blokes tended to push things until a wedding band was firmly in place. When she'd told Jamie she was looking forward to being left in peace, he'd said that if he'd met her with a wedding ring on her finger he'd have been hard-pressed not to try his luck.

"Lucky I wasn't married then," she'd said.

"Nah. You'd have left him for me," he'd teased.

Her heart twisted. With Jamie gone she knew Sam saw her as fair game, and he wasn't alone. Sometimes living in a town with more men than women was exhausting.

Ignoring Sam, she kept walking. She'd almost reached the door of the ladies when she felt a hand on her arm. "Hannah."

She turned and faced Freya. Her mind instructed her to force the word "congratulations" past the lump in her throat. Instead, she heard four accusatory words. "You lied to me!"

"No." Freya's hair swung around her pale face. "When you asked me, I didn't know. I only found out later and I wanted to tell you in person, but Lydia and Ian insisted on picking you up from the airport and there was no time today. If you have to be mad, be mad at Ryan. I am!"

Hannah didn't understand. "Why?"

"For announcing it tonight."

Hannah tried putting herself in Freya's shoes. If she was living her old life she could totally imagine Jamie doing the same thing and she would have been fine with it. Ecstatic in fact. There was nothing like soaking up the joy of other people's love and delight for happy news.

"It's the perfect occasion to tell everyone," she said.

"It's too early. I haven't had any tests."

Hannah frowned. "You mean an ultrasound?"

"No, I mean blood tests. I'm thirty-five and this baby's an acc—a surprise," Freya said quickly. "I wasn't taking any prenatal supplements and I was drinking, so I just need to make sure it's okay."

Hannah stared at her, stunned. "Are you saying that if there was something wrong, you'd get rid of it?"

Freya's face sagged. "I have no idea what I'd do."

"Then why find out?"

"Because ..." Freya's hands fluttered. "Because I don't want to spend the next nine months wondering."

"Seven months," Hannah heard herself correcting. How could Freya get that wrong? If Hannah was pregnant she'd know down to the day how long was left until she cradled her baby in her arms.

"Hannah!" Ryan appeared, his face contrite. He kissed her on the cheek. "Thanks for coming. We know it can't be easy for you."

"It's not, but you're my closest friends so ..." She tried for a smile.

He picked up Freya's hand. "And don't be mad at Frey. That's my bad. I'm sorry I let the cat out of the bag before she had time to tell you, but I'm so damn excited it just spilled out."

"It is exciting. Congratulations," Hannah said automatically. "And don't stress. You're forgiven. Jamie would have done exactly the same thing."

"Hear that, gorgeous," Ryan said to Freya, his eyes pleading for absolution. "Hannah forgives me."

Without saying a word, Freya abruptly pulled her hand away and pushed open the bathroom door. It closed with a whoosh of air behind her.

Hannah stared, unable to believe what she'd just witnessed. Freya and Ryan were the sunniest, most even-tempered couple she'd ever met. In all the time she'd known them, not once had she ever seen them have a public falling out or even a snipe inside their own home.

She glanced at Ryan—his brow was furrowed and his gaze confused.

"Hormones, I guess," he said ruefully. "She's pretty tired and feeling sick doesn't help, but ..."

"But what?" Hannah asked, curious as to what he'd stopped himself saying.

At that moment Lexie came out of the ladies and grinned at Ryan. "You're in the shit, brother, dear."

"I know." Ryan rubbed his face. "Problem is, I don't know this Freya. Got any tips?"

"Once she gets to twelve weeks and stops throwing up she'll be back to her old self," Lexie said confidently. "Until then, roll with the punches. Oh, and don't go making any big decisions without consulting her."

"Fair point. Is there anyone else in there?" Ryan asked, his hand on the door.

"Nah, all good. Go and beg hard."

Hannah watched a worried Ryan disappear into the bathroom and pain spiraled through her. Jamie wasn't here to be a listening ear for him. Was that her job now? But even as the thought landed she knew she didn't have the emotional stamina for anyone else's problems.

"Drink?" Lexie asked.

An urgent need to leave hit Hannah hard. "Actually, I'm a bit jetlagged."

Lexie scoffed. "How? Singapore's the same time zone. Besides, Ryan and Freya are paying so it's party time!" She marched to the bar.

Since Lexie's husband had walked out, Hannah had noticed a new edge to her that was both steely and brittle. She certainly partied hard and had done so for months. Sometimes Hannah found it hard to reconcile that Freya and Lexie were sisters. She knew Freya worried about her, but Hannah had always sensed that Lexie milked that concern rather than appreciating it.

Lexie was now flirting hard with Sam, and Hannah took it as a sign she was off the hook to keep her company. She should do a round of goodbyes, but just the thought turned her feet towards the door. She'd text Freya and Ryan—they'd understand.

She was halfway across the room when Lydia stopped her. "Are you ready to head home? Ian and I can leave too. Save someone else driving you."

As much as Hannah appreciated Lydia and Ian's care and concern, she craved the space to spend time alone with Jamie. To be in their house, comforted by the scent of his clothes and their possessions that gave truth to the life they'd shared.

She gave Lydia what she hoped was an appreciative smile. "Thanks, but you stay. I'm going to walk."

Lydia frowned. "You're staying at the house tonight? Are you sure that's a good idea? I mean, is there even milk in the fridge?"

"Freya filled the fridge for me. Besides, Ozzie's there, remember? I'll come out to the farm in the morning to pick up my bag."

"Well, if you're sure ..." Lydia sounded unconvinced.

"I am." Hannah kissed her goodbye and exited through the glass doors.

The streets were quiet as she walked the familiar path home—one block north, one block east. It wasn't like she hadn't walked home alone or been alone in the house before. She had many times when Jamie was away for work.

As she turned into their road, the diesel throb of a four-wheel drive broke the silence of the night. When it pulled away from the curb she realized it had been parked close to the house. It was probably Rob Pettigrew—he'd told her at the party that he'd had dinner with his elderly parents. Then he'd said he wanted to discuss replacing their shared side fence because his father was worried Ozzie was going to escape and dig up his vegetable garden. Hannah had been too stunned to point out that Ozzie had never escaped, and had escaped herself by grabbing a drink from a passing waiter. She gave a silent vote of thanks that she hadn't arrived at her door a few minutes earlier, because knowing Rob he would have bailed her up on the doorstep to "nail a time to hammer out an arrangement."

As the taillights disappeared around the corner, she opened the gate to the old stone schoolhouse. She slid her key into the front-door lock, pretending it was a night when Jamie was in Perth and tied up entertaining clients so unable to call her. The door swung open and the fresh scent of citrus wafted out to meet her. She frowned. Why did it smell like lemons?

She flicked on the lights and blinked twice. The last time she'd been in the house was before the accident and back then wedding-related paraphernalia had rested on every surface. Jamie's moleskins, shirt, tie and jacket had hung in the hall, and beneath them his buffed and gleaming RMs, neatly side by side, ready for their big day. Now his clothes and all the associated wedding gear had vanished. Every surface was clean, dusted and tidied to the point of being unfamiliar.

Hannah automatically dropped her keys on the dresser and opened the sliding glass doors to the deck. Ozzie barked and bounded up to her, his eyes alive with delight.

"Oh, Ozzie, how I missed you."

She was sinking down to his level when he rushed behind her into the house, his nails tapping on the bare boards and his body fishtailing on the rugs in his haste to run down the hall. Her joy at seeing him was quickly drowned in grief as she realized he was looking for Jamie. When Ozzie had explored every room he returned to her, head drooping, then sank at her feet. Hannah buried her face in his fur and let her tears flow.

At some point Ozzie stopped licking her tears and nudged her with his muzzle —a sign he was hungry. Hannah pushed herself to her feet and filled his food bowl.

With leaden legs, she walked down the hall, past the cricket trophies and the photo wall: Jamie in the heritage-listed shearing shed on the farm; Jamie with Ian and Lydia at his graduation; Jamie skiing in New Zealand; Jamie and Ryan dressed as penguins on the Big Bash ... She paused at the only photo of the two of them together. It had been taken at the airport by a stranger who'd insisted on recording the moment after Jamie proposed. Hannah was holding the roses and her ring sparkled on her finger. The picture had been snapped as she'd gazed up at Jamie but he was grinning straight into the camera.

She suddenly remembered how she'd wanted a different photo of them on the wall—one taken on the farm where they were both looking into each other's eyes—but Jamie had laughed. "That's such a cliché, poss. This is the one. It says our future's coming and it's gonna be amazing."

"Oh, Jamie." Hannah stroked the glass over his face.

One life lost, one life saved—it was brutally unfair. Not the saving of the child, never that, but why had Jamie's act of bravery been rewarded with death? It should have been recompensed with a long and happy life and a medal. The wrongness of it raged inside her. Why had the child even been on a bike on a busy road? That question had arrived recently, along with many others now the initial fog of shock was lifting to expose a battleground of anger, despair and an incomprehensible new reality.

She tugged off her party dress and pulled on an old soft T-shirt of Jamie's, then crawled into bed not caring that she hadn't removed her make-up or cleaned her teeth. As she pulled the covers over her head, she breathed in the scent of laundry powder. A sob broke from her—Jamie's scent had been washed out of the bed.

CHAPTER SIXTEEN

DURING HER TIME IN SINGAPORE, Hannah had slept fitfully but the city noise had filled her mind and helped distract her from her own thoughts. Now, the cloaking silence of a small town pressed in on her, thick and heavy, making it difficult to breathe. She threw off the bedclothes and swung her feet to the floor, tossing up between making herself chamomile tea or taking two of the sleeping tablets Declan's doctor had prescribed her. Perhaps both were the solution.

As she padded towards the kitchen she glanced into Jamie's office. For the first time since their final phone call, she heard his voice clearly in her head: *Our office, poss. Our office, our business and our future.* They'd shared this space, working together—surely she'd feel him here. She flicked on the light and stepped in.

Jamie had wanted their desks to face each other but Hannah had pointed out that as she spent far more time at hers than he did at his, her desk should sit under the window. She loved looking out onto the garden and watching a variety of birds—big and small—fluttering in the birdbath. She was especially fascinated by the little New Holland honeyeaters that hung precariously as they sucked sweet nectar from the grevillea flowers.

As she sat in her chair, the familiarity of its papers and her diary pierced the numbness of her grief and she thought about work. Xavier, the young programmer Jamie had employed, was good but he was pretty junior. Was he coping? Was Ian on top of the business? He hadn't asked her any questions about it while she'd been away so she assumed he was, although could the business even function without Jamie? Since Jamie's death, Hannah found recalling things was like hauling on a weighted line encased in mud. She reached for her phone to tap out a reminder to talk to Ian about the business, but it was in her bedroom so she scrawled on a sticky note instead.

She turned towards Jamie's desk. The last time she'd been in the office its surface had been empty as usual—Jamie's commitment to paper-free was laudable. But now a utilitarian brown cardboard box with a black lid rested on the polished wood.

Curious, Hannah lifted the lid and briefly scanned the contents. Her chest cramped and her fingers dropped the lid back into place. This must be the box of Jamie's personal possessions that Ian had emailed her about in Singapore.

Breathing hard, she turned around three times, hating that she wanted to both delve into the box and ignore its existence completely. Then she hefted it onto the floor and sat.

More than anything she wanted to tip out the contents and lie on top of them knowing they'd been with Jamie on the day he died. Instead, she forced herself to be slow and methodical—to savor the pleasure as well as the inevitable shocks of pain.

Starting with the big items, she pulled out the fire extinguisher and the first-aid kit—two of the three things Jamie always insisted were in the car. For some reason the old tartan picnic blanket was missing. So was his computer. Ian probably had it—she'd ask tomorrow.

She caught a flash of red and her heart soared. She immediately broke her self-imposed rule about starting with the big things and grabbed Jamie's phone.

"Why do you have a red phone?" she'd asked early in their relationship, intrigued by his choice of color.

"Power and success," he'd deadpanned, then he laughed. "Unlike your boring black one, mine's so damn bright I never lose it."

She raised the phone to her cheek. In the immediate days after his death, she'd called it hourly until the battery had died and with it his voice message. Instead she'd got an unknown woman telling her "This phone is switched off or out of range." Scrambling to the charger, Hannah plugged the phone in. The screen stayed black, and she knew it would take time before it gained enough charge so she could hear his cheery *G'day, this is Jamie McMaster* ...

Next, she pulled out a can of energy drink. They'd argued about what she considered Jamie's over-consumption of it, but he'd claimed he only drank it on late-night drives. "It keeps me awake and focused so I make it safely home to you," he'd said.

"Oh, Jamie." She rolled the unopened can in her hand, wishing he'd drunk this one on that fateful afternoon, seen the child earlier, reacted faster and avoided the tree.

There was a medium-sized black box wrapped in red and gold ribbon, its bow now flat. It was obviously a gift and she tugged it open, wondering what was inside. She gasped. Nestled in black tissue paper was a sheer lace red bra, a tiny triangle of lace thong and a matching garter belt. There was also a tiny vibrator, its packaging stating: *Solo fun or give your partner control via the app.*

Jamie's wedding present to her.

Hannah's heart somersaulted then lodged in her throat as she hugged the lace to her. It was such a surprise and far more luxurious and expensive than the set she'd bought for their honeymoon. During their time together she'd tried on and off to inject some fantasy into their lovemaking but Jamie had always resisted, telling her he loved her exactly as she was and he didn't need props to find her sexy. In fact, he'd given her a few pairs of fun shortie pajamas to stress his point. And now this.

Tears welled and she sniffed loudly. She spread out the underwear, examining it more closely, and sighed. Just like the pajamas, he was clueless on getting her size right and these would swim on her. She carefully folded the set and wrapped it in the tissue paper, her initial joy tarnished by the reality that keeping it would be yet another reminder of what she'd lost. But he'd obviously wanted her to wear it for him, so perhaps she could exchange it next time she was in Perth.

She glanced at the vibrator. Was masturbating to the memory of a dead man weird and sick or normal and healthy? Unable to answer the question, she closed the lid of the gift box and set it aside.

A charging cord lay at the bottom of the big box. As she fished it out, she realized it wouldn't fit Jamie's phone so it probably belonged to a client. It amazed her how forgetful men were—Jamie's clients in particular. They were forever leaving charging cords, earbuds and other small items in the car. It happened often enough that she'd put a small plastic cube in the back for lost property, making it easier for Jamie to return items to their owners the next time he was in Perth. She looked for the cube but the only thing remaining in the box was an envelope.

She tipped the contents onto the floor and surveyed them. Chewing gum, a packet of wet wipes, a pen and an empty keyring—all items branded Porsche. She stared at them. Jamie had done some consulting with the Ferrari dealership for their new IT system earlier in the year. Had he mentioned Porsche contacting him? Probably, but like so many things since the accident, Hannah had forgotten.

She was musing about how keyrings were now a collector's item since the invention of the key fob, when she recalled Anthony Carbone saying something about cars at the party. What was it? But all she could remember was her instant rage at the word "wanker," Anthony's backpedaling and reassurances that Jamie was "a great bloke." The blast of adrenaline had left her nauseous and skittish. What else had he said?

She tugged at her hair, hating that she couldn't remember but wondering if it even mattered. She dropped the keyring into the envelope with the pen and Anthony's words suddenly pealed in her head as clear as St Paul's newly renovated bells. *Luxury car wanker.*

That couldn't be right. Jamie had driven a reliable but battered four-wheel drive that was comfortable for long journeys and doubled as a farm vehicle. She picked up the keyring again. Porsche was a luxury brand, but surely if Jamie had died driving a Porsche, Brett or the McMasters—someone, anyone—would have told her?

Had they told her?

The week following the accident was a blur—the dash to Perth, the sperm retrieval, the funeral—and then she'd run to Singapore to hide from the horror of Jamie's death. She had a hazy recollection of screaming at Ian after being told that Jamie had died saving a child, then telling him that she didn't want to see or hear any details about the accident. Jamie was dead and nothing could change that. Knowing exactly when, where, and how it had happened would only sink her. Keeping that information at bay was the one small protection she'd had. But now questions rose and popped like a volcano spitting rocks.

Jamie driving a Porsche made no sense. But if he had been, why? And where the hell was his four-wheel drive? It wasn't here in the driveway and it wasn't at the farm. At least she didn't think it was at the farm. She hadn't seen it parked next to the homestead, but perhaps it was in a shed because the McMasters couldn't cope with seeing it every day and being reminded of Jamie's absence.

She fingered the keyring. "Oh God, Jamie. Were you really driving a Porsche?"

Despite the hour, she retrieved her phone and rang the police station. She got a recorded message stating the opening hours and the advice to call the emergency code if it was an emergency.

As she cut the call, Jamie's phone screen lit up—finally it had gained enough charge. Suddenly nothing else mattered except hearing his voice. She called his number, closed her eyes, and gave in to tears as his deep rumbling timbre wrapped around her.

The following day, overwhelmed by grief and pain, Hannah closed the blinds, locked the doors, cuddled Ozzie and stayed in bed.

Lydia and Ian arrived mid-afternoon and let themselves in.

"Hannah?"

She groaned at the sound of Lydia's voice, but even as she pulled the pillow over her head she knew it wouldn't save her from having to face the McMasters.

"I'm just getting into the shower," she called. "Be five minutes."

When she eventually entered the kitchen, the table was set for afternoon tea, and scones decorated with jam and cream graced a plate.

Lydia hugged her. "Three's late for a shower, darling. Are you okay?"

"I went for a run," Hannah lied.

"Exercise is a good idea." Ian helped himself to a scone. "By the way, while you were away Brett gave me a box of Jamie's things from the car. It's mostly odds and sods but there's a present in there for you."

"Thanks, I found it."

Lydia's eyes lit up. "What was the gift? Can I see?"

A flush of heat crawled up Hannah's neck. "It's ... um ... it was for the honeymoon."

"Oh, I see." Lydia busied herself pouring tea.

"If you don't want to keep the fire extinguisher and the first-aid kit," Ian said, "I'll have them for the farm."

Hannah's mind finally kicked in. "Last night at the party, people were talking ... Anyway, I just assumed Jamie was driving his four-wheel drive, but—and this sounds crazy—was he driving a Porsche?"

Ian nodded and Hannah heard herself ask a shaky, "Why?"

Lydia exchanged a look with Ian. "We thought it was something you'd arranged for the wedding."

Hannah shook her head. "I didn't know anything about it."

"Jamie probably wanted to surprise you. You know how he loved doing things like that," Lydia said.

Did he? In their everyday life, Jamie wasn't big on surprises, although he had gone to a lot of effort when he proposed. And the lingerie and sex toy were certainly a surprise, so perhaps the Porsche was connected. But Hannah was still struggling to align Jamie with the vehicle.

"He wasn't a sports car type of bloke," she said. "He always made cracks about status symbol cars, and he didn't care what he drove as long as it was reliable and got him safely from A to B. I mean, his four-wheel drive was always filthy."

"He knew how much you wanted great photos and it would have been a stylish and memorable way to leave the wedding," Lydia said. "It fitted perfectly with that very exclusive Tahitian resort you booked."

A prickle of unease chilled Hannah. "Are you saying his death is my fault?"

"No, of course not." Lydia grabbed her hand. "It was a combination of unfortunate events. An unfamiliar car, a child, a bend, a tree and a gravel road."

"The Great Southern isn't gravel," Hannah said.

This time Lydia looked confused.

"Hannah, the accident wasn't on the Great Southern Highway," Ian said.

"Of course it was. Jamie was coming from Perth."

Yet again Ian and Lydia exchanged a glance. "That's as may be," Ian said slowly, as if talking to a child, "but the accident took place on the old Garringarup road."

Hannah stared at them, unable to absorb the words. "But that's not the way from Perth."

"That's correct," Ian said.

"But he was coming from Perth," Hannah insisted.

"Perhaps he had a meeting in Northam," Lydia suggested. "Didn't he have a contract with an engineering company there?"

"Yes, but he texted me when he left Perth."

"Did he actually say he was leaving Perth?" Ian asked.

Even though the last texts Jamie had sent her were burned onto her brain, she picked up her phone to check: *Leaving now xxxx*; *Bloody roadworks*; *Be later than I thought but will still make it in time*

Lydia peered over Hannah's shoulder. "Your mind was full of the wedding so you probably assumed it was Perth."

Hannah reread the texts and conceded they weren't specific. She supposed Jamie could have driven from Perth via Northam, but he'd never mentioned an appointment. Had he?

Normally she knew his plans for the day and the week, but on his suggestion she'd taken leave from the business before the wedding. "Trying to juggle work and the wedding will just stress you, poss," he'd said after she'd hung up from a fraught cake conversation with the baker.

The idea of having the freedom to only think about the wedding had tempted her like French champagne. "But what about the billing and your appointments?"

"You're forgetting that before you started working with me, I handled everything. I can manage again for a few weeks." He'd kissed her on the nose. "I want a relaxed bride, so forget about work and concentrate on our special day."

She'd taken him at his word and hadn't once glanced at his calendar or the business accounts. If she had, she'd have known about the rental car and the meeting. But even if he'd added a client visit to his schedule, why choose the old road when there were better options?

"The old Garringarup road's awful," she said to Ian. "It's not even direct. Why didn't he take the one twenty?"

Ian read the texts. "He probably did and then got off it because of roadworks. You know Jamie hated being held up."

Hannah did know that—he organized his day down to the minute and got frustrated when people ran late. She studied the time stamp on the first travel-related text Jamie had sent the day he died.

"But if he'd been leaving Northam when he sent this, even with roadworks he should have arrived earlier than the accident. Unless he sent the text then got delayed and didn't leave until later, but that would have been more than an hour and he would have messaged again."

"I imagine he thought it was better to drive so he'd arrive on time rather than waste time texting," Ian said.

Except unlike Ian, Ryan and Declan, and so many other men Hannah knew, Jamie had only ever been thoughtful and considerate. If anything changed for him that impacted her, he always let her know—especially when it involved driving long distances. "Can't have you worrying, poss," he'd say, and her heart would expand just that bit more. She'd never felt so loved as she did with Jamie.

Hannah read the texts yet again. Words she'd accepted as straightforward and informative were now changing shape yet giving her nothing. Unexpected rage jetted through her, breaking her out in a sweat.

"None of this makes any sense!" She shoved the phone across the table. "I mean, if Jamie had been on the Great Southern he wouldn't have needed to swerve in an unfamiliar car to miss a child and he'd still be here!"

"Bargaining isn't helpful. Jamie's dead and nothing can change that." Lydia's tone whipped Hannah. "He died saving a child, which is exactly the sort of selfless thing he's known for. Yes, it's tragic and heartbreaking. *My son* is dead, but if he had to die, at least we can find solace in his actions."

Lydia's voice suddenly broke and she took in a deep breath. When she spoke again her voice was steadier. "Hannah, we need to focus on the positives. That child lives because of Jamie, and now there's a big chance Jamie's child will live too, that his death won't be in vain. Instead of tying yourself up in knots about things you can't control and answers we'll never get, hold onto the thought of your child. His baby."

Hannah's rage subsided as fast as it had flared, leaving her shaky. She hauled her thoughts towards the special vials nestling in liquid nitrogen—Jamie's sperm and their future babies. Lydia was right. For all that Hannah wished Jamie hadn't decided to surprise her with a luxury car, or take a meeting in Northam, or dodge roadworks by taking a narrow road, all of it had happened. His death was her reality. All she could do now was honor him.

"I'll call the IVF clinic tomorrow," she said. It felt good to be taking control.

As Lydia patted her hand, Hannah suddenly remembered the note she'd scrawled the previous night. "Ian, how's the business?"

"Nothing for you to worry about," he said.

Hannah thought about Xavier, who was in his graduate year, and the load he'd be carrying. "And Xavier's coping?"

"We had to let him go," Lydia said.

The small grip Hannah believed she had on her life loosened. "What? Why? Jamie would hate that."

Ian sighed. "Jamie *was* the business, love. Without him, most of the accounts got leery and left. That makes selling goodwill a lot harder. It's on the market, but if we don't get a nibble soon it will probably be wound up."

Anxiety raced Hannah's heart. "Did Xavier get his last month's salary and annual leave payout?"

"Not yet. There's a lot to process with all the other debtors and creditors. We're chasing money from the accounts so it's going to take a few months."

Months? Her ostrich weeks in Singapore roared back to bite her. "So that means I've lost my job too ... When do you expect probate to go through on Jamie's personal financial affairs?"

Ian sighed. "It's tricky because of the business."

"So are you talking a few weeks or ...?"

"I don't want to give you a date when I really don't know, but I think it's more likely to be months rather than weeks."

Hannah pictured her own bank balance drained by wedding deposits. Jamie had offered to transfer the money to her, but to save numerous transactions she'd told him to wait until after the wedding when she had the final figure.

Full-blown panic hit. "Oh my God! What am I going to live on for now?"

"Focus on the positives," Ian said.

"What are they?"

"You don't have to find rent every week," Lydia said matter-of-factly. "And if you truly can't manage on what you have in the bank, then I'm sure we can start a tab that can be settled when probate goes through."

Hannah thought of the thousands of dollars in upcoming medical procedures. "And the IVF?"

"Please don't worry," Lydia soothed.

Hannah clung to Lydia's reassurances and slowly her anxieties receded to a dull buzz. Lydia was right—she had enough stress in her life without piling on fictional scenarios. She could live frugally for a few months, and it wasn't like she was being kicked out of her home. *Their home.*

The house resonated with Jamie's presence. Soon it would ring with the gurgles and cries of a baby. There was no better place to raise their children.

CHAPTER SEVENTEEN

FREYA WAS DROWSING when she felt Ryan's weight tilt her side of the bed. Waking was like swimming up through mud and she wondered if it was worth the effort—she'd much prefer to sleep.

"Frey," he said gently.

His tone annoyed her—it implied she was an unexploded bomb and he had to tiptoe around her. She wasn't a bomb, she was just bloody furious that he'd announced the pregnancy to the entire town without her permission.

He'd apologized profusely and she'd accepted. She prided herself on being fair-minded but, for reasons she was yet to fathom, a kernel of irritation remained. It was a new feeling and it unsettled her. She sighed. Everything to do with pregnancy was a new feeling.

She forced her eyes open, and when they focused, she saw Ryan was proffering a mug and a plate.

He smiled. "I read that ginger tea and crackers before you get up helps with the nausea."

Her generalized irritation with him subsided—he really was the best. She sipped the tea and nibbled a cracker, her stomach thankfully not rebelling.

"Thanks. This is great."

"Too easy." He kissed her cheek. "Sorry, but I have to love you and leave you."

"Really? What time is it?"

"Eight."

She was suddenly wide awake. "What happened to the alarm?"

"I switched it off. You've been so tired I thought you could do with a longer sleep."

"Ryan!" She threw back the covers. "I've got a huge day. Christmas stock's being delivered, I have to take Mum to the clinic and Lexie's dropping Mia here any minute."

She ran to the shower and flicked on the faucets.

Ryan followed and dropped a bathmat onto the floor for her. "Why's Mia coming?"

"Because Lexie's shift got changed and there's no childcare until 10:00."

Freya spun around to grab a towel and the ginger tea shot to the back of her throat, burning all the way. Sweating, she dropped to her knees as the paste of crackers joined it, making her gag. She threw up in the toilet bowl.

Ryan rubbed her back, then passed her a damp cloth and a glass of water. She silently accepted them, wiped her face and rinsed her mouth while Ryan turned off the shower. Then he was squatting in front of her, his eyes filled with concern.

"I think you're doing too much," he said.

She shook her head. "I'm doing what I normally do."

He gave a wry smile. "Yeah, but you're pregnant."

"You think I don't know that!" Oddly angry and utterly confused, she was suddenly blinking back tears.

"Hey, hey, it's okay."

Ryan hugged her and she leaned in, wanting him to assuage the tumultuous mix of emotions that were her constant companions now she was pregnant.

"I feel like an alien's invaded my body and completely taken over."

He wiped her tears with his thumbs. "But the best type of alien, right?"

"I guess."

He laughed and sat next to her, holding her hand. "Everything I've read says the first few weeks are the toughest, then things settle down. So maybe you need to cut yourself some slack. Instead of running around looking after everyone and getting exhausted, just look after yourself and the baby."

The irritation scurried back. "Isn't that looking after someone else?"

He shoulder-bumped her. "You know what I mean. Can't Lexie ask Vivian for some help this morning?"

Freya sighed. "Mum's not up to coping with Mia at the moment. She's barely managing her own life. Her diabetes is all over the shop."

"Right ..." He rubbed his jaw. "Would Vivian let me take her to the clinic?"

"Aren't you in Northam today?"

"Yeah, but if she shifted her appointment I could—"

"There's no wriggle room with appointments. Angus and Leah are going to Perth for a medical conference next week. I'm fine to go. It just would have been better if you hadn't turned off the alarm and I didn't have to rush."

He grimaced. "I was only trying to help."

And she knew that, but somehow it felt like yet another demand on her.

The doorbell pealed and then Lexie and Mia were inside and calling out hello.

"You can help by entertaining Mia for five minutes while I have a quick shower," Freya said.

"Sure, but I'm serious, Frey. Talk to your mum and Lexie, because when the baby comes things will change. They may as well start now."

Ryan left the bathroom and she heard him saying, "Mia, my Mia, are you a plumber and is that your wrench?" And Mia's giggle and reply: "No, silly, I'm a fairy and this is my wand."

"Are you going to magic me?" Ryan asked.

Freya could picture his dancing eyes and Mia's delight. She held no doubts that Ryan would be an amazing parent. All doubts lay squarely at her own feet.

After the shower and swallowing ginger tablets, Freya managed some toast and tea. She stuck Mia in front of the iPad while she checked her online orders, answered emails, and posted a photo she'd styled last week of a new collection of colorful crossbody bags on her Instagram account. It reminded her she needed to create and photograph a variety of different hampers—body products to gourmet food and kitchen essentials, along with some funky socks and fun pajamas—all part of her Christmas campaign. Freya justified the screen time for Mia as her visit was both unplanned and during business hours, therefore compromises needed to be made. That and she had no energy or time to play.

What about when you have the baby?

She tried to picture running the business with a baby. Initially, the baby could sleep in the back room of the shop and Freya could go there to breastfeed—the locals would understand. She had more trouble imagining all the other administration that went with running Just Because and how she'd juggle it all as the baby got older. A toddler in a homewares and gift shop geared around stylish curated displays was the equivalent of a bull in a china shop. And permanent screen time wasn't an option.

She suddenly heard Lexie's voice in her head: *Finding decent childcare is harder than winning Oz Lotto.*

Oh God, did she need to register her unborn baby at the childcare center?

The alarm on her watch croaked and Freya grabbed her bag and keys. "Come on, chicken, into the car. It's time for day care."

"No!" Mia didn't look away from the iPad.

"We had a deal, remember? When the frog sings it's time to go."

This time Mia just ignored her.

She'd always been a sunny child, but since Kane had lost interest in his marriage and his daughter, leaving Lexie lurching between being switched on and coping and barely there and floundering, Mia understandably experienced some difficult days. On a rational level, Freya knew that today's disruption to her niece's routine wasn't helping and that she should have given her a five-minute warning, but she had neither the emotional energy nor the time to deal with a recalcitrant child. She needed to be at the shop by 10:00.

"You're going to day care and I'm going to work."

"I want Ryan!"

"He's at work. We've all got jobs."

Freya picked up the iPad and put it high on the bookshelf. Mia screamed.

Freya flinched. "I think you know that's not going to make me give it back to you."

Mia hit her with her wand.

Normally, Freya would have given her a timeout and later chatted to her about using her words and appropriate behavior, but the clock was ticking.

She grabbed Mia's wrist and wrenched the wand away. "You do not hit me. Understand?"

Mia tried to bite her.

Picking up the screaming child, Freya angled her body to minimize being kicked and marched out of the house. If she missed the delivery truck she'd have to wait another week for the stock and that wasn't an option.

Mia balked at getting into the car seat, arching her back and fighting Freya with the seatbelt.

"Stop being such a brat!"

Mia landed a kick on Freya's tender breasts. Pain ricocheted through her, making silver spots spin in her eyes. In a haze of agony, she lost control and smacked Mia's leg.

Mia stilled, her big brown eyes wide with shock, and fat tears rolled silently down her cheeks.

The tremors started at Freya's toes as guilt and shame flooded her. Dear God, what had she just done?

"I'm sorry, Mia."

Somehow she managed to guide the seatbelt latch into the lock, then she pulled her niece's soft toy emu out of her backpack and handed it her. "Edwina needs a cuddle."

Mia buried her face in the toy and Freya wished she could do the same. With a still-racing heart, she drove to the childcare center.

"Mummy will pick you up after work," Freya told Mia before bending down to kiss her. She added to Caprice, the childcare worker, "It's been a bit of a rough start."

"We all have those," Caprice said cheerfully. "Come on, Mia, let's go outside and look at the rabbit."

Mia took Caprice's hand and walked angelically by her side as if she was a completely different child from fifteen minutes earlier. Freya made it back to the car before bursting into tears.

Three hours later the delivery truck still hadn't arrived. Freya had called the courier company and been told roadworks were causing delays, but the order would be delivered today. Usually the unspecified time wouldn't be much of a problem, but her mother's medical appointment was in half an hour and, as her father used to say, Sod's Law guaranteed that the moment she left the shop the truck would arrive. As it had taken her two visits and one phone call to convince her mother that either she or Lexie should accompany her to her next medical appointment, Freya knew if she failed to attend, it would be even harder to get Vivian to agree again.

There weren't many occasions when Freya needed a second pair of hands. In the past during the Christmas rush her sister had helped out, but that was before Lexie had been forced into fulltime work. This year Freya was interviewing some Year Eleven students for the job but even if she'd already hired someone, right now was school hours.

She watched the minute hand move on the French provincial clock and knew she was running out of time. She ducked out onto the footpath, hoping to spot someone she both knew and trusted who could spare her half an hour, but a cannon could be fired down the main street and not hit a soul.

As she stepped back into the store her gaze fell on the cheery gingham outdoor cushions, reminding her of the wedding present she'd given Hannah. Guilt pinched. Freya hadn't seen or heard from Hannah since the engagement party and that was on her. She should have made the effort to check that Hannah was okay and coping with her re-entry into Garringarup, but with the baby sucking all of her energy, and exhaustion running like glue in her veins, she barely got through the basics of each day.

The bell rang behind her and she turned. "Oh my God, Hannah. I was just thinking about you. I'm so sorry. I should have called."

"I should have called to thank you for the party, but ..." Hannah shrugged as if the last few days had been impossibly hard. "Anyway, I needed to get out of the house so I'm doing it now and in person. It was a great party, and you better have forgiven Ryan."

"Always." Freya hugged her. "How are things?"

"The days are long and the nights are never-ending." Hannah's voice wavered. "I miss him so much." She glanced around the store taking in the increased stock. "I also wanted to ask if you need someone here."

Freya blinked. "As in a job or a way to fill your day?"

"Both." Hannah grimaced. "Apparently, due to the business Jamie's estate is hellishly complicated and probate's going to take months. I'll get the money eventually, but I don't have a lot in the bank and I hate asking the McMasters for advances. They've already paid for the funeral, the sperm retrieval and six months of freezing."

Freya thought that as the McMasters had suggested the sperm retrieval it was only fair that they contributed to the ongoing costs, but she didn't have the time or energy to have that conversation today.

"I'm really sorry about the probate stuff," she said. "And as much as I'd love to have you in the shop, I don't need anyone fulltime."

"Maybe not right now, but you will in six and a half months. Between now and then, I can work part-time—which is about all I'm up for—and it gives you plenty of time to teach me everything about Just Because." The first glint of enthusiasm since Jamie's death lit up Hannah's eyes. "Then, when you go on mat leave you can relax knowing that everything here is under control. You can throw yourself completely into motherhood and focus all your attention on your beautiful baby because I'll be taking care of this one."

A sharp pain caught Freya under the ribs. She couldn't imagine not being involved in Just Because—it had been her baby for six years. It certainly felt more real to her than the unseen collection of cells dividing inside her.

"And," Hannah continued, "by the time you're ready to return, hopefully I'll be pregnant, so it's win-win. We can both work part-time." She grabbed Freya's hands. "It will be so great having babies together and supporting each other."

Freya wasn't only struggling to keep up with Hannah's plans, she couldn't seem to form words.

"So what do you think, Freya? It's the perfect plan, right?"

"It's um ... It's something to think about." There was so much to think about. So much to worry about. "I'll have to run the numbers ..."

"Of course. But I've got marketing and business experience, and you know how much I love Just Because. I'll look after it and nurture it as if it was mine."

The alarm on Freya's phone croaked, kicking her mind back into control. "Can you look after it now for half an hour while I take Mum to the medical clinic?"

"Hundred percent!"

Freya grabbed her bag. "I'm expecting a delivery so if it comes there must be fifteen cartons."

"Fifteen, got it."

"Call me if there's a problem."

"Sure, but email me the order so if anything's missing I'll know what it is."

It was a sensible suggestion. "Will do. Thanks. I won't be long."

"Take as long as you need." Hannah's smile suddenly drooped. "It's not like I have anywhere to be."

Freya hugged her, compassion welling. Less than three months ago they'd both been happy and content with their lives. Now they were grappling with unexpected and life-altering changes. Perhaps Hannah was right—supporting each other may just get them through.

Freya watched Leah Cameron frown at the computer screen. The doctor had been frowning a lot during the consultation—when she'd taken Vivian's blood pressure, when she'd run the plessor along the soles of Vivian's feet, and when she'd tested her urine.

"So, Vivian, how have you been feeling in general?" Leah asked.

"Fit as a flea."

Freya cleared her throat and Vivian shot her a tight-lipped glare. "I'm not unfit. I go to exercises."

"Did you tell Leah you've been getting short of breath?" Freya said.

"Have you, Vivian?" Leah asked.

"Everyone gets a bit puffed—that's the point of exercises." Vivian leaned towards the doctor. "You don't have to worry. I sit down if I get dizzy."

"I see." Leah made a note. "How's the new insulin?"

"It's going great," Vivian said.

Freya's hand gripped the arm of the chair so tightly her knuckles ached. "You've had more hypos and spikes in the last month than you've had in two years."

"It will settle down. My body just has to get used to it, right, Leah?"

"Not exactly. Considering the tweaks we've made and the fact things haven't improved as quickly as expected, it's time to go back to the endocrinologist," Leah said.

"I'll see him next time he's in town," Vivian said firmly.

Leah checked the visiting consultant's schedule. "He's not back until after Christmas so I'm afraid you need to go to Perth." She raised her hand to pre-empt a complaint. "And while you're there I'll organize for you to see a cardiologist, ophthalmologist and a urologist."

"Gracious!" Vivian laughed. "Is that really necessary? You're making me sound sick and I'm not."

"Judging by your latest blood tests, I think a thorough check-up's necessary. That way we have a baseline so we can monitor changes." Leah smiled. "Besides, a night in Perth could be a bit of a treat. I hear Michael Bublé's coming to town."

"I'm not a fan," Vivian said. "And I don't like the drive."

Leah glanced at Freya. "Perhaps Freya can take you?"

Before Freya had opened her mouth Vivian was objecting. "I don't think so. You know she's pregnant, don't you? And just look at her—she's exhausted."

This time Leah's glance lingered on Freya. "Congratulations. I did see Trudi's notes and I was about to chase you up. Considering your age, I thought you would have already been in to organize your ultrasound and blood tests."

"I was just getting the engagement party out of the way," Freya mumbled, unhappy at Leah's disapproving tone and the way Vivian had cunningly swung the spotlight away from herself.

"I think we can kill two birds with one stone," Leah was saying. "You'd have to go to Northam for the ultrasound anyway, so I'll arrange for you to have it in Perth." She suddenly smiled. "Ryan mentioned he's got an in-service there next week so leave it with me. I'll make some calls and pull some strings so you can both have your appointments on the same day Ryan's in Perth."

"Sounds like a plan," Freya said faintly, once again feeling powerless against the pregnancy juggernaut.

Leah got a misty look in her eyes. "The first ultrasound's a truly special experience. Even better that you get to share it with Ryan and Vivian."

Vivian wasn't the most demonstrative mother on the planet but she reached out and squeezed Freya's hand. "That sounds so much better than Michael Bublé."

Her mother's smile reassured Freya. Suddenly she couldn't wait to tell Ryan they were going to see the baby—his grin would be wider than the Milky Way.

CHAPTER EIGHTEEN

FIFTEEN MINUTES AFTER FREYA LEFT, the delivery truck arrived. Hannah dutifully counted off fifteen boxes, supervised their positioning in the back room and signed the electronic screen. By the time the truck drove away the thirty minutes was up, but instead of Freya returning to the store she called to ask if Hannah could stay until closing because Vivian needed her help.

"Absolutely, not a problem."

Hannah's only concern about being alone in the shop was dealing with well-meaning but cloyingly sympathetic locals. She found it easier to deal with strangers—they didn't tiptoe around her like she was glass that may shatter at any moment. Nor did they say, "How are you, good?" in the hope she wouldn't tell them that her heart was broken and bleeding, and that getting up in the morning was the bravest thing she did each day.

While the store remained free of customers Hannah used her time to prove to Freya she was an asset. Inspired by the new stock, she created four gardeners' gift baskets featuring gardening tools, decorative gloves and rejuvenating hand cream. Then she used the new planter pots as a focus in a pretty display on the small table she knew

Freya used as her "testing the product" space. Pleased with her handiwork, she took several photos and filmed a video for Just Because's Insta account. It was fun dusting off her marketing skills. Although she'd done some marketing for Jamie's business, it had never given her a creative buzz. Then again, it was hard getting excited about IT.

A dozen septuagenarians on a tourist bus popped in and raided the children's section, buying everything from clothes to wooden puzzles for their grandchildren. Soon after they'd left, a bloke hovered just inside the door.

"You're very welcome to browse,' Hannah called from the counter.

"I'm terrified if I try to walk around that lot I'll knock something over."

Hannah took a closer look at him. He was as broad as he was tall, and if it hadn't been for the battered Akubra hat his wide hands were turning over, she'd have guessed he was a rugby player. He'd have to breathe in and turn sideways to navigate half the shop and even then it was a risk.

"Is there something in particular you're after?" she asked.

He grimaced. "My baby sister's twenty-first."

"Oh, I'm sure we can find something. What's she interested in?"

"Anything on her phone."

Hannah laughed. "We're all guilty of that. Basically, twenty-first gifts fall into two categories. Something practical she can use, like a handbag or quality kitchenware, or something personal, like a piece of jewelry."

"She's still in student housing so maybe jewelry?" His hat almost collided with a glass Christmas ornament. "She's mad about horses."

"I'm just minding the shop so give me a minute to find the key to the jewelry cabinet." As she checked the bunch of keys Freya had given her and hunted through a drawer, she said, "I'm Hannah by the way."

"Mac Downie." He cleared his throat. "I was sorry to hear about Jamie."

Blindsided, Hannah felt her grief invade the ordinary situation,

freezing her hands, trembling her legs, swooping her blood to her feet
and threatening to pull her under.

"Oh, shit, are you okay?" Mac grabbed a display chair, sending a
stack of coffee-table books tumbling. "Sit!"

Hannah sat, then heard a crash, swearing and the thud of RMs on
the floorboards.

Mac returned with a wet glass half-filled with water. "Drink it."

She drank and then laughter bubbled out of the black hole that was
her sorrow. "You're a sheep farmer, aren't you?"

"Yeah, sheep and crops, why?"

"You've just told me to sit and drink. I'm expecting heel next."

Embarrassment pinked the tips of his ears. "Sorry. I spend more
time talking to Daisy, my dog, than anyone else."

The shock of hearing a stranger mention Jamie was receding, and
even though Hannah was certain she would have remembered this tank
of a man, she asked, "Have we met before?"

Mac shook his head. "Nah, and I probably shouldn't have said
anything, sorry. It's just his death was mentioned in the recent
Penthurst school alumni newsletter. He was the same year as my older
brother and we were in the same house. I haven't seen him in years."

"So if we haven't met and you haven't seen Jamie in years, how did
you know I was his fiancée?"

"The condolence page on Facebook. I recognized you from the
photos."

A zip of adrenaline raised the hairs on Hannah's arms. This bloody
town and its men! Had this farmer come deliberately to seek her out?
He made Sam Dillinger look like a saint.

She stood and rounded the counter, putting the wide piece of
jarrah between them. "You don't have a sister who's turning twenty-
one, do you? You just thought you'd come into town, offer your
sympathies and what? See if you got lucky?"

Mac took a step back, causing the teacups on the dresser to rattle in
their saucers. Bafflement shone bright in his eyes along with the
suspicion that he was talking to a crazy person.

"Georgie's turning twenty-one on Saturday and there's a hundred and twenty people coming to the party at the Beverley town hall. The reason I'm in Garringarup today is because I'm buying sheep. When I was at the bakery grabbing lunch, I asked the bloke if there was anywhere in town I might buy her a present. He suggested here. And I'm not desperate or a dickhead, thanks very much."

He turned to leave and the Christmas tree swayed. Hannah could picture the chaos if he stormed out, but mostly she knew she'd grief-jumped to the wrong conclusion.

"Wait ... Mac, I'm sorry." He turned back to face her. "It's just ... there are a lot of dickheads about."

His brows rose, his face clearly stating: *And this is your apology?*

She rubbed her face. "Sorry. If you'd met me before Jamie died, you'd know I'm not usually so ... No one ever tells you that grief drives you crazy."

"It leaves you reeling, that's for sure." He tapped his hat against his thigh. "And although I don't appreciate being lumped in with the dickheads, I'm running out of time so can you show me the necklaces?"

"Of course!" Pleased to have a task, she pushed her misery back into its well and opened the cabinet. "This one is gorgeous." She picked up a sterling silver pendant. On first glance it looked like a horse's head and mane, but on a second look the silhouette of a girl appeared. "Or perhaps you could get her name engraved on this horseshoe? Or—"

"The horse girl," Mac said firmly. "Can you wrap it for me? I always end up with a crumpled mess."

"Sure. You choose a card while I'm wrapping."

He laughed. "Next you'll be asking me if I want fries."

"Not at all, but we've got a great collection of matching Australian floral ties, socks and pocket squares to get you schmick for the party."

A look of horror crossed his face. "All good, thanks."

She laughed. "As long as you know you can't wear your blue work shirt."

He ducked his head and she got a glimpse of him as a kid. "Yeah, Georgie already told me that."

"Approved your outfit, has she?"

He gave a rueful smile. "I see you've met my sister."

In the end, along with the card and the necklace, Hannah convinced Mac to buy a pair of socks patterned with flowering gums. Freya was going to be impressed and grabbing Hannah's idea of running the business together with both hands. Hannah couldn't wait.

The following morning while Hannah sat in the Ferguson & Associates office waiting for Rowan to arrive, she sketched some of her ideas for the Christmas displays she planned to create when Freya was in Perth. It was another opportunity to show her friend what an asset she was to Just Because and how her being involved was beneficial to them both.

"Morning, Hannah, you're bright and early." Rowan stood in front of her, puffing slightly, and ushered her into his office. "Coffee?"

"No, thanks." He looked disappointed. "But you have one. Looks like you've got a snazzy new machine."

He beamed. "Geraldine's suggestion. I'm quite partial to a latte."

He pressed some buttons, and while the machine gurgled and hissed he insisted she take a seat. Then he whipped papers out of his briefcase and switched on his computer.

"So what can I do for you today?" he asked after taking his first sip of the brew.

"I want to start IVF."

Rowan's grandfatherly features softened into sympathy and care. "Ah."

His tone surprised her. "Ah, what?"

"Jamie's only been dead ... what, two months?"

Hannah couldn't believe the date wasn't engraved on his mind. "Ten weeks, six days and four and a half hours."

"Right. Of course."

"Anyway," she said, desperate to get the conversation back on track, "I've spoken to Angus and I rang the IVF clinic to make an appointment to get the ball rolling. They said I needed permission to use Jamie's sperm. I said we got that when Jamie died. Then they said I needed to talk to you, which doesn't make a lot of sense but here I am."

Rowan ran a hand through his thick white hair. "We got permission to harvest the sperm, Hannah."

"Yes, I was there."

"That's different than permission to use it."

"What? But that's crazy." Some of the details of the days immediately after Jamie's death were hazy, but she clearly remembered the rush to get the documents together to present to the Supreme Court. "Why would anyone go through all that stress and effort to harvest the sperm if they weren't going to use it?"

"Well, the law around reproductive technologies is complicated," Rowan said. "It has to be satisfied that the deceased—"

"Jamie!" Hannah hated the way people stopped using the given name of people who had died. It had happened with her parents.

"Jamie," Rowan said evenly. "The law needs convincing that Jamie wanted to be a father in life and that subsequent offspring will thrive when their biological parent—in this case their father—is not alive."

"So we just submit the same affidavits to the court again, get a new order and I'm good to go?"

Rowan gave a small indulgent smile. "I'm afraid it's a little more complicated than that."

"Of course it is." Hannah worried a dry piece of cuticle on her thumb. "Please tell me exactly what's involved."

"We need to return to the Supreme Court, but this time with affidavits from the immediate family and from people who knew Jamie well. Friends, work colleagues, community members, that sort of thing."

Hannah pulled out her phone and brought up a note. "Freya and Ryan will sign. Who else do we need? Someone from the cricket club?"

"Half a dozen would be good. Ideally all with different connections to Jamie. Basically, anyone who ever heard him say he wanted a child."

Hannah added Xavier to the list. As much as she didn't want to ask Sam Dillinger, she typed his name and added a question mark. She'd never understood his and Jamie's friendship—they were chalk and cheese—but Jamie's friendship group had been eclectic. Considering his propensity to look after people and Sam's need to be looked after— he was stuck in adolescence—their bond had been strong. Still, there had to be other blokes at the cricket club who would help.

"What about you, Rowan?" He was an obvious choice.

"I'm sorry, dear. I never actually talked to Jamie about his desire to have children."

"But you know he wanted them, right? I mean, he dotes on Ozzie and—"

"I'm afraid assumption doesn't play a role here. To sign the affidavit, people need to have heard Jamie say he wanted children."

Oh, for heaven's sake! Everyone who knew Jamie knew he wanted kids. But she stifled her ripples of annoyance at the stodgy old lawyer's pedantry. She needed his help.

"Okay," she said firmly. "I understand. Where do people make their declarations?"

"They can make an appointment to see me or at their local magistrates court." He tapped on his computer and the printer whirred into life. He handed her a piece of paper. "Here's a template that needs following and the statements must be typed."

"Great, thanks." Hannah rose to her feet. "I'll get onto this right away."

"Hannah, please sit."

She instinctively sat, getting a flashback of being in her high school principal's office. "There's more?"

Rowan nodded and laced his fingers. "Remember I said the law needs to be satisfied that the child will thrive despite the death of its biological father?"

A muscle twitched around Hannah's eye. "Our baby is wanted and will be loved. And not just by me but by Lydia and Ian and Maddie—"

"I don't doubt that, but again, it has to be proven. As I said, this is new territory, but there's an unstated opinion that applying for permission to use the sperm less than a year after the dec—Jamie died is a red flag."

"Why?"

"Grief."

A flare of fury lit through her. "There's no magic formula to ending grief, Rowan. It doesn't just stop at twelve months! I'll be grieving Jamie forever."

He nodded, the action full of gravitas. "The twelve months isn't legislated. It's a worldwide guide so there's adequate time for grieving and counselling before assisted posthumous reproduction."

"So I have to get counselling?"

"The court would view that favorably. I strongly recommend it."

Hannah closed her eyes, her temples throbbing. What had started off as a straightforward request was now a series of difficult hurdles. Anger bubbled and spat.

"So I have to prove Jamie wanted children and get counselling to show I'm not nuts and very capable of being a mother. And yet there are teens out there who are far too immature to be mothers having babies after unprotected sex!"

Rowan startled at her tone and leaned back into his chair. "Are you sure you wouldn't like a coffee?"

"You softening me up for yet another problem?" She tried to joke, embarrassed she'd raised her voice.

Not meeting her gaze, Rowan cleared his throat and rose. "Latte? Cappuccino? Espresso?"

"Just tell me, Rowan."

He pressed a button on the coffee machine, then leaned on the edge of his desk. "Western Australia's *Human Reproductive Technology Act* doesn't allow for gametes—"

"Gametes? What are they?"

"Gametes are sperm and eggs." He shifted uncomfortably. "The Act doesn't allow for them to be used after a donor's death."

"You have got to be fuc—kidding me!" Hannah threw her hands into the air. "This is as insane as allowing the sperm to be retrieved but not stored. Why didn't you tell me this when Jamie died? Why did you let me carry this hope around in my heart—the only thing that's keeping me going—when you knew it could never happen? How dare you! What was all this? A money-making proposition for you?"

Rowan carefully placed a latte on a coaster in front of her. "Hannah, please. I need you to hear what I'm saying."

He waited as Hannah worked hard to calm her roiling fury. She tried harder not to succumb to the devastation that always followed these blasts of intense pain and laid her low for hours. Caffeine was probably the last thing she needed, but she took a sip of the foamy beverage to buy herself time. When she set the glass down, Rowan spoke.

"There is a solution. The eastern states do posthumous assisted reproduction, so we apply for the gametes, the sperm, to be moved to one of those states. Before we do that, we need to find an IVF clinic that's happy to assist you. My contacts tell me not all of them are, but it's already happened in Queensland, so I suggest we make that our first port of call.

"Once that's dealt with, we jump through that state's legal hoops and prove Jamie wanted a child. Once we have the court order you have treatment over there, but the moment you're pregnant you can complete your pregnancy care back here."

Apart from the uncertainty of winning approval for both the transfer and the use of the sperm, and finding a clinic happy to treat her, the costs stacked up like gold ingots. There'd be legal fees in two states, the IVF treatment, and the added travel and accommodation costs—it would tally in the tens of thousands of dollars. Her chest strained with tension and she breathed deeply, trying to keep her focus on the first stumbling block.

"Am I likely to win the application to move the sperm over east?" she asked.

"I've been advised that with strong affidavits, you have an eighty percent chance."

She straightened her spine against the desire to sag in her seat. "Why do they make it so hard?"

Rowan's mouth pulled down on one side. "It's not so much hard as it is taking into account the many and varied ethical considerations this brave new world offers us."

Hannah thought it was more a case of putting the boot in when her life had been derailed and all she had left was a smoldering pile of grief and angst.

If Jamie was alive, she'd probably already be pregnant and everyone would be teasing them with honeymoon jokes. No one would be asking her why she was pregnant or asking Jamie if he wanted to be a father. They'd be slapping him on the back, proud that he'd knocked her up so fast. But Jamie was dead and she was half-living. If their baby had any chance of coming into this world it rested with her.

Determination fought its way clear of the resentment that she had to work so much harder than most women to have the child of the man she loved. So much harder than Freya, who seemed shocked by her pregnancy rather than overjoyed. Damn it! Hannah had the right to bring their longed-for baby into the world and she'd move heaven and earth to make it happen. It was going to take commitment, time and money. But Jamie's estate would cover the costs and hopefully there would be enough left over to live on.

"When will Jamie's affairs be settled?" she said.

"Best to discuss that with Ian."

Yet again the attorney surprised her. "But aren't you doing the legal stuff?"

"Under Ian's direction. He's my client and, as such, our dealings are confidential."

Hannah studied Rowan, uncertain what it all meant. "Are you saying I'm locked out of the discussions about my fiancé's financial settlement? Money that's coming to me and is legally mine?"

"I'm saying that as Ian's the executor of Jamie's estate, you need to ask him these questions."

"Right." But as reasonable as Rowan's words sounded, unease stirred and bumped against her confidence.

She stood, giving herself a mental shake. This was just lawyer-speak and lawyers were circumspect and cautious. Of course there was nothing to worry about. In fact, the few times she'd asked Ian about the business and probate, he'd told her not to worry and so had Lydia. They were giving her much-needed space to find her feet, and if there were any issues, they'd tell her. After all, they were a team. They wanted a grandchild as much as Hannah wanted a baby.

CHAPTER NINETEEN

FREYA AND RYAN sat in the shade on the deck of a café in Kings Park overlooking the lake.

Ryan slid his hand into hers. "This is nice. Just us."

She ran her thumb over the back of his hand. "It is. And we've got tonight. Mum's insisting we go out to dinner without her."

The waitress delivered their order—a cappuccino for Ryan and a chai latte for Freya, along with a slab of iced ginger slice and two forks.

The moment they'd thanked her, Freya reached for the slice and cut it in an approximation of half. She speared the biggest piece and when the tangy sweet taste of sugar and the hot burn of ginger hit her tastebuds she sighed. Ryan laughed.

"What?" she said after she'd swallowed.

"First you scarfed eggs and bacon at breakfast and now this." He grinned, his love for her racing to his eyes. "It's great you've got your appetite back."

"So great. I don't miss waking up feeling chucky every morning."

"Yeah, that can't have been fun." Ryan checked his watch for the third time in quick succession.

"Relax. We've got time."

"I know. I'm just pumped. In less than an hour we get to see Sprocket."

A bubble of excitement rolled through Freya's generalized anxiety. When she'd told Ryan how Leah had arranged the joint appointments and about Vivian's enthusiasm to attend the ultrasound, Ryan had gone quiet. It was a sure sign he wasn't thrilled her mother was coming, but he hadn't objected. At the time, Freya hadn't pressed him for an opinion—she'd been too tired and too busy concentrating on not throwing up. But it was amazing the difference a week made. Without the constant companion of nausea she had more energy and, thankfully, more emotional stamina. She wanted him to know she understood his disappointment.

"I know Mum coming isn't ideal ..."

He shrugged. "It's Leah I'm pissed with, not you. Besides, I've had a chat with Vivian. I told her I've got pole position sitting next to you and holding your hand. She's fine taking the other chair."

Freya kissed him, grateful for his understanding. "And she'll take that better from you than me."

Ryan had been great with Vivian on the trip so far, but then he had loads of experience transporting older people with health challenges to their appointments.

"Besides, it will be a nice treat for her after her raft of tests," he added.

The waitress delivered the bagged sandwich Ryan had ordered for Vivian and he stood. "We better get going. We have to pick up your mum from the cardiac clinic. Is your water bottle full? You still have to drink six hundred mill."

She rolled her eyes. "Yes, Dad."

Ryan slid his arm around her, his eyes shining. "I can't wait to be called that."

. . .

After telling them her name was Marilyn, the first question the female radiographer asked Freya was, "Can a student perform the ultrasound under my guidance?"

Part of Freya wanted to say no. With Vivian and Ryan in attendance it already seemed like a crowd. But Ryan trained volunteer paramedics and she knew all about the juggle involved with students gaining enough experience.

"Sure, no problem," she said.

"Thanks." Marilyn beckoned the student forward. "This is Lachie. He's in his final month and will be working here next year."

"Hi, Lachie. I'm Freya and this is my partner, Ryan, and my mum, Vivian."

With the pleasantries out of the way, Lachie patted the examination sofa. "Do you need a hand getting up here?"

Freya laughed. "I'm pregnant, not old."

As she got settled, Ryan engaged Lachie with questions about the specifications of the ultrasound machine.

"Freya, I just need you to pull up your blouse and roll down the top of your pants so your belly's clear of clothing," Lachie said. "I'll tuck this towel around your clothes to protect them from the gel."

Freya still remembered the icy hit of gel on her breast a few years earlier when a possible lump was being investigated. "Is it warm?"

Lachie held up a jug warming the gel. "Always. Ready?"

Freya had no idea if she was or not. Excitement and trepidation beat in unison and she looked at Ryan, needing his reassurance. His eyes scrunched up above his mask and she pictured his smile. He slid his hand into hers and gave it a squeeze.

"Ready," she said.

"Are you turning on that big television so I can see?" Vivian asked.

"I'll turn it on once there's something to look at," Lachie said. "Freya, you'll feel a bit of pressure but it won't hurt."

Freya's bladder was fit to explode. "Don't push too hard or I may have an accident."

"So you're twelve weeks?" Lachie pushed some buttons and ran the probe over her belly.

"Almost thirteen." Freya watched the small screen on the machine turn into a snowstorm. She felt Ryan leaning forward.

"Are you sure there's a baby in there?" she joked.

"Sometimes they like to hide," Lachie said.

He moved the probe lower on her belly and she flinched as shockwaves vibrated through her bladder.

"Here we go." Lachie pointed to the screen. "There's baby's head and spine."

Freya squinted at the screen. All the ultrasound photos she'd been shown on women's phones always pictured a baby floating on their back, their face in profile.

"He's got his back to us," Ryan said. "Come on, buddy, turn around."

"Don't worry. There's plenty of time for that while I do the measurements and complete the examination," Lachie said.

"Can I see?" Vivian asked.

"Of course." Lachie turned on the big television.

Freya stared at the screen, trying to recognize the baby. Before now she'd struggled to picture it and she'd hoped the scan would do it for her. So far it looked like a tiny dugong.

"This is baby's head, baby's bum, and this is a hand and that's a leg," Lachie said.

"Oh, Frey." Ryan's hand tightened on hers. "It's really a baby."

"Right now it looks more like an alien." Anxiety crawled through her. "There is only one in there, right?"

"Yes, it's a singleton pregnancy," Lachie said.

Two crosses appeared on the screen connected by a dotted line.

"What's that?" Freya asked.

"I'm measuring the crown-rump length," Lachie said. "It helps determine the gestation." He clicked a few more buttons. "So we have the date of your last period as August twenty-fourth. Any ambiguity around that date?"

"What do you mean?" Freya asked.

"Had you forgotten the actual date and just guessed a ballpark?"

"We know the exact date of conception," Ryan said, a hint of sadness under his joy. "No ambiguity about it at all."

"Right." Lachie clicked more buttons and moved the probe. The full picture of the baby disappeared. "I'm looking at the spine now."

A jolt of fear tightened Freya's chest. "I wasn't taking folic acid or any other pregnancy vitamins. The baby's a bit of a surprise."

"Best surprise ever," Ryan said.

"Absolutely," Vivian said. "It's so exciting."

"The spine's looking good." Lachie moved the probe again and more crosses and dots appeared.

"What about Down syndrome?" Ryan asked. "Freya's had the blood test and the doctor said you'd look for it."

"We measure the nuchal translucency at the back of the baby's neck. It's not a diagnosis but it can point to a possible problem." Lachie clicked more keys.

Freya lay rigid. It was hard enough picturing herself as a mother, let alone the mother of a child with a chromosomal abnormality.

"Nothing out of the ordinary there," Lachie said.

Air rushed out of Freya's lungs. She felt Ryan's head touch her shoulder.

"Well, that's good news," Vivian said. "It's always a risk when you leave it so late to start a family."

Freya was too relieved to argue with her mother.

"There's more risk of having a Down syndrome child at nineteen than at thirty-five, Vivian,' Ryan said lightly.

"Really? I had no idea," Vivian said. "When are we going to hear the heartbeat, Lachie?"

"Sometimes it's tricky to find," he said.

Freya squeezed her eyes, hoping the narrowed focus would make the blob on the screen look more like a baby. "I thought it would look different."

"It's looking straight at you, not side-on." Lachie turned to Marilyn, who'd been standing quietly behind him.

She stepped forward and accepted the probe, moving it across Freya's belly and pressing firmly.

"Oh!" Freya clenched her pelvic floor. "Will it be much longer? I really need to pee."

"Sorry, Freya. Hopefully not too much longer." Marilyn tilted her head towards the door and Lachie left the room.

"Can we get a photo?" Ryan asked. "Mum will want to see it."

"But it looks like two blobs," Freya said.

"Yeah, but it's our beautiful blob. It's the first photo for their album."

"At least you said 'their' this time."

"Are you going to find out the sex?" Vivian asked.

"No," Freya said at the same time as Ryan said, "Yes."

The door opened and Lachie returned with a woman. "Freya, Ryan, this is Doctor Indra Sharma."

"Hello." The doctor accepted the probe from Marilyn. "I'm just going to have a bit of a look. This may be uncomfortable," she said as she repeated what the radiographer had been doing.

Searing pain pierced Freya and she thought her bladder would explode. She gripped Ryan's hand so hard he flinched. "Uncomfortable is an understatement."

"Is there something wrong?" Ryan asked.

"That's what we're trying to find out," Doctor Sharma said.

Freya wished she knew what it was on the screen that was worrying the staff. She turned to Ryan, hoping he may know, but his eyes only held unease. Vivian moved her chair closer and placed her hand on Freya's leg.

The clicks and whirrs of the machine were amplified by the lack of conversation and they filled Freya's ears with a roaring buzz. Time slowed—each second excruciating—and Freya wanted to leap off the bed and run far, far away.

Doctor Sharma returned the probe to its holder and gently wiped

Freya's belly before removing the towel. "You can reassemble your clothes."

The moment Freya had pulled up her pants and lowered her blouse, Ryan grabbed her hand again. Something made her sit up and dangle her legs over the side of the bed.

"What's going on?" Ryan asked the doctor.

"The baby's measuring ten weeks rather than twelve. Initially that wasn't a concern, but I'm afraid we can't find a heartbeat. I'm very sorry."

Freya stared at her, every part of her numb. "Are you saying the baby's dead?"

The doctor nodded as Ryan said, "But if it was a miscarriage, Freya would have bled."

"This is what's called a silent miscarriage. Or in medical terms, a missed abortion. The baby has died, but for some reason the body doesn't recognize the pregnancy loss yet and the placenta keeps producing hormones. That's why there's no bleeding."

"Oh, darling." Vivian's voice cracked. "I'm so sorry."

Freya's mind slipped and slid over the news. She was pregnant but not pregnant. There would be no baby. For weeks she'd struggled to believe she was pregnant, and just as she'd accepted that she was, the baby was dead.

"But it's still in me," she heard herself say as Marilyn turned off the television.

"What happens now?" Ryan asked.

"There are three options, Freya," Doctor Sharma said. "You can wait for your body to realize it's no longer pregnant and pass the tissue. Or we can give you a drug to speed things along, although it may also take a couple of weeks."

"Two weeks?" Freya didn't want to be pregnant/not pregnant for another two weeks. "What's the third option?"

"You have a minor procedure under general anesthetic and I remove all the pregnancy tissue."

"Yes, that," Freya said quickly. "Can I have it today? I've got private health insurance."

"We live in Garringarup," Ryan said, "but it's possible to stay in Perth longer if necessary."

The doctor nodded her understanding. "I'll do my best to fit you onto the end of today's list. It depends on staffing. I'll call you as soon as I know. Meanwhile, don't eat or drink anything from now until you hear from me."

"Where do we wait?" Ryan asked.

"Feel free to go for a walk in the park but don't stray much further. I'll talk to you soon."

Freya slipped on her shoes. As she left the room with Ryan's arm around her waist and her mother close behind, the radiographers murmured their condolences. The words spun around her without landing. It was as if she'd already been administered the anesthetic.

CHAPTER TWENTY

HANNAH WAS ENJOYING her time in Just Because while Freya was in Perth. The morning had vanished without her realizing as she threw herself into the joy of dressing the front window. Now she was in the back room packing the orders she'd promised Freya she'd dispatch. At least that was the plan but she was staring off into space when her phone rang. It startled her so much she dropped the packing tape on her foot. God, she didn't even know she'd been holding the tape, let alone for how long. Ten seconds? A minute? Longer?

She scrambled amongst the mess on the workbench and eventually glimpsed her phone on top of a half-packed hamper. Man, she really was losing it. As she accepted the call, she was surprised to read Ryan's name. She could count on one hand how many times he'd called her.

"Hey, Ryan. What's up?"

There was a beat of silence. "Hi, Hannah. We, ah ... We just got some bad news. The baby ..." He cleared his throat. "Frey's had a miscarriage. She's having a D&C right now."

Rafts of prickling sensation ran up and down Hannah's limbs. "Oh, Ryan. I'm so sorry!"

"Yeah. We're gutted." A long sigh rumbled down the line. "Anyway, Frey's worried about the orders."

Hannah had no idea how Freya could even be thinking about the business; then again, she knew how crazy grief could be. Unlike the devastating news that her baby had died, dealing with shop orders was simple and achievable—although Hannah was currently struggling to concentrate.

"Tell her not to worry," she said. "I'll sort them out. And I'll open the store each day until she's ready to come back."

"You sure you're up to it?" Ryan asked.

"It'll be good having something to get me out of bed in the morning."

"Thanks, Hannah."

"Give Freya my love."

"Will do. Bye."

"Ryan! Wait."

"Still here. What?"

Hannah took the chance to ask the question that had been eating at her for weeks. "Did Jamie tell you about the Porsche?"

Again there was strained silence on the line. "No."

"So he never mentioned it at all?"

"No. Sorry, Hannah, I have to go."

"Of course, sorry. Go. Do what you need to do. I've got the shop covered." But he'd already hung up.

Hannah mulled over the fact that neither Jamie's parents nor his best friend had known about the Porsche. Was that odd? Yes. Although not if it was part of the wedding surprise. But who organized a big surprise without involving other people?

Jamie. He'd bought her engagement ring all by himself and he hadn't hinted to anyone else that he was about to propose. She still remembered everyone's shocked delight when they told them the news, and Jamie's wide grin that he'd pulled it off without anyone suspecting, not even her.

But a Porsche? Perhaps Jamie had mentioned it to Xavier?

She texted.

> Hi, Xavier, when's a good time to chat?

If she spoke to him, she could ask him about the car *and* signing the affidavit.

Her phone rang in her hand. "Hi, Xavier, how are things?"

"Pretty shit, really. You?"

"Much the same."

He made a harrumphing sound. "Look, I get that without Jamie the business will probably be wound up, but I could have finished the McGuire and the Be Right Back contracts."

"I'm so sorry, Xavier. Letting you go wasn't my decision. In fact I wasn't even consulted. Jamie's father's the executor of his will."

"Yeah, why? You have more of a clue about the business than a farmer."

Hannah sighed as her own frustrations burned her. "Do you have an up-to-date will, Xavier?"

"I don't have a will."

"Then go make one, okay? Let one positive come from this awful mess." When Xavier murmured his agreement, she said, "Did Jamie tell you about any surprises he was planning for the wedding?"

"What sort of surprises?"

"I dunno. Like hiring a Porsche?"

"I didn't know that was for the wedding. I just know he was pretty PO'd about it."

"Was he?" She heard herself saying the words but her brain seemed disconnected from her mouth as it frantically churned through the whys, hows and what the hells.

"Yeah," Xavier said. "He said you wanted a Lamborghini. Sorry, Hannah, I've got another call about a job. Talk later."

Hannah managed, "Sure, bye," then sat staring at the phone, willing it to explain why Jamie would have said she wanted a Lamborghini.

. . .

Hannah sat in a cane chair on the homestead's veranda looking out into the garden. In the distance she could make out the fallen tree trunk straddling the creek. How could she have thought a flattened wedding marquee was a catastrophe when so much worse had followed?

She hated how life went on as if hers hadn't been shattered. The damaged garden bed was recovering—established plants were putting out fresh shoots and new bedding plants were flowering. Soon there'd be no evidence of the disaster.

Oh, Jamie.

Sensing her wave of grief, Ozzie laid his snout over her feet.

Trying to hold back tears, Hannah gulped the remaining tea in her cup—crying in front of Lydia made her uncomfortable. It wasn't that Lydia wasn't grieving—the death of her son was clear in the new lines on her face—but she always held it together in public. Hannah was working on trying to do the same.

Lydia pushed a plate towards her that was loaded with fluffy scones generously dolloped with jam and cream. Since Jamie's death, Hannah's appetite lurched from consuming everything in sight to barely eating, although the former happened less often than the latter. Today, hunger had deserted her.

"You're too thin and thin women struggle to conceive," Lydia said.

Anxiety fluttered in Hannah's belly. "Do they?"

"Apparently. It's a bit like animals in a drought—they stop ovulating."

"I'll have drugs making sure I do that," Hannah said.

"But you need to be a healthy weight to give the embryo the best chance."

Hannah forced herself to pick up a scone and take a bite. Like most food she ate, it tasted like dust. There was a certain irony in the fact that grief flattened her appetite but presenting her with food was the way so many people showed their sympathy. Her overloaded freezer couldn't squeeze in another lasagna.

She'd told Lydia about her conversation with Rowan, and Lydia was listing people who may sign affidavits.

"Don't forget his Penthurst friends," she said. "It's probably best if you contact them to arrange a time to meet. These things are best done in person." Lydia leaned forward. "I could come with you if you wanted the company."

"Thank you. I'd like that."

"We could do some Christmas shopping too." Lydia gave a sad smile. "I know Christmas will be difficult, but as much as we may wish to ignore it, the grandchildren won't let us. I wish Maddie lived closer …"

Hannah almost said, "Every day is difficult," but there was no point —Lydia knew it too. They needed something positive to come out of this nightmare and that was Jamie's child. The sooner she was pregnant, the sooner they could focus on looking forward. Enjoy hope instead of this gut-wrenching and unrelenting grief.

Her mind immediately went to Freya's miscarriage and fear burned in her chest. What if that happened to her? No! The universe wouldn't dare do that to her on top of taking Jamie. Would it?

Her worry must have shown on her face because Lydia asked, "Is it to do with Christmas?"

Hannah shook her head. "I was thinking about Freya. Did you know she had a miscarriage?"

"I did hear," Lydia said.

Hannah waited for Lydia to say more—something along the lines of "how upsetting" or "poor Freya"—but instead her mother-in-law was reaching down for something. She straightened and handed Hannah a yellow B4-size envelope.

Hannah peeked inside and saw a white envelope, a pile of small white cards, pieces of ribbon and a Ziplock bag containing carefully pressed flowers. She pulled out a few of the cards—some were handwritten, others were printed, but most were stamped with the Garringarup Florist's logo.

"What's all this?" she asked.

"Cards from the funeral flowers and the ones left at the accident site," Lydia said. "I held onto them to make sure everyone received a thank-you card, but now they've been sent I thought you may like them."

A burr of annoyance prickled Hannah's skin at the weeks it had taken for these cards to reach her. "Shouldn't I have sent the thank-yous?"

"None of these cards were personally addressed to you. In fact most were written directly to Jamie. Anyway, you were in Singapore."

Hannah couldn't decide if Lydia's tone was disapproving or not. She shook away the thought. If Lydia hadn't wanted her to go to Singapore she would have said something at the time.

"The thank-you cards went out on behalf of the entire family, including you and Maddie," Lydia said. "I've put one in the envelope for you. I've taken copies of the condolence cards and I'm making a memory book. People have said such lovely things about Jamie." Her voice wavered and she blew her nose, taking a moment to compose herself. "You could do something similar and include the funeral speeches. It would be the perfect book for his—your child to read so they know their father."

Hannah breathed deeply. It was a lovely idea, but she wasn't certain she had the skills to do it justice. "I guess I could ask Freya to help."

"Freya doesn't scrapbook." Lydia's mouth was a firm line. "She just sells the supplies with a hefty markup. You'd be wiser to order online."

"Why are you so harsh on Freya?" The question Hannah had wanted to ask since she'd moved to Garringarup slipped out.

"Because she was the reason Jamie went to Perth."

"Surely Monique was the reason?"

"Monique broke Jamie's heart and I've never forgiven her for that, but at least she had the decency to leave town. Him moving to Perth was Freya's idea. She kept pushing that barrow when it was none of her business. She should have left well alone."

Hannah spun her engagement ring, discomfort needling her. "I'm glad Freya pushed it. If Jamie hadn't lived in Perth we would never have met."

Lydia released a long sigh and patted Hannah's hand. "You're the only positive to come out of his time away. Even so, Freya should have stayed in her lane. Back then, Jamie needed the support of his family and friends, not being isolated and alone in Perth. And Ian needed him here on the farm. It was a difficult time for all of us."

Back at home Hannah poured herself a glass of wine and sat down to read the condolence cards. The printed messages ranged from detailed missives to a few single Xs with no other identifying features. All oozed love and grief for Jamie.

Garringarup Cricket Club: Keep hitting sixes, mate.
Garringarup Chamber of Commerce: Taken too soon.
The best of friends and forever missed. Lots of love, Ryan & Freya x
Sam Dillinger: Hope the beer's flowing up there.

Many of the cards said *Rest in peace*, which bothered Hannah because rest was something Jamie rarely did. He was a constant whirl of activity, either planning something or physically doing it.

The next card read: *With heartfelt condolences, Monique, David and Will Llewellyn-Jones.* Once, Hannah would have experienced a rush of jagged emotions at seeing Monique's name, but she remembered how kind and respectful the woman had been at the funeral before Lydia had lost it. How much her words "I can see why he loved you" had helped hold Hannah up on that horrendous day. She hoped that if their roles had been reversed, she would have the same dignity and poise. Then again, Monique had fallen out of love with Jamie so perhaps that made it easier to be gracious.

There were signed cards from various members of Jamie's extended family—some printed, others handwritten—as well as an unsigned card with the words: *It wasn't meant to end like this.* Hannah turned it over, seeking a name, but the card was blank.

She flipped it back and stared at the handwriting—it was a mix of printed letters with occasional cursive connections. The ink had smudged. Was that from tears? Water from flowers? Rain? She had no idea and set it aside, picking up the next card.

Andrew and Annika Anderson: Keep laughing, Jamie.

Something about how the As were written on this card made Hannah return to the one that had snagged her. *It wasn't meant to end like this.* Most people wrote the lower-case "a" like a squished circle with a tail as they'd been taught in elementary school. Whoever had written this card—and Hannah would bet her life it was a woman—had used a calligraphy style with a hat over the top of the "a" and a tail.

And why would they write *It wasn't meant to end like this?* Easy! Because Jamie's life wasn't supposed to have ended like it had or so soon. Except ... wasn't it a strange thing to write when someone died? All the other messages were far more straightforward, but this one sounded cryptic. Was it hiding something? Saying something more? And if so, what?

Deciding she was overthinking things, Hannah stood to refill her glass and realized she was hungry. Her freezer was full to overflowing with meals people had cooked, but making a decision was beyond her. She plunged her hand into the cold, leaving the choice to chance, and pulled out a disposable foil container with a cardboard lid.

The contents were labelled in marker pen and Hannah instantly recognized the swirly, decorative handwriting as Freya's—she'd been reading similarly written signs in the store. She put the container into the oven and was about to drop the lid into the trash when she noticed the three lower case "a"s in "lasagna"—they looked similar to the ones on the card.

She immediately told herself she was being ridiculous. There was no way Freya would have written *It wasn't meant to end like this.* And even with the extremely long odds that Freya had written it, she would have signed it with her distinctive back to front F accompanied by an "x", like she'd signed the lasagna lid. And she'd have added Ryan's name. Freya always signed cards *Lots of love, Freya & Ryan.*

Hannah rummaged in the envelope and pulled out the typed card with both their names on it to prove the point. Even so, she found herself lying the unsigned card and the lasagna lid side by side on the counter. There was no disputing the shape of the "a"s.

Hannah's heart thumped in her chest like the kick of a horse. Why the hell had Freya written this and not signed it?

Xavier's words suddenly tumbled through her head: *He said you wanted a Lamborghini.*

Hannah froze. Were Freya and Jamie secretly driving sports cars together?

The sound of a hysterical laugh circled her. Ozzie looked up from his mat, a quizzical look in his eyes.

"Sorry, mate," Hannah said. She was being ridiculous. Of course Freya and Jamie weren't doing that.

She was the reason Jamie went to Perth—Lydia had said those words at afternoon tea. Was there more to Freya pushing for Jamie to go to Perth than getting over Monique? Did Freya visit him on her buying trips so they could be together driving fast cars far away from the prying eyes of Garringarup? Hannah's mouth dried at the thought.

Stop it! One: Jamie would never cheat on her. And two: Freya had gone out of her way to welcome Hannah to Garringarup and help her settle in. She'd repeatedly told her how thankful she and Ryan were that Jamie had met Hannah and how happy she made him. A lover didn't do or say things like that!

Camilla Parker Bowles befriended her lover's fiancée and look how that turned out.

Hannah rubbed her face and reminded herself that Jamie loved and adored her. He'd have walked over hot coals for her. If he and Freya had been involved, she would have noticed. Garringarup was too small to hide an affair. Wasn't it?

And Freya loved Ryan. God, they were the poster couple for a successful relationship. It took less than half an hour in their company to be impressed by the love, trust and respect they held for each other. Hannah wasn't even sure Freya noticed other blokes. She couldn't think of a single time when Freya had joined in the fun of girl chat, discussing who was hot and who was not.

People talked about grief in terms of denial, anger, bargaining and depression, but no one mentioned insanity. And this sort of thinking was bat-shit crazy—it was time to jump off this ride and grip tightly onto logic. Hannah had absolutely no reason to suspect either Jamie or Freya of anything other than love, care and devotion to her. And yet ...

Blowing out a long breath, she narrowed her gaze and stared at both sets of writing until her eyes stung. The card lacked the decorative swirl Freya always used on capital letters and there was no little flick on the "w". She studied the "a's again and this time she noticed they weren't as carefully rounded as Freya's. Even when Freya wrote a shopping list her script was faultless. Despite some water damage on the card, Hannah knew for certain it hadn't been written by her friend. But on a day when everyone was numb from the trauma of a life cut short far too soon, a woman had scrawled these words. She just had no idea who.

And the Porsche?

She chewed her lip. The reason behind the car was less clear, but like everything else there would be a logical explanation. Xavier had told her that Jamie—

The tantalizing aroma of garlic and tomatoes hit her nostrils accompanied by a tinge of burning cheese. *Yikes, the lasagna!*

As Hannah headed to the kitchen, she got a flash of memory. It had been just prior to her birthday and as she'd entered the office Jamie had clicked his mouse to send his screen to black. In all the months they'd shared the space, he'd never done that before.

"You buying my birthday present?" she'd teased.

He'd grinned. "Better than that."

Excitement had fizzed and popped. "Really?"

"Yep. Honeymoon surprise."

The statement had confused her because they'd already booked the honeymoon resort package that offered everything from diving and paddleboarding to mountain-bike riding and spa treatments.

"But everything's included," she said.

"*This* surprise is before we get to Tahiti."

"In Perth? Sydney? Do I get a hint?"

"No."

"Please," she'd begged.

"All I'll say is that the theme is red."

"What do you mean red?" she'd asked. Her favorite color was blue and Jamie preferred green.

But he'd just laughed, pulled her onto his lap and kissed her long and deep until she was wet with need. She'd reached for his fly, wanting to have sex right then in the generous chair, but he'd pulled back from her, a look of horror streaking over his face.

"Hannah! Anyone could walk in."

Before she could say, "Who?" his phone had rung and then hers had too and

all thoughts of sex and the red-themed surprise had been overtaken by chasing money from the Pederson account.

Now Hannah sagged against the door frame as everything fell into place. The lingerie was red. The Porsche was red, and there was a newly opened boutique hotel in Perth called Red. Lydia was right—the car had been a honeymoon surprise.

Embarrassment followed on the back of her relief. How could she have gone down the insanity rabbit hole, no matter how momentary, of thinking Freya and Jamie had been having an affair?

That Jamie had died trying to surprise her left her both gutted and buoyed in equal measure, so she did the only thing she could do. She held onto the essence of the surprise—Jamie's love for her—and let go of everything else.

CHAPTER TWENTY-ONE

ON THE DECK, Freya cupped her coffee mug with both hands and gazed at the white streaky clouds scudding across the intensely blue sky. After the hospital and the noise of the city, the joy of being home slid through her. She lowered her gaze, taking in the bright profusion of color from her pelargoniums. They were plants that took little in the way of water and care yet gave and gave.

She sipped her coffee—oh, how she'd missed it—and sighed in delight as the caffeine streaked into her bloodstream giving her an alertness that had been absent during her pregnancy. When she'd woken this morning, she'd momentarily forgotten she was no longer pregnant until she'd felt the dampness between her legs. Then the awfulness of the last few days had flooded back. The silent ultrasound. The concerned faces of the hospital staff. The scratchy hospital gown, the itchy paper hat and the cool steel of the hospital gurney. Her mother's uncharacteristic sympathy. Ryan's ashen face.

A missed abortion. She knew abortion was the medical term for a miscarriage, but somehow it made it sound as if she'd been the one to make the decision to end the pregnancy.

"You're up early." Ryan joined her on the deck, dropping a kiss on her lips. "Couldn't sleep?"

"It's not early."

"I thought after the last couple of days you'd want a lie-in."

"I thought I'd go in to work."

His eyes registered surprise. "There's no need to push yourself. Hannah's got things under control."

Irritation bubbled in her gut. "I'm not pushing myself."

"Sweetheart, they gave you a narcotic pre-med, you've had an anesthetic, you lost more blood than normal and you're still bleeding. You're not supposed to drive a car yet, let alone make business decisions."

His tone was the calm and patient one she'd heard him use the few times he'd gone into work mode at a social function when someone had fainted or hurt themselves. More recently she'd heard him using it with Vivian. Why couldn't he have been an accountant?

"I'm not bleeding much."

His brows rose. "I've got bedsheets soaking in cold water. I want you to see Leah today, just to make sure everything's okay."

Freya was suddenly uncomfortable that Ryan knew so much about her body. Although she'd never hidden her period from him, she didn't discuss it with him either. Now he knew she was losing too much blood after the D&C *and* he was commenting on it.

"Okay, fine. But I'm seeing her on my own," she said, the words coming out unexpectedly terse.

Hurt flickered across his face. "Okay, but I'm driving you."

Guilt slammed into her and she dropped her head onto his shoulder, blinking back tears. "I'm sorry. I shouldn't have said that. I thought I'd feel like myself again, but I'm still not me. I just feel numb."

"No one expects you to be yourself." His voice cracked. "I mean, hell—it's been a shit time. We lost Jamie and now we've lost our baby."

"I'm sorry."

"It's not your fault. It's just one of those things. I did some reading and miscarriages happen to ten percent of pregnancies. Next time will be different."

A wave of fatigue hit her, accompanied by skips of panic. "I can't even think about that yet."

"Hey, breathe, it's okay." He stroked her hair. "How about you go back to bed and I'll bring in breakfast?"

This time she only felt gratitude and relief. "That sounds wonderful, but I may nap first."

He kissed her. "Good idea. Yell when you want food."

When Freya opened her eyes, the clock beamed 10:00 and she heard the sound of running feet.

"Freya!" Mia jumped on the bed.

"Mia!" Lexie followed her daughter into the bedroom. "I said you had to be quiet."

"Sorry, Mummy."

"Say it to Freya," Lexie said.

"Sorry, Freya." The little girl snuggled in next to her. "Do you have a sore tummy? I can kiss it better."

Freya's head swiveled to Lexie. Surely she hadn't told Mia about the baby.

"Ryan didn't want to wake you, but he asked me to check in on you before I start my shift," Lexie said. "And to tell you he's taking you to see Leah at 4:00. You want me to make you brunch? I could do eggs or pan—"

"Pancakes!" Mia scrambled off the bed and ran out of the room.

"I think it's been decided," Freya said. She knew she should throw off the covers and get up, but her legs felt as heavy as the tree trunk that had flattened the wedding marquee.

Lexie sat on the bed. "You okay?"

Freya had no idea what she was—she barely recognized herself. She was circled by a void that distanced all sensation from her. Doctor Sharma had told her that in a couple of days she'd feel more herself.

God, she hoped so. She hadn't felt like herself in weeks but these sensations were different again. Surely they were due to the drugs and the remnants of pregnancy hormones in her system.

"I will be okay," she said, more to reassure herself than Lexie.

"Ryan looks like shit too. As bad, or worse even, than when Jamie died." Lexie put her hand on the covers. "I never told you, but I had a miscarriage before Mia. The only thing that helped, besides buckets of wine, was getting pregnant again."

Freya felt a jolt of sadness that Lexie had hidden her miscarriage from her, and then remembered she'd been four months pregnant when she'd married Kane and they'd only been together six months. Did that mean the first pregnancy had been Kane's child or someone else's?

In so many ways her younger sister remained a mystery to her. They had always been different, but as the years passed there were days when Freya wondered if they shared any DNA at all.

"At least there's only a few weeks left of this crappy year," she said. "Next year's going to be way better for the Quayle sisters."

"The only thing that will make next year less crappy for me is meeting someone and winning Powerball so I can quit my job," Lexie said.

"I thought you loved your job," Freya said.

When Kane left, Lexie had been forced back to work, but her previous jobs as a shearers' cook, nanny, ski-lift attendant and waitress weren't child-friendly. Ryan had heard about the ward clerk position at the hospital and gave her a crash course in medical records and Freya gave her one on spreadsheets.

Lexie rolled her eyes. "You love your job. Ryan loves his. I endure mine."

Old memories fluttered to the surface—Lexie raving about a new job and a few months later hating it and quitting to try something new. It hadn't been an issue when she was only responsible for herself, but now she had Mia to care for and permanent positions with good conditions in Garringarup weren't exactly plentiful.

Dismay dragged through Freya and she was preparing to talk up all the positives of Lexie's job when her sister said, "Mum called. Something about test results."

Freya sat up. "And?"

"She wants someone to go with her to see Leah."

"That doesn't sound like Mum."

"Right. So can you take her at the end of the week?"

Freya was having trouble imagining getting out of bed now, let alone dealing with Vivian in a few days' time.

"It's just you're better at this sort of thing than me," Lexie said. "You've always coped better with her diabetes and you're not alone like I am. You've got Ryan to explain all the medical stuff so it makes more sense, you know."

Freya tried not to let her frustration swamp her. She'd dispute that as a child she'd coped better with their mother's diabetes—it was more a case of her being five years older than Lexie. But they were both adults now and the age gap was irrelevant.

She was about to insist Lexie accompany Vivian when Mia yelled from somewhere in the house, "Mummy! Freya! Pancakes!"

Lexie jumped up. "You stay in bed and enjoy not being at the beck and call of anyone."

As Lexie left the room, the now-familiar waves of fatigue rolled back. Freya hauled the covers over her head and gave in to the welcoming darkness.

Lexie left in a whirlwind of "gotta go, rest up, Ryan will wash the dishes when he gets home," and Mia body-hugged Freya, insisting she keep her snow dragon to cuddle "just for today." Freya closed the door behind them and sighed in relief. Her sister's brand of sympathy was exhausting.

She opened her computer, checked her business bank account, then looked at the online orders. Hannah appeared to be on top of things as the only outstanding orders had been placed less than two hours ago. She could hear both Ryan and Hannah saying, "We've got this. You relax."

She snapped down the lid of her computer and picked up a book. Five minutes later she might have turned six pages but she hadn't absorbed a word. Agitation thrummed her body—she needed to be at Just Because. She had enough time to shower, visit the store and be back before Ryan arrived to drive her to the clinic.

She was drying her feet after her shower when she suddenly swayed and needed to sit on the edge of the bath until her head stopped spinning. It was bad enough that she felt detached from everything around her without her body acting out with physical symptoms.

She checked her blood loss. Too much.

"Why are you doing this to me?"

Her body refused to supply an answer.

She managed to blow-dry her hair to a reasonable standard, then peered at the black smudges under her eyes—she needed the full complement of make-up today.

With blusher and concealer doing their job, she heeded Ryan's instructions not to drive and walked to the store, taking her time and enjoying the sunshine. As she pushed open the shop's door, the thrill she always got at the sound of the bell ran up her spine. She breathed in the floral scents of the handmade soaps and a long-missed calm wrapped itself around her like a cloak. She'd created this beautiful store on the back of a lot of hard work and a long-held dream.

A few steps inside the shop and she stopped, her thrill ebbing. Something was different, but it was so subtle it took her quite a few seconds to work out what it was. Hannah had created themed Christmas displays and, in the process, had reorganized the store.

Pique pinged along Freya's veins. *It's my shop!* Hannah was supposed to be minding it, not changing it. Her belly cramped again and she sucked in a deep breath, trying not to double over.

"Freya!" Hannah rushed towards her from the back of the shop and enveloped her in a hug. "I didn't think you'd be coming in today. I was going to visit you after I locked up. How are you?"

Freya's skin prickled from the touch and she extricated herself.

The shop's bell rang and Chrissie Lancefield walked in with Anita Carson. The two women exchanged a glance with Hannah before turning their attention to Freya.

You idiot! In her disordered thinking, she'd come into the shop assuming it would be free of the mess that was her miscarriage.

"Freya? Goodness. Shouldn't you be at home?" Chrissie said.

"That's what I was thinking," Hannah said. "You've been through a lot."

"Not as much as you." Just as Freya was wondering how Hannah coped with the town's solicitude, she saw the moment her words landed. Shock was clear on the three women's faces.

"You just lost a baby," Hannah said.

Freya thought of the tiny dugong she'd seen on the ultrasound. "It was early."

Hannah looked aghast. "Oh God, is that what they told you? That doesn't make it any less sad. It was the baby you dreamed of and imagined holding in your arms."

The prickles returned in stinging rafts. "Can we talk about something else, please?"

"That's not healthy, Freya," Chrissie said. "For hundreds of years women have been having miscarriages and people have stayed silent because they blame themselves, or worse, others blame them. Back in the day, the local priest told my mother that her miscarriage was God's will and she should go to confession. She was so furious she told him that God should be stopping wars instead of taking longed-for babies. She never went back to church and she started a support group. It was groundbreaking stuff and it sounds like it's still needed."

Chrissie whipped out her phone. "The community health center runs the group now." Freya's phone croaked. "That's the contact details. Give them a call."

"Thanks," Freya said, fervently wishing that Garringarup wasn't so enlightened about miscarriage. She had no intention of making the call.

"As sad as it is, sometimes miscarriages happen for a reason," Anita said. "Perhaps there was something wrong with the baby. And it's all very well for people to say 'I'll love the baby no matter what," but what about my cousin, Esther? She's got two severely disabled children and Harvey's scarpered. It's no life for her or the kids. And the one kid that's normal—her childhood's being destroyed by looking after her siblings. I'm sorry, but if there was something wrong, Freya, your miscarriage is a blessing. Have they suggested genetic testing?"

Hannah and Chrissie stared at Anita, their mouths slack with shock.

Chrissie finally spoke. "That's incredibly insensitive."

Anita shrugged. "I'm only stating the truth."

Freya thought Anita had just articulated one of her own worst fears. From the moment she'd learned of her pregnancy, she'd feared that her lack of prenatal vitamins and all the alcohol she'd drunk after Jamie's funeral might have inflicted damage. But right now she selfishly took advantage of the tense situation between the women—anything to move the spotlight off herself.

She picked up a basket. "It sounds like Esther could do with one of the fabulous pamper packs Hannah's put together for Christmas. Dario's olive oil, mango butter and lemon myrtle moisturizer is like satin on your skin, and you know The Grove makes beautiful soap."

Anita patted Freya's hand. "I was only trying to help. And you're right, Esther will love this. I'll give it to her with a voucher for some house cleaning."

"Did you need anything else?" Freya asked. "You always say Rick's hard to buy for, but I noticed his hat was looking tatty last time he was in town. What about a new one?"

The bell rang and half a dozen customers walked in. Freya gave thanks they were tourists. Better yet, they were strangers who had no idea she'd been pregnant and had lost the baby.

CHAPTER TWENTY-TWO

MUCH TO HANNAH'S RELIEF, Freya had asked her to stay on at Just Because until Christmas. "If you work in the shop it frees me up to pack the online orders," she'd said. "After that interview in *Country* magazine, they've exploded."

"Using the park for the Instagram photos has helped too," Hannah said. "You get the outback dirt along with pretty wildflowers. City slickers love that sort of stuff, especially the east-coasters."

Freya had smiled at that—the first smile Hannah had seen since the miscarriage. But it wasn't lost on her that by packing orders, Freya was hiding from the town.

Ryan must have noticed too because he'd called Hannah a few days ago. "How does she seem to you?" he'd asked, clearly worried.

"I haven't actually seen her," Hannah confessed. "I think she comes to the store when I'm not here. We call and text but it's always about Just Because. Each time I've suggested an IRL catch-up she says soon, but she won't commit to a time."

"She's exhausted," Ryan said. "But she won't admit it. At least she's keeping you on."

Hannah's relief that she still had the job—one she intended to keep by proving to Freya that she was indispensable—tangled with guilt that Freya was struggling.

"I think she came back to work too early," she said.

"You and me both," Ryan said. "I wanted her to take time to absorb what's happened, but she's not listening to me or Leah."

"She doesn't want to talk about the baby at all," Hannah said. She knew that talking about Jamie had helped her so she'd been surprised when Freya deflected every conversation about the miscarriage. It hadn't only been with her—she'd noticed Freya did it with other women too.

Ryan sighed. "I think she's still in shock and it hasn't fully hit her yet. But it's going to land one day. I worry that when it does, she's going to fall in a heap."

Hannah thought about her own grief. There were times when the thick morass of devastation lifted and it was less of a struggle to go about her day. Then wham—it hit again like a runaway train, driving her back inside and under the covers.

"Thank goodness Freya has you," she said.

"Yeah."

The word dripped with melancholy and Hannah's heart ached. Ryan had lost a baby too.

"How are you?" she asked.

"Bloody sad." He sighed. "And missing Jamie. Aw, shit, Hannah, I'm sorry—"

"No, don't be. I love that you just told me you miss him. So often I feel like it's only me and the McMasters who notice he's gone."

"Believe me," Ryan's voice was ragged, "I notice."

His despair at having lost his best friend reached down the phone line. Hannah latched onto it as a way of staying close to Jamie. "He would have taken you out for a beer and listened."

"Yeah. Or taken me to the driving range and got me whacking golf balls, or bowling to him in the nets."

"I can listen, Ryan."

"Thanks, Hannah, but you've got enough on your plate."

"I think you'd be helping me as much as I'd be helping you. Especially until Freya's back on her feet."

"God, I hope it's soon. I hate seeing her like this." There was noise in the background. "I have to go, but thanks, Hannah. Not just for minding the store, but for the chat. Talk soon."

Since that phone conversation, Hannah had only seen Freya briefly. She'd come into the store, adjusted one of the displays and asked for an inventory of gift-wrap before rushing out again. Last week she'd moved a lot of stock to her garage and was now packing hampers at home.

The shop bell tinkled and a tall woman walked in, all grace and style. Her clothing choices marked her as one of the Wheatbelt's farming elite—casual country elegance with jewelry to match.

It took Hannah a moment to recognize her. "Monique?"

The woman turned and her eyes widened. "Hannah? Has Freya sold the store?"

"I wish it was my store, but no. I'm helping her with the Christmas rush."

"That's why I'm here," Monique said. "David's at the Garringarup stock sale today so I'm Christmas shopping here instead of Northam." She took a few steps closer to the counter, her face filled with concern. "How are you?"

"Okay." Hannah struggled against the odd sensation of being alone with a woman she didn't know but who had known Jamie as intimately as she had. "Taking it one day at a time."

"That's all you can do." Monique nodded sympathetically, then glanced around the store. She pointed to a novelty apron embroidered with the words: *The last time I cooked almost nobody got sick.* "That could have been made with Jamie in mind."

Hannah remembered some of the questionable meals Jamie had cooked for her and laughed. "It really could. I adored him but he couldn't cook."

"He really couldn't." Monique's look was that of an indulgent older sister. "When we were together he made a tuna mornay once, but he couldn't get the white sauce to thicken. Turns out he'd used icing sugar instead of corn flour."

Hannah laughed. "Oh my God, what did it taste like?"

"Absolutely disgusting." Monique's phone beeped and she glanced at the screen, her smile fading. "David's ready to leave a lot earlier than I expected so it looks like I'll be Christmas shopping in Northam after all. It was nice to see you, Hannah. Take care."

"Thank you. You too." Hannah watched her leave, savoring the unexpected gift of a new Jamie story.

The moment Monique had cleared the doorway, a young woman entered. Hannah gave her time to glance around and get her bearings.

When delight lifted the woman's mouth, Hannah said, "Welcome to Just Because. Is there anything I can help you with or are you enjoying a browse?"

"Both really. You have a gorgeous shop. I had no idea this place existed and I can't believe that my brother actually stepped inside, but I'm so glad he did." Her fingers rose to her necklace. "He bought me this for my twenty-first."

Hannah recognized the horse pendant. "Are you Georgie?"

"That's me."

"Your brother gave me heart failure every time he took a step on these old boards. Everything wobbled."

Georgie laughed. "Yeah, he's not built for being around fragile things."

"I'm Hannah and I helped him choose the necklace. I'm glad you like it."

"I love it!"

"How was your party?"

Georgie's eyes lit up. "So good! The olds all left at 11:00 and we kicked on until 2:00. Mac's band was awesome."

Hannah couldn't imagine the beefy bloke in a band. "Is he the singer?"

"Mac can't sing to save himself."

"Drummer then?"

"Saxophone and piano."

Hannah's jaw dropped slightly as she tried picturing Mac's huge hands moving dexterously over piano and saxophone keys.

Georgie laughed. "I know what you're thinking, but he's good. He won a music scholarship to Penthurst. Oh, cool!' She picked up a pair of black and white socks covered in musical notes. "I never thought Mac would wear fun socks but he wore some to my birthday. I'll get him these for Christmas."

"Great." Hannah produced a basket for Georgie. "Are you shopping for the whole family?"

"That's the plan."

Half an hour later Hannah knew that Georgie's mother loved flowers, her father enjoyed puzzles and her grandparents were barbecue devotees. She'd just put the finishing touches on a hamper of gourmet meat rubs, sauces and salad dressings when the shop bell pealed.

"You ready, George? We need to get going before—" Mac stood in the doorway and suddenly pulled off his hat. "Oh, g'day Hannah."

"Hey, Mac. Thanks for recommending Just Because to Georgie."

"No worries."

Georgie laughed. "Don't make it sound like you were doing Hannah a favor. You just wanted me to do your Christmas shopping for you."

Mac grinned. "I offered you the chance to go to the farm supplies, but you said you wanted to see where I got the necklace. Anyway, did you actually choose the gifts or did Hannah do her present-whispering thing?"

"Present-whispering?" Hannah had no clue what he was talking about.

"Somehow you got me to buy socks with flowers on them," Mac said, sounding bewildered.

"And you wore them," Hannah said.

"Hah! Sprung bad!" Georgie spun around to Mac, who'd taken a few steps into the store. "You told me you'd chosen them to match Mum's flower arrangements."

"And you believed me?" A loud belly laugh rumbled out of him. "Who's the dummy now?"

Georgie swatted him on the arm. "You can pay then."

"I was always going to pay." He handed Hannah his credit card. "Do I want to know how much I've spent?"

Hannah smiled, enjoying the siblings' banter. "Your presents will be a huge hit."

"Lucky lamb prices are up, eh?"

Hannah nodded as she always did when farmers rabbited on about stock prices and the weather. "I've put the receipt in the bag. On the rare chance someone isn't happy with their gift, Freya will happily exchange them after Christmas."

As if saying her name had summoned her, Freya entered the shop.

"This is Freya Quayle, the owner of Just Because," Hannah said. "Georgie and Mac Downie. Mac and his brother were at boarding school with Jamie."

Freya said hello and smiled as Georgie gushed about the store. "You can follow me on Instagram if you like."

Georgie had her phone out in a second.

Mac's murmur sounded far more parental than brotherly. "Great to meet you, Freya," he said, "but we have to get back to Beverley. Come on, G. Daisy needs a drink."

He strode to the door and Freya's hands reached for the wildly swinging glass Christmas ornaments as everything on the shelves rattled.

When Mac and Georgie had left, Hannah said, "Let's have a coffee to celebrate return customers and a big sale."

"How much?" Freya asked.

When Hannah told her the total of the eight purchased gifts, Freya high-fived her.

With an ear on the shop bell, they sat in the back room sipping lattes.

"I think I'm falling in love with Just Because," Hannah said. "I'm loving the creative side of retail, that's for sure."

Freya's smile was oddly tight. "It's been a slow build, but if the pre-Christmas sales keep on like this I'm on track for my best year ever. More and more tour buses are coming through town and the gray nomads love buying things for the grandkids."

Hannah eyed Freya over the top of her glass. "Talking kids, how are you?"

"I'm fine."

"Really?"

Freya closed her eyes for a moment, then opened them. "Like you, I can't change what happened. I can only learn to live with it."

Hannah railed at the comparison and her words rushed out unchecked. "But you can get pregnant again. I can't get Jamie back."

When Freya didn't say anything, a wave of nausea hit Hannah. "Have you been given bad news about getting pregnant again?"

Freya shook her head. "The only thing I was told was not to have sex for a couple of weeks."

"That's good news. So you've started trying again?"

"I'm so exhausted that the thought of sex is beyond me, let alone doing it." Freya sagged into the sofa. "Can we go back to talking about everything other than the miscarriage?"

"I didn't mean to upset you."

"I appreciate your concern, but can you please let me bring it up when I'm ready?"

"Sure." But she couldn't shift a kernel of hurt that Freya didn't want to share.

She cast around for a new topic of conversation. Freya's miscarriage had shelved her own plans of talking to her and Ryan about the affidavit. Was now the time? She licked her lips. "How do you feel about me talking about my pregnancy plans?" A flicker of something crossed Freya's face. "Too soon for you?"

Freya shook her head. "It's not too soon for me."

Hannah heard criticism in Freya's voice and immediately checked her face for confirmation. The only thing she saw was fatigue. She tried to settle her chaotic feelings and reminded herself that Freya had only ever been a supportive friend.

"Remember how I had to get a court order to retrieve Jamie's sperm and another to allow it to be frozen," she said.

A look of confusion crossed Freya's face. "Why did you need a separate order for it to be frozen?"

"Because WA law only allows for the immediate use of gametes—eggs and sperm." Hannah sighed. "Obviously I couldn't use them then and there."

"Right ..." Freya sipped her coffee. "Well, the law exists for a reason ..."

Hannah huffed out a tight laugh. "It exists to make my life difficult. I'm ready to start IVF but there are more legal hoops to jump through. The easy bit is I need statements from friends and colleagues to prove that Jamie wanted to be a father. The problem part is WA law won't let the gametes of a deceased person be used so I have to apply for the sperm to be released to a place that does allow it."

Freya's eyebrows hit her hairline. "How far will you need to go? Just east or overseas?"

"Queensland." Hannah sighed. "And I have to apply to the court there to use the sperm. But there's a doctor who will treat me so Rowan says it's just a matter of going through the motions."

"It sounds expensive." Freya leaned in, her face serious. "Hannah, are you sure it's worth it?"

The words burned like the sting of a scorpion.

"Of course it's worth it! If Jamie was still alive I'd already be pregnant. Instead, I'm all alone and—"

"You're not alone, you've—"

"Dec's my only living relative!" She realized she was yelling and tried to lower her volume. "Freya, I want our child. I want the family I was always going to have. Surely with what you're going through, you understand that?"

But Freya's brows had arrowed down so sharply that they'd turned the bridge of her nose into a series of creases. "But having a child on your own is—"

"What I want." Hannah refused to allow the conversation to head in this unwanted direction. She didn't need to justify her decision to anyone except the WA legal system. If Jamie was alive, no one would be questioning her choice to become a mother. "But due to my situation, I need help from the people who love me and who knew, loved and respected Jamie. You and Ryan are Jamie's best friends—"

"Ryan was his best friend."

The clarification surprised her. "Sure, but you know what I mean. You knew Jamie for a long time too. I need you and Ryan to sign individual affidavits stating that Jamie wanted to be a father. You can either say it in your own words or use a template that Rowan's set up. I'll send it now."

Hannah pulled out her phone and dispatched the email she'd had sitting in drafts for over two weeks. Freya's phone pinged.

"That's all the information you need. Rowan's on leave, but you can sign it at the magistrates court in Northam. In fact, why not go on a day Ryan's working there and have lunch at that new bistro everyone's talking about?" She gave what she hoped was an encouraging smile. "I'll mind the shop for you at no charge."

Freya hadn't said a word and now she was engrossed in the email.

Hannah waited, impatience ticking inside her. Why was it taking her so long to read a short and straightforward paragraph that basically reiterated what she'd just said? She blew out a breath, seeking calm. Of course Freya was taking her time. No matter the situation, she was meticulous with details—it was why Hannah had asked for her help with the wedding. Freya would be reading every word three times so she understood the contents completely. Even so, that didn't stop bubbles of agitation popping in Hannah's gut.

Unable to wait a second longer, she broke the silence. "Do you understand it? I can answer any questions."

She bit off adding, "Or Rowan can." She didn't want to suggest Freya could talk to Rowan, because by the time he got back from his

Busselton vacation Hannah planned to have all the affidavits signed and ready for him to lodge.

Freya nodded, the action slow and contemplative. "I need some time."

"Time?" Hannah didn't follow. Time was something she wanted to speed up, not slow down. The sooner she collected the affidavits, the sooner she could get pregnant and welcome her and Jamie's baby into the world.

Freya blinked, her dark eyes unusually luminous. Oh, hell, was that because of tears?

Hannah's heart cramped, although she wasn't certain if it was with disappointment for herself or compassion for her friend. Then a spurt of irritation fizzed in her veins. Why couldn't Freya just cry and talk and grieve her baby like other women, and then look forward? From what Hannah had gleaned from talking to Chrissie, the usual response to a miscarriage was a driving need to conceive again as soon as possible.

However, Hannah's own months of pain had taught her that grief wasn't linear. But despite knowing that reality, Freya's delay ran smack bang into her own craving for a deadline.

"Do you need a week? Or just a few days?" Hannah hoped that Freya only needed a couple of hours and a chat with Ryan to absorb the request.

But before Freya could reply, her phone rang and at the same time the shop bell pealed. Hannah had no choice but to leave Freya and return to the store.

CHAPTER TWENTY-THREE

WHILE VIVIAN FLICKED THROUGH A MAGAZINE, Freya approached Janet, the medical receptionist. They'd been waiting forty minutes and all Freya could think about was how many orders she could have packed during that time.

"Any idea how much longer Leah will be?" she asked.

"She'll be as long as she needs to be," Janet said curtly. "And then she'll give your mother all the time she needs."

"Yes, I appreciate Leah's good that way, but if she's likely to be another half an hour, I could use that time and pop back at 4:00."

"I'm not going to interrupt her to ask as that'll just slow things down. Use the time to do some meditation." Janet handed her a pamphlet. "You look like you need it."

Freya stopped herself from saying that crying babies, toddler tantrums and old men coughing in the waiting room weren't conducive to meditation. Janet was like most medical receptionists and it would be detrimental to turn her into an enemy. She returned to her seat.

Vivian sighed. "I'm sorry it's taking so long."

"Not a problem, Mum. Happy to be here.'

Vivian laughed. "As a child you were never good at lying, darling, and you haven't improved."

"I'm more than happy to be here. I just wish doctors ran to time is all."

Vivian patted her arm. "Is everything okay? You look tired."

Freya was fast getting sick of being told variations on that theme. Just like she was completely over the pitying glances from the local traders, customers and everyone she shared a passing glance with. If Ryan hadn't told the entire town they were pregnant, coping with the miscarriage would be a lot easier. Now she was actively dodging people to avoid unwanted conversations.

"I'm *always* tired at this time of year, Mum."

Vivian's mouth pursed at her snappy tone and she rummaged through her voluminous handbag before handing Freya a small black tube. "Here. Cover the black rings with some concealer and then no one will bother you with their concern."

Freya closed her eyes and blew out a long breath. She was seriously considering meditation when she heard Leah's voice calling, "Vivian Quayle."

After some quick pleasantries, Leah said, "What can I do for you today?"

Vivian produced a sheaf of papers. "I want you to translate all this mumbo jumbo they sent me."

Leah glanced at the papers, clicked on her computer and returned them to Vivian. "They sent me copies too. The cardiologist put you on medication for your heart condition. How's that going?"

"What heart condition?" Freya glanced between the two women.

"Vivian's developed atrial fibrillation. It means her heart's been beating irregularly and that's why there are times when she's short of breath, dizzy and has palpitations."

Worry gnawed at Freya. "And the medication can stop it from happening?"

"That's the aim." Leah turned her attention back to Vivian. "Have you been feeling better?"

"I didn't get dizzy at exercises last week."

"That's a win then." Leah checked the screen again. "There are a couple of other concerns connected with your diabetes. Your kidney function's down on what it should be so I'll be keeping a close eye on that."

Vivian sighed. "Does it mean more trips to Perth?"

"No, we can do the blood tests here."

"That's something," Vivian said.

"What's the other thing?" Freya asked.

"Vivian, your eyesight's deteriorated." Leah hesitated for a split second. "Until you have cataract surgery you shouldn't be driving."

Freya thought about her mother saying she didn't want to drive to Perth anymore, but she was still driving around town.

"Did the ophthalmologist in Perth tell you not to drive?" she asked. Vivian didn't meet her eyes. "Mum?"

"I'm only driving on roads I know," Vivian said defensively. "And I'm not driving at night."

"Mum, that's not the point. If you can't see properly it doesn't matter if you know the roads or not."

Leah cleared her throat. "I see you're on the waiting list for surgery."

"You can't expect me not to drive for over a year," Vivian said.

"How much would the surgery cost if she went private?" Freya asked.

"All up, including the hospital and anesthetist's fees, around $7,500 for both eyes."

Vivian gasped.

"And if we went that way, how long's the wait?" Freya asked.

"Vivian could probably have the surgery as soon as the consultants are back from Rottnest after their Christmas break," Leah said. "As you've already been seen by Doctor Morton, it's just a matter of booking in a surgery date with her receptionist."

"Mum, do you have contact details for the ophthalmologist?"

"I do, but you're not paying for my surgery."

"I'll let you two discuss that later," Leah said. "I'm sorry, Vivian, but legally I have to let Brett know you can't drive for the time being." Vivian's mouth thinned at the mention of the police sergeant's name. "But cataract surgery's a game changer. Once you've passed the eye test you'll be back driving again. Meanwhile, have you given more thought to an insulin pump?"

As they left the clinic, relief rolled through Freya that her mother's myriad health issues had consumed all of Leah's attention. It had left no time for the doctor to ask her how she was feeling or whether she'd seen the counselor she'd recommended, or to comment on the inky shadows under her eyes.

"Would you like a coffee at my place?" she asked Vivian as they got into the car.

"Not at this time in the afternoon. I'll never sleep."

"Tea then?"

"I'll make you one at mine."

Vivian didn't say anything more until she'd set a mug of steaming tea in front of Freya. "I can't ask you to pay for my surgery."

"You're not asking, Mum. I'm offering. There's a difference."

"You can't offer without discussing it with Ryan."

Freya tried not to sigh. "We share a mortgage and all expenses, not a joint account. Of course I'll tell him, but it's my money to spend."

Vivian frowned. "What about when you have a baby?"

Freya flinched. "What about it?"

"You won't be working and Ryan will be supporting you."

"Of course I'll be working. I have a business to run."

"You'll have the extra expense of employing Hannah."

Freya blinked. "How do you even know that was a suggestion?"

"Hannah and Ryan told me."

Not for the first time, Freya got an overwhelming sensation that her life didn't belong to her. "If I get pregnant again—"

"Of course you will, darling." Her mother's hand shot out and gripped hers. "The Quayle women have never had any difficulties in that department. Old Doctor Ferguson told your grandmother that if Pa got in the bath with her she'd get pregnant. And Lexie fell fast. Too fast really, considering the type of man Kane turned out to be ..."

Freya swooped on Vivian's reflective pause. "I know how much you value your independence and the sooner you have the surgery, the sooner you'll be back driving. If it makes you feel uncomfortable, consider it your birthday and Christmas present."

Vivian huffed. "For the next twenty years."

"Mum, it's my choice. I wouldn't be offering if I didn't want to pay. You and Dad gave me loads of opportunities. If Dad was still alive, you'd be able to afford it yourself. But he's not, so let me help. Please."

Vivian stared into her tea as if the slice of lemon was a constantly changing kaleidoscope. When she finally raised her head, she said, "Talk to Ryan and sleep on it. If you still feel the same way at the end of the week, I'll accept your offer and book the appointment."

Freya smiled, relieved that her mother was able to set aside her pride to maintain her independence. "It's a deal."

At 6:30, Freya walked into the house from the garage that was currently doubling as her packing room and into a wall of music. She was surprised to see Ryan in the kitchen making a salad.

"You're home early," she said. "I thought you were at Goomalling today."

"I got an early mark so I grabbed some steaks from the gourmet butcher in Northam on the way home." He pulled her in close and picked some shredded packing tissue from her hair before kissing her. "I thought I'd fire up the barbie and we can open a bottle of red. All you have to do is put your feet up."

She rested her head on his shoulder and breathed him in, feeling the stresses of the day—Hannah's request, the worry of her mother's health—receding. From the moment they'd met, Ryan had always been her shelter from the world, the one person in her corner no matter what.

"That sounds wonderful," she said, not moving.

"Good."

He was the one who eventually broke contact. "You sit, I'll pour the wine."

As she sat, she noticed a small blank piece of paper on the floor under the table. She reached down, picked it up and turned it over. Sweat doused her.

"Ryan? Where did you get this?"

He turned and noticed the ultrasound photo in her hand. "I asked for it when we were at the hospital."

"Why?"

"Because it makes it feel real."

"I don't understand."

Sadness ringed him. "You knew you were pregnant and going to be a mum because you felt different. But I didn't have any tangible evidence that I was going to be a dad. This is it."

She stared at him, stunned. "But it's a photo of death."

"Nah, it's hope." A slow smile broke over his face. "We got pregnant once so we can do it again."

She studied the black-and-white blur of their dead baby and waited for misery to hit. Waited for hope to land that she would conceive again. Waited for anything that resembled a reaction, but the numbness remained.

Ryan kissed her, then took the photo out of her hand and slid it inside the Gillet family history book his mother had written. "It belongs here. It's our history."

He returned to the wine and cracked the seal.

As Freya watched the deep ruby liquid swirl into the wineglass she tried not to think about the evening two nights before the wedding when Jamie had presented a dozen bottles to Ryan as a thank you for being his best man. About Hannah's dreams. Her request Freya sign the affidavit. As much as she loved a big bold red, she wondered if this one might choke her.

"Tell me about your day," she said, desperate to flee her own thoughts.

Ryan cheerfully launched into stories about his new group of volunteer trainees and she lost herself in the mix of comedy and drama. It was the first time since Jamie's death and the miscarriage that he looked and sounded more like his old self. When she'd been pregnant and waking during the night to pee, she'd often found him standing on the back deck staring at the stars as if they might offer up answers to the question she assumed he was posing—*why Jamie?* Since the miscarriage she knew another question had been added. But tonight her Ryan was back and she was ringed in comfort.

He was outside retrieving the steaks when her phone beeped with a message. *Hi, guessing Mum overreacted and news was good? Can Mia sleep over on Saturday?*

Freya needed a phone call or a face-to-face chat with her sister about Vivian, but minding Mia was easy. *No worries re Mia. Talk tomorrow re Mum. Fx*

Ryan slid a plate in front of her. "With the blood stopped, just as you like it."

"You're amazing."

He sat adjacent to her. "I'm glad you noticed."

Something in his tone made her check his face, but he was smiling and passing her the salad. Blaming her weariness for misinterpreting him, she loaded her plate with the spinach, avocado and mango concoction then tucked in. The meat was so tender it melted in her mouth. She sighed.

"Good?" he asked.

"Sublime."

"That was the aim." He raised his glass. "To us."

She forced away the memories that clung to the wine and joined him in the toast. "To us."

"I love you, Frey."

"I know you do. I love you too."

"It's been a crap time with Jamie and the baby ..." He slid his hand into hers. "At least we've got the wedding to look forward to."

The tender meat she'd just swallowed hardened into a lump. Since she'd gotten pregnant, all thoughts of the wedding had been vanquished by nausea and fatigue and the reassurance that the occasion could be a fast affair with just immediate family. Since the miscarriage, she hadn't even thought about it.

"So with that in mind," Ryan continued, "I've booked us in this weekend at that B & B in York you love so much. We can check out Barton Park, Faversham House and Laurelville Manor."

"But they're for big weddings," she said faintly.

"Yeah." His smile was wide. "Let's go the whole hog."

"But I thought you wanted to get married sooner rather than later. Places like that have to be booked at least a year in advance."

"Way ahead of you. We can easily get a booking for a midweek wedding. Even with the Perth rellies, no one has to travel more than ninety minutes."

She thought of the tens of thousands of dollars it would cost them and immediately thought of her mother's surgery. "Ryan, it's too much money."

"We can afford it." He studied her face. "Unless something's going on with the business you haven't told me about."

She sighed. "It's not the business. I went with Mum to see Leah today. She's not allowed to drive until after cataract surgery and the waiting list is over a year. I offered to pay for it."

"Before talking to me?"

His quiet words jolted her. "She's my mother and it's my money."

"Yeah, but we're a team. If it was the other way around I would have discussed it with you."

"Your mother has private health insurance and can afford whatever she needs."

A grim look settled around his mouth. "You know what I mean. We always talk things through before we make a decision."

"You just booked a weekend away without talking to me about it."

"As a surprise! God knows we both need some time alone and a bit of pampering. And you love York."

"I do, but it's crazy season for work. Anyway, while you were bringing in the steaks, Lexie asked if we could mind Mia on Saturday night. I said yes."

"Freya!"

She threw out her hands. "I'm sorry, but the diary was clear."

"I was five meters away on the deck. All you had to do was yell or wait one minute before you replied."

"Okay. But to be fair, I thought it was a no-brainer. Since I started the business, we've never had a weekend away during the Christmas rush. As for offering to pay for Mum's surgery, I honestly thought you'd be on board with getting her independent again as fast as possible—unless of course you want us to drive her everywhere for a year?"

Ryan shifted in his seat. "Yeah, okay. Fair points."

Her heart ached at his dismay and she stroked his face. "As much as I love the idea of a night in York with you, I can't spare the time until after Christmas. And I'm so bloody tired I don't have the headspace right now to be planning a wedding."

"When do you get the results of your blood test?"

"What blood test?"

He took a long, deep breath as if he was trying not to yell. "I keep telling you that you're probably anemic. Which is why you're so damn tired, acting out of character and irritable all the time."

She didn't want to hear this. "It's the silly season. I'm always like this."

He shook his head. "You're not. In all the years I've known you, you've never been like this."

"I've never been pregnant or had a miscarriage before."

"True." He slumped. "And Jamie died."

The complicated mess that was her feelings for Jamie clashed in her gut. She directed the focus away from herself. "You're struggling too."

"I'm okay."

If you were, you wouldn't be pushing so hard to copy Jamie and insist we get married.

"Are you really?"

He closed his eyes for a moment, and when he opened them sorrow reflected back to her. "It's a lot, but we've got each other. I know we can come back from this, but right now it feels like part of you disappeared with the baby and I can't reach you. Talk to me, gorgeous. Please."

But talking to him was beyond her when she had no idea what to say about the baby, about Hannah's request, the wedding—any of it.

So she stood and held out her hand. "There's fresh sheets on the bed. Let's go and pretend it's the flash B & B."

Ryan was on his feet in an instant, his face alight with hope and desire. "You sure?"

She nodded, despite being uncertain about absolutely everything.

CHAPTER TWENTY-FOUR

HANNAH STRAPPED on her running shoes, pressed in her earbuds and set off with Ozzie on a run before the heat started to bite. As she turned at the gate, she noticed a white four-wheel drive parked opposite the Pettigrews'. It was a popular model and probably belonged to the carer helping Mrs. P with her shower.

Ozzie barked his approval at being out. He was desperate for the exercise and now she was working more hours at Just Because she'd missed some walks and runs. She should probably take him out to the farm so he could race around to his heart's content, but she needed him to come home to at the end of the day. Without him, the house felt like a tomb.

But this morning's run wasn't just for Ozzie. She needed it to flatten the constant unease that simmered in her gut. It turned out that collecting the affidavits wasn't as straightforward as she'd expected. Lydia was putting pressure on her to set a date to go to Perth but she was yet to hear back from the three Penthurst connections she'd reached out to. She'd emailed Xavier and received an autoreply stating he was in Bali. It hadn't mentioned a return date so she'd set a calendar reminder for next week to try again—not that she needed it. Organizing the affidavits was all she thought about.

She'd been on tenterhooks since her conversation with Freya, but her friend was yet to raise the topic. Since the miscarriage, the only thing Freya talked about was Just Because. Holding back from asking her if she was ready to sign was killing Hannah, but this week Freya looked and sounded brighter, so Hannah reassured herself it meant she would sign soon.

Today Freya wouldn't be in the shop and Hannah had everything crossed that the reason was because she was going to Northam with Ryan to sign the papers. God, she hoped so. There were only a few weeks before Christmas, then everything shut down like a drum until after the new year.

Ozzie barked again, alerting Hannah to an approaching car. Readying for it to pass, she moved farther onto the red gravel shoulder and kept running. When it didn't overtake her she turned and recognized Ryan's work four-wheel drive. She waved.

He pulled over and lowered the passenger window. "Hey, Hannah. Good to see you back running."

"I have a love-hate relationship with it but I sleep better, or at least Ozzie does."

Ryan laughed. "That dog can outrun us all."

Hannah saw that Freya wasn't in the car. Perhaps Ryan wasn't going to Northam today.

"Where are you headed?" she asked.

"Northam.'

Disappointment twisted her gut. "Freya's not going?"

He tilted his head, clearly confused. "Did she say she was?"

"No ... it's just ..." She shook her head. "It doesn't matter."

"Sounds like it may." Ryan opened the passenger door. "Hop in and tell me what's up?"

She hesitated, but the kindness in his eyes called to her so she swung into the passenger seat and the bliss of air conditioning. "Freya's told you about the affidavit?"

He frowned. "As in a legal document? Is this something to do with you working for her?"

"It's nothing to do with Just Because. It's the next step in being allowed to use Jamie's sperm to have our baby."

"Sounds complicated."

"It is. Anyway, I asked her last week if she'd sign one saying that Jamie wanted children. It has to be done at the magistrates court and I was hoping she'd catch a ride with you to Northam and do it today."

"I guess that would have made sense." His fingers tapped the top of the steering wheel. "The thing is, this is the first I've heard of it."

Hannah stared at him. She thought that Freya and Ryan talked about everything. "She didn't tell you?"

"No, but she's been going through a lot." His hands flew up like stop signs. "Not that I'm comparing our loss to yours, Hannah. God, no. But since the miscarriage—before that even—Freya's concentration's been a bit hit and miss. And now with the Christmas rush ... Sorry, none of that helps you, does it?"

She shrugged. "I know it's a crazy time of year, and maybe I should wait until everything goes back to normal in January, but waiting's so damn hard. Asking now makes me feel like there's some forward movement, you know, even when there isn't. Xavier and the Andersons are away, and I'm not sure which of Jamie's clients would be best to ask."

"You haven't asked me."

"I guess I thought you and Freya were a package deal."

He grinned. "I can't promise to get Freya to Northam before Christmas, but I'll do my best."

"Thanks."

"How are Lydia and Ian?"

"They don't say much, but they're as keen as me to get this dealt with. They want our baby as much as I do."

"I get that." Ryan checked his watch. "Sorry, I have to get going. Do you want a ride home?"

"I want to say yes, but Ozzie needs the run." She opened the door. "Thanks, Ryan. I really appreciate your help."

"Too easy." He rubbed the back of his neck. "I miss him, Hannah. I can only imagine how much worse it must be for you. If the tables were turned, I know Jamie would be looking out for Freya. Don't hesitate to reach out, okay?"

"Okay." She leaned in and kissed his cheek before slipping out of the car. Just before she closed the door she added, "Keep me posted."

"Will do."

She watched the vehicle merge back onto the road and recognized that although her gut still bubbled, it had shifted from agitation to excitement. With Ryan involved, she knew he'd make it happen. Two signed statements from Jamie's closest friends would be the best Christmas gift ever.

Hannah was reconciling the till when Freya arrived unexpectedly holding a basket with a bottle of wine peeking out of the top.

"It's the silly season and we both deserve a drink," Freya said. "I thought here was quieter than the pub."

For a bare second Hannah wondered why, if Freya wanted quiet, she hadn't invited her over to Kitchener Street. But then a starburst of hope rained in her chest. The locked store with its cozy back room was the perfect place for an uninterrupted chat.

Thank you, Ryan! He had woven his magic and Freya was here with good news.

As Hannah plucked wine glasses from the shelf, Freya produced a charcuterie board. The familiar arrangement of cheeses, meats, olives and quince preserve speared Hannah with memories. The beautifully arranged board was always a feature of the relaxed evenings she and Jamie had spent with Freya and Ryan at Kitchener Street. Jamie sitting on a sofa, a bold red in one hand, his other hand resting on her shoulder as she snuggled into him. Ryan and Freya in a similar position on the opposite sofa. Her excitement suddenly flattened under a brick of grief.

"Hannah?" Freya's voice sounded muffled. "You okay?"

She fought free of the darkness threatening to claim her. "I just got a flash of the four of us together at your place."

Sorrow and dismay flitted across Freya's face as she followed Hannah's gaze to the board. "That's why I thought meeting here would be better, but I should have changed the nibbles. Sorry. I make this board on autopilot and—"

"No, it's fine," Hannah said, desperate not to continue down this conversation path. "And Ryan isn't here so it's not remotely the same." She lunged for the wine bottle and poured two generous glasses. "To another profitable week and my Just Because pay cheque."

"And to many more." Freya smiled. "I don't know how you managed to sell that khaki picnic blanket, but kudos to you and thank you. All the others just flew out the door."

Hannah grinned. "I sold it to Hamish Ruthven. I might have mentioned that a romantic picnic was a way to a woman's heart and that, along with a fire extinguisher and the first-aid kit, a blanket was a vital piece of equipment to have in his ute. Let's face it, most blokes around here aren't going to reach for a bright and cheery gingham check."

"Are you saying I should always stock a brown or khaki one?"

Hannah laughed. "Let's wait and see if Hamish gets lucky."

Freya hacked into the camembert, slathered it with quince preserve and sighed as she ate it. She caught Hannah's smile. "I missed lunch."

"It's good you're hungry again," Hannah said without thinking.

Freya's hand paused on a second hunk of cheese, but instead of looking stricken she looked as if she'd been caught raiding the candy jar. "How's your appetite?" she asked.

"Pretty much MIA. But I need to stay healthy in preparation for IVF so I'm concentrating on grazing rather than three big meals." She scooped up some almonds to demonstrate the statement.

Freya sat back on the sofa and sipped her wine. The knot in Hannah's stomach tightened and she had to stop herself from babbling on about a new display idea to showcase the Indigenous Christmas baubles.

Freya finally broke the portentous silence. "Thanks for giving me time to think about your request."

Hannah wanted to say, "What's there to think about?" but nodded instead.

"You've said that if Jamie was still alive you'd be pregnant by now," Freya went on.

"Hopefully, yes."

"So you and Jamie talked about a honeymoon baby?"

She heard Jamie saying, *Poss, how about we concentrate on one big event at a time, okay? Let's get through the wedding first.*

"He was super busy with work before the wedding so we were going to talk about it in Tahiti," she said.

Freya's head tilted. "What other baby conversations did you have?"

"What do you mean?"

"I dunno." Freya shrugged. "The five-year plan?"

"A five-year plan?" Hannah laughed. "You know Jamie believed in living in the moment so he never missed an opportunity."

"Sure. But had he talked about seizing that moment?"

Hannah didn't follow. "What moment?"

"Did he ever suggest you throw away the contraception to see what happens?"

"I was on the pill until a month before the wedding."

"So you'd discussed stopping the pill?"

"Not exactly. I just thought I should get my body ready."

"Did he know you'd gone off the pill?"

Resentment flared at the barrage of personal questions. "I think I told him."

Freya shifted on the sofa. "And when you told him, did he insist on using condoms?"

"What has any of this got to do with you?" Hannah said, far more sharply than she'd intended.

Freya ducked her head for a moment, but when she looked up her gaze was direct and unapologetic. "You've asked me to make a statement under oath. I can't do that without all the facts."

Hannah stared at her. "All you have to say is Jamie wanted to be a dad. You don't need to know about our contraception and sex life to do that!"

"It's connected."

How? But Hannah needed Freya's statement and she didn't want to do anything to jeopardize it. She was suddenly torn about revealing the next part of the story, but she needed Freya to understand why Jamie wouldn't have insisted on using condoms when she was off the pill.

"Okay, fine. If you must know, the month before the wedding Jamie suggested we stop having sex to make the honeymoon special. I wasn't keen. I suggested the night before or perhaps the last week, but ..." She realized her fingers were twisting the fringe on the throw blanket. "Jamie had some old-fashioned ideas about sex."

Freya's face didn't betray a single reaction to this news.

Hannah relaxed and took another sip of wine. "So after our imposed celibacy, the honeymoon sex was going to be amazing and we'd make a baby," she added when Freya didn't speak.

"Except you're assuming Jamie would agree to trying for a baby. And that's the problem," Freya said.

"How is it a problem?"

"Because in all the years I knew Jamie, I never heard him say he wanted a child. You've just told me that he never actually said those words to you either. I'm sorry, Hannah, but I can't in good conscience sign a document stating that he did."

Every cell in Hannah's body jerked in pain as if she'd been tasered. She stared at her friend as if she'd never seen her before. "No. That's wrong." Her voice rose. "You can't do this to me!"

A slight ripple of movement wove across Freya's body. "I'm not doing anything to you, Hannah. I'm respecting the law."

"Jamie knew how much I wanted a family of my own after losing my parents." Her voice cracked. "Him being dead doesn't change that."

"That's not what I'm being asked to sign." Freya closed her eyes for a moment. "I get you want a baby, Hannah, I do. The issue is, did Jamie?"

Anger made her slap the sofa. "Of course he did. Everyone thought they knew Jamie, but he kept his heart's desires close. *I* knew him. I knew Jamie better than anyone!"

Freya's face pinched in pain and an odd chill settled over Hannah.

"Are you punishing me because you lost your baby?" she said. "Is that what this is all about?"

Freya's pupils dilated so fast that her milk-chocolate irises vanished under inky discs. "God, no! This has nothing to do with that."

"Then why are you denying me his child?"

Freya glanced at the ceiling, then the stock shelves, then at her feet, as if she was seeking something. When her gaze finally settled, it locked onto Hannah's and was devoid of any ambiguity. "Why do you think it's taken me so long to talk to you about this? I'd do anything to protect our friendship—"

"Then sign the form!"

"I'm sorry the truth's hurting you, I truly am. But I can't lie on a legal document."

"You keep saying that, but I think you're the one who's lying now. Jamie wanted children. I know it, the McMasters know it, Ryan knows it—"

"Ryan's assumed," Freya said softly.

Hannah imagined daggers flying out of her eyes and stabbing Freya in the heart. "Ryan loved Jamie."

"Signing is not about love."

"It's everything to do with love."

"It's so much more complicated than that." Freya's voice was weary. "Because you weren't actively trying to conceive, the law says I had to hear him say words to the effect of "I want children." In all the years I knew Jamie, he never said anything like that to me."

"This is crazy. You never heard him say he wanted kids, but I bet you never heard him say he didn't want them either."

A pulse beat in Freya's throat and she dropped her chin to her chest.

"Freya?"

Freya's silence leached into the room, making it hard for Hannah to breathe. Urgency clawed at her until she was prepared to do almost anything to shake a sound from Freya. Risk her friendship—or what she'd believed to be a friendship. Risk her job—what was money compared to this woman's treachery? How could Freya have declared moments ago that she didn't want to hurt Hannah yet take a hatchet to all her hopes and dreams? To her life?

Somehow she managed to grind out words from a clenched jaw. "Did you ever hear him say he didn't want children?"

Freya swallowed hard and raised her head. This time Hannah saw distress bright in the other woman's eyes—distress for her. It reached out and choked her. "I did."

"That's bullshit."

"I wish it was."

"When? When did he tell you?"

"After Monique left him."

"Oh my God! You can't be serious." Hannah stared at Freya, barely recognizing her. "You must really hate me."

"I don't hate you."

"Yeah, right. You're using ancient history—a time when Jamie was heartbroken—as a reason not to sign? He'd recovered from all that before he met me."

"He'd gotten over Monique, but I never saw or heard any evidence he'd changed his mind about having children."

Hannah gripped her wrist to stop herself grabbing Freya by the throat. "You knew I wanted kids! If you believed he didn't, why didn't you tell me?"

"When you got engaged I asked you if you'd talked about having kids."

Hannah didn't remember the question.

"And I told him you wanted a family." Freya's gaze implored her to understand.

"So you want a medal for that?"

"That's not what I meant. I—" Freya sucked in a deep breath. "I was hoping the engagement meant he'd changed his mind. I was hoping I'd never have to tell you this. It's why the day before the wedding, when you said he was stressed, I told you to talk to him."

Hannah suddenly remembered Freya's urgent suggestion prior to the tree felling the marquee. A chill settled over her. "Tell me."

Freya twisted her hands. "Two nights before Jamie died, he brought over Ryan's best man gift and—"

"The night of the cricket club bachelor bash?" Hannah laughed, suddenly relieved. "The night he was so drunk he could barely stand?"

"He wasn't drunk then," Freya said tightly. "He arrived early and we were waiting for Ryan to get home. Jamie was talking about the business expansion and when I said, 'And family expansion,' he shook his head."

Hannah threw up her hands, fury and frustration slamming into her like waves on a reef. "That's not definitive! He could have been shaking away a fly. He was probably telling you that he didn't want to discuss *our* personal life with you. Something that's none of your business!"

Freya flinched. "It wasn't an ambiguous shake of his head. It was three slow back-and-forths and he looked straight at me when he did it. I wish I'd never asked him the question! I wish he'd never told me."

Hannah felt like she was walking through a dark and endless tunnel seeking the light. "But that's the thing—he didn't tell you. What did he say when you told him I wanted children?"

"It was when you got engaged. He said you were young and there was plenty of time."

Only there hadn't been any time at all. A wave of devastation caught her, threatening to pull her under. She felt herself pitching towards the great sucking hole lined black with grief, then everything stilled.

It was incomprehensible that Freya was holding onto old words and vague gestures and calling them truth. But Freya was only one person. There were others in her corner, like Ryan. He was Jamie's closest friend and his statement carried far more weight than Freya's. Hannah's world steadied and she pushed to her feet.

"You're big on ethics, Freya, but what about your moral responsibility to me? You say you're my friend yet you're stealing my chance at happiness and destroying my life because you didn't know Jamie as well as you think you do. If you did, you wouldn't be clinging to words he said years ago and a stupid misunderstanding. You're the outlier here. Everyone else will sign and you'll be alone with your principles, so good luck with that. I hope they're good company because I don't need you. We're over. I never want to see your traitorous face again."

"Hannah, please."

She ignored the pain in Freya's voice and slammed the back door behind her.

CHAPTER TWENTY-FIVE

When Freya arrived home after the gut-wrenching conversation with Hannah, she was greeted by an unusually taciturn Ryan. He gave her a perfunctory kiss and relieved her of her basket, noting its contents before he set it on the kitchen counter.

"Where have you been?" he said.

It was a question she rarely heard him utter and she laughed.

"I'm serious, Frey."

"Oh. Okay." She started unpacking the basket. "I was at Just Because."

"With a charcuterie board?"

"Is this Twenty Questions?"

"Asking questions may be the only way I get told things," he grumbled.

She paused in her unloading and took in his folded arms. Ryan rarely got snarky and the last thing she needed today was another difficult conversation. "What do you think you haven't been told?"

"Hannah said she asked you to sign an affidavit about Jamie wanting children."

He knew? Shock zapped her, raising the hairs on her arms. What sort of crazy thinking had she been indulging in, hoping she could avoid this issue with him?

She took a steadying breath. "She did."

"Jeez, Freya! When were you going to tell me?"

"I didn't deliberately not tell you."

Liar liar, pants on fire. She'd purposely avoided telling him so she didn't have to deal with something she'd been determined to bury with Jamie. Yet here it was raising its head for the second time that day.

"I needed time to sort out my thoughts," she said.

"What's to sort? Hannah wants to have our best friend's child and she needs our help to do it."

"*Dead* best friend's child."

Ryan grimaced. He grabbed the opened bottle of wine and poured a glass. "If you died, I'd want your child so I could hold onto you. Hannah's not only lost Jamie, she's lost her future with him. Making the statement is the least we can do, so why are you dragging the chain?"

"I'm not. I've just come from talking to her about it."

His face creased into a warm smile and he hugged her. "That's great. So we can sign together."

The gaping maw of hell opened in front of her, flames leaping. She grabbed a newly arrived bottle of plum pudding gin and sloshed a generous amount into a glass. This conversation held even more risk than the one she'd just had with Hannah.

When Jamie died, Freya had thought she was safe from ever having to tell Ryan or Hannah what he'd said to her. Safe from the fallout, which would cause her the most suffering because when had the messenger of difficult news ever been welcomed with open arms? But that bastard had played her in life and now he was doing it in death. Part of her seriously considered just signing the damn affidavit, but she couldn't. She might have disliked Jamie, but death shouldn't change his wishes.

"I told Hannah I couldn't sign."

Ryan's mouth fell open, closed, then opened again.

Freya grabbed her drink and the leftover platter and carried both to the living room. Ryan followed.

"Why the hell did you say no?" he finally asked.

"Because Jamie didn't want children."

"Of course he did! He loved kids. He started junior cricket for God's sake."

"Because it was good for the club. He organized the sponsorship and dealt with all the paperwork for Cricket Australia, but you're the one who's hands-on with the kids. When did Jamie ever come to practice?"

Ryan's eyes flashed. "He was always in Perth on Wednesday nights. This is crazy, Freya. He was marrying Hannah!"

A deluge of conflicting emotions pressed down on her. "People get married for all sorts of reasons, Ryan. Commitment, companionship, family pressure, religion, tax breaks ... His engagement to Hannah isn't enough to prove that he wanted kids. The law says we have to have heard him say words that reflected his intent, or we have to know that he and Hannah were actively trying to conceive."

"They might have been."

"Hannah told me they didn't have sex in the month before the wedding."

Ryan's brows rose. "You're kidding? No wonder he was stressed in the lead-up. Still, that doesn't mean he didn't want kids."

"We both heard him say it after Monique. And before you say he was heartbroken then, I never heard him recant it. But I heard him moan about Maddie's kids every time they visited, and he questioned if Mia really needed to be in the wedding party."

"He also questioned Ozzie's involvement. That's just Jamie carrying on," Ryan said firmly. "Don't read more into it than there is."

"I'm not. We can only do what our conscience tells us." She knew she sounded pompous but she really didn't want to explain herself any further.

Ryan was staring at her as if she was a stranger. "I know things have been difficult since we lost Jamie and the baby—"

"This has *nothing* to do with the miscarriage."

"What then?" His eyes blazed with a fury she'd never seen before. "You and your conscience need to explain yourselves right now, because you're looking like a vindictive woman denying another woman happiness."

The gin surged on a wave of fear that burned all the way to the back of her throat. "I wish I could do what everyone wants, but I can't."

"Why?"

More than anything she didn't want to answer, but Ryan's gaze bore into her. "The night Jamie brought over your best man's gift, he basically told me he didn't want children."

Ryan looked baffled. "But I was here that night. I cooked dinner before we left for the club."

"Jamie arrived before you."

"No." He shook his head. "I clearly remember him walking up the drive with me because he was obsessing about the wedding rings. Remember?"

Freya slid her hand into Ryan's, feeling his agitation skipping under his skin. "The card he'd written for you had fallen out of the bag and he went back to his car to get it. That's why you thought he'd just pulled up."

Ryan seemed to chew on that, then he tilted his head to one side. "The thing I don't get is, why you? I mean you and Jamie never talked about anything more serious than the weather, sparring about footy teams and the occasional book chat. How on earth did you end up having a D&M about kids?"

She thought about Hannah and how disclosing Jamie's statement had broken something integral in their friendship. If she gave Ryan the full details of the conversation with Jamie she risked losing even more.

"Jamie raised it. It put me in a panic." Both statements were true. "I mean, he and Hannah—I thought they were a good match."

You convinced yourself of that.

Shut up!

"They were a good match. It sounds like wedding nerves to me,"

Ryan said. "Remember how intense Hannah was and obsessing over every tiny detail. Jamie got pretty drunk at the bachelor bash and that's when blokes usually bare their souls even if they don't want to." He shifted on the sofa, his hurt shining as bright as a warning beacon. "Frey, I was his best man *and* his best mate. If Jamie really didn't want to have kids, he would have told *me*."

An ache throbbed deep inside her. *I wish he'd never told me. I never wanted to know.* "What did he say to you that night?"

"That he wished the wedding had been a week earlier and they were already married." He ran his hand through his hair. "God, I wish it had been too. Then he would have been honeymooning in Tahiti instead of dead and we wouldn't be having this bloody conversation!"

Ryan lurched to his feet and paced. "You must have got it wrong, Frey. Jamie and I grew up together. I knew everything about him and what he wanted to do with his life. For starters, he never wanted to leave Garringarup and go to boarding school. He hated it. All he wanted to do was farm, but Ian pushed him to do computer science so he had a backup plan in case he changed his mind. But Jamie was never going to do that. When he was at UWA and I was at Flinders, he'd call me saying all he wanted to do was come home, take over the farm, fall in love and settle down."

That wasn't how Freya remembered Jamie's plans, but then she and Jamie had talked about different things.

"People change," she said gently.

"The only person who changed was Monique," Ryan said grimly. "She ripped out his heart then stomped on it and he only threw himself into the business to forget. It was when he met Hannah that all his long-held dreams returned. Why else would he have brought her to Garringarup?"

Freya didn't think it had anything to do with the farm. Hannah had talked often of Jamie's business, its growth and her role in that. She trawled her memory for any conversations that mentioned plans to farm and drew a blank. Freya couldn't picture urban Hannah as a farmer's wife—taking care of Ozzie was as close to animal husbandry as she got. Not that it mattered now.

Ryan suddenly stopped pacing and sank onto the sofa, his chest heaving as if he'd run a marathon. "I hate that Jamie lost his chance to restart his life. I miss him like I've lost a limb."

His pain leached into her and once again she compartmentalized her feelings to support him. She considered the seismic shift in their lives since Jamie's death: their sudden engagement, the pregnancy and Ryan's new restlessness and obsession with "living now," which seemed more like "rushing things" to Freya. Up until the accident that had never been his way.

She stroked his hair. "Perhaps you should talk to someone?"

Please talk to someone.

"I just want to honor him."

Freya's mind was drifting to perpetual trophies and a bench seat at the cricket club when Ryan raised his head and wiped his face with the back of his hand.

"I'm going to make a statement for Hannah," he said.

She stared at him, wondering if he'd been deaf to everything she'd said. "But you'd be lying under oath."

He moved away from her, his face tight. "Jesus, Freya. This is one of those times when the strict truth doesn't serve anyone. Not you, me, Hannah or Jamie. How can you be prepared to do incalculable hurt to Hannah? How's it going to look to her, the McMasters and the town when you're pregnant again but you're denying her a child?"

It was exactly what Hannah had accused her of. "This has *nothing* to do with Hannah's desire for a child," she said, knowing she sounded like a cracked record. "The law exists to protect the deceased's wishes. It operates on facts, not implied truths. And what about the child?"

Ryan looked baffled. "What about it?"

"Is it fair that they'll never have the chance to know their biological father?"

"They'll have Jamie's love through his parents."

"But they're not Jamie!"

Ryan's arms jerked into the air ringed by exasperation. "The McMasters will give their grandchild Jamie through stories, photos and the strong bond of family that he thrived on. Hell, that's a closer connection than Mia has with her rat-bastard father and he's alive."

Freya flinched at the vitriol in Ryan's voice. His care and understanding for almost everyone fell short when it came to Kane and she didn't really blame him. Mia missed her father and didn't understand why he'd left her. She wasn't alone there. Freya accepted that sometimes relationships broke down, but she railed against any father who removed themselves from their child's life for no other reason than to hurt their ex-partner.

"But Kane chose to be a father and now he's chosen to be absent," she said. "Jamie doesn't get that choice. We have to consider his wishes."

Ryan made a derisive sound.

She glared at him. "What?"

The air between them vibrated with hostility.

"When did you actually ever care about Jamie's wishes?"

"What are you talking about?"

"Perth."

Memories of Jamie assailed her. "Not this again! He needed a change. And I was right—he met Hannah."

"Yeah, but you treated him differently when he came back."

"No, I didn't," she said, too quickly. Ryan's face clearly disagreed, but she wasn't prepared to continue along this particular conversation highway. "And even if I had, *this* has nothing to do with how I felt about Jamie on any given day. This is me being honest about never once hearing him say he wanted children."

But Ryan was digging his phone out of his pocket—something he never did mid-conversation unless he was on call.

"What are you doing?"

He faced her—back straight, shoulders squared, chin up. "I'm starting a WhatsApp group and I'm organizing an affidavit party for Hannah. I've sent you an invitation if you change your mind."

"Ryan, it isn't a matter of me changing my mind. I can't hear unspoken words."

"And I can't allow my best mate's wife to suffer any more than she already has."

A spasm of pain rocked her as she registered that Ryan found it easier to disbelieve her than deal with the hurt that Jamie hadn't shared the information with him.

CHAPTER TWENTY-SIX

THIS WAS the first time Freya and Ryan had ever been on opposite sides of anything more significant than how to load the dishwasher. Freya spent a restless night lying next to a rigid Ryan, missing his warmth spooned into her. When she woke, he'd already left for work, although he'd written her a note saying that if she changed her mind the appointment at Northam magistrates court was 2:00.

She'd never been more grateful for Just Because and the Christmas rush. It consumed her and whenever the rest of her life tried to intrude she batted it away, rationalizing that she had no space in her brain to think about anything else. Especially now she was one hand down. Hannah hadn't formally quit but neither had she arrived at work.

Freya's phone rang. "Hi, Mum."

"Hello, darling. The eye doctor's receptionist has sent a quote and given me some dates. I didn't want to book anything until I'd spoken to you."

"Are any in January? With summer break, it's my quiet month."

"It's day surgery but I have to be in Perth the day before. Will Ryan mind?"

She heard the reluctance in her mother's voice—her fear of being a burden.

"Of course Ryan won't mind. It's not a problem, Mum."

"Well, I'm paying for our motel," Vivian said firmly. "So don't think about arguing with me. Have you spoken to your sister?"

The shop bell rang. "I've got customers, Mum. Talk later." Freya hung up and walked back into the store. "Oh, hello," she said, recognizing the young woman. "Georgie, isn't it?"

"That's me." Georgie gave a self-deprecating smile. "I can't keep away."

Delight spun through Freya—she loved Just Because and it was reassuring to know others did too. "You've just made my day. Are you looking for something specific?"

Georgie seemed to take a deep breath before plunging her hand into the leather satchel on her shoulder. She pulled out an intricately decorated bridle and a horse made out of wool. "I make these."

Freya turned them over in her hands, taking in the detail and the artistry of the two very different pieces. "They're gorgeous."

"Thanks." Georgie's smile was tentative. "I was wondering ... you know ... 'cos you promote locally made products on your Insta, would you like ... be interested in selling them?"

Freya took in the hope in Georgie's eyes and the quality of the products, and thought about her clientele. "My customer base is interested in homewares and knickknacks so the fiber-art horse may be a fit, but a saddlery would be better for the bridle. Or selling them from your own Insta account?"

"I've been doing that, but you have so many followers."

"True, but it's matching the product with followers' interests that's key."

Georgie's face fell and Freya remembered her own retail journey—trying to catch a break.

"What's your Instagram?" she asked.

"I'm on Insta and TikTok." Georgie pulled out her phone and showed Freya her grid.

The photos were art: the products displayed against a typical Wheatbelt scene of red earth, scraggly gums and an endless outback sky. But it was the photos and videos of Georgie with her horse that reached out and grabbed Freya.

"This photo says it all."

"Really?" Georgie peered at it. "I only put it up because Mac took it. It was the first time he'd used his camera since—in ages. Why does it say it all? I mean it doesn't even show the bridle."

"It's the love in your eyes for your horse. *That's* what will sell your stuff." Freya thought about her followers. "A few of my customers probably ride or have kids who ride, so tell you what. Write me an article for my newsletter saying why you started making your pieces and I'll include it along with your social media and buy links."

Ideas started popping. "But more importantly, for all the women who've secretly wanted to ride but have never had the opportunity, get another photo like this one but with your horse wearing the bridle and find a way to include the fiber-art. Maybe in your hand? On the horse? No idea. Just experiment and see what works. Use your love of horses to sell your product."

"Oh, wow! That's so great. Thank you!" Georgie suddenly looked uneasy. "Um, Mac says I need to ask what commission you charge."

"Mac's right. And the fee varies, depending on the price of the product." Freya doubted she'd sell many fiber-art horses and she had a more immediate problem. "Georgie, I don't suppose you could work for me today?"

"With Hannah? Oh my God, yes! I'd love it."

"Hannah's not in today."

"Oh, is she okay?" Georgie looked worried. "It's just Mac said her fiancé died."

"Yeah, it's not a great time for her. Any chance you can stay till 3:00?"

"Totally. Mac's busy until 2:30 but he can wait half an hour."

"The first tourist bus arrives in ten minutes so let's get cracking with a quick tutorial on the POS system. I know it's a baptism by fire, but I'm just in the back if you need help with anything."

As Freya packed orders she listened to Georgie's cheerful enthusiasm and patience with some of the older and very particular customers. There were only a few times that she needed help.

Freya was insisting Georgie take a twenty-minute break when her brother arrived with coffees and paninis.

Georgie flushed every shade of red. "Mac, I'm working!"

"And you need lunch," he said equably.

"Which is exactly what I was telling her." Freya got the feeling that this bear of a man was checking she wasn't one of those retailers who played free and easy with employment conditions.

"Will you need Georgie tomorrow?" he asked.

"Mac!" Georgie sounded horrified.

"What?" Mac looked genuinely confused. "I need to know if you're ditching the farm tomorrow. If you are, I'll call Brady and get him to work."

"Freya and I haven't talked about it yet. Anyway, Hannah may be back tomorrow, right?"

Freya doubted it. Part of her knew she should call Hannah and the other part of her wanted to hide.

"How far away do you live?" she asked Georgie.

"Just this side of Beverley."

Disappointment slugged her. "That's a fair drive with the price of diesel. You'd keep more money working for your brother."

"Yes, but—"

"Freya!"

Freya turned to see Lydia McMaster determinedly weaving her way through the shop and for a moment she thought that her displays were more at risk from Jamie's mother than from Mac. Freya was used to a cool reception from Lydia, but today, if Lydia's eyes had been guns, she'd be dodging a spray of bullets.

She opened her mouth to greet her but Lydia spoke first. "You call yourself a friend and then you do this to Hannah? Why? Don't you think she's suffered enough already without you putting the boot in?"

The words peppered Freya and her mind seized in shock. She wanted to suggest to Lydia that they talk later, but the woman had mission written all over her.

Freya was aware of Georgie's wide-eyed reaction and the way Mac's gaze was flicking between Freya and Lydia, trying to work out what was going on. It was bad enough that the Downies were witness to this—Freya didn't need anyone else coming into the store.

She opened the door to the back room. "We can talk in here," she said.

Lydia didn't move.

The bell rang and Chrissie Lancefield stepped inside the store.

Freya's stomach went into free fall. "I'll make you a cup of tea, Lydia."

Whether Lydia heard the touch of desperation in Freya's voice or she'd never had any intention of taking the conversation out of the public arena, Freya didn't know. But she recognized the moment Lydia made the decision to stay put.

"Why would I want to have a cup of tea with a toxic woman determined to destroy my family?" Lydia said. "I should have known you'd wade in on this, just like you did with Jamie and Perth. Sticking your oar in where it doesn't belong. Getting in the way of Ryan and Jamie's friendship—"

"I never stood in the way of their friendship," Freya said, knowing she spoke the truth.

But Lydia hadn't come to listen. "And now, in Hannah's darkest hour, you do this to her! What the hell is wrong with you?"

Both Mac and Georgie looked longingly at the door, clearly desperate to escape the drama, but they were hemmed in by Lydia and Chrissie.

Chrissie's eyes were alight with the euphoric hit of solid gold gossip.

"Lydia," Freya tried, "this isn't personal. The law requires me to—"

"The law!" Lydia spat the words. "Your behavior has nothing to do with the law and don't you dare say the word 'ethics' to me. This is everything to do with you and the self-centered way you live your life. Everything has to be about Freya. You lost a baby so Hannah can't have one either. That takes you from selfish to cruel."

"Jesus, Freya," Chrissie said. "You're not signing for Hannah?"

Despite knowing she should keep her mouth shut, Freya said, "Chrissie, this is a private conversation."

Chrissie's arm gestured around the store. "I don't think so."

"Thank goodness Ryan's doing the right thing," Lydia said. "And the Andersons, the Garibaldis and Sam Dillinger."

"I'm happy to sign a petition," Chrissie said.

"It's not a petition," Freya ground out. "And you hardly knew Jamie!"

"I know Hannah wants a baby and that's all that matters."

"No, it's not!" The pressure in Freya's head threatened to splatter her brain all over the shop. "I don't need to discuss this with anyone except my own conscience."

"Lucky you've got that, because it's the only thing in this town on your side," Lydia said.

Mac picked up a box of Indigenous hand-painted Christmas ornaments. "How much are these?" he said loudly.

Chrissie spun around to face him. "We're in the middle of something."

"Twenty-five dollars," Freya said just as Georgie asked Chrissie, "What can I help you with today?"

But Lydia was exiting the store, and Chrissie muttered something about the time and followed her onto the street.

Freya sank onto the stool behind the counter. "Thank you, Mac. But you don't have to buy the ornaments."

He shook his head. "My tree's a bit bare."

Georgie looked at him, a small smile lifting her worried mouth. "You're decorating a tree?"

"Yeah." He glanced at his feet before lifting his head and smiling at her. "Thought it was time."

Freya's phone rang—it was Ryan. She walked into the back room to take it. "Hi."

"Hi," he said. "Listen, Hannah just called me. Just a heads up—Lydia's on the warpath."

"I know. She was just here."

"Shit. Are you okay?"

She wanted to say no, she wasn't okay and she was being accused of things she'd never done, but that would only open a can of worms she'd gone to great lengths to keep shut during Jamie's life. If she let it all spill out now, "Saint Jamie" would win. Hell, he'd won anyway. She was the outlier.

"Frey?" Ryan said.

Despite their opposing opinions regarding Jamie's desire to be a father, she heard the care in his voice and his love for her.

"It sounds like Hannah's got enough people to sign," she said.

"Yeah."

"I didn't want to hurt her, Ryan."

There was silence on the line and she braced herself for more pain-inflicting words, but instead he said, "How does chicken satay sound for dinner?"

Barbecue chicken satay was one of her favorite meals in Ryan's repertoire. Was it an olive branch now that Hannah had the signatures she needed? A sign he'd forgiven her?

What about you? Do you forgive him?

She knew how hard Ryan had found it to refuse Jamie anything, and by default this extended to Hannah. And when Jamie was alive Freya had protected his and Ryan's friendship, so she could hardly expect Ryan to do an about face now.

"Satay chicken sounds perfect, thanks."

"All things being equal, see you at 6:00."

"Love you," she said.

"Love you too."

Her world righted as she closed out the call.

CHAPTER TWENTY-SEVEN

HANNAH SPENT the weekend at the farm. She hadn't intended to, but when Lydia had arrived at the house on Friday at noon and found her in bed sobbing, she'd insisted. Hannah's energy levels had barely been enough to get her through the day, let alone to stand firm against a very determined Lydia.

Over a cup of tea and a scone, she had poured out her devastation that Freya was refusing to sign the affidavit. Lydia's reaction had been nuclear. She'd grabbed her handbag and left the house, returning calmer but insistent that Hannah and Ozzie were to stay the whole weekend at the farm instead of just Saturday. Maddie was visiting and it was the perfect time to scatter Jamie's ashes.

"Not all of them," Hannah said, surprising herself. "I want to keep some."

For a moment it had looked like the deep frown on Lydia's forehead was heralding a no, but then she'd said, "Of course."

The private family moment took place down by the creek at dawn. As streaks of peach and apricot crawled across the sky, and the cacophony of birdsong mixed with the low bleat of sheep, they scattered Jamie's ashes on the land he'd loved.

Maddie stared along the creek. "Remember how we swam here as kids?" she said. "I hope there's a waterhole and a swing rope wherever you are. And one day your child will play here with their cousins and I'll tell them all the stories. Well, the G-rated ones anyway." She laughed, then squatted and sprinkled some ashes onto the water before wiping her face with the back of her hand.

Ian picked up a handful of red dust, stirred some of Jamie's ashes into it and returned it to the ground. "I miss you, son." His voice cracked. "Every day."

"You should be here with us, working the land like you planned," Lydia said, her chest heaving. "But as we can't have that, at least you're here and part of this place where your heart belongs." She drizzled ashes around the base of a tree that Jamie had carved his initials into years earlier.

The McMasters' sorrow and grief echoed Hannah's own, yet she didn't recognize their version of Jamie. Yes, he'd loved the farm—that was a given. So was the fact that he'd been happy helping his father during peak periods. And sure, she'd occasionally seen him reading articles on improving soil that Ian had given him, but in all conversations about their future not once had he mentioned—or even hinted at—taking over the farm. Yet it was clear Lydia and Ian assumed that was his intention.

She ran through some of their significant discussions about the business—how to approach the next growth phase, her detailed marketing plan. She could picture Jamie's wide smile, hear his words, "You've got it all organized, poss," and feel his kiss—

Did he say he wanted children? Freya's unwanted question interrupted her thoughts. As she tried to throw it off, another question loomed. Had Jamie said he wanted to build the business? Or had he just listened to her plans and she'd taken his smile as agreement?

Before she could stop herself, she blurted, "Did Jamie tell you he wanted to farm?"

The McMasters turned towards her, surprise clear on their faces.

Maddie laughed. "Only since he was ten."

"But the business ..."

"The succession planning was all in place, Hannah," Ian said. "It was a gradual handover, taking five to ten years depending on who wanted what and when."

All in place? Hannah stared at him, utterly flummoxed. She searched her memory for any mention of taking over the farm but drew a blank. Was this a case of Ian hoping Jamie would succeed him?

"Do you have it in writing?" she said.

Ian glanced at Lydia, clearly disconcerted, before returning his gaze to Hannah. "Jamie had invested financially in the farm, dear."

Hannah's mind was spinning. Even if she'd had coherent words to ask when Jamie had invested in the farm, she couldn't have spoken them—her tongue seemed stuck to her palate.

"And that makes you the investor now, Hannah," Lydia said, reassuringly. "Ian can explain it to you at a more appropriate time. Now is all about honoring Jamie."

As if to emphasize this, Lydia opened the picnic basket and busied herself setting out breakfast croissants, fruit salad and a thermos of coffee on the rugs.

Maddie gave Hannah's shoulder a squeeze. "I heard about Freya. What a bitch! Thank God for Ryan."

"He's been amazing," Hannah agreed.

"With those six statements plus ours, can you get the go-ahead before Christmas?"

"Rowan says it's best to get at least one from someone outside of town," Hannah said. "Xavier's not responding, and Jamie dealt directly with the clients so I don't have a relationship with any of them. And to be honest, I'm not sure if Jamie deviated from business into personal, although there were enough lunches and dinners so I suppose it was possible."

"Mind you, he was a bloke."

Hannah bristled. "He was more in touch with his feelings than most."

Maddie gave her a sideways look. "We still talking about my brother?"

The nebulous sensation that her Jamie wasn't the same Jamie other people believed they knew returned. She tried to shake it off and focus on *her* Jamie—the man she knew and loved. But thoughts kept intruding and blocking her view: Jamie driving a Porsche on the old road; Freya's insistence that he didn't want a child. And now farm succession?

Jamie had often suggested improvements to the farm, just like he did for his own business—his mind had rarely stopped. She thought about the family dinners and how Ian dominated the conversation with farm matters. She'd always thought Jamie's interest was filial politeness, but viewing it through a succession lens she now recognized the dinners as business meetings. Was this why Jamie had never actually said the words "I'm taking over the farm"? Was it like him wanting children—implied in everything he did?

Lydia called them over for breakfast, and the McMasters told stories of a young Jamie growing up on the farm.

"He was forever bringing home injured birds and animals," Ian said. "For years the home paddock was a wildlife rescue center. I think he thought himself a modern Gerald Durrell."

"Jamie rescued them, but Ryan rehabilitated them," Maddie said.

"Your brother was a big-picture person. His skill lay in inspiring others and delegating," Lydia said. "And Ryan adored him. Such a shame he fell for Freya." She looked at Hannah. "You've quit Just Because."

Despite the rising inflection, it wasn't a question and Hannah saw the steel of loathing in Lydia's eyes.

Her own feelings were pretty clear—she hated that Freya had cast doubt on Jamie's desire to be a father. What sort of friend did that? Thank goodness for Ryan. He understood and respected friendship and loyalty. Hannah experienced a fizz of schadenfreude for Freya— the so-called perfect relationship must be battered and bruised now that Ryan had rallied behind Hannah and organized people to support her.

"The less you have to do with Freya the better," Lydia added tartly.

"I still have to eat."

"We won't let you starve, love," Ian said. "I could do with some help in the farm office. You any good with Excel?"

Hannah bit off the comment that she had run Jamie's office and was all over the full Office suite. "Not too shabby."

"I was thinking Hannah could help me with the Women in Agriculture conference program," Lydia said.

"I'm sure I can do both."

Lydia leaned over and took Hannah's hands in hers. "We're here for you, darling. Jamie loved you so we love you too. You're family and you'll always have a home here."

Tears stung the backs of her eyes and her heart ached for the loss of Jamie and her own parents, and for Declan being so far away. She felt herself falling into the fathomless black hole. Lydia's arms caught her and Hannah sobbed.

On Sunday, Hannah woke from a deep medicated sleep—Lydia's suggestion—and tried to defog her brain as she listened to Lydia and Maddie discussing Christmas plans.

"I thought a change in tradition this year may help," Maddie said. "And the kids are keen to have a Christmas at home."

Was that code for "we'll miss Jamie less in South Australia than here on the farm," Hannah wondered. How could anyone think that? But she heard herself agreeing to accompany the McMasters to the Eyre Peninsula for Christmas. It wasn't like she had any other options. Flying to Singapore again wasn't in her budget, and there was no way in hell she was spending Christmas with Freya.

Maddie departed after breakfast and the McMasters went to church. Hannah declined their invitation to join them and offered instead to cook the Sunday roast. Since Jamie's death, her relationship with all deities was on shaky ground. What loving God would steal the love of her life from her?

Alone in the house she prepared the vegetables and the lamb for baking and slid them into the oven. Job done, she had no idea what to do with herself. As often as Lydia and Ian said "Make yourself at home," she still felt like a guest.

She wandered into the library, which was also Ian's office, looking for something to read and immediately saw Jamie's computer. A thought almost knocked her off her feet—the details about the red-themed honeymoon surprise would be on it! Even though she was certain the reason Jamie had been on the old Garringarup road was connected to the surprise, if she read his full plans she'd know for sure. With Freya's refusal to sign the affidavit and yesterday's farm news, she needed the reassurance.

She opened the lid and was immediately met by a password request. She'd never needed to know the password because she had her own computer. The lingering fug from the sleeping pills had slowed her mind. Had Jamie ever given her the password? Did Ian know it? He hadn't asked her about it so she assumed he did.

She tried Jamie's Oz Lotto numbers and the date they'd met before getting a "forgot your password" prompt. She sighed.

The clack of nails on floorboards distracted her and Ozzie came in, giving her a hangdog look.

"Okay, let's go for a walk." Hopefully it would clear her mind.

Instead of doing the usual kilometer walk along the drive to the main road, she cut across the yard intending to stroll along the creek. As she passed the last shed, she caught sight of Jamie's four-wheel drive. So that's where Ian was storing it.

The familiar vehicle called to her and she squeezed between it and the tractor, opened the door and swung up into the passenger seat. The faint aroma of Jamie's cologne filled her nostrils. She could picture him in the driver's seat, his head swiveling to her and a grin streaking across his face as he switched on the ignition. Then Ozzie whined and hairline fractures crawled across the fragile moment before collapsing it completely.

Hannah realized the dog was nosing around in the back of the car. "What have you got there?"

Ozzie had a shirt in his mouth and he offered it to her. She didn't recognize it, but Jamie had a huge shirt collection. She held it to her face and breathed deeply. Disappointment socked her—it smelled of warehouse and soft plastic packaging. She took a closer look and saw there were still shop tags attached. He'd never worn it.

She'd assumed that Ian had emptied the vehicle of all belongings and put them in the same box as the contents from the Porsche. Had he missed anything else?

She hopped out of the vehicle and opened the rear door. The back was empty bar the obligatory fire extinguisher, tire-changing equipment and jumper cables. The back seats and footwells were also empty, apart from the shop bag that must have held the shirt, and the lost property cube.

She moved the driver's seat back and found a water bottle before repeating the action with the passenger seat. She directed her phone's torch under the seat and made out a shape. When she brought it out into the light she realized it was a sleek black phone.

It wasn't the first time she'd found a client's phone—they often slipped out of men's pockets. Jamie always returned them to the client so why hadn't the owner of this one reached out? Perhaps because Jamie had died and they wouldn't want to intrude? Or perhaps they had reached out while she was in Singapore and Ian had taken a "boy" look.

She grimaced. There were many possible scenarios and she hadn't been there to follow through. She pocketed the phone—she'd charge it when she got home and see if it had a contact number on the lock screen.

She closed the back and studied the mud-splattered vehicle. It had always been Jamie's car—the few times she'd driven it she'd struggled with the clutch and been happy to return to her own vehicle. She imagined loading a baby in and out of it and realized her car was better suited to the purpose.

And their baby plans were getting closer. By Christmas, the Supreme Court should have approved her application to relocate Jamie's sperm to Queensland. She could start the new year by applying to use it in the Sunshine State, and if all went to plan she'd be starting her first cycle of IVF by the end of January.

The need to start the new year debt-free sang loudly. Jamie had been financially responsible and Hannah owed it to their unborn child to be the same. She took another look at the four-wheel drive. Could she sell it?

She let the thought sit, and when no sense of loss accompanied the idea she ruffled Ozzie's ears. She'd talk to Ian about selling it. In fact, it was time for another sit-down with Ian about the state of play of probate.

The timer on her own phone beeped. Hell, the roast. She ran back to the house to turn the vegetables.

CHAPTER TWENTY-EIGHT

ON HER RETURN from the farm, Hannah opened the cherry red front door, dropped her keys next to a smiling photo of Jamie and called out, "Hi, I'm home," before realizing what she'd said. Hollow silence greeted her, fast followed by a falling blanket of grief.

She swallowed the lump in her throat and marched to the kitchen. As she switched on the kettle she saw her charging cable and remembered the phone in her pocket. She tried plugging it in, but it required a different cord. Did she have one that matched this phone?

She went into the office and rummaged around in her desk drawer. She was about to give up when she noticed the storage box in the corner. She had a vague memory of a cord in there so she pulled off the lid. Curled like a snake on the brown cardboard bottom was a red charging cord with a USB C tip. Bingo! She returned to the kitchen and plugged in the very flat phone, then made a cup of tea she didn't really want to drink.

She missed Jamie every hour of every day, but there was something about late Sunday afternoons that bit hard. It was the time they'd kicked back in preparation for their busy week ahead. After syncing their diaries and talking through the logistics of their working week, they'd relax with a bottle of wine. It was a magic time—just the two of them.

The urge to pour a glass of wine right now tugged hard. "It's past 4:00," she said out loud, as if that gave the idea credence despite it being a hundred minutes earlier than her and Jamie's tradition. Ozzie gave her a quizzical look.

"Okay, fine." She stomped down the hall and cleaned the bathroom, adding twenty minutes to the time. Then, without looking at Ozzie, she cracked the seal on a Margaret River sauvignon blanc.

Not bitch diesel, she heard Jamie saying, his voice loud in her head.

Her anticipation of the refreshing fruity taste took a slight hit. "If I drink one of your big bold reds I'll cry," she said.

Just teasing, poss. You do you. But one day—

"Come on, Oz," she said loudly, drowning out Jamie's voice. It was the first time she'd done it, but now that "one day" would never come she didn't need an extra reminder of what she'd lost.

Sitting on the sofa with Ozzie lying at her feet, she aimed the remote at the television. As she drank she tried losing herself in the trivial worries of a young American in Paris. She was refilling her glass when she heard a beep. It was followed by a rapid series of them, then silence. Then another two beeps.

Had she been added to a group chat that was going off? She checked her phone but there were no notifications. Then she remembered the phone in the kitchen. It must have charged enough to connect to the network and been hit with a deluge of texts.

Much to Ozzie's dismay, Hannah returned to the kitchen. The locked screen was lit up with a generic design. She waited for a permanent message to scroll across it saying something like *If this phone is found please call* and a number. But there was nothing beyond the time.

There were over a hundred notifications on the locked screen, many missed calls but no names assigned to the numbers. As she scanned them, she realized they were all the same number. She picked up her phone to call it, then stopped. She had no idea who she'd be calling, and they didn't know her so they might not pick up. Surely it was better to call from the lost phone.

Yeah, right. Everyone locked their phone and there were a million possible passcode combinations. She had no clue who owned this device so she had no hints to take even a calculated guess.

She thought about how often Jamie had said that when it came to passwords people were stupid. Just to prove it she typed in oooo. Nothing happened. She tried 1234. Nothing. Then she randomly tried Perth's postcode. Her jaw dropped as the phone opened.

"It's a sign, Ozzie! Fingers crossed whoever owns this phone will be the professional colleague of Jamie's I need to sign the affidavit."

She pressed the number. It rang three times and Hannah realized she was holding her breath. Just as she blew it out, the ringing stopped.

"Jamie?" A woman's voice. "Oh my God! Jamie?"

Hannah dropped the phone on the counter and stepped back as if it was a grenade about to explode and that small distance would protect her.

She heard the woman saying, "Hello?"

Heart racing, she violently jabbed at the red button. The phone fell silent.

What the hell? Under the deluge of shock, her brain struggled to compute. The unknown woman thought this was Jamie's phone, except it wasn't. His phone was red. His phone was a different brand entirely with a different operating system. Jamie had always been very vocal about his choice, arguing down anyone who favored the other side. He would never own this type of phone or this color.

The phone rang.

Hannah jumped and agitation skittered and throbbed in every cell. It was the same number. Did she answer it? Or did she let it ring out and see if the woman left a voice message?

Each long peal was like razor blades slicing into her skin until she couldn't stand it a moment longer. With shaking fingers she managed to slide up the arrows.

"Who is this?" she demanded. "How did you know Jamie?"

The call cut out before the woman said a word.

Hannah rang back, but the call was silenced and no voice mail was offered. She used her own phone to dial the number and the same thing happened.

"God damn it!" Hannah looked for voice mail on the phone, but it wasn't set up. She searched the call log, but this phone had only ever called one number—the woman who had answered. Who was she? Why was she the only person ever called on this phone?

Hannah's gut cramped and her mind spun with unwanted and unexpected scenarios.

Stop! Do not go there—it's where crazy lies.

"Just because a woman answered this phone ... There's a rational explanation, right Ozzie?"

The dog raised his head for a moment then lay it down again.

Hannah tried to recall the woman's voice. She hadn't immediately recognized it but there was something familiar about the well-modulated vowels. It had sounded a little bit like Lydia—the type of woman who wore pearls and tailored jackets. It had to be someone connected to the business.

Hannah grabbed a pen and listed the companies Jamie had been working with. The first four gave her nothing, but when she wrote *McKenzie Enterprises* it all came rushing back. She sagged against the counter, relief softening her tension.

Jamie had spent a lot of time grumbling about the company—always demanding, always wanting last-minute changes—but they paid well so he'd put up with them. Hannah was rarely required to go to work functions, but Jamie had begged her to accompany him to the McKenzie Enterprises product launch last year. "If you're there, Janet won't spend the night badgering me about moving the delivery date forward."

Initially, Hannah had been daunted by the elegant sixty-year-old woman with her perfectly styled white bob, tailored clothes and terrifyingly correct posture. But once she'd discovered the high-powered businesswoman was also a devoted grandmother, she'd steered the subject towards family and the conversation had flowed.

Now she knew it was a McKenzie Enterprises bat-phone, it no longer plunged her into a blind panic. Janet was just the sort of person to insist Jamie have a dedicated phone for immediate contact, and he would have obliged but kept it hidden to save himself from the pile-on if anyone who knew him well saw him using it.

As she returned the phone to the counter, Hannah realized it was also the answer to her prayers. A well-respected businesswoman like Janet McKenzie attesting to Jamie wanting a family would not only add gravitas to Hannah's application, it would also be the signature to strengthen her application to the Supreme Court.

She punched the air. First thing tomorrow morning she'd ring McKenzie Enterprises and request an appointment.

Five days later Hannah was at the farm again, waiting for the call that would decide if she could proceed with her plan to have Jamie's baby. She was trying to distract herself by wrapping Christmas presents, but her phone was on the table next to her with the volume turned up as high as it would go so she didn't miss any calls.

"I've got champagne on ice," Lydia said.

Hannah wanted to appreciate Lydia's confidence, but her body popped and fizzed with worry. "They may rule against me."

Lydia shook her head. "They won't. We gave them everything they asked for."

Janet McKenzie had listened carefully to Hannah's request and had executed it by close of business. Hannah had floated out of the sleek Perth office and ridden the elevator down to the ground floor on a stream of happiness that had propelled her all the way home.

It took until the following day for her to realize that she'd forgotten to return the phone. She'd immediately emailed, offering to snail-mail it to Perth. The reply from Janet's PA was *keep it.* Hannah had no use for the phone. She'd momentarily considered selling it, but decided to pay

Janet's kindness forward—after all, it was the season of giving. She'd returned the phone to factory settings and donated it to a local charity.

Ian came in through the back door, bringing the aroma of sheep with him.

"Boots, Ian!" Lydia said.

"Sorry, love. Any news?"

"Not yet."

With Hannah's dash to Perth and Ian busy making hay, she was yet to sit down with him and get an up-to-date report on where Jamie's estate was at probate-wise. And today wasn't the day. Waiting for the call meant no one could concentrate on anything else.

Hannah's phone rang. She froze. Lydia made a squeaking sound.

"Answer it, Hannah," Ian said.

She picked up the device and let go of her breath. "It's Maddie."

"Put her on speaker," Lydia said.

"Have you heard?" Maddie's voice sounded tinny and anxious.

"Darling, we said we'd call you," Lydia chided.

"I know, but this baby will be my niece or nephew. You're all there together sharing it. I wish I was too."

Hannah's heart swelled. This was her future child's family—her family—and they wanted this as much as she did.

"As soon as we know, I'll video call you," Lydia said. "Hang up now."

"Thanks, Maddie," Hannah said. "Hopefully we'll talk soon."

Lydia told Ian to have a shower and returned to writing gift tags for the presents Hannah was wrapping. They'd run out of conversation, their minds elsewhere, and if Hannah's gaze hadn't been fixed on the kitchen clock, watching the hands moving forward, she'd have sworn time was going backwards.

Rowan had said they'd hear no later than 4:00. It was 4:00 o'clock now—why the hell hadn't he called? She checked her phone's battery, then her reception. All good.

Lydia suddenly lurched to her feet. "I can't stand this. I'm calling Rowan."

"Are you sure?" If it was bad news, Hannah didn't want to invite it in.

But Lydia was already making the call, pacing back and forth as she waited for Rowan to answer. Hannah watched, her heart in her mouth.

"Rowan, thank goodness. We need to know if there's been ... Yes, I understand, but you need to understand that—" She continued pacing as she listened. "How long have you been our family's attorney? We can always review that if you can't meet our needs."

She turned to make another cross of the kitchen, then made a garbled sound before her hand flew to her mouth.

Ian ran into the room, his face creasing in confusion when he saw Lydia on the phone instead of Hannah. "What's happened?"

"I don't know. She called Rowan," Hannah managed to say, although her heart felt like it had stopped.

Lydia was nodding now. "Yes. Fine. I understand. Thank you." She ended the call.

"What?" Hannah demanded. "Have they made a decision?"

"They ruled in our favor!"

Relief and joy flooded Hannah. After all the hours of waiting and worrying, she could hardly believe it.

Then Lydia was hugging her tightly and Ian was hugging them both.

"Oh, Hannah. After such an awful, awful time, it's the perfect Christmas present," Lydia said.

"It is. It really is."

Hannah's phone rang.

"Oh, dear," Lydia said. "That will be Rowan. I promised him I wouldn't tell you—something about privileged information or some such nonsense. I mean, why does it matter who he told first when we're all family? But he's an old duffer so pretend you don't know, okay."

Hannah wondered how on earth she could contain her joy, let alone hide it, but she gave it her best shot.

CHAPTER TWENTY-NINE

FREYA WOKE on Christmas morning feeling like she'd run a marathon. With Christmas Eve falling on a weekday, the shop had been frantic with locals—mostly men—buying last-minute Christmas gifts. Of course none of them arrived with any idea of what they wanted to purchase so each transaction took time as Freya and Georgie tried to get a sense of what their partner, mother, daughter, sister would enjoy. As tempting as it was to sell them anything within their price range, experience had taught Freya that it came back to bite her in January with returns and exchanges and the inevitable pressure to refund so the giftee could keep the money.

During the weeks since their argument Freya had written, called and texted Hannah asking to meet, but Hannah refused her calls, didn't reply to her texts and had even crossed the street the one time they'd come into each other's orbit. Freya didn't experience any remorse at not signing the affidavit, but she ached with regret for the loss of Hannah's friendship. It had highlighted how superficial her relationships were with other women in the town, and emphasized the chasm that existed between her and Lexie.

Georgie had continued to work at Just Because, and tactfully avoided mentioning the scene with Lydia. However, many people had dropped in on the twentieth of December to tell Freya that the McMasters had been successful at court.

"They deserve this, wouldn't you agree?" people said, studying her closely and hoping she'd say no so they could berate her.

But Freya refused to explain her actions to the town. Despite some locals threatening to withdraw their custom from Just Because, none had. The shop was too convenient when they'd left their gift-buying to the last minute.

It was Ryan who'd broken the news to Freya after Hannah had messaged him. "I didn't want you to hear it from anyone else," he'd said.

"Thank you."

"Are you going to be okay with it?"

The sigh that now seemed to be part of her rose once again from the depths of her soul. Why was it no one could understand? She desperately wished Jamie was still alive and able to express his own choices.

"This was never about me, Ryan. It wasn't about Hannah either. It's what Jamie told me. I wish to God I'd never heard him say it."

"Me too." Ryan sighed deeply. "Especially when you didn't always recognize when he was teasing. He'd hate what's gone down, and not just between you and Hannah, but with us. He loved us. He only ever wanted the best for us."

Freya thought "the best" was open to interpretation and exploitation.

Ryan pulled her close. "We're okay, aren't we?"

"Yes." She checked his face, seeking understanding. "We don't always have to agree as long as we respect each other's decisions."

"You're a person of integrity, Frey, and I love you for it even if I found it hard to accept your decision." He stroked her cheek. "But I've been thinking—as relationship tests go, if we got through this and the last few months, we can get through anything, right?"

Relief slid through her like the soothing cool of silk on sunburned skin and she'd kissed him.

Now, five days later, she watched him sleeping beside her: the rhythmic and reassuring rise and fall of his chest, the ripple of his eyelids, the twitch of his fingers. Her heart flipped with gratitude and love.

She rolled into him and he opened his eyes.

"Merry Christmas," she said softly.

He smiled at her. "Merry Christmas."

She trailed her fingers along his chest. "Do you want your present?"

His eyes twinkled. "Is this a joint gift?"

"I think so."

"Perfect."

And it was.

Afterwards, lying in his arms flushed with the remnants of euphoria, she wished they could stay wrapped together in their blissful cocoon where nothing in the real world could touch them.

The moment the thought landed, the world rushed back in the form of Mia's running feet and her joyous shouts of, "Santa's come! Santa's come!"

Ryan laughed. "And we're on."

"What time are your parents arriving?"

"I said 11:00. That okay?"

"I'm making coffee," Lexie yelled, as if Mia's shouts hadn't been enough to wake them.

It was Lexie's and Mia's first Christmas without Kane. Although Lexie had asked if they could sleep over at Kitchener Street so Mia could have the magic of a big tree surrounded by presents for seven people, Freya thought it was more to do with Lexie not wanting to wake up in her own house. Not that Freya could recall Kane being much of a Christmas fan—"grinch" was a far more accurate description.

"You've got five minutes," Lexie added.

Freya groaned. "I guess we're lucky Mia slept until now."

Ryan grinned. "It's good practice for us. Besides, it isn't Christmas without kids. I just love the wonder on their faces."

His comment surprised her. In the past they'd enjoyed many childfree Christmases both in and out of Garringarup. A few times, on Ryan's suggestion, they'd lain around a pool in Bali and high-fived themselves on their freedom.

"And the over-excited meltdowns," she teased him.

"And the joy of watching them open the present they wanted."

"You better get into the shower this second then or you risk not seeing Mia tear open your gift."

He threw off the covers and pulled her into the shower with him.

They arrived in the kitchen seven minutes later and were body-slammed by Mia.

"Presents!" she squealed.

Lexie was drinking a mimosa but handed them both coffees. "You're gonna need it."

Mia was like a blowfly—buzzing in wild circuits, landing briefly, then taking off again. Freya tried unsuccessfully to focus the little girl's attention on one thing.

"How about I take her outside awhile to help her run off some steam on her new scooter?" Ryan suggested. "Or you can and I'll get started on lunch prep?"

Freya eyed her sister, who was pouring a second mimosa—this one barely touched by orange juice. "How about you take both Lexie and Mia."

"But that leaves you with a big load."

"Mum will be here soon." She shoved a box of Danish pastries at him and poured coffee into two insulated mugs. "Brekkie picnic in the park."

He grinned at her. "See? This is why we're going to be awesome parents." He kissed her, then hustled Lexie and Mia outside to join the caroling magpies.

Freya consulted her list and tried to ignore the glue-like fatigue rolling through her. While she'd been working eighteen-hour days she'd deliberately ignored the fact that her period was late. She could do a test—there was a spare in the bathroom cabinet leftover from when she couldn't believe Trudi's test so she'd done another two at home. But today, on top of everything else, she had no space in her brain to be thinking about a pregnancy.

Ryan, however, was very focused—too focused?—on the coming year and the hope of a baby. He'd been wishing away the last weeks of the year and urging the new one to start, seeming to believe that pushing forward was all it took to recover from their recent losses. Freya wished he'd talk to someone, but he continued to resist her suggestion.

She gave herself a shake, hoping it was enough to kickstart her energy and get her through the day. She should have insisted they go to the pub for Christmas lunch, but when she'd raised the idea everyone had looked so aghast that she'd forced a laugh and said, "Kidding!"

Why was it that those who wanted a Christmas like the ones they'd enjoyed as a child seemed unaware of the work involved in making it happen? Granted, their mothers understood—they'd done their share, and Freya saw the fairness in the passing of the baton. It was just that even before Lexie's marriage had collapsed she'd never hosted because of Kane. It had left—still left—Christmas falling on Freya and Ryan.

She phoned her mother. Vivian's voice had the reedy quality of someone who'd suffered through a difficult night.

"Everything okay, Mum?"

"Merry Christmas, darling. Bit shaky today, but as you've got Lexie and Ryan there to help, I won't rush over. I'll come with Sally and Barry."

Freya decided not to mention Lexie's early start on the sparkling wine. "Good idea. See you then."

She turned to the pile of potatoes. At least she'd bought the washed variety.

When Ryan returned, Freya was looking forward to working with him in the kitchen—the camaraderie of being in the trenches together. But Mia was demanding someone help her build her dinosaur park, and Lexie had perched herself on a kitchen stool, poured herself another drink and was picking up a peeler.

"Want me to top and tail the beans?" she said.

Freya momentarily toyed with suggesting that she and Ryan had everything under control in the kitchen and Lexie could help Mia with the toy, but experience had taught her that when her sister visited she took a step back from parenting. It was never explicit, but outside of her own home Lexie allowed others to attend to her daughter. Hell, lately it happened inside her home.

"Thanks." Freya flicked on the kettle. "I'll make us tea."

Lexie gave her a flinty look. "Is that code for I'm drinking too much?"

"No, it's code for pace yourself, it's a long day."

Lexie slumped. "You and Ryan give Mia a better Christmas than her parents."

"Than her father perhaps, but that wouldn't be hard." Freya gave her sister a quick shoulder squeeze. "She loves the scooter you gave her."

"I hate that I miss him today." Lexie gave a loud sniff. "I mean, God! He hated Christmas."

"Yeah, well, emotions often don't make any sense."

"You got that right."

The kettle whistled, breaking their contemplative silence.

"I'm looking forward to this year being over," Freya said. "Although Mum's health is a ticking time bomb. I think we need to accept she may need more help."

"Once she gets her eyes done and she can drive again, things will improve," Lexie said, ignoring Mia's calls of "Mum-me, come see."

"The cataract surgery is the easy bit," Freya said. "Her heart and kidneys are the worry."

"Mum-meee!" Mia appeared at the door. "Come look at my trice-tops."

"I'm busy," Lexie said.

Freya caught the droop of Mia's mouth and the flash of resigned disappointment in her eyes.

Come on, Lexie. It's Christmas, Freya urged silently. But her sister was doggedly peeling beans, so Freya dried her hands and turned to her niece. "Show me quick before it eats Ryan."

Mia giggled and grabbed her hand.

Vivian arrived at 11:00 with Sally and Barry. Freya appreciated how Ryan's parents had always made her feel welcome and how they included Vivian in social arrangements.

Vivian unpacked a large basket filled with baked goods and her famous brandy cream sauce. Technically it was for the pudding but some people treated it as a drink.

Lexie's eyes lit up. "Egg nog!"

"After lunch," Freya said firmly, picturing Lexie asleep on the sofa before she'd served the first course.

As Freya watched everyone troop into the living room to open presents, she said to Ryan, "I don't understand Lexie. She has the day off, we're hosting and all she has to do is take pleasure in Mia enjoying the day. Instead, she's drinking herself into a stupor before lunch."

Ryan slid an arm around her. "She's had a rough year."

"We've all had a rough year!"

He pressed his forehead against hers. "But we've got each other."

"Come on, lovebirds." Barry reappeared in the kitchen. "We're dying of thirst out there and Mia's set to take the tree apart."

Freya ducked between the gift-opening frenzy and the kitchen, checking the turkey and the vegetables and prepping the prawn entrée. Each year Sally and Barry contributed the seafood—Freya just wished they'd peel the prawns as well.

Ryan wrangled Mia and maintained a conversation about interest rates and classic cars with his father as well as clearing up gift-wrap. Sally drifted into the kitchen and Vivian followed, and somehow the first two courses were plated, served, eaten and enjoyed.

"So when's pudding?" Lexie asked as soon as Ryan and Barry had cleared the plates.

Freya took a long deep breath, burying the words, "When you serve it." "I thought people might like a walk to make room."

"And leave the air-conditioning? I don't think so." Lexie reached for the bottle of sparkling wine. "Besides, Mia's happy."

Mia was under the table playing with her new keyboard. Ryan had wisely connected it to her headphones so she could plink and plonk to her heart's content and none of them had to listen to the noise.

General murmurs of agreement wove around the table in response to Lexie's claim so Freya didn't push the walk, but there was no way she was serving pudding until she'd sat with her feet up for at least half an hour. She reached for the water jug Ryan had just refilled.

"It's not like you to turn down Barry's sparkling burgundy, Freya," Sally said. "Does it mean good news and you're pregnant?"

Stunned, Freya stared at her. In all the years she and Ryan had been together, Sally had never asked such a direct question.

"Oh, so *that's* why you're so judgy about me drinking today," Lexie said. "Because you can't."

"No!" Freya thumped the jug back onto the table. "I just think five drinks before lunch is about three too many."

"Girls," Vivian said. "It's Christmas."

Freya had no idea what that meant and she wasn't going to ask. Instead she replied to Sally. "I had a glass of the burgundy."

"So that's a no to being pregnant then?" Disappointment rang in Sally's voice.

"We'll let you know when we know, Mum," Ryan said, his eyes questioning Freya as he squeezed her hand.

"I hope for both your sakes it happens quickly," Sally said. "Meanwhile, I haven't received my 'save the date' for the wedding."

"Now the Christmas rush is over we're getting onto the wedding plans, right, Frey?" Ryan said.

"It's going to be small," she said.

"But at St Paul's," Vivian said firmly.

"With Mia as flower girl and me as maid of honor," Lexie said.

Freya's head pounded. "Without Jamie, it's—We'll just have two witnesses."

Ryan frowned. "I do have other friends, you know."

"Of course you do," she said quickly. "It's just I thought—"

"You've waited long enough," Barry said. "Go the whole hog. It's not like Maeve's gonna give us a wedding anytime soon unless that bloke she's seeing commits bigamy."

"Barry!" Sally admonished.

Lexie laughed and replenished her drink. "More power to Maeve."

"I think the power lies with Dan," Barry muttered.

"I just hope next Christmas there's a baby lying under the tree fascinated by the baubles and the light coming through the window," Vivian said.

"Yeah, sis," Lexie slurred. "Christmas is all about kids and you're dragging the chain."

Freya's exhaustion collided with her exasperation at keeping so many balls in the air. "If Christmas is all about children, why have Ryan and I been entertaining yours all day?"

Ryan's hand tightened on hers in warning as Vivian said sternly, "Freya Diane."

Lexie's eyes flashed behind their unfocused gaze. "Sorry we're such an imposition."

Freya sighed and rubbed her temples. "You're not. I'm sorry. I'm tired is all."

"Just tired?" Lexie queried. "Last time you were this snippy you were pregnant."

"Oh my God!" Freya's hands came down hard on the table, making the silverware jump. "Why are you all so obsessed by this?"

"Lexie's got a point," Ryan said quietly. "Normally nothing fazes you."

It sounded like betrayal. As the pressure from five sets of eyes almost propelled her across the room, Freya found herself blinking back tears.

She stood abruptly. "If I do a pregnancy test right now, will you *all* back off? Never ask me if I'm pregnant ever again?"

Everyone exchanged cautious glances as if they were being addressed by an unstable person waving a knife.

Eventually Ryan looked up and down the table. "You all promise that, right?"

They nodded their agreement.

"Right then. I'll go pee on a stick," Freya said.

"Will I come?" Ryan asked.

Her mouth was suddenly a rifle and her "No" shot around the room defiant and determined.

The hurt on his face wounded her and she heard herself apologizing for the second time in as many minutes against a backdrop of knowing looks.

Damn it! They were probably right—she was almost certainly pregnant. Her uncharacteristic short fuse was all too familiar, along with the tender breasts and overdue period she'd been ignoring, blaming both on the stress of the season. Did she really need to do the pregnancy test? Probably not, but she needed five minutes by herself.

She kissed Ryan and heard the buzz of voices start up again the moment she left the room. She closed the bathroom door and leaned against it, taking some long, slow, deep breaths.

"Pregnant"—the word rolled in her mouth and clogged her throat.

Last time it had been a shock. This time it felt inevitable, as if from the moment of the miscarriage there'd been external forces at play far greater than her, propelling her to this point. The sensation dragged, pulling at her belly, her legs, her whole body, until she sank onto the cool tiled floor. An oppressive feeling encased her.

What the hell was wrong with her? Everyone in the dining room wished her pregnant. They'd be thrilled; for her and Ryan, as well as for themselves. Ryan would be ecstatic, and why not? A baby was everything they wanted.

Everything Ryan wanted.

It's not what I want.

All the ambivalence and indecision of the preceding weeks suddenly fell away, revealing a shocking truth she could no longer hide from.

She didn't want to be pregnant. She didn't want a baby. She didn't want to be a mother. Not now. Not ever.

Too late for that.

Christmas lunch lurched into her mouth, bitter and scalding. She forced it down, hauled herself to her feet and ripped open the pregnancy-test packaging. Hoicking up her dress, she whipped down her panties and was preparing to pee on the stick when she noticed spots of blood on her panty liner. She stared at them, then grabbed at the toilet paper to wipe herself. When she pulled the tissue away it was stained a bright ruby red.

She sagged with relief. *Thank you.*

But her euphoria was short-lived as she remembered reading about implantation spotting. The blood could be the sign a baby was settling into the lush lining of her uterus, readying to take over her body. Her mind. Her life.

Panic thrummed and she struggled to relax enough to urinate on the test stick. She set the timer on her phone, then sat on the floor with her head in her hands. *No, please, no.*

After what seemed an eternity, the timer rang. She froze. It took two commands from her brain before she managed to force her gaze to the test. She heard a sound coming from her mouth—an odd combination of fear and release. She'd just been gifted the best Christmas present ever.

There was a gentle knock on the door. "Everything okay, Frey?" Ryan asked tentatively.

She wanted to yell, "Yes! More than okay," but she couldn't. Not when her elation was equal to his disappointment. Equal to the dismay of their family.

The weight of their expectations flattened her. What the hell happened now?

CHAPTER THIRTY

HANNAH ENDURED Christmas on the Eyre Peninsula—she felt like a stranger dropped into a world where she didn't speak the language or understand the customs. She spent the week-long visit counting down the days, hours and minutes until the summer slumber was over, businesses and services returned to normal, and Rowan could secure a court date in Brisbane.

Back home in Garringarup, January rolled out and Hannah discovered that "helping" Lydia with the Women in Agriculture conference was actually a twenty-hour-a-week unpaid job. She was currently wrangling an agreement with a conference center, as well as setting up a newsletter account so that all interested persons' email addresses were stored in the one place.

"I knew you'd know what to do," Lydia said. "And it's good to keep busy."

It was, but the work didn't challenge her and she found herself missing Just Because. *And Freya?* No. What Freya had done to her was unforgivable.

Hannah tried to reframe the work in her mind. It wasn't all that different than what she'd done for Jamie, except she'd viewed that job as their business and their future. She was never going to be a woman in agriculture. Although, with a current financial stake in the farm she supposed she should take more of an interest, but she couldn't muster much enthusiasm. After probate went through it may be wiser to sell her farm shares and invest the money on the stock market rather than wait on the once-in-twenty-five-years boom year. She'd talk to Dec about it.

Helping Ian was more straightforward than assisting Lydia, although it took a lot of prodding to get information out of him about probate.

"As part of winding up the business, Rowan's placed a creditors notice," he said.

"So that means probate will go through soon?"

Ian sighed. "Still a few hoops to jump through yet, I'm afraid."

Disappointment slugged her. "I've been thinking of ways to bring in some cash. Could we sell Jamie's car?"

Ian rubbed his chin. "It's done a lot of kays, love. You wouldn't get much."

"But I'd get something," she urged.

"It's part of the estate though, so we can't sell it just yet."

Hannah tried to keep her frustration from her voice. "Can I see the accounts so I can get an idea of what's coming? You know, for planning purposes?"

"They're not going to give you an accurate picture."

"Can you at least give me a ballpark?"

"At this stage it's a bit hard to tell and I wouldn't want to steer you wrong." His smile was tinged with resignation. "I'm sorry, it's a lot more complicated than we expected."

She thought about Jamie's honeymoon plans and hoped she could at least get one definitive answer to her long list of questions. And, while she was at it, get a peek at Jamie's personal bank balance. She had no clue what he was worth.

"I was wondering if you could log me into Jamie's computer, please?"

Ian frowned. "I don't have it."

She almost said, "Yes, you do, I saw it before Christmas," then realized that would prove she'd been snooping.

"It's with Rowan." Ian patted her hand. "I know it's hard, Hannah, but bear with us. We've only got your best interests at heart, and it's better to take our time and get it right rather than rush things and make a dog's breakfast of it."

Despite her rising exasperation, she sensed she'd pushed Ian as far as she could. On the drive home she called Declan.

"How long should probate take?"

"How long's a piece of string?" he said.

"Not helpful. Is four months too long?"

"Depends how complicated it is and how on top of things Ian is. I've heard of executors spinning it out for a year."

"What? No! Why?"

"All sorts of reasons, although in some families it's often got nothing to do with problems and everything to do with power or spite. They hold onto the money to piss off their siblings, especially if they know they're desperate for money. But that's not an issue for you. It's probably Jamie's business that's causing the delay. But the McMasters are taking care of you while everything's being dealt with, right?"

"Yes, but I hate being dependent on them."

Declan laughed. "You're planning on having their grandkid so that means you'll be leaning on them for years."

Her chest suddenly tightened and she didn't understand why. "I won't be financially dependent!"

"Han, is everything okay?" His laughter had been replaced by concern. "Do you need some cash?"

"Yes. No. I wish you were closer."

"Sorry." He cleared his throat. "How about I drop five hundred into your account."

Gratitude and relief tangoed with unease. "I don't like the thought of owing you money too."

"Consider it an early birthday present. Love ya, sis, talk soon."

The line went dead.

Hannah got a sudden urge for sugar and carbs. Between probate and baby plans, it felt like her life was reduced to waiting for other people to make decisions about her that she was powerless to control. She parked the car in the main street, leashed Ozzie and sat under a large white market umbrella outside Duc's Bakery.

She was logging into her bank account to check her balance when Ozzie suddenly stood. As he and another dog greeted each other by sniffing butts, Hannah became aware of someone standing by her table.

She looked up, immediately recognizing Mac. "Oh, hi." She quickly turned her phone screen down. No need to show anyone else her terrifying bottom line.

"G'day." His fingers worried the brim of his Akubra. He didn't look quite as ill at ease as he had in Just Because, although it was a close call.

"Is this Daisy?" Hannah asked, tilting her head towards the other border collie.

He looked surprised. "It is. How do you know her name?"

"You've mentioned her each time we've met."

"Well, she is the most important woman in my life." His face suddenly flushed sunburn red and he stammered, "I mean, on the farm. Shit. I mean she's a working dog."

"Not a working girl?" Hannah teased. "Oh, right, that's the sheep."

"We're not in bloody New Zealand," he muttered.

"Oh, hey, Mac. You're looking hot," Duc said. "I'll get you some water."

Hannah took pity on Mac and kicked out a chair. "I'm having coffee and cake if you'd like to join me."

Mac gave his order to Duc and sat down, ruffling Ozzie's ears. "Your dog?"

"He is now."

"Oh, right." His left leg jiggled up and down. "How are things?"

She shrugged.

"I heard you're trying to have his—Jamie's baby?"

The idea that the news had spread beyond the town limits was disconcerting.

"How?" she said. "You don't even live here."

He glanced down for a moment then met her gaze. "I was in the gift shop with Georgie when Mrs. McMaster tore strips off Freya."

Hannah blinked. She hadn't doubted that Lydia would have eviscerated Freya with words, but she'd assumed it had happened in private. "That had to be uncomfortable."

"Little bit."

She expected him to ask her the same questions about having Jamie's baby as everyone else. She started marshalling her standard answers of, yes it's unusual, but no, she wasn't the first woman to do it; yes, she knew exactly what she was doing and it made perfect sense to her; no, she didn't think—

"You have the advantage on me," he said.

"Sorry, what?"

"Being able to have Jamie's baby."

"You wanted to have Jamie's baby?"

He gave a wry smile. "I did not want to have Jamie's baby. I did not fancy him, and just to be clear, I do not fancy blokes. To be honest, Dan and I didn't exactly see eye to eye with Jamie at school."

"I find that hard to believe. Jamie got on with everyone."

Mac shrugged and bit into his pastry.

She didn't want to hear anyone badmouthing Jamie so she changed the subject. "What were you saying about an advantage?"

Mac swallowed and chased his bite of pastry with a sip of coffee. "You have a uterus. When Chelsea died, my dreams of a family died with her."

Hannah had assumed Mac was single because he was awkward and shy, not because they shared the fallout of an event that had exploded their worlds. Her heart ached and she noticed she was gripping Mac's hand.

"I'm so sorry. How long ago did you lose her?"

"Two and a bit years."

"Does it get easier?"

"Yes and no."

Dismay bit and she tugged her hand away. "How is that reassuring?"

He gave a sad smile. "I know you want a yes, but all I can offer you is that my grief's changed shape. At first it was this massive lump of hard clay that filled every part of me, making it impossible to function."

"I know all about that."

"Yeah." He took a reflective pause. "I hated it when people said 'time heals all wounds' and crap like that."

"They don't get it's not helpful."

"For sure. But as much as we rage against it and wish things were different, the world keeps turning around us. Time slowly molded that lump of clay into different shapes and sizes. Don't get me wrong—grief still flares and catches me off guard, but I've noticed I recover faster."

He ran his finger around the rim of his cup. "There's always going to be some sadness when I think about Chelsea, and not just because I didn't get the life with her that I planned. Hell, she didn't even see thirty-one and that's bloody tragic. For a while the guilt that I wasn't in the plane with her slayed me. It kept me on the farm and away from people, away from my life."

Hannah thought about all the times she dived under the covers and never wanted to face the light again. "What changed?"

His blue eyes met hers and his mouth tweaked up, rueful and shy. "I was in the middle of lambing season and it suddenly hit me that if I stayed a miserable shit, making everyone who loved me hold their breath around me, keeping them constantly worried I'd do something stupid, then the bloody plane crash was stealing two lives."

"And Chelsea's was one too many," she said.

He nodded. "So I did what more blokes, especially farmers, should do. I got some help. I wouldn't call it fun, and I still check in—but hey, I enjoyed Georgie's party and eighty percent of Christmas."

Hannah remembered Jamie grumbling about Christmas. "How much of Christmas did you usually enjoy?"

"You got me." He laughed, his tension rolling away. She was suddenly looking at an entirely different person. "Nah, Christmas is alright. It was definitely better this year. And having Georgie home for the summer helps. Mum and Dad are too busy worrying about her and the party circuit so it takes the pressure off me."

He gave her hand a quick brush. "Just take one day at a time, and lean on your family and friends."

Hannah thought about her parents, about Declan so far away, and Freya. A sharp pain sawed in her chest and she sucked in her lips.

"Did I say the wrong thing?" Mac asked.

She shook her head. "I ... it's ... I only have my brother and he's in Singapore." She blinked frantically, trying to hold back tears—falling apart on the main street was not an option. "And the McMasters, of course. Jamie's baby will make us a family."

His brow creased in a slight frown, but before he spoke her phone buzzed. She reached for it automatically and had turned it over before she realized it was incredibly rude.

"Sorry," she said. "I've spent too much time on my own lately."

"No worries, you're preaching to the choir." He stood and jammed his hat on his head. "I have to go. Georgie's car wouldn't start this morning so I ran her in. She finishes at 3:00."

Delight scampered through Hannah. "Georgie's working in Garringarup? Where? I'd love to say hi."

Like a turning tide, ill-at-ease Mac rushed back. He shoved his hands in his pockets and avoided her gaze.

"Mac?"

He screwed up his face as if the answer hurt. "She's at Just Because."

A stab of something complicated caught Hannah under the ribs. Even though Freya had betrayed her, and Hannah knew she'd never work for her again, it stung that Freya had hired Georgie.

"I think G only said yes because she was hoping to work with you," Mac said, recognizing her discomfort. He pulled out his phone and handed it to her. "Give me your number and I'll pass it on to her. I'm sure she'd love to catch up."

As Hannah typed in her digits and handed Mac his phone, her mind was stuck on Freya's double betrayal.

You ignored all her pleading calls and texts.

SHUT UP!

"Take care, Hannah," Mac said, then he called Daisy and walked away.

Hannah remained seated. She pushed away thoughts of Freya and concentrated on what Mac had said about his grief changing shape. She knew the only thing that would change the shape of her grief was holding her and Jamie's child in her arms.

CHAPTER THIRTY-ONE

WHILE FREYA WAITED for Vivian to be discharged from the day surgery center, she checked in with Georgie.

"All good, Freya. I packaged up the orders and did a stock take on the condiments. Most are well within their use-by date, but I've moved the stock around. You need to order more of the lemon myrtle spice packs and I've put them on the stock list. But the best news is, I sold one of my fiber-art horses!"

"That's great!" Freya could imagine Georgie talking about her love of horses to a customer and how her passion would have sold the decoration. "Fingers crossed it's the first of many. I won't be back before you lock up, so drop the keys in the key safe at my place, please."

"Too easy."

"I'll see you tomorrow."

Freya appreciated how reliable and responsible Georgie was, as well as her eye for design—it was as good as Hannah's. But none of it made up for the loss of her friend. Sometimes talking to Georgie was like visiting another planet.

After the events on Christmas Day, and the expectations of her family, Freya needed to talk to someone. Usually her go-to person was

Ryan, but this time he was involved so she couldn't use him as a sounding board. Many women would have turned to their sister, but as much as Freya wished that time and adulthood had closed the five-year age gap between her and Lexie, it only seemed to have widened it. Recently, Lexie seemed to both want and resent Freya's help with Mia —her comments on Christmas Day had more than conveyed that—and Freya wasn't certain her sister could be an impartial advisor.

And you really think that Hannah would understand you not wanting a baby?

That was the problem. Freya wasn't certain anyone in Garringarup would understand.

"Freya Quayle?" a nurse called, pushing Vivian in a wheelchair into the waiting area.

"That's me. Hi, Mum." Freya bent and kissed her mother on the cheek. "How are you feeling?"

"Fine. I've had a cuppa and some sandwiches, and my blood sugar's great so we can drive straight home."

The nurse ran through the post-operative care then handed over a bag of eyedrops. "Be good, Vivian, and we'll see you back here for the other eye soon."

Freya had convinced her mother to stay the night with her and Ryan before returning to her own place the following day. Once back at Kitchener Street, her mother called Lexie while Freya poured cool drinks.

She could hear Vivian telling Lexie, "the private hospital was like a five-star hotel," and then her voice changed. Freya realized she was talking to Mia, although it sounded like a very one-sided conversation.

When the call ended, Vivian said, "I'm worried about your sister." It was an old refrain.

"About what exactly?" Freya asked. There were many reasons to worry about Lexie.

"She's drinking more than she should, and Mia's spending far too much time on that iPad. She should be outside playing in the fresh air."

Freya recalled Vivian ushering her and Lexie outside as kids with drinks and snacks, then locking the back door. By the time Vivian unlocked it—which felt like hours later but had probably only been fifteen minutes—she and Lexie were usually engrossed in some activity and had to be called in for dinner. But they'd had each other for entertainment. Mia was by herself.

"Mia gets a lot of outside play at day care," Freya said. "Besides, we're in the middle of a heatwave and all of us are doing what we need to survive."

Vivian made a harrumphing sound.

Freya set a glass of sparkling water in front of her mother. "It's hard work juggling a fulltime job and a child."

"I juggled your father, the two of you, part-time work and volunteering," Vivian said. "And it wasn't like Kane was much help when he was here. She's better off without him. She *must* know that."

Freya wasn't so certain. "Kane rejected her and Mia. Logic doesn't make up for that emotional hammering. I think her partying and drinking are connected—proving to herself she's worthy of being loved maybe? I dunno." She sighed. "I worry about the impact her distraction is having on Mia."

"Your sister's a very good mother," Vivian said briskly.

The criticism was clear: only Vivian was allowed to worry about Lexie; Freya was supposed to listen, not give an opinion. It was a well-worn path and Freya swallowed a sigh.

"I'm not saying she isn't. I'm saying that at the moment, whenever I see her, she seems disconnected from Mia. When she visits us, she lets me and Ryan do everything."

"Because she needs the rest," Vivian said firmly. "The daily grind of parenting is tough—as you'll find out soon enough."

Freya glanced at her mother. Was this an opening she should take?

"How did you know you wanted a baby?" she asked.

Vivian laughed. "Darling, your dad and I got married.'

Freya didn't follow. "But you had contraception. You had a choice."

Her mother gave her a blank look. "What do you mean?"

Freya moistened her lips. "I mean you could have kept using contraception and not had children."

Vivian laughed.

"What's funny?"

"Darling, back then contraception was something you used to avoid getting pregnant before you got married. After the wedding, you bought a house and had babies. Nowadays, young couples buy the house, have the babies and then get married."

Freya traced the condensation on her glass. "So you always knew you wanted children?"

Vivian shrugged. "I can't really say I thought a lot about it."

Freya almost choked on her water. The decision to have—not to have—a baby was all she could think about. "So you had Lexie and me without any conscious thought?"

"Of course not!" Vivian said indignantly. "We waited until we'd bought the house."

"It sounds like you were checking items off a list!"

Vivian gave Freya a reproving look—one she hadn't received since she was eighteen and had missed a family dinner with her grandparents because she'd been out with a boy.

"When your dad and I got married, having children was a given. I suppose people who didn't want children didn't get married. And if you couldn't have a child naturally, you adopted." Vivian's face softened. "I had some misses because of my diabetes and my pregnancies weren't easy, but it just made me more determined. To be honest, it was extremely hard being the only one in our friendship group without children. I felt quite isolated for a long time."

Freya didn't understand. "But motherhood doesn't define a woman. You were living in Perth. You were working as an accountant. Surely you and Dad had friends without children?"

"Only Steve and Lewis, and they wanted kids too. In the eighties, Perth wasn't the place it is today. They had to live as "confirmed bachelors" and housemates sharing the rent. Back then gay men couldn't adopt. In the end they did a deal with some lesbian friends and shared a child."

A sensation of separateness hit Freya in the solar plexus. "So you've never regretted your non-decision to have us?"

"Freya! What a thing to say. Of course not. What on earth's got into you?"

I don't want a child.

"Nothing." But as much as she knew she should change the conversation before she hit dangerous currents, her words kept coming. "It's just ... sometimes I find it hard to imagine being a mother."

Vivian gave her an indulgent smile. "That's normal and nothing to worry about. I promise you, once you hold your baby in your arms you can't imagine your life without them."

Freya bristled. "That's not always true though, is it? Some women get postnatal depression."

Her mother tsked. "Sometimes, Freya, I wonder about you. You're normally full of common sense so why are you looking for problems? There's no history of postnatal depression in our family, and even if there was, these days they know how to treat it."

She gave Freya's hand an awkward pat. "It's okay. I know what you're doing."

Hope soared. Did her mother understand without her needing to voice the words? "What am I doing?"

"You're overthinking things as usual. You did it before you moved in with Ryan and before starting Just Because, and both of those things are the best decisions you ever made. You're just feeling bruised by the miscarriage and the disappointment at Christmas. I promise you, being a mother is the most rewarding job you'll ever do."

A faint roll of nausea washed through Freya. Why had she even considered the possibility that Vivian was in tune with her when she rarely was? At that moment, she desperately missed her father.

· · ·

Three nights later Ryan arrived home at 9:00, gray with fatigue, and fell onto the outdoor sofa next to Freya. "Thank God today's over."

"Nasty call-out?"

"None of them nasty, just a lot in one day. I don't care what the boffins say about full moons, we're always busier." He leaned in for a leisurely kiss and when he drew back said with wonder in his voice, "Listen."

Freya strained to hear whatever it was that was making him smile. She could only hear cicadas. "What? I can't hear anything."

He grinned. "Exactly. We have the house to ourselves again."

She snuggled into him, having missed the intimacy that came with them being alone.

"It's been a bit like a hotel here," she agreed, "but Mum's coping with the drops and thankfully the surgery didn't send her blood sugar all over the shop."

Ryan ran his fingers through her hair. "Fancy an early night?"

She did—she almost always did. Their sex life had always been good—except for when she'd been pregnant and exhausted.

"It's close to peak baby-making time, right?" he said.

Freya's heart sank. She'd put off having the baby conversation with Ryan—why introduce a difficult topic when they'd been enjoying a honeymoon period after the affidavit issue.

A few nights earlier, when she'd been home alone and Ryan was out on a call, she'd drunk too much wine and come up with what she'd thought was a brilliant plan—go on the pill and not tell him. But in the light of day—apart from the fact that she couldn't take the pill for medical reasons—the idea of hiding contraception from Ryan looked like a cancerous growth.

Their relationship had always rested on a bedrock of respect—something she never wanted to lose. It was time to pull on her big girl pants and tell him her true feelings about having a baby.

"You've had a huge day. Aren't you hungry?" she said.

"Always for you."

She rolled her eyes at the corny line. "I made a Thai beef noodle salad."

"In that case ..." He pulled her to her feet and they walked inside.

When the food was eaten and the day discussed and deconstructed, they relocated to the sofa with half a glass of Riesling each. It was companionable and easy, and Freya almost changed her mind, but the fear of another accidental pregnancy forced her to speak.

"Ryan, I don't think I'm ready for a baby."

"What?" Shock rode across his face. "But it's what we want."

"It's what you want."

"No ... I mean yes, but ..." He leaned forward, his gaze intense and searching. "Where's this coming from?"

She took a deep breath. "When I got my period at Christmas and everyone was sad and disappointed, all I felt was relief."

His frown almost buried his eyes. "Why relief? Are you scared of having another miscarriage?"

"No."

"What then?"

Her hand tightened on her glass. "I'm scared of getting pregnant and having a baby."

Bewilderment ringed him, and his mouth opened and closed twice before he managed to speak. "But I don't understand. If you hadn't had the miscarriage you'd be five months pregnant. We'd be preparing. Painting the nursery, choosing strollers, names—"

"I know. And all that terrifies me."

"But why? You'll be a great mum."

She set down her glass and noticed her hand shook. "I don't think I want to be a mother. I don't think I've ever wanted it."

"No." He shook his head. "No way. That's not right."

"I'm starting to think it is."

She recalled being sixteen and sitting cross-legged on the netball courts while her schoolfriends clucked over photos of some celebrity's baby in a magazine. Freya hadn't understood their over-the-top reactions of "Aww, so cute! OMG, I want one!"

"When I was at uni, women talked about wanting kids but I was never that person," she said.

"Of course you weren't," Ryan said reassuringly. "You were in your twenties, you had things you wanted to do and," he shot her his impish grin and winked, "you hadn't met me." His grin faded, seriousness taking over. "You're amazing with Mia."

"Not always. And anyway, that's not the same as being a mother."

"Sure it is." He kissed her. "Stop overthinking this."

But she couldn't let him use her family's default argument to dismiss her concerns. "Until Jamie died, you'd never mentioned wanting children or getting married. Now it's all you think about. I'm worried it's your grief talking."

"It's not," he said tightly.

"But what if it is?" She leaned forward, needing him to really hear her. "What if you wake up one day having changed your mind? You decide you don't want to be a father and you leave me to raise a child on my own—" Her voice cracked.

"Hey." He stroked her face. "I'm not Kane or any other of those dropkick bastards."

"I know that." She let her forehead rest on his for a moment before pulling back. "But I'm worried you're rushing into this."

He snorted. "Rushing would have been having a baby ten years ago. Let's face it, we're the last ones in our group without kids."

She thought about her mother's reasons for having children. "Keeping up with everyone is not a reason to have kids."

"Well, duh," he said easily. "And again, if we were into that sort of thing we'd have done it years ago."

She took his hands and looked into his eyes. "Can you honestly tell me that this sudden need to have a child isn't connected to your grief about Jamie? That you aren't daydreaming about his kid and ours growing up together and being mates like you were with him?"

He hesitated a split second too long and she sighed.

"Yeah, okay, a bit," he said. "When I found out what Hannah was planning, the thought might have crossed my mind. But it's only a tiny part of the reason."

"Is it really? Because before Jamie died you never mentioned having kids."

He tilted his head, his look contemplative. "You keep saying I never talked about having kids, but you didn't either. Us not talking about it didn't mean I didn't want them. I just wasn't ready. But like with Jamie, it was always implied. It's what 'one day' means. I thought we were on the same page about getting our careers established, paying down the mortgage and getting some travel under our belts before we started a family. And to be fair, Frey, we've done all that. I'm ready. I thought you were too. Hell, we've been pregnant!"

"With an unplanned baby!" She tried to slow her suddenly racing heart. "The thing is, the whole time I was pregnant I didn't feel like me. I wasn't me. I felt like I was outside of myself looking down on someone I didn't recognize. You can't honestly tell me that you enjoyed tiptoeing around that woman?"

"I'm a grown-up, Freya. I know pregnancy's an assault on the body, and hormones can make you cra—short-tempered. I knew that you yelling at me wasn't personal." He stroked her face. "Pregnancy is a temporary state. The payoff is the baby."

Agitation riffed and pulsed, making her jumpy. "And what if I'm still crazy after the baby's born? How long will you be happy to put up with that? God, I don't want to be like that. I'm already busy being your partner, a sister, an aunt, a daughter, a business-owner ... I'm divided into so many parts there's not much of me left. I don't think a child deserves only a part of me."

He rubbed the back of his neck as if it might help him make sense of what she was saying. "But it will be *our* baby. Surely they take priority?"

She drained her glass. "If we have a baby, you, Mum, Lexie and Mia, Sally and Barry don't stop being family. And Just Because is my livelihood. It demands constant attention to keep it thriving and turning a profit. Without that, it dies and I risk massive debt. With all the claims on my time, I just don't think I have anything else left to give."

"But that's the beauty of the human heart, Frey. It's not finite. Once you hold our baby, it will expand its love."

How could she make him understand?

"I'm not talking about love, Ryan. I'm talking about *time*—to do my very best for you and the family we've already got. On top of everything else, I don't need the guilt of failing."

"You've never failed at anything, Frey. You're not going to fail at this."

His words swirled around her, full of love, but they weren't enough to assuage her anxieties. "You don't know that."

"I do."

She tried again. "Name me any parents we know who aren't stressed with the constant juggle of childcare, work, school and after-school activities. Tiffany told me that she and Jackson are lucky to have sex once a month. Worse than that, she'd rather come to book club because she gets to walk out of the house and none of us there wants or needs anything from her."

Ryan scoffed. "You know Tiffany can't organize herself out of a brown paper bag. You're the most organized person I know."

He wasn't hearing her. She tried to think of something to say that might jolt him out of problem-solving and into listening.

"Look at Lexie. She was desperate to have a baby. Now Mia's crying out for her attention and Lexie's too caught up with her own needs to see her."

"You're nothing like your self-obsessed sister."

Freya didn't want to admit she thought Lexie was selfish because it felt like a betrayal, but Ryan had a point.

"Kane isn't helping," she said.

"He's a first-degree asshole for sure." Ryan wrapped his arms around her and drew her close. "I get you're floundering. I get that you're always scared about big changes, but you're forgetting you've got me in your corner. I know I can't be pregnant for you, but we'll share everything like we always do. Or we will once you've finished breastfeeding."

She suppressed a shudder at the thought of having a baby tethered to her—one more person needing something from her.

He stroked her hair. "We're nothing like Lexie and Kane or Tiffany and Jackson or anyone else you can name. We'll make awesome parents of amazing kids."

"Our DNA's not that special."

He laughed and her stomach knotted. He didn't get it.

"Ryan, I don't want to get pregnant."

The edges of his mouth tightened. "This month? This year?"

Never. But he was looking at her as if she was a stranger.

Something greater than the fear of having a child roared through her and the truth faltered on her tongue. "I'm not sure."

He smiled then as if his world had just righted. "Well, that's what you told me when I suggested we move in together and when we bought this house. Look how great those decisions turned out." He pulled her onto his lap. "What I'm hearing is that you need time to wrap your head around us being parents. So, let's take a few months, go back to using condoms, and we'll keep talking until we've ironed out all your misgivings."

Everything, from the hairs on his head down to his bare feet planted firmly on the floorboards, said he would use those months to change her mind.

Freya didn't know what was more concerning—his belief or hers.

CHAPTER THIRTY-TWO

Mac TEXTED Georgie's number to Hannah. When it arrived, she wondered why he hadn't given her number to Georgie and left the ball in the younger woman's court. Surely someone who'd just turned twenty-one would find Hannah too old? She thought it very possible that Mac had only sent the number because he'd felt uncomfortable about his sister taking over her job. Did Georgie feel that way? Hannah had no idea and plonked it all in the too-hard basket.

But a few nights later, when she was home alone with only Ozzie for company and loathing herself for missing Freya, she snatched up her phone. Before she could second-guess herself, she texted Georgie suggesting they catch up.

Georgie responded with a thumbs-up, leaving Hannah wondering if that was a "yes, I've received the message" or "yes, let's catch up."

Not wanting to look desperate, she jumped onto the socials to see if she could get a sense of who Georgie was and if she was likely to be interested in meeting up. Her TikTok account was mostly horse videos, but her Instagram was filled with intricate fiber-art sculptures of horses, dogs, cows, sheep and other bushland creatures. Hannah recognized Daisy—Georgie had captured her markings perfectly.

Impressed, she texted her again. *OMG, I just looked at your Insta. You're so talented. Also beautiful horses*

A smiling emoji came back. *Do you ride? You should come out to the farm!*

The closest Hannah had gotten to riding a horse was watching *Saddle Club* as a kid. Jamie had talked about teaching her and she'd wanted to learn, but between work and his cricket club commitments it had fallen to the side. She hadn't pushed it because she'd thought he had a lifetime to teach her.

Another text came in. *If you don't ride, I can teach you! Bullet is the best teacher*

Bullet?

Mac's old horse. He's the best

Hannah almost dismissed the idea. What was the point in learning to ride when she'd be pregnant soon? But she'd put off learning once before and lost the opportunity. Her weekend diary was utterly empty and the idea of spending Saturday watching cricket followed by a night at the pub dodging Sam Dillinger didn't appeal. Nor did going out to the McMasters' farm now that she spent part of every weekday there.

Before she talked herself out of it she replied. *Does Saturday or Sunday work?*

They'd settled on an early Sunday-morning ride before the wind rose and the heat of the day broke over them. Bullet defied his name by walking sedately around the paddock railings, giving Hannah time to learn the importance of steady hands and holding the reins correctly to protect his mouth. Keeping her heels down and not bouncing all over the saddle when he was trotting was far more challenging.

When she dismounted an hour later and carried Bullet's saddle back to the stables, Hannah discovered she had inner thigh muscles she'd never met before and got a glimpse of what walking may be like when she was eighty. She also realized she'd been so busy listening to Georgie's instructions and concentrating on what she was doing that she hadn't given any thought to the list of things that usually occupied her mind in a never-ending loop: Jamie, their baby, probate, IVF, the delayed court date in Brisbane, Freya ... It was liberating. She'd do it again just for the peace.

"Thanks, Georgie. That was amazing."

Georgie grinned. "You did really well. Hungry?"

"Starving."

"Me too."

Georgie led the way out of the stables and across the yard. Hannah was admiring the old stone homestead with its wide verandas and row of gnarled weeping peppermint gums that provided extra shade, when Georgie suddenly veered right, exited the yard and walked towards a cottage nestled in another grove of gums.

"You have your own place?" Hannah asked.

But Georgie was busy levering off her boots, greeting three border collies and issuing instructions to sit as the dogs rushed Hannah. She recognized Daisy and gave her a scratch under her chin before following Georgie inside.

"We need coffee," Georgie said, but she indicated the bathroom. "When you're done the kitchen's just through here."

When Hannah entered the kitchen she was surprised to see a table filled with platters of eggs, bacon and baked beans, bowls of fresh fruit and yogurt, and a rack of toast. She was even more surprised to see Mac leaning against a long counter drinking coffee.

He gave her his shy smile. "Morning, Hannah. I hear you're a natural horsewoman."

"I think your sister's being generous."

Georgie shook her head. "I've tried to teach townies to ride before and it's been a disaster. You actually listened."

"Grab a seat and start eating," Mac said. "Coffee? Latte, right?"

"Yes, please." She sat and immediately reached for the wholewheat toast as a base for her cooked breakfast. "You made all this?"

Mac placed her coffee on her right. "After an early start and a riding lesson I thought you deserved more than a muesli bar and bottle of water. It's all Princess here can cook."

"Hey!" Georgie protested. "I can do more than that."

"That's right." Mac facepalmed. "I forgot about two-minute noodles."

Georgie gave him a gentle punch on the arm. "It's not my fault Mum loves to cook and won't let me use the kitchen."

"And yet others of us learned," Mac said drily, passing Hannah the bacon. "Sorry you missed out on Mum's Sunday crepes and champagne breakfast. Our parents are in Perth this weekend."

"This looks great," Hannah said. "I haven't felt hungry in months, but I'm famished. It must be all the fresh air and concentration."

"That'll do it," he said.

"Thanks for cooking."

He smiled. "Too easy, especially as Georgie's washing up."

"I never get why cooks think that's a hardship." Georgie loaded her plate with food. "I turn up the tunes and watch the wind in the trees and the horses while I wash."

"It's not a bad view," Mac conceded. "Although I'd appreciate you taking more notice of the sheep."

Hannah glanced around the kitchen-dining area. The cabinetry was old, but freshly painted; however, the appliances were new, including an expensive-looking coffee machine. An aerial photo that she assumed was of the farm hung on one wall. On another was a triptych of wildflowers. The first photo depicted a vivid carpet of yellow, red, orange and pink strawflowers, with an oddly shaped tree in the distance that Georgie had pointed out earlier as where all three Downie kids had broken their arms. The second photo narrowed the focus to a closer view of six flowers, all different colors; and the third was a close-up of a pink flower unfurling from its tight bud with a bee hovering over its bright yellow center.

Hung above the boarded-up fireplace was an abstract acrylic painting of red earth, yellow, brown and white boulders, and scraggly gum trees with their long and pointed narrow leaves—quintessentially the Wheatbelt.

Below it, on the mantelpiece, rested two photos. The first was of Georgie and Mac, and a man she assumed was their brother, standing next to older versions of themselves. The second was of Mac with his arm around the waist of a woman wearing a pilot's uniform—Chelsea.

"So this is your cottage?" Hannah asked Mac.

"Yeah. I moved out of the homestead after uni."

"It's the perk for the first child to express an interest in taking over the farm," Georgie said.

Mac rolled his eyes. "You and Dan didn't want to farm." He looked back at Hannah. "Georgie's been offered a cottage when she finishes uni."

"It's eight kays away," Georgie told Hannah in a tone that implied it was eight hundred kays.

"A perfect distance to save the contents of our fridges," Mac teased.

"Just wait," Georgie said. "When I'm rich and famous, I'll build my own place down by the stables with a view over the creek."

"Good." Mac pointed his knife towards the painting. "And I'll sell that and make a killing."

Hannah turned to Georgie, stunned. "You painted that?"

Georgie nodded. "The photos are Mac's."

Hannah thought the photos were pretty, but the painting was something else. "Do you have a gallery contact in Perth?"

For the first time since Hannah had met her, Georgie's keen enthusiasm for life seemed to falter. "No, I'm not good enough. My tutor says there's more things wrong with it than right. Mac took pity on me and hung it here."

"Bullshit," Mac said.

"I'm with Mac," Hannah said. "Has the tutor ever left Perth and stood on this land?"

Georgie shrugged. "No idea, but carded wool is cheaper than paints and canvas. Anyway, people think less about spending under a hundred dollars than over. I've sold six of my fiber-art horses since they went up on the Just Because website and Freya thinks—ouch!"

Mac was shaking his head at Georgie and her face flushed pink. "Sorry, Hannah."

"No," Hannah said quickly, thinking about Georgie's kindness today and not wanting her to experience any discomfort. "It's my friendship with Freya that's broken. It doesn't mean you can't mention your business arrangement with her. Just make sure you have things in writing and don't assume she'll always support you."

"Mac made sure I nailed down the commission," Georgie said. "And Freya's always paid me on time."

"Freya's good at business," Hannah said. "It's friendship she sucks at."

Daisy whined at the door.

"Do you need to get back to Garringarup or do you have time for a tour of the farm?" Mac asked.

Horse-riding was one thing. Listening to dry facts and figures about sheep and wheat was another thing entirely. "As great as that sounds, I have to get back."

Mac nodded. "Another time then."

Hannah filled her mouth with food so she didn't have to commit.

"But you'll come out for another lesson?" Georgie asked, her enthusiasm returning. "I've only got a few weeks before I'm back at uni, but if you can manage twice a week I'll have you cantering by then."

"Look out," Mac said. "She'll be signing you up to pony club next."

Georgie grinned. "That's a great idea!"

Hannah laughed.

At first she didn't recognize the sound, but then a memory stirred. She was in Kings Park with Jamie, their heads thrown back, their bodies shaking as the noise of their laughter mixed together and rained over them infused with joy and happiness.

Jamie would never laugh again.

Guilt slammed into her. The overwhelming need to be back home and surrounded by his things followed.

Somehow she managed to make her thanks, say her goodbyes and get to her car. She cried every moment of the forty-five-minute drive home.

CHAPTER THIRTY-THREE

"Sold to number twenty-two!"

Freya smiled at the auctioneer, thrilled she'd made the winning bid. She'd driven to York Auctions hoping to discover something Ryan could renovate into a display case for the store, and the old meat safe was perfect.

While the auction-house workers loaded it into the ute, she crossed the road for a coffee. She'd just finished ordering when she heard someone call her name. She turned and her stomach dropped.

"I thought it was you!" Monique was smiling and holding a toddler on her hip.

"Monique. Hi." Freya's brain was playing catch-up. The last time she'd seen her was at the funeral, and prior to that? Not since she'd left Garringarup. "This is a bit random."

"Not really," Monique said with her usual decisiveness. "Anywhere in the Wheatbelt is local."

Old memories rose—Freya had always felt wrong-footed around this woman. She changed the topic by inclining her head towards the child. "Is this Will?"

At the mention of his name the curly-haired boy buried his face in

Monique's shoulder. "It is." Monique sounded surprised that Freya had remembered.

Will suddenly lurched sideways, reaching for his cupcake. Monique laughed and sat him in the highchair before turning and indicating a spare chair. "Please join us while you wait."

Caught off guard by the unexpected invitation, Freya found herself sitting.

Monique made general chitchat about the weather—after the intense summer heat her husband, David, was sweating on an early autumn break; Just Because—Freya should investigate the line of organic cotton children's clothing her friend had designed as possible stock: "so very cute"; and the challenges of not losing herself under the demands of motherhood and the farm.

Monique took a sip of her coffee, then looked straight at her. "How's Ryan coping without Jamie?"

Freya had nodded her way through most of Monique's comments, but she couldn't avoid answering a direct question. "Oh, you know. A bit lost."

"I can imagine. I mean, they were inseparable." Monique leaned forward, her tone conspiratorial. "There were times I was jealous."

This surprised Freya. "Of Ryan?"

"Yes. Weren't you?" Monique must have read her confused face. "Jealous of Jamie, I mean?"

Freya had no idea what to say to that. Of all the complex emotions she'd had around Jamie, being jealous of his friendship with Ryan wasn't one of them.

"Ryan and I have never lived in each other's pockets," she said.

"Oh, that's right. You like to think you're an evolved couple."

Freya bristled but she couldn't find a way of replying without sounding defensive. Thankfully the waitress had arrived with her drink, so she took a sip and let the comment slide.

As Monique gave Will the second half of his cupcake she said, "How's his fiancée? Hannah, right?"

"I'm not sure."

Monique raised a perfectly shaped brow. "I thought you and Ryan would have circled her in friendship."

The barb stung. "We welcomed you too." *Until you left and everything went to hell.*

Monique's mouth flattened momentarily as if she disagreed. "Is she selling Jamie's house and going back to Perth?"

"It's her house now."

"I suppose it is. So ...?"

"I'm not sure of her plans."

Perhaps Monique heard something in her tone or read more into the pressure of Freya's hands on the mug because she said, "What did you fall out over?"

Freya really didn't want to revisit the story. "It's not important."

"That's a lie. You read her words for Jamie at the funeral so you were obviously close." Monique studied her. "Did Lydia get in her ear?"

Freya saw the determined look in Monique's eye and knew from experience that she wouldn't stop questioning her until she caved. And did it matter if Freya told her? To be honest, she was surprised the news hadn't already reached Monique through the Wheatbelt grapevine.

"Hannah wants Jamie's baby."

Monique's eyes widened and she seemed momentarily lost for words. "How? I mean ... Were they on IVF when he died?"

"No. And that's the problem. Jamie didn't leave any written instructions about wanting children."

"Who does?"

"Right? And because there were no specific written instructions, people close to Jamie were asked to sign affidavits stating he wanted children."

Monique leaned forward. "And?"

"And I never heard him say he wanted children so I told Hannah I couldn't sign."

A look of understanding crossed Monique's face. "I can't imagine that went down well."

Freya shuddered. "That's the understatement of the year. Lydia came into the shop and screamed at me."

Monique gave an ironic smile. "Welcome to the club."

Freya laughed, then sobered as she remembered Lydia's vitriol towards Monique at the funeral. "I don't know why I'm laughing. Sorry. Anyway, I can live without Lydia's good opinion, but I miss Hannah."

"No important choice is ever easy." Monique fiddled with her teaspoon. "Our decisions come with gains and losses, but ultimately we have to be able to sleep at night. Good for you sticking to your guns."

Freya blinked, stunned at the unexpected support. "Thank you. I think you're the only person to express that sentiment."

Monique shrugged and Freya expected her to say something more, but Will was squawking, tired of the highchair. Monique lifted him free and they both stood and walked to the door.

"It was good to see you, Monique," Freya said, surprising herself with the sentiment.

"You too." Monique laughed.

"What?"

"I don't think that's something either of us ever expected to say to each other."

Freya smiled. "You're right, but I'm glad we got here. Take care, Monique." She walked away feeling lighter.

On her way to a community council meeting about upgrades to the main street, Freya dropped in to check on her mother. She was loading the freezer with meals when Vivian asked about Ryan.

"He's good," Freya said. "He's doing an awesome job on the old meat safe."

He was also honoring his promise to give her space about getting pregnant, and by default that seemed to include wedding plans as he hadn't raised them either. Thankfully, his parents had also gone quiet on that front.

Most importantly, after the months of ups and downs since the accident, things between them were back to normal and they were enjoying the delights of shared interests, long talks and companionable silences. They'd even had a weekend away glamping and indulged in some naked moonlight swims—bliss.

"So I gather you're not pregnant yet?"

Vivian's words hit Freya like a sledgehammer. "Mum! We had a deal, remember?"

Vivian shrugged as if the Christmas pact was irrelevant, and Freya decided to draw a line under the topic once and for all.

"Actually, we're taking a break until we're both sure it's what we really want. If anything changes I'll let you know."

Her mother was uncharacteristically quiet after that, but as Freya was leaving, she hugged her with unfamiliar tightness. "Darling, if you don't have a child, who's going to look after you when you're old like me?"

"Mia," Freya said lightly, trying to ignore the ratcheting tension in her chest.

"Mia will have her hands full looking after Lexie," Vivian said.

All semblance of calm fled. "First of all, sixty-nine isn't old. Second of all, you can't be serious about me having a child so there's someone to look after me in my old age. A thousand things can happen between now and then. They may hate me!"

Vivian rolled her eyes. "They won't hate you."

"Fine, but there's no guarantee we'd even be living in the same town. Even if we were, is Lexie looking after you?"

"Your sister's got a full plate," Vivian said tightly.

Freya stared doggedly at her mother—not just because her own plate was full to overflowing, but because the statement glossed over the day-to-day issues with Lexie and ignored the big ones. Like Vivian had done ever since their father had died.

When Vivian's gaze slid away, guilt slapped her. "Sorry, Mum."

"You need to understand that children give you far more than they take—"

"I'm late, Mum. I have to go."

As Freya slipped into the community meeting, she was relieved to see an artist's impression of a play space projected onto the wall. Great! She hadn't missed the discussion about how the upgrade works on Main Street would impact on the traders.

Peter Jessop was outlining the park plan, and by the time he'd emphasized that the town council had "consulted widely," murmurs were whipping around the room like embers from a wildfire. While Freya half-listened to the criticisms and complaints, she studied the plans and waited for someone to point out the obvious. When discussion slowed and no one had mentioned it, she decided to raise it.

"Is it really necessary to move the toilet block? It means we lose one of our few significant trees."

"Spoken by someone who doesn't have kids."

Freya looked along the line of chairs and realized the woman who'd spoken was Ainsley, a pre-school mother she'd met once when she'd been picking up Mia. The woman's words infuriated her. Why did not having kids mean she could never have an opinion on anything connected to children? And worse than that, what if she was a woman who did want kids, was still grieving her miscarriage and trying to get pregnant? Or going to massive lengths to conceive, like Hannah? The words "doesn't have kids" would burn into those women's souls.

"Actually, they're spoken by someone who regularly takes her niece to the park," she said firmly.

"Hah! Try taking *three* kids and supervising them when one needs to pee and the toilets are at the opposite side of the park," Ainsley retorted.

Freya pointed to the projected image, indicating the eastern end of the playground. "The toilets could be built there *and* save the tree."

"Access to the sewer at the eastern end isn't possible," Peter said. "And as you can see, five trees will be planted to ameliorate the loss of one."

"Yes, but that tree's got twenty-five—"

"Even if the sewer wasn't the issue, that's too far from the parking area," Ainsley said, her shoulders rolling back with the joy of a win. "You'd know that if you unloaded kids and strollers and bikes and scooters every second day. Come spend an hour with me and learn what being a mother's all about."

Freya suppressed the urge to give Ainsley the bird. She would have left the meeting, except she really needed to know how many weeks the parking on the main street was going to be unavailable as part of the "beautification" works.

As it turned out, the construction of new garden beds, seating and sculptures that would weave the length of the main street as part of a green wedge to connect the historic precinct to the river would take at least three months. Freya knew "at least" meant longer, and that dust and disruption would be part of the business-owners' lives for all that time and impact on foot trade. Thank goodness Just Because had a well-established online presence—the locals may need to use it too.

After the meeting, Freya checked her phone to see a message from Ryan. *Been called out.* No need to rush home then.

She hadn't seen much of Lexie lately other than a quick "hi" and "bye" when she dropped Mia off. Lexie was always too excited about a night out to stay for a chat, and too subdued the morning after with a hangover and ringed in "don't talk to me" vibes. Perhaps tonight was a good opportunity for them to hang out together on the sofa and have a real conversation about Vivian? Freya needed to get a re-commitment from Lexie to stick to her agreed plan to help. So far, instead of visiting Vivian as promised, Lexie had asked Freya to babysit so she could go to farewell drinks for a work colleague.

Freya texted her sister. *Up for some company?*

The reply was swift. *Sure. Bring wine*

Freya arrived at the house five minutes later and was taken aback to see that Mia was still up and dressed in her day clothes.

"Auntie Frey!" The little girl threw herself at Freya's legs, almost knocking her off balance. "Come and play!"

"Okay, let me get through the door."

At least it made a change from "I want to sleep at your house!," which Mia requested with increasing frequency. Last Sunday after a bike ride with Ryan, she'd thrown a tantrum when he'd said it was time to go home.

"Follow me," Mia squealed and ran out of the room.

Lexie sat at the table in her work uniform, shoulders slumped, looking bone-weary. Scattered plates displayed the remains of dinner—possibly baked beans on toast. Mia loved "brinner," as did all the Quayle women—it was the ultimate comfort food.

"Hi!" Freya shot for upbeat. "Did Mia go to a birthday party today?"

"No, why?"

"She's pretty wired."

Lexie sighed. "That's normal. I think she's hyperactive."

"She's not hyperactive. She's probably just tired."

"You saying I don't know my own child?"

Freya almost said "I know my niece," but the bite in Lexie's voice on top of Ainsley's comments at the meeting cautioned her.

She blew out a long breath. "How about I run Mia through the bath and get her into bed and you clean up here? Then we can both relax on the sofa."

Lexie instantly brightened. "You brought wine?" When Freya shook her head, Lexie grabbed her phone and keys. "I'll just nick down to the bottle-o."

"We can have a cup of tea," Freya said, but she was talking to a closed door.

Mia lurched between cute and difficult, splashing Freya with water and insisting she wasn't tired *at all* despite talking around ginormous yawns.

Amid the chaos of Mia's room—toys were strewn everywhere—Freya found Monkey, Clownie and Bear. She and Ryan had learned the hard way that all three were required if Mia was to fall asleep.

Freya selected a book from the shelf. "Come on, into bed. The toys are waiting for a story."

"Where's Mummy? I want Mummy to read me a story!" Mia wailed, barely able to keep her eyes open.

Freya strained to hear the clink of dishes. She didn't want to interrupt Lexie—she knew how frustrating it was being interrupted mid-job with a request for a new one. *See, Ainsley, I don't need kids to know all about that!*

"Mummy's finishing a job," she said.

Mia's hand grabbed Freya's, the touch unexpectedly fierce. "Mummy's gone. You stay."

"Sweetie pie, Mummy's not at work. It's not that kind of a job," Freya reassured her. "How about I read you a story, then Mummy can? That way you get two stories."

Mia took her time absorbing the information, her eyes flicking between Freya and the door. "Mummy's here?"

"Yes. She's in the kitchen, washing dishes. Come on, in you get." Freya tucked Mia and the toys under the monkey-patterned bedsheets she'd bought her for Christmas.

She was only halfway through *Imagine* when Mia finally gave in to the over-exhaustion that had run her ragged. Freya closed Mia's bedroom door and returned to the kitchen. The mess remained untouched and there was no sign of Lexie.

Not wanting to call out and wake Mia, Freya checked the living room, Lexie's bedroom and the bathroom, even though she'd just walked past it and scooped up the wet towels. Now she opened the laundry door, dumped the towels in the laundry basket and stepped back into the kitchen, having gone full circle.

She pulled out her phone. *Hi, Mia's asleep. Where are you?*

Got delayed. On way

Delayed? Freya knew all about ducking into a store, running into someone and losing ten minutes, but the drive-through bottle-o wasn't like that. Even if Lexie knew the attendant, there was no way people behind her in the queue would tolerate a long conversation.

All Freya wanted to do was kick back on the sofa, but leaving a table covered with dirty cups and plates was beyond her.

Go sit in the living room where you can't see it.

But there was mess in the living room too, and clearing the table was an easier prospect. She rinsed the plates and loaded the dishwasher, but she drew the line at washing up the sundry items by the sink.

Your sister's got a full plate.

Freya swore. "Okay, Mum, I get it." She donned gloves, kept an eye on the back door and washed the remaining dishes.

She made tea and let it brew. By the time she'd put milk in her mug, the small ball of anxiety that had been turning since she'd discovered Lexie wasn't home had gained the speed of a spinning top.

"This is nuts." She called Lexie. The phone rang out. "Where the hell are you?"

She reminded herself that it was a two-minute drive from the house to the bottle-o. If Lexie had been in a bad accident Freya would have heard the sirens. If Lexie was involved in a minor accident, even one that needed a tow-truck, Brett would have called Greg Eccles and dropped Lexie home. Or if Brett thought she needed medical treatment, the hospital would have rung by now.

Freya called the pub. "Hey, Stuart, it's Freya. Is Lexie there?"

"Hang on, Freya." The sound of the receiver clattering onto the bar reverberated in her ear, followed by music, the hum of conversation and the occasional bark of laughter. "You still there, Freya?"

"Yep."

"I checked the bistro and the lounge, so unless she's in the ladies, she's not here. If I see her, I'll ask her to call you, yeah?"

"Thanks, Stuart."

She hung up and drummed her fingers. It was now almost an hour since Lexie had left the house. Had she popped in to see Vivian? It was unlikely, and Freya didn't want to worry their mother by asking if Lexie was with her.

She wanted to go out and look for her sister, but she couldn't leave Mia. Anyway, outside of the pub and the hospital, she had no idea where to start.

She called the hospital.

"You know I can't say who's here," the urgent care nurse said, "but Lexie isn't. And the bat-phone hasn't rung, so chill, Freya. There's no need to panic."

Freya wasn't reassured and she did something she'd never done before—she called Ryan at work.

The phone rang five times before he picked up. "Frey? You okay?" His concern rode down the line.

"I'm fine, but I'm worried about Lexie. I'm at her place and she popped out for five minutes. That was almost an hour ago and she's not answering her phone. I've called the pub and the hospital but she's not there either."

Freya heard the beeping of a machine and Ryan murmuring something that sounded like, "Sorry, mate, I need you to move your arm this way."

"Ryan?"

"What?"

"Did you hear what I said?"

An exasperated breath huffed into her ear. "I'm busy, Frey. I only picked up because I thought you calling meant something bad had happened. Lexie skiving off doesn't qualify."

"But this is out of character!"

She heard his muffled voice saying, "Take some long sucks on the green whistle," before full volume returned. "I have to go. I'll talk to you when I get home."

The rapid disconnection beeps filled her ear. She stared at the phone, working on quelling the rafts of annoyance running up and down her spine. She wanted to give in to the indulgence of being cross with Ryan's short response, but he had a point. He was busy saving lives and her sister was probably fine, and yet ...

God, sometimes it was exhausting trying to be fair-minded. She stomped into the living room and, ignoring the urge to pick up the chaos of toys and sort the basket of clean laundry, lay on the sofa.

CHAPTER THIRTY-FOUR

FREYA HAD no idea how long she'd been asleep when a crashing sound jerked her awake. Heart pounding, it took her a second to work out where she was.

"Hello?" she called, then instantly berated herself. Had she just greeted a burglar?

She heard another thump and glanced around the room for something that would double as a weapon. The plastic ice castle had pointy edges.

As she reached for it she heard giggling and then Lexie staggered in holding one shoe.

Freya sank back onto the sofa. "God, you gave me a hell of a fright."

Lexie fell onto the sofa. "Soz."

Freya checked her phone. "Shit, Lexie! It's midnight."

"Shhh!" Lexie growled. "Don't wake Mia."

The words fell like a spark on dry grass. "You don't get to play the mother card when you disappear on me for hours!"

"Don't have a menty b."

Fury burned through her. "Where have you been?"

Lexie grinned. "Out."

"Obviously. Where?"

Lexie leaned forward and tried tapping her nose, but her lack of coordination meant she bumped her chin. "Top secret. You wouldn't approve, oh judgy one."

You got that right. Except Freya didn't disapprove of Lexie enjoying herself, just the way she'd gone about it. "Let's get you into bed."

Lexie giggled. "Already done that."

Freya took a deep breath so she didn't say, "Who with?" or "Please tell me you weren't so drunk you didn't use protection?" Instead she tried steering Lexie towards the bathroom. That's when she realized her sister reeked of alcohol and the sickly-sweet smell of weed.

Oh, Lexie. Even though she knew her sister was responsible for her own behavior, Freya got an overwhelming urge to track down Kane and punch him in the face.

She helped Lexie wash and, with a great deal of cajoling, managed to get her to drink some water. Leaving the water bottle by the bed, she tucked Lexie in like she'd done for Mia, then she texted Ryan. *Hi, Lexie needs me here tonight. Wanna come for a sleepover too? Fx*

Sorry, gorgeous. In Perth after transfer. Home after breakfast. Luv ya xx

Freya borrowed some pajamas, hauled fresh sheets out of the linen closet and made up the spare bed.

She woke again to Mia sitting on her.

"I'm hungry." Mia didn't seem to think it at all unusual that Freya was sleeping in the spare room.

"Is Mummy up?"

Mia shook her head and said with all the resignation of a world-weary four-year-old, "She sleepy. She always sleepy."

Freya checked her phone: 7:45. Lexie was due at work in forty-five minutes. She couldn't believe that Mia had slept so late—normally she was a natural alarm clock. Then again, she'd been beyond tired last night. Freya was glad Mia had enjoyed a solid catch-up sleep, because Lexie wouldn't be up to coping with the hair-trigger emotions of a weary child this morning.

"Okay, kiddo, time for breakfast."

She set Mia up with cereal and juice before entering Lexie's room. Her sister was tangled in the bedsheets as if she'd had a restless night.

"Lex?" When she didn't stir, Freya opened the curtains.

Lexie swore and pulled the sheet over her head. "What are you doing here? Go away."

"What do you mean what am I doing here? I slept here."

"Why?"

Freya laughed then didn't know why. "I wanted to make sure you were okay." *And be here if Mia needed anything.* "I've made coffee. Do you want it before or after your shower?"

Lexie pressed her hands to her head. "Let me sleep."

"It's almost 8:00. If I take Mia to childcare, you'll still get to work on time."

Lexie made a sound that was half-groan and half-sob. "I can't."

"Sure you can," Freya said, reminded of when Lexie was thirteen and going through a school refusal phase. "After a shower, coffee and some paracetamol you'll be a new woman." Lexie stayed silent. "Start by sitting up slowly."

Lexie half-rose from the pillow and fell back. "I'm gonna throw up."

Freya grabbed the bucket she'd left by the bed and gave it to her.

Lexie hugged it. "Ring work for me. Please."

Freya took in Lexie's pallor and conceded defeat. "Okay but drink some water."

"Mummy!" Mia jumped onto the bed and threw herself on Lexie. "Get up, sleepyhead."

Lexie vomited.

After cleaning up the mess, giving Lexie painkillers and leaving her to sleep, Freya got Mia ready for day care and drove her to the center. She kissed her goodbye and explained that she'd be picking her up "because Mummy's sick." That's when she remembered she was supposed to have called the hospital.

Back in the car she made the call and was put through to Lexie's supervisor. "Hi, Natalie, it's Freya Quayle. Lexie's woken up with a stomach bug so she won't be in today. Sorry for the late notice."

Freya anticipated a "Sorry to hear that, hope she feels better soon," but all she heard was silence. "Natalie? Are you there?"

"Yes, I'm here. Tell Lexie she'll need a sick certificate."

"For one day off?"

"She's long out of single sick days."

"Really?" Although Lexi often asked Freya to babysit so she could go out, she'd never asked for help because she was sick.

Natalie sighed. "Look, I probably shouldn't say anything but you're her sister. She's missed a lot of days and sometimes she turns up looking really rough. Her work performance is less than average."

Freya knew Lexie had been partying hard but she'd thought it was limited to the weekends. There'd been that one time after their mother's second operation when she'd asked Freya to mind Mia midweek, but Natalie was implying there'd been many more occasions. Who'd been minding Mia then?

Natalie was still speaking. "When I've suggested she talk to someone, she insists she's fine. She's not. We're worried about her."

"How long have you been worried about her?"

"A while."

What did that mean? Freya tried to get a sense of the period. Lexie had hated being forced back to work when Kane left. "From when she started?"

"No, she started off okay." Freya heard the sound of fingers tapping on a keyboard. "But the last few months have been bad. She's missed so much work since Christmas she's received a final warning."

The call left Freya reeling. The last thing Lexie needed was to lose her job. And if she was missing work, it meant nights like last night had happened before.

She always sleepy. Freya's stomach dropped. She'd assumed that Lexie only drank when she was out, but were the guileless words of a four-year-old telling a different story? Was Lexie writing herself off at home during the week?

A horrifying thought tightened her chest. *Mummy's gone. You stay.*

She immediately told herself not to jump to conclusions. Lexie would never leave Mia home alone. Never. If Lexie wanted to go out she would have asked Freya to mind her.

Oh, judgy one. Guilt skewered her. Okay, perhaps not midweek. Especially not after the time she'd tried to limit Lexie's drinking by insisting she'd only mind Mia if Lexie was home by 11:00 o'clock.

But Lexie would ask someone else to mind Mia. Vivian? Not lately.

One of her friends from work or one of the mothers from netball? Not if she was coming home in the state she was in last night.

Surely when Mia had said "Mummy's gone," she meant gone as in sacked out asleep in bed.

She's four! Gone means physically absent.

Suddenly the increase in Mia's requests to sleep over at Kitchener Street and her tantrums about going home took on a very different meaning.

Freya raised her hands over her ears as if that was all it took to silence her fear that Lexie's drinking had spiraled to the point of putting her beloved daughter at risk. Then her stomach cramped so violently she doubled over.

Impotence was more terrifying than taking action. She picked up her phone.

"Georgie, I know you're getting ready to move back to Perth for uni, but any chance you can run Just Because for me today?"

With the store organized, she called Ryan.

Freya used the work-required sick certificate as an excuse to get Lexie to the doctor and Leah took her straight into the treatment room. Freya felt queasy as she and Ryan sat with Lexie while the intravenous ran—she was betraying her sister and, in a way, her mother.

Half an hour later, a considerably less glassy-eyed Lexie was anxious to go home. "Thanks, Leah. I feel heaps better. If you give me the sick certificate, I'll get out of your hair."

"Do you want to talk about last night?" Leah asked.

Lexie shrugged. "Nothing to talk about. Who hasn't been dumb enough to have a few too many?"

Leah's face stayed impassive. "I think the issue is more that you left home without telling Freya where you were going."

Lexie shot Freya a killing look. "Last time I checked she wasn't my mother."

"But in the past you would have told me," Freya said.

Lexie gave a self-deprecating shrug. "Look, we all agree that last night was a mistake. But onwards and upwards, right?"

"Would you say you're drinking more than you did a year ago?" Leah asked.

"No."

"Freya says there are fourteen bottles of wine in your recycling bin. That's more than one bottle a night, which is—"

"Fuck you, Freya!" Lexie lurched to her feet and stormed out of the room.

Freya rose to follow, but Ryan said, "I'll go. You talk to Leah."

"I'm sorry," Freya told the doctor. "She's not herself."

Leah shrugged as if she'd seen far worse behavior. "There are two key concerns. Lexie's mental health and Mia's safety."

"Lexie wouldn't have left her alone." The words had become Freya's mantra—her life raft in the middle of this crisis.

"Addiction is an illness, Freya. It changes behavior so even though none of us wants it to be true, it needs investigating."

"I must have misunderstood Mia." *Please let me have got it wrong.*

"It's possible. Mia's age means we can misconstrue what she's saying or not actually understand it. And she could interpret the question 'Has Mummy ever left you alone at home?' as being alone in her room, or the back garden while Lexie was in the house. And the question is muddied by the fact that when she's at childcare or with you, Lexie has technically left her. We'll talk to the childcare workers and see if they have any concerns, but to be honest, the fact you have them is enough."

. . .

When Freya walked into the house, Lexie raged at her. "How dare you tell Leah I have a drinking problem!"

"You said you were going out for ten minutes and you disappeared for four hours!"

"I came home," Lexie said sulkily.

"That doesn't make up for all the worry and the fact you abandoned Mia."

"Oh, come on! I didn't abandon Mia. I left her with you," Lexie said. "Despite what you think, I'm entitled to let my hair down now and then."

"But that's the thing, Lexie. According to Natalie, it's been far more now than then."

Lexie's eyes bulged with fury. "Oh my God! First you snitch on me to Leah and now you've talked to my boss about me? Thanks for nothing!"

"You asked me to phone in sick for you!"

Freya's head threatened to explode from Lexie's failure to see there was anything wrong with her behavior. She looked to Ryan for support.

"Lexie, there's letting your hair down and there's craving something so badly you lie to get it," Ryan said. "Last night you lied to Freya to get it."

"Aww, look at the two of you all loved up and nauseatingly happy." Lexie hurled the words at them as if their last six months had been heaven on a stick. "What the hell do you know about my life?"

"We know enough to be worried," Freya said, her heart thumping. "We know you've been drinking heavily for months and now I'm stressing about drugs. Last night you came home reeking of weed."

"Did it ever occur to you that I was in a room where it was being smoked but I didn't join in? No, of course it didn't. I'm a single mother working fulltime. You don't have the right to stand here and judge me."

Doubt crept in. Was Freya being unfair? It was true that she'd never really understood her younger sister, who'd flitted from job to job, chasing adventures rather than pursuing a career. Back then Freya had put it down to Lexie being young and grabbing life by the throat, and who didn't want to do that? But even then Lexie's party lifestyle had bothered her and she'd despaired that her sister would never grow up. She'd even expressed the thought to their mother, who'd rolled her eyes and said, "Just because you and your father knew what you wanted to do with your lives from an early age doesn't mean we all do."

"You went straight into accounting," Freya had reminded her.

"She'll settle down," Vivian had said with infuriating insouciance.

And Vivian had been right. Once Mia had arrived, the wild child in Lexie was replaced by an earth mother—the polar opposite of how she'd lived her life up to that point. She'd embraced motherhood in its entirety, even the bits many women found mind-numbingly boring. She'd loved nothing more than being a stay-at-home mum.

When Kane walked out, Freya had held her breath, worried that Lexie would fall apart. But her sister had surprised her with her determination to show Kane she didn't need him and had impressed her by stepping up to the responsibility of meeting the mortgage.

However, the woman standing in front of Freya now closely resembled the teen and early twenties thrill seeker. The one who'd always lost interest in a project when a newer, shinier one tempted her. Even so, was Lexie right? Was Freya letting the past cloud her judgment?

Hesitating, she looked at Ryan, who was shaking his head and mouthing the word "facts." Freya nodded and took a deep breath.

"This is what I know. Last night you lied about going out. When you got home you could barely stand and this morning you couldn't remember why I was in the house. You threw up, you couldn't get out of bed and you asked me to call work. When I spoke to Natalie, she told me she's worried about you, that you've missed too many days, your concentration's poor and you're close to losing your job. Mia's not hyperactive, Lexie. She's anxious and acting out because—like me—she doesn't understand what's going on."

Freya indicated the unkempt house. "This isn't you either. Since you bought this place you've always been so houseproud. I'm really sorry you're struggling, I truly am, but writing yourself off isn't going to bring Kane back—"

"I don't want that bastard back!"

The vitriol slammed into Freya like a brick to the chest.

"If you got a phone call from Natalie right now saying you're sacked, what does it mean to you in real terms?" Ryan said.

Lexie scoffed. "They're not going to fire me."

"That sounds like magical thinking. Unless you stop pulling stunts like last night, you will lose your job," Ryan said calmly.

"You bastard! I thought you were supposed to be the kind and caring one!" Lexie stomped into the kitchen and pulled open cabinets, her hands frantically searching the contents.

"If you're looking for the bottle of Jack, I've borrowed it," Freya said.

Lexie whirled around. "You can't do that! It's my property. God, next you'll be giving me shit about my credit-card bill."

Freya could pay an outstanding credit-card bill, but something about the pallor of Lexie's face told her it was more than that.

"Lexie? Are you in financial trouble?"

Her sister's chin jerked up. "You'd love that, wouldn't you?"

"What? No. Of course not. I just want—"

"Could you make us a cuppa, Lexie?" Ryan didn't wait for an answer but ushered Freya outside.

"This is classic addict behavior," he said quietly. "She's feeling cornered so she's lashing out because we're threatening the one thing she's come to depend on to block out her pain. I know it's hard not to take it personally, but if you follow her down this emotional rabbit hole she's determined to suck you into, you're the one who's going to get hurt."

Addict behavior. The horrifying awfulness of the words pierced the numbness that had settled over her since her phone call with Natalie.

"She's my sister, Ryan. I love her. I just want to help her. Maybe I've overreacted. Maybe it's just booze, not drugs, and—"

"Just booze?" He wrapped his arms around her. "It might be legal, but for some it's an addictive drug. You've been worried about her for weeks and now you have backup evidence from Natalie. Lexie's sick, Frey. This has gone way beyond you giving her a cash advance and some extra childminding."

"That's why she needs to see a counselor, but you've heard her—I'm the problem! It's like she's a teen again." Tears fell and she dropped her head onto his shoulder. "If she had something like diabetes or cancer she wouldn't question she was sick. I'm scared, Ryan. What's it going to take for her to accept help?"

Freya heard a car pull up. She raised her head and saw Brett get out with a woman she didn't recognize.

Ryan swore. "I think forced help just arrived."

CHAPTER THIRTY-FIVE

HANNAH WAS on her third video call with Ashley, the IVF counselor. She could hardly believe she'd reached this point and was still pinching herself. Two weeks earlier, after two shifted hearings, Rowan had finally called with the news that the Queensland Supreme Court had granted approval for her to undertake fertility treatment using Jamie's sperm. She'd immediately called the clinic for a preliminary appointment, which had turned into a detailed rundown on fees. On top of the legal fees there were treatment costs, flights and accommodation—it was eye-watering.

When she told the McMasters, Lydia had brushed off her concerns. "We've been through all this, Hannah. Let us worry about money, and when I say worry there's nothing to worry about. Your job's to focus on the baby."

A baby. Hannah hugged herself, fizzing with joy. Their child was worth all the money, all the legal hassles and the fractured friendship with Freya. An unwanted tug of regret pulled on her and she batted it away. What sort of a friend wouldn't support her decision to have Jamie's child? No friend at all, so really she hadn't lost anything.

"Hannah, have you received the hormones?" Ashley asked.

"Yes. They're in the fridge."

The clinic was being amazing, allowing video consultations with all of the team and working with Leah to arrange the blood tests and ultrasounds and supervise the hormone injections. This meant Hannah only had to go to Queensland a couple of days before the egg pick-up, saving on accommodation. Although she was tempted to stay for two weeks after the embryo transfer and laze on the beach to give the baby every chance to nestle in tight and deep. But despite her mindfulness app telling her that all thoughts were transitory and to let them float past in the moment, there was one that refused to budge: *It may take more than one implantation.*

"You must call us the day your period starts," Ashley said. "You do understand how important that is?"

"I do." There was still no sign of her period and that was another worry. "Hopefully it's soon."

Ashley's smile held restraint. "IVF's a marathon. Best to take it one day at a time."

The call ended, leaving Hannah unsettled rather than excited. She was glad she had her final riding lesson—a ride would settle her mind.

As she drove through the gates of Baile Na, she noticed the paddocks were freshly plowed in anticipation of some sort of crop. If Mac had mentioned the type in any of their passing conversations after a riding lesson it hadn't stuck.

Hannah's visits to the property were always a guilty mix of pleasure and sadness. Riding gave her so much joy—a way of leaving behind all the stress—but guilt struck when she realized she was living moments of happiness without Jamie.

Over the last few weeks she'd met the senior Downies, who'd welcomed her warmly and easily into their home. Mac had been correct—his mother's crepes were a definite culinary experience. Hannah loved watching the way the Downies interacted—some teasing, some praise, some thoughtful suggestions. At times it made her miss her parents and Declan in ways she'd never experienced with the McMasters.

And Mac's quiet understanding of her grief was a balm, but no matter how hard she tried to hold onto his words—"don't let death steal two lives"—she often left the farm gutted by sadness. The emotional rollercoaster was exhausting and, in a way, it was a relief that Georgie's return to university was bringing Hannah's visits to a natural end.

She released Ozzie from the car and he bounded around in exuberant circles, sniffing all the wondrous smells of dogs, sheep, mice, rabbits and probably foxes before taking off towards the cottage.

"Ozzie! Come!"

The dog slowed, ears drooping, then turned and stared at her as if to say, "you've got to be kidding me." He slunk back as he did every Wednesday, clearly unhappy that Daisy was out working, but he submitted to being tied up on a long rope in the shade of a peppercorn tree outside the stables.

Hannah headed inside, her eyes slowly adjusting to the dim light. Bullet was in his stall and on hearing her voice he swung his head towards her, anticipating the apple in her pocket.

Hannah was surprised that Georgie wasn't waiting for her. Usually they saddled up together and Georgie double-checked that Hannah had the girth and throatlatch buckled at the correct tension.

Bullet nuzzled Hannah, then enthusiastically bit into the apple resting on her palm. While he chewed, she threw on his saddle blanket and saddle, all the while murmuring to him about Jamie and her IVF plans.

"G'day, Hannah."

Surprised, she spun around to see Mac striding towards her holding a riding helmet. She looked beyond him for Georgie, but all she saw were dust motes spinning in the sunshine.

"Georgie got called into Just Because," Mac said.

"Oh, I thought she'd finished up?"

"Yeah, but Freya's got some personal stuff she needs to deal with."

Despite not wanting to care, concern lanced her. Was Freya dealing with another miscarriage? The last time Hannah had asked Ryan about baby plans he'd changed the subject.

"Is Freya okay?"

Mac shrugged. "I don't know any more than that."

Hannah checked her phone, wondering if she'd missed a text from Georgie cancelling the lesson, but the only message was Freya's Just Because newsletter. She really needed to unsubscribe.

"Georgie didn't want you to miss your last lesson so you've got me instead," Mac said.

"Oh, that's kind, but are you sure you've got the time?"

"I could do with a break from the tractor engine's determination to defeat me." He gave a wry grin. "At least Bix will go when I tell him."

Hannah watched as Mac led the large bay horse from his stall. "Bix as in short for Biscuit?"

"Nah, Bix as in short for Bix Beiderbecke."

"Who?"

Mac feigned horror at her ignorance. "Only one of the most influential jazz soloists of the 1920s and my teenage idol."

She laughed. "Pardon me. I'll try to rectify that gap in my musical lexicon."

"I can send you a playlist."

The seriousness in his voice took her by surprise, but he was giving up his time to supervise her ride so it was only polite to accept. "Um, okay, sure."

She realized that while they'd been talking they'd walked far beyond the mounting block. "Oh, I need to go back."

"Nah, we can do it the old-fashioned way." Mac linked his hands.

"I can't stand on you!"

"You won't be, not really. Put your hand on the pommel then rest your foot on me, and as you pull up I'll give you a boost. Ready? One, two, three."

The next moment she was sitting on Bullet.

As Mac checked her stirrups, he automatically adjusted her foot just as Georgie always did and said, "Heels down."

Apart from Lydia and Ian's kisses hello and goodbye, this friendly tug on her heel was the only other human touch she'd experienced all week.

The warmth of his hand caught the tiny band of exposed skin between the top of her boot and her jeans, and a tingle whooshed through her, tensing her thighs against the saddle. Shocked, she realized she'd pressed forward as well, seeking pressure, as if her body was willing the sensation to last longer. It was the first time she'd experienced anything close to arousal since Jamie had died. As the tingle faded, shame followed.

"That's the way," Mac was saying cheerfully, oblivious to her roiling emotions. "You've got a nice seat."

Heat walloped her and she felt her cheeks flame. She frantically pulled at the reins, turning Bullet so she didn't have to face Mac. She heard him chatting to Bix, his slight grunt as he mounted, and then he and his horse walked past her.

"I thought we could ride the east boundary," he said. "It's pretty at this time of year."

He urged Bix into a trot and Hannah followed them across the paddock, her gaze constantly slipping to rest on Mac's behind rhythmically rising and falling in his saddle. Another wave of traitorous heat burned through her, immediately followed by self-loathing.

She hauled her gaze away, pressed her heels into Bullet's sides and urged him into a canter, thankful that staying on the horse took every ounce of her concentration and left no room for wayward thoughts and unwanted lust. She overtook Mac and didn't stop until she reached a closed gate.

Mac pulled up next to her and leaned down to swing open the gate. "That was fun, but Bullet's not a pony anymore."

Remorse got tangled with her own feelings. "Oh God, I'm sorry. I should have thought. It's just I needed the speed."

"I get that." Mac smiled. "And there's nothing to be sorry about. He enjoyed having his head, but he'll appreciate the recovery time."

They passed through the gate and entered a completely different ecosystem—one filled with trees.

"Oh, this *is* pretty," Hannah said.

"Yeah. Imagine trees like this as far as the eye can see and that's what this land looked like before white settlement. For the last eighty years we've been planting trees, but some of these are the originals."

"How did they survive the great clearance?"

"Family graveyard."

Mac held Bullet's reins so she could dismount. There were a dozen graves, the oldest dating back to 1898.

"Is Chelsea buried here?" she asked.

"Nah. We weren't married."

"Oh, I thought ... when you said your dreams of a family had died with her ..."

He rubbed the back of his neck. "My dreams of a family with Chelsea died. At the time, I couldn't see beyond that."

She understood completely, but the way he'd emphasized "with" made her ask, "And now?"

He glanced at his feet, then gazed off into the distance before swinging his intense blue gaze back to her. "Now, I can picture it with someone else."

The air around her stilled. Her heart thumped so hard she heard it in her ears and she had the crazy urge to take two steps and close the gap between them.

Bullet snorted, thankfully breaking the moment and restoring her sanity.

"Good for you." Determined not to allow any more confusing moments of attraction, she inserted Jamie firmly into the conversation. "I'm all set to start IVF."

"Wow. So it's really happening?" Mac pulled two water bottles from his saddlebag and passed her one.

She accepted it, careful not to touch him. "Well, it will as soon as my—" A wave of embarrassment hit her. For all that Mac was kind and understanding, he wouldn't have signed up to talk about periods and hormone injections.

"Guess it's a bit like AI," he said, meaning artificial insemination.

Oh God, this was worse. She cast around for another topic. "The

McMasters and I are keen to start a memorial trust in Jamie's name. You know, so his memory stays alive."

Mac took a long slug of his water.

She moved her gaze to his left shoulder. "I thought something connected with kids' cricket, but Lydia suggested a sports scholarship. Do you think the Penthurst alumni may embrace a fundraising dinner? Support like that would really kick things off."

Mac's attention was fixed on tightening Bix's girth. When he didn't answer, Hannah repeated her question.

He finally looked up. "I dunno. Maybe. I don't get to many functions."

"What about your brother?"

"He's over east."

"But you could put me in contact with someone on the alumni committee, right?"

A pained look crossed his face and she wondered if Mac's Penthurst experience hadn't been the positive one Jamie had enjoyed.

"I'll make some inquiries and see if I can get you a name," he said.

"Thank you!" She moved to hug him and stopped herself.

"No worries." Except his body language was at odds with the laidback words.

She realized she hadn't seen him this tense since the first time he'd stepped into Just Because. "Is everything okay?"

His mouth tightened and she braced herself for something she sensed was going to be awkward and uncomfortable.

"It's just ... The thing is ... Sorry, Hannah, I need to get back."

She laughed then, flooded by relief that it was only his concern about a shortened ride that was bothering him. "There's no need to apologize. I totally get it. The tractor waits for no man, right?"

She expected a flash of his shy smile, but instead she received a brisk nod before he urged Bix forward and started the ride back.

She followed, feeling as if she'd just missed something important.

. . .

The following afternoon Hannah was doing a guided meditation and focusing on willing her period to come when the doorbell rang. Ozzie barked.

"Sit," she told him. "It's probably Kevin delivering the cleaning products I ordered."

She pulled open the front door and her greeting died on her lips. Instead of burly Kevin, a young woman with dyed jet and purple hair stood on the porch jiggling car keys in her hand. She wore skyscraper heels and a short skin-tight dress with a very low neckline that left little to the imagination. As the cloying combination of smoke and perfume hit Hannah's nostrils she tried not to recoil. At the same time she worked on stalling the judgment that put this woman in a particular socio-economic and educative box far removed from her own life.

"Can I help you?"

The woman blinked, her thicker-than-natural eyelashes beating like moth's wings. "I'm looking for Ray."

Hannah noticed a late-model Ford with a missing hub cap parked across the street. "I think you've got the wrong address."

"This is Monash Street, right?"

"It is." Hannah realized the woman was a lot younger than she'd first thought. "Sorry, I'm Hannah. And you're ...?"

"Tameeka."

"Hi, Tameeka. Who are you looking for again?"

"Ray."

It rang no bells. "Is Ray a Ray or Raylene?"

"Bloke. Six foot. Old."

While Hannah ran through all the tall men she knew over sixty, trying to recall if any were Ray, Tameeka added, "Like nearly forty."

Hannah laughed. "How old are you?"

"Nineteen. Nearly twenty, but."

Making forty old. "I know most of the men in town between thirty and forty and none of them are called Ray."

"I got told he lived here."

"Who told you Ray lived here?"

Tameeka screwed up her face as if answering the question was difficult. "I've come from Perth." She jiggled her keys again. "Can you help me find him? It's really important."

Something about the way she said it reached out to Hannah. "You look like you could do with a cold drink. Why don't you come in and we'll go from there."

Tameeka stepped inside and glanced around. "Nice place. Cute dog."

"Thank you." Hannah walked through to the kitchen. As she pressed a glass under the cold water dispenser she realized Tameeka hadn't followed. "Tameeka?"

When there was no reply she set down the glass and went looking for her. Tameeka was standing in the hall peering at the wall of photos. Her forefinger jabbed at the photo of Jamie and Ryan at the big bash.

"That's him. That's Ray."

"Oh, you mean Ryan?"

Tameeka shrugged. "He likes dressing up."

"Not as much as Jamie. The penguins were his idea. I remem—"

"So is he here?"

Hannah swallowed as grief rose again. "No, Jamie's not here."

Tameeka rolled her eyes. "I meant Ray—Ryan."

"Oh, right. Sorry, yes, Ryan lives in town. Come into the kitchen and I'll write down the address."

Hannah assumed that Tameeka's need to see Ryan was connected with his job. Freya had once told her that after accidents and health emergencies, patients and their relatives often reached out, either wanting to thank him or trying to get answers. Hannah understood all about wanting answers, but she'd never discussed Jamie's accident with Ryan. She didn't want to put either of them through the trauma again.

While Hannah reached for a notepad, the sound of keys landing on wood made her turn. God, she hoped they hadn't scratched the table. She picked them up and realized they all hung off a bright yellow Ferrari keyring—a stark contrast to the battered car parked outside.

"I'll just put these on the counter if you don't mind," she said.

"Whatevs." Tameeka drank the water. "You've got a lot of photos of Ray—Ryan."

Hannah handed her the note with Ryan's address. "Just the one in the hall."

"What do you call these then?" Tameeka indicated the photos of Jamie on the windowsill and the dresser, and the one on the small writing desk next to the fresh vase of flowers Hannah arranged every few days.

"That's Jamie."

"You said Ryan and he told me it was Ray. How many names does the guy have?"

Hannah suddenly remembered one of Jamie's middle names was Raymond. "You knew Jamie?" *My Jamie.*

"Sort of."

Hannah's mind tripped over itself. Why had Jamie given his middle name to this girl? Why was she in Garringarup looking for him?

She took a breath and tried to sound vaguely interested rather than interrogating. "How did you know him?"

"Perth."

Tameeka said it in a tone that implied everything Hannah needed to know was contained in that one word. But even excluding their age difference, Tameeka wasn't from the same side of the tracks as Jamie. They'd hardly have mixed in the same social circles.

"Oh, right." She hoped she sounded casual. "Where exactly in Perth did you meet?"

"Can I just talk to him?"

Hannah closed her eyes and summoned the will to say the words she hated. "You can't."

"Look, lady—"

"He died a few months ago."

The teen's head snapped up, her face pale under her heavy make-up. "You serious?"

"It's not something I'd lie about!"

Tameeka studied Hannah as if the statement was questionable. "How'd he die then? Did he wait too long before—what happened?"

"It was an accident. He swerved to miss a child on a bike and his car slammed into a tree." Hannah suddenly heard herself asking, "Do you know what sort of car he drove?"

Tameeka shrugged and a ridiculous sense of relief rode through Hannah that she hadn't said Porsche.

"A Ferrari," Tameeka said. "He gave me a keyring."

"He took you for a drive in a Ferrari?" Her voice sounded a thousand miles away.

Tameeka scoffed. "As if. We never went nowhere together."

The reply didn't settle Hannah's unease. "Why did you want to see him today?"

Tameeka raised her thumb to her mouth and bit on the nail. Hannah noticed the nail polish was chipped. Then she saw the colored tattoo of Elsa, the Disney character, on the girl's wrist, and farther up a silhouette of a swimming mermaid. She was so young.

"You can tell me," Hannah urged. *Tell me now!*

Tameeka's flinty gaze assessed her. "He never wanted no one to know. Said it had to be our secret."

A tingle whooshed over Hannah's skin so violently she itched. *Do not jump to illogical conclusions.* Tameeka was a teen and Jamie was a kind and caring man. No woman would actively seek out a bloke who'd been abusing her—especially when he hadn't made contact in months.

Hannah put her hand gently on Tameeka's. "He's not here to get mad."

"Yeah, but you might."

"The fact you drove all the way out here today to see him means it's something important. The fact he's dead doesn't change that for you, does it?"

Tameeka shook her head.

"Can I help instead?"

Tameeka took a long look at the Hamptons-style kitchen, her gaze lingering on the white subway-tiled backsplash, the Shaker-style cabinetry and the quality appliances. She brought her gaze back to Hannah.

"You have nice stuff."

"Thank you?"

"Like Ray. He was paying for my beauty therapy course. Semester's starting and I need money to pay the fees."

The words fell like boulders, unexpected and out of context.

Hannah stared at the girl. "Why was he doing that?"

She stared back. "Said it was his social responsibility."

That sounded like Jamie. Hannah knew he'd volunteered at Outpost, a Perth-based charity supporting the homeless and financially challenged, and she'd always been proud of his social conscience. In a way it made sense that he might use his middle name to put some distance between the clients and his everyday life. But paying for a beauty course? She thought Outpost ran more along the lines of providing hot meals, clothing and accommodation services.

"I needed money and he had money to give," Tameeka said.

"Sure, but there must have been someone else involved? A caseworker?" Hannah probed.

Tameeka fiddled with her hair. "Yeah."

"Have you talked to them?"

She shook her head. "After the first time, Ray said it was easier to pay the money direct. You know, so I got it all."

Hannah knew charities had to cover running costs but even so, this didn't make a lot of sense. Not that she could donate to Outpost or give money to Tameeka directly—she barely had enough money for her own living expenses.

"Of course I'd like to continue supporting Jamie's charitable work," she said, "but things are a bit complicated at the moment."

"You sayin' no?"

Guilt dug in—Hannah had a temporary cash-flow problem that would resolve, but Tameeka was dependent on assistance until she qualified.

"I can talk to your caseworker. Help you find another sponsor."

Tameeka stood, grabbed her keys and gave Hannah a sharp-eyed look as she flicked the metal Ferrari fob against its leather backing. "How about a fifty for fuel?"

Hannah pictured the small amount of cash in her wallet and fought an internal battle between privilege, philanthropy and a sense of being shaken down. She handed Tameeka a twenty.

Tameeka stared at the note as if it was offensive. "It won't buy lobster."

Hannah flinched—it was something Jamie always said whenever he used a twenty.

"He said that to you?"

"Yeah. Told me lobster was overrated and yabbies tasted better, as if I gave a shit. God, he could be boring. He banged on about catching yabbies on a stick at some place on a river. Said it was magic and how I'd love it there. As if!" She pulled open the back door. "See ya."

Stunned, Hannah watched her walk away, her mind lobbing a hundred questions as she replayed the conversation. *It was our secret. Nice stuff like Ray.*

She sprinted across the road, reaching the car as Tameeka switched on the ignition. She banged on the window. "How did you really know Jamie?"

Tameeka ignored her and drove away.

CHAPTER THIRTY-SIX

"We should be able to see her," Vivian fumed down the phone. "Lexie needs her family, and what about poor Mia? They don't have the right to deny us a visit!"

"Mum," Freya said carefully, trying to stay calm. "I've explained this and so has the clinic. We can visit Lexie as soon as she moves out of the detox program and into residential care. Right now she needs all her energy to deal with withdrawal symptoms. And for Mia's sake, Lexie needs to be in a good place before we take her to visit."

Mia was waking up most nights crying, and Freya was dealing with her own nightmares. Faced with Brett's unrelenting questions, Lexie had finally admitted that she'd left Mia alone in the house "once," then later, "no more than twice," to buy wine. Freya hated that she'd had no idea how much pain her sister was in and that things had reached this point without her knowing. Then again, she was learning how much lying occurred when someone feared being found out and losing access to the substance they craved.

Brett had vouched for Freya and Ryan, so thankfully Mia had avoided foster care and come straight to them. To her really—Ryan had left three days later for Geraldton. He was a keynote speaker at two conferences and was away for ten days.

The few times she'd talked to him, he'd been high on the exhilaration of spending time with like-minded people. He'd told her in great detail about the new techniques he'd learned and how he planned to rewrite the current training program. "It will be a lot of work, but so worth it," he'd said.

Freya, who'd always had empathy for Lexie's unwanted plunge into single parenting, now had a vivid understanding of the day-to-day challenges. Even without the added emotional baggage of abandonment it was a lot. She'd written a daily schedule so she and Mia got out the door on time with everything they needed for the day, but for all her organization, the chart didn't allow for the meltdown mornings or the broken sleep. For the first time since Freya had moved in with Ryan, she was counting the days until he walked through the door.

"Can you drive me to Perth the moment Lexie can have visitors?" Vivian asked.

"I'll try, but if I can't there's always the bus."

"If Mia can't go then Ryan can mind her," Vivian said with the confidence of someone who'd given the topic a great deal of thought. "I've found a cheap place near the clinic and I thought I'd stay for a couple of weeks."

Freya knew better than to say, "Are you sure you're feeling up to that?" so instead said, "That means you're in Perth without a car. Have you booked your driving test with Brett?"

"Yes, but even when I get my license back I'm not driving in Perth. The traffic's terrible."

"Let's discuss all this when we know more." Freya picked up her keys and locked Just Because. "I'm on my way to pick up Mia. Can I drop her off with you for forty-five minutes while I do the grocery shopping? She can sit on the sofa and watch something, and I can do your shopping at the same time?"

There was silence.

"Mum?"

"I'm sorry, darling, but I've been light-headed all day. I've got a late appointment with Leah."

Freya's temples throbbed. "What's your blood sugar?"

"That's not the problem, it's my blood pressure. I was hoping you could drive me to the clinic."

Freya glanced at the clock and recalculated. She couldn't be late for Mia—not just because she'd get hit by a late fee, but because right now Mia needed to be surrounded by cast-iron security and being the only child left at the center didn't qualify. And she knew that taking a tired child grocery shopping wasn't ideal, but with Georgie back at university and it being a two tourist-bus day in town, she hadn't been able to leave the shop.

"I'll pick up Mia then come and get you," she said.

"I'll be ready," Vivian said firmly. "And thanks for offering to shop. I'm out of everything."

When Freya arrived at the supermarket it was filled with harassed parents—mostly women—and tired and hungry children, many dressed in sports uniforms. Freya clutched her mother's list and planned her assault in aisle order so she could execute the task in the least amount of time.

"Ready?" She bent to lift Mia into the trolley, but her niece was reaching for a plastic child-sized trolley. "Don't you want to ride up high?" Freya cajoled.

"This is *my* trolley," Mia said.

Freya heard the tone and calculated the extra time in the supermarket versus the risk of a tantrum if she overruled it. "Okay, but we're only getting things on the list."

"Okay," Mia said cheerfully and ran off with the trolley.

Freya caught her by the back of the T-shirt, fearing for people's ankles. "And stay with me."

Mia chatted happily as they walked the aisles, telling her about a story Caprice had read at day care. Freya lifted Mia so she could pluck light items from the shelves and proudly put them in her own trolley.

On the way to the fruit and vegetables section, Freya was taking a moment to check the list and mentally running through her own when Mia spied the candy aisle. She took a sharp left, and by the time Freya caught up with her she was dropping bags of snakes into her trolley.

Freya squatted down so she was at Mia's level and, even though Mia couldn't read, showed her the list. "There are no snakes on the list."

"They on my list!" Mia grabbed for another bag.

"Stocking up are you, chickee?" A silver-haired man dressed in the well-heeled rural uniform—chinos, checked shirt, moleskin jacket and polished RMs—gave Mia an indulgent grin.

Freya ignored him. "Mia, there's candy at home. We're not buying more."

"One bag won't hurt," the bloke said.

Freya swung around. "Excuse me. This has nothing to do with you."

"Candy is more appropriate than some of the other things in her basket," he muttered.

Freya had no idea what he was talking about. She scanned the contents of Mia's trolley: teabags, toothpaste and a box of tampons decorated in swirls of blue and green. Mia had demanded they go in her basket because she liked the colors.

Freya noticed the lapel pin on the man's jacket—the logo of a family-focused political party. She recognized his face from election posters—Tom Kroger.

"It's not your job to comment on my groceries," she said.

"As her mother, you should know better." Judgment oozed from him like slime.

"I'm not her mother, I'm her aunt," Freya said wearily.

"Oh, well, that explains it then."

Freya narrowed her eyes. "Explains what exactly?"

His mouth curled in distaste. "You have no idea what you're doing. No mother would put those things in her child's shopping basket."

Fury burned through Freya so hot and fast she expected to ignite. First she was judged as a failing mother and now she was judged because she wasn't a mother.

"The last time I checked, the act of giving birth wasn't followed by a how-to book. Oh, wait, fathers don't give birth either and yet somehow they parent with the same qualifications as me." It took every gram of restraint she had not to press her forefinger into the man's chest. "And if I was her mother, those tampons would still be in her basket because at her age she likes the colors and that's all that matters. But as she gets older they'll be there because I want her to know they are a normal monthly purchase that doesn't need to be hidden. And I'll be teaching her to recognize misogynistic bastards like you and how you shame women to make yourself feel better."

Mia wailed then, tears streaming down her cheeks. Horrified, Freya realized she'd been yelling. People had stopped shopping and were openly staring.

"It's selfish, unhappy, dried-up women like you who are destroying society," Kroger said. "Get that child home to her mother before you traumatize her even more." He turned and strode away.

Freya wanted to yell that Mia wasn't safe with her mother at the moment, but she couldn't do that to Mia or to Lexie. As hard as it was to separate the person from the illness, she reminded herself every day that Lexie's addiction was the problem, not Lexie. She refused to join the narrow-minded people judging her—like that bastard.

Shaking, Freya picked up Mia. As she soothed her, she told herself that of course the ultra-conservative right was threatened by women who wanted to be childfree. In their view, all women belonged at home, barefoot in the kitchen, incubating babies and caring for children and grandchildren. His opinion didn't matter.

But she couldn't shake the memory of Ainsley's comments at the community meeting, or her mother's concern that children were the only way for a woman to be completely fulfilled. With or without a religious overview, society assumed—expected—women to have children. Even infertile women were expected to spend tens of thousands of dollars and explore every possible avenue to have a child. Freya had no quarrel with women who wanted children—go them—but why did people denigrate those who decided to remain childfree? Why did they take those women's decision as a personal affront to their own values?

She managed the last of the shop with Mia clinging on her hip and eating snakes. She ignored all the looks and the comments by other shoppers that ranged from the sympathetic "you do what you need to do" to "ready for the sugar high, are you?"

After she'd dealt with dinner, bath and bedtime, Freya logged onto the supermarket's website and set up a home-delivery service for herself and her mother. Then she poured a glass of wine and closed her eyes, anticipating the first sip—the taste, the warmth, the way it would roll away the stresses of the day.

Her eyes flew open. Horrified, she returned the wine to the bottle and texted Ryan a message she'd never sent before.

> When are you getting home?

CHAPTER THIRTY-SEVEN

HANNAH HAD CALLED Outpost the moment Tameeka drove away and got a recorded message about opening hours. She'd rung back the next day and a volunteer had promised to pass on her message.

When she finally spoke to a staff member and asked about Tameeka, she was told that client confidentiality precluded them from providing specific details.

Against pulsing frustration she switched to general questions about the program. Yes, she was told, support was provided for education. Yes, they had a specific fund. Would she like to make a donation?

Hannah told herself the fact that education fund existed was a good thing. Any donations would be confirmed by looking at Jamie's tax return. She was halfway through typing a polite email to Rowan asking for the return of Jamie's computer when she remembered Tameeka saying, "Ray said it was easier to pay the money direct." Had Tameeka made that up to try and get more money out of Hannah now Jamie was dead?

The girl certainly hadn't wanted Hannah to talk to her caseworker, and the mention of lobster and yabbies meant Jamie hadn't been a faceless benefactor. But that didn't automatically mean anything sinister—after all, Hannah had heard the same story about catching yabbies. And yet as much as Tameeka's story rang true, it also rang off-key.

He never wanted no one to know. That could be viewed as true philanthropy or as hiding something. If Hannah could study Jamie's bank statements—

The moment the thought landed she knew that even with Jamie's computer she couldn't access his bank records. Only the executors could do that.

She swore loudly. Ozzie whined.

Hannah blew out a long breath. She was supposed to be focusing on calmness and serenity so when she started her IVF journey she was in the best possible state of mind to nurture a baby. Instead, she was stressing out over why and how Tameeka knew Jamie.

She grabbed her keys and drove to the farm. Lydia was out, which suited Hannah because she hadn't come for scones and conversation. She expected Ian to be in the paddocks and that she'd have to go looking for him, but by some miracle he was in the office.

After a hello hug she got straight to the point. "I need to see Jamie's bank statements."

He sighed. "Hannah, we've been through this. It's not going to give you an accurate picture now we're dealing with debtors and creditors."

She didn't want to tell him that she needed to see the statements to decide if Jamie was a philanthropist or a man taking advantage of a young woman's disadvantage.

"It's just I've been approached by a charity in Perth—Outpost. They said Jamie was a sizeable donor and I want to confirm they're legit before we consider them as trust beneficiaries."

Ian rubbed his forehead. "You're jumping the gun a bit there, love. Let's get probate through first before we worry about the trust."

Hannah was about to insist when Ian added, "We need to talk about the house at Wilberforce. I know you and Jamie chose it because of its lovely spot on the river, but it's pretty isolated. Now you're on your own, you're probably better off staying in town closer to us, especially with the baby plans. Rowan's suggesting we sell it to improve your bottom line."

She almost said, "Jamie and I never chose a house together," but the massive red flag waving wildly in her head stopped her. Jamie owned a house she knew nothing about and his parents assumed she'd been involved in the purchase decision—what the hell was going on? Her mind spun out on yet another Jamie mystery—they were piling up now as fast as falling leaves.

Somehow she managed to make her voice sound perfectly normal. "I should probably take a last look at it so I know for sure if I can let it go."

Ian nodded, understanding bright in his eyes. "Will you be okay on your own, or do you want Lyd or me to come with you?"

"I'd like to go on my own." *I just have no idea where the hell it is.* She gave a self-deprecating laugh. "The thing is, Jamie always drove and you know how easily I get lost."

Ian gave her an indulgent smile. "And Google isn't much use out there. I'll draw you a map."

Hannah bumped down the rough road in a haze of red dust. Kangaroos lazed under scrubby acacias and flocks of corellas wheeled, whitening the sky, but she was immune to the bucolic scene. Why on earth did Jamie have a house way out here?

And where the hell was it? She'd been driving for over an hour, had left the main road thirty minutes ago and for the last two kilometers she'd been parallel to the river, glimpsing it through a pretty grove of eucalypts and she-oaks.

She slowed and reread Ian's instructions. *Cross the ford. Track on right.*

The road swept left, the first deviation in ten kilometers. Suddenly she was driving over a large drain that channeled the river underneath the road—it would easily become a ford after heavy rains. She turned right onto a rutted track that immediately threatened to consume her car. With limited phone reception she really didn't want to get stuck, so she pulled over and walked the final hundred meters.

The track approached the house from behind—it looked like a kit home—but she imagined the view down to the river was exactly as Ian had described. As she rounded the side of the house to climb the veranda steps she saw a white four-wheel drive parked in front. Had Jamie bought the house as an investment property and it was rented? If he had, it still didn't explain why he'd never told her about it.

As she knocked on the door she realized it was the same cherry red as her own front door. After about fifteen seconds had passed she knocked again and strained to hear footsteps. Nothing.

She cupped her hands around her eyes and peered through the large window that provided the occupants with a stunning river view. The room was tastefully decorated, with a large acrylic painting dominating one wall. Underneath it she saw a side table filled with knickknacks and framed photos. There was a wood heater, a two-seater sofa and a Moroccan-style rug on the floor—the vibe was comfortable and cozy.

Hannah crossed to the window on the other side of the door and realized she was staring into a small kitchen. The kettle and toaster glinted silver in the sunshine, and a small vase of flowers sat in the center of a wooden table.

"Excuse me?" a voice said behind her. "Can I help you?"

Hannah's heart thumped in shock and she turned, her palm pressed against her chest. A woman wearing a baseball cap, large black sunglasses, a Liberty-print T-shirt and capri pants stood with her hand on the front door.

"I'm sorry," Hannah stammered. "I knocked but when no one answered—"

"You thought you'd have a sticky." The woman pushed open the door. "You better come in then, Hannah."

Startled at the use of her name, Hannah followed. Who was this woman? The voice was vaguely familiar but the sunglasses and baseball cap effectively hid her face, and her straight back gave no clues.

"Have we met?" she asked.

The woman removed the cap and glossy dark-brown hair fell to her shoulders. Hannah realized who she was a second before she took off her glasses.

Monique held up the kettle. "Tea? Or would you prefer whisky? I find a stiff drink to be a great comfort."

Hannah fought the increasingly familiar sensation of being flung out of her known world and into one that was unrecognizable. "What ... Why are you here?"

"I have the same question. I didn't think you knew about this place."

"I didn't until today." Hannah hated that she was answering questions when she should be the one asking them. "I thought you lived in Barraboolup."

"I do. This is my second home."

"How? According to Ian, it's part of Jamie's estate."

Monique's look was one of sympathy mixed with sharp edges. She made two mugs of tea and brought them to the table, then poured two shots of whisky. "Sit. Drink. You're going to need it."

Hannah didn't want to sit. She had an overwhelming urge to run.

Monique took a generous slug of whisky. "This place was ours. Mine and Jamie's."

Hannah willed logic to support her. "You mean you and Jamie owned it before you split up and then he bought you out?"

"No. We bought it just before you moved to Garringarup."

The words boomed in Hannah's head and the room tilted. She dropped into a chair.

"If you think this is some sort of joke, it's not remotely funny."

"It's not a joke." Monique looked almost contrite. "I'm sorry, Hannah. If there was an easier way to tell you this, I'd use it, but there isn't. Truth be told, I hoped you'd never need to know, but once Jamie died that became wishful thinking. To be honest, I'm surprised we didn't have this conversation months ago, but then again, the grapevine says his estate's in a hell of a mess."

Hannah barely heard the words. Her brain was refusing to budge from "we bought it just before you moved to Garringarup."

"But you dumped him! You broke his heart, moved away and married David." The words came out like a script—the one she'd learned from Jamie on their very first date. "We were hours from being married. He loved me, not you!"

"You were getting married, that part is true. But I didn't break up with him. He broke up with me."

There were certain words and phrases connected with Monique that had been engraved on Hannah's heart by Jamie, his parents, Freya, Ryan, the town ... "That is *not* what happened."

"It is," Monique said serenely. "He proposed. I accepted."

Hannah's heart thundered so fast the sound deafened her. "I'm the *only* woman he ever proposed to."

"He might have told you that ..."

Monique swiped her phone a few times then pushed it across the table. It was open on a photo—a selfie of her and Jamie with their heads together and her hand close to the camera. A pink diamond ring sparkled on her left ring finger. It was identical to the one Hannah wore.

Hannah heard a gurgling gasping sound and realized it was coming from her. She sucked in air and tried not to vomit.

"No ... that ... I don't understand."

Monique sighed, the sound filling the room with something that was neither happiness nor regret. "When we broke up, I returned the ring and I honestly thought he'd sell it. I never expected him to give it to you. In fact, we argued about it. I said you deserved your own ring."

Monique sounded like she was defending Hannah to Jamie, but not in any universe did that make sense.

"If you'd been engaged to him, people would have told me," Hannah said.

"No one knew. Jamie called it off before we went public."

She broke my heart, poss. I thought I'd never recover.

"No, that's not right." Hannah was shaking her head so hard her brain hurt. "You broke up with him. You broke his heart."

Monique's impassive demeanor faltered. "He fractured mine."

Hannah was intimate with Jamie and Monique's story—Monique was lying.

Jamie never told you they'd been engaged.

She couldn't unhear the unwanted thought. "How did he fracture it?"

"I wanted children."

Hannah scoffed. "So did Jamie."

Monique's mouth pulled into a tight grimace. "No, he didn't, Hannah. He was adamant. So adamant, in fact, that he was prepared to walk away from the love of his life."

The sudden need to hurt Monique burned hot. "You were not the love of his life! Did it ever occur to you that he actually wanted children, just not with *you?*"

Monique's face didn't alter nor did she flinch. "He told Freya the same thing—it's just you don't want to believe her. And I get why, but it doesn't change the truth."

The words slashed and burned. "You wouldn't know the truth if it rose up and bit you!"

"I knew Jamie better than anyone and even I didn't understand all his complications."

Hannah rebalanced on steadier ground. "Jamie wasn't complicated! He loved me, cricket, his family and his community."

"Then how do you account for me and this house? Our house." Monique encompassed the room with her arm, before pointing to the photos.

Now Hannah was closer to them she saw they were all of Monique and Jamie together. She desperately wanted to discount them as photos taken years earlier. She wanted to paint Monique as an unstable ex who'd never got over Jamie and kept this house as some sort of crazy shrine to him. And she could have, except the shirt Jamie was wearing in one of the photos was the one she'd given him on his last birthday.

She gulped the whisky, welcoming the burn and yearning for its numbing qualities, because right now she wanted to rip off her skin.

Monique refilled their glasses. "I loved him and he loved me—that was the simple part. But I wanted children and he didn't, so he left. I was devastated and furious. How could he walk away from the best thing that had ever happened to either of us? How, when we were soulmates, could he not give me what I wanted? I raged for a long time, but when Will was six months old I finally understood."

Hannah recoiled, her heart breaking for the child. "Are you telling me you regret having your son?"

"God, no. I love him to pieces. I'd die for him." Monique stared into her drink. "Jamie lived different lives in the same skin and he was far more honest about what he wanted than most of us. In the end he did me a favor. David gave me Will and the love and security a child needs. Jamie gave me everything else."

Don't ask. Do not ask.

"What was everything else?"

Monique's smile turned dreamy. "The antithesis of monogamy. Never underestimate how erotic and exciting an affair can be, Hannah. All the planning, the clandestine meetings, the secret phone calls, this house—it saved my marriage." Her voice caught. "I miss him so much."

Hannah was flashing hot and cold like she was in the grip of a fever. As hard as she tried to hold onto the belief that Monique was telling her lie upon lie, it slipped through her fingers, smashing at her feet. A slew of phrases bombarded her: *The accident took place on the old Garringarup road. Bloody roadworks, be later than I thought. He was driving a Porsche. He said you wanted a Lamborghini.*

The pain that corkscrewed through her almost knocked her off her seat. Jamie had been driving to Monique when he died.

"You killed him!" Hannah launched herself at the other woman. She wanted to scratch and bite and hit. Hurt her as much as she was hurting.

But as Monique's arms blocked hers in a defensive strike, Hannah slumped, and for the briefest moment an attack became a hug. Horrified, Hannah pushed her away.

"It was an accident," Monique said softly.

"Because he was driving an unfamiliar car!"

"No. We'd rented it before."

When Jamie died, Hannah thought she'd never known pain like it. This was worse.

"Why?"

A sympathetic look crossed Monique's face. "Jamie got off on fast cars and sex."

"No, he didn't!"

Monique brought up more photos. She and Jamie, arms entwined, leaning on a black Ferrari and a red Corvette.

"I know this is hard for you, Hannah. It's not exactly easy for me. We've both lost a man we loved."

"Don't you dare compare your loss to mine!" But as Hannah heard the words she wondered exactly who she had lost. She didn't recognize the Jamie that Monique spoke of in such soft and loving tones.

"When Jamie was with you," Monique went on, "he was the man his family and the town expected and needed him to be. When he was with me, he was the man he wanted to be."

"What the hell does that mean?"

"He could be curious and open-minded. We took risks. We pushed boundaries. We explored."

Hannah wasn't that naive. In this context, open-minded, curious and exploring wasn't going on a picnic in a fast car. It was the antithesis of vanilla sex—the sort of lights-out, missionary-position sex Jamie had favored with her. Another wave of fury engulfed her, only this time it wasn't directed exclusively at Monique. She thought about the lingerie in the luxury black box she'd thought was part of Jamie's wedding present to her. The lingerie that was the wrong size—Monique's size.

She lurched to her feet and threw up in the sink.

Monique silently handed her a damp cloth and a glass of water. Hannah hated herself for accepting.

"How did you live with yourself knowing what you were doing to me?" she said.

"I wasn't doing anything to you, Hannah."

"You were fucking my fiancé!"

Monique grimaced. "We went to great lengths to protect you."

Hannah's breath was so shallow she saw spots. She sank to the kitchen floor.

Monique handed her a brown paper bag. "Long, slow, deep breaths."

When Hannah finally got her breathing under control, Monique said, "Have you found any more phones?"

"Phones?" Hannah could barely keep up.

"Cell phones. You obviously found one because you called me."

"No, I didn't. I'd remember if I had."

"It was in December. When the number lit up on my phone, I had a crazy moment that it was Jamie and I'd only imagined him dead all those months. It was one of the numbers he always called me from and I couldn't help myself—I called back. When I realized it was you I hung up."

"That was you? I thought it was Janet McKenzie ... Hang on, why would there be other phones?"

Monique blew out a long breath. "Like I said, Jamie was complicated."

Hannah didn't recognize anything about the Jamie Monique maintained she knew. "You need to be more specific."

"He liked to experiment. We both did."

Hannah was torn between wanting and not wanting to know more. "Experiment? What does that mean?"

Monique gave a slight shake of her head as if she couldn't believe she had to explain. "We were part of the sex-positive community. Swinging, threesomes, that sort of thing. But after the engagement—"

"Yours or mine?" Hannah said savagely.

Monique's smile was a grim line. "Yours. I think it was the stress of the wedding, but Jamie suddenly wanted to take things to another level. Try things I worried weren't safe."

"Like what?"

Monique flapped her hand as if the question was irrelevant. "Although he never asked again, I knew him. I think it's very likely he went looking for it in Perth. He had a cell phone for me and a cell phone for you, so it makes sense he'd have a phone for that."

He never wanted no one to know. Said it had to be our secret. Tameeka's voice squealed like feedback in Hannah's mind. Horror filled her at what a vulnerable young woman might have agreed to for money.

"So he was cheating on both of us!" she said.

"That's a very WASP paradigm," Monique said.

"You make that sound like it's a bad thing."

Monique shrugged. "It places a very narrow definition on love. So much so, is it even love?"

Hannah stared at the married mother of one who was dressed in the classic clothes of the WASP elite and tried to align her with a long-term affair that sounded like it was built on a foundation of kink with a man she no longer recognized. Rage engulfed her and she pushed to her feet.

"You do not have the right to lecture me on love, marriage and morality! Start packing, because tomorrow this house is going on the market."

Monique paled. "No."

Revenge energized Hannah. "Yes."

"No," Monique said firmly. "You got to share your grief with everyone who knew him. I had to hide mine."

"What? You suddenly want my sympathy?"

"I do. I deserve it."

Hannah's laugh hurt her chest. "You deserve squat." She suddenly remembered the time Monique had dropped into the store. "Why did you come into Just Because?"

"I needed to talk about Jamie with someone who loved him."

Hannah remembered how much she'd valued that conversation, how she'd hung onto a new story about Jamie as if her life depended on it. Now she loathed herself. Loathed even more that she saw the pulsing heartbeat of Monique's grief and how it mirrored her own. She pushed the recognition away—Monique didn't deserve a single thing from her.

Monique's moment of vulnerability faded and she crossed her arms, the action all business. "The fairest arrangement is for you to keep the schoolhouse where you shared your life with him, and I keep this one."

"Fair?" Hannah screeched. "Fair doesn't exist anywhere in this equation. I was his fiancée. I get to make the decisions about his estate."

"That's not what I'm hearing."

"I don't care what you've heard. Ian McMaster is taking advice from Rowan Ferguson and he says sell this place so it's happening."

"Oh, Hannah, be careful."

The respect in the warning upended her. "What the hell is that supposed to mean?"

"Jamie loved me. There's no way he would abandon me with nothing."

She hated Monique's smug confidence. "Oh, yes, he would. He died without a will!"

"That's more your problem than mine."

Ice chilled her veins. "What do you mean?"

"Jamie set up a shell company to buy this place for us. It's why it's taken so long for Rowan to discover it, but once he does a title search he'll find my name. So you can walk away now and keep your dignity or face a very public battle in court."

The power shift almost knocked Hannah off her feet. "You're an absolute piece of work, you know that!"

Monique closed her eyes for a moment. When she opened them the antagonism had faded. "I don't want to fight you, Hannah."

"Oh, how very gracious of you! What a shame your impeccable manners didn't stop you from fucking my fiancé."

"I didn't have a choice."

"Of course you had a choice. *He* had a choice."

"Jamie and I found a way to be together that worked for us both, and we did it in a way that protected you, David and Will."

"Protected me?" Hannah's laugh was jagged and ugly. "You're living in la-la land."

"No more than you. Freya told me about your baby plans. Jamie didn't want to be a father, Hannah. If you truly loved him, you should honor his decision like I did."

The words plunged into Hannah's heart as deep and as violently as a dagger. "Honor it? What? Like you and Jamie honored me and David?"

"David and I have an open marriage. He knows all about Jamie, and since his death he's been my rock. He lets me come here when I need to be on my own with Jamie. He knows I'm here today."

At that moment Hannah didn't know what was worse: Jamie's utter betrayal of her; the fact that Monique's grief for him matched her own; or that instead of being alone with her pain, Monique had a man and a child in her life who loved her.

CHAPTER THIRTY-EIGHT

THE RAIN HIT, sharp as needles, just as Hannah reached the car. It was as if the universe knew her life was caught in a violent storm and had sent weather to match it. In less than an hour everything she'd believed to be true about her life, about Jamie and his love for her, had been picked up by a tornado, hurled around and smashed into a thousand tiny pieces.

She thumped the steering wheel and screamed, the sound reverberating around her. What had just happened to her were the sorts of things scriptwriters wrote to keep viewers watching. It wasn't supposed to happen in real life. Not in *her* life when all she'd done was love and trust a man who'd purported to do the same for her.

Between the rain and the drop in temperature that fogged the windshield, Hannah struggled to see the road. She was rubbing the glass when the car fishtailed wildly, tires spinning on gravel. All her instincts commanded she brake but she resisted. Instead, as the car slid ominously sideways, she accelerated until she felt the tires grip again and the vehicle straighten. Heart hammering, she eased back on the pedal, gently pumping the brakes until the car rolled to a stop next to a stand of towering gums.

"Oh God, oh God, oh God."

She closed her eyes but the skidding sensation rushed back. Not caring about the rain, she pushed open the door and got out, patting her body to confirm she was still alive and in one piece.

Now that the front had passed the rain was easing, but water sluiced off the trees, running in rivulets down the trunks to form puddles at the base. As she followed the trajectory of the water something colorful caught her eye. She took a few steps and squatted at the base of the tree. She found a small piece of blue and white plastic. A soggy ribbon. A decaying bunch of flowers.

A chill ran over her. *No!*

But her fingers were already searching inside the cellophane and pulling out a water-damaged card. *I miss you more than words can say* was written in a script she'd seen once before—Monique's handwriting.

Hannah shot to her feet and backed away. She'd never wanted to visit the accident site, had never wanted to be haunted by any visual reminders of where Jamie had died.

She released an ugly, raw bellow of rage. "You bastard! How dare you hide behind me and my hopes and dreams so you could indulge in whatever the hell it was that got you off! How dare you die a hero idolized by everyone you knew. I fucking hate you!"

An odd sensation washed over her. It certainly wasn't peace—how could it be after the bomb that had just exploded her life? Her fury burned so red and hot it would be visible in space, so what the hell was it? It felt like a heavy coat had slid off her shoulders, and now that she was free of its weight she could stand straighter.

She remembered Mac talking about grief changing shape and laughed grimly. Her grief hadn't changed shape; she'd shed it because it was no longer required. There was no point mourning a man who'd never existed.

Cold fury propelled Hannah home. She immediately tore the house apart looking for phones, receipts, anything that pointed to the activities Monique had hinted at.

She pulled every item of Jamie's clothing off the hangers—clothes she'd been unable to part with because she needed to touch them and inhale their scent to keep Jamie close. Now her hands tugged at them, turning pockets inside out, looking for evidence of treachery. She found a hundred-dollar bill.

She dumped the contents of Jamie's bedside drawers on the floor. Condoms and coins fell out, along with receipts from places they'd visited together.

She plundered his bookcase, shaking out books, and ended up with a small pile of boarding passes he'd used as bookmarks. They gave her nothing—she'd accompanied him on every flight.

"Arrgh!" She spun around, propelled by fulminating anger. Where next? Was there a point to searching the office? Surely if anything was there she would have discovered it while Jamie lived. Except back then she'd had no reason not to trust him.

Leaving the mess on the bedroom floor, she entered the office and took apart the main filing cabinet. It had always been her domain and, as neat files fluttered to the floor, it appeared still to be very much hers.

She kneeled in front of the two-drawer cabinet that was part of Jamie's desk. It had always held chocolate and Jamie had teased her that he needed to keep it locked or she'd eat the lot. When she'd been stress-eating before the wedding she'd appreciated the lock. Was it hiding more than Jaffas? She jammed the small key into the lock, gave it a vicious turn and tugged the drawer open. The only thing inside was a hamper-worthy array of chocolates, including her favorite Swiss white-chocolate balls. Jamie rarely bought them, saying they didn't constitute chocolate, and yet here was an unopened box with a note in his handwriting: *Sweet chocolates for a sweet Hannah.*

Her anger was momentarily swamped by loathing for herself. How could she have shared a house and an office with this man and never worked out that he was leading a secret life?

When Jamie was with you, he was the man everyone expected and needed him to be.

"Shut up, Monique!"

She shredded the note and threw the box. Chocolate balls rained down and rolled across the floor.

Ozzie wandered in, drawn by her shouts and screams.

"Sit," she commanded, and scrambled to scoop up the chocolates.

She stomped down the hall, planning to bin them, and tripped over the stepladder she'd abandoned when she'd been searching the hall closet. She cried out, sank to the floor and pressed her fingers over her throbbing toes.

As she waited for the pain to subside and the silver flashes of light behind her eyes to fade, she glanced up at the ceiling and found herself staring at the rectangular entry to the roof space. Jamie had stored memorabilia and old tax files up there—at least that was what he'd told her. Hannah had never been up there because small dark places terrified her, but she knew today was the day she needed to confront that fear.

She maneuvered the stepladder into place, climbed the steps and, ignoring the pain in her toes, rose on them and reached for the ring pull.

Her fingers only just grazed it, but she managed to open it and concertina stairs appeared.

Ozzie barked.

"Glad you think I can do this," Hannah said.

She heaved herself up until her head and shoulders were in the roof. The heat hit her like a wall as she waited for her eyes to adjust to the dim light. She was looking at boxes labelled *Kitchen, Bathroom, Bedroom, Living room, Odds and sods*. She suddenly remembered the packing boxes from the Perth apartment that Ian had organized when she was in Singapore. Sweat trickled from her hairline. Which of the boxes was likely to yield something useful?

She tried shifting the bedroom box closer to the manhole entrance, but whatever was in it weighed a ton and it wouldn't budge. She gave the odds and sods box a hard tug and it shot forward so quickly she almost fell backwards. It was unwieldy, but she managed to hold it close to her body with one arm while gripping the side of the ladder with her other hand. By the time she was back down on the hall floor she was panting hard.

Unable to rip open the box due to the generous amount of packing tape, she carried it into the kitchen and used scissors as a blade. When she flipped off the lid, all she could see was scrunched cream packing paper. She pulled it out, then started unwrapping the items.

A TV remote. A phone. A silk plant. A phone. A bottle of whisky. A tangled mess of charging cords and plugs. A phone. A book. A USB stick. A bunch of keys. A blister pack of paracetamol. A phone.

Four phones?

She lined them up and registered that they were the same make and model as the one she'd found in Jamie's car. She thought burner phones were supposed to be cheap, but these were all smartphones.

"Did you get a bulk discount, Jamie?"

She plugged the phones in to charge, binned the plant, removed the batteries from the remote for recycling, then took a slug of the whisky.

"Come on, phones!" The batteries were still too flat to display the screens.

She picked up the book. It was a blockbuster novel, the type Jamie had always eschewed. Of course it was. It was just another piece in a new and horrible puzzle that revealed the man she'd loved as a stranger.

She plugged the USB stick into her laptop and was clicking on the first folder when the screen of one of the phones lit up. She grabbed it and navigated straight to contacts.

She blinked, swiped up, then reopened contacts. Empty. She checked the call log. No incoming or outgoing calls.

She flicked back to the home page but the only apps she could see came with the phone and the text messages were also empty. Had this phone ever been used?

The other phone screens were lighting up and she systematically checked for signs of use. For an incriminating phone number. Anything. She got nothing.

Granted, she was unfamiliar with the operating system. Had she missed something? She must have, otherwise why would Jamie have four unused phones? Phones that Monique had suggested might exist.

Jamie was complicated.

She picked up the first phone again and swiped randomly until she found a list of apps. She opened the only one she didn't recognize—a community for couples and singles to explore their desires—and fell down a rabbit hole. The profile said Jez, and Jamie had used a photo from when he was twenty-five. *Fun-loving and open. FWB.* She opened the chat facility and read what "open" actually meant.

Dropping the phone, she picked up the next one. This time his profile said Jace and the photo was different, but it still implied he was at least eight years younger. Jace was *non-judgmental* and interested in *kink* and *ONS*, whatever the hell that meant. On the third phone he was Paul who was *looking to experiment, midweek hook-ups only, no single men*; and on the final phone he was Ray. Desires included BDSM, dominance and breath play. *CNC. Perth only.*

He never wanted no one to know. Said it had to be our secret.

Hannah gagged and dropped the phone. It was the proof she'd been looking for since Tameeka had rung her doorbell, but it was so much worse than she'd imagined. It was one thing for Jamie to cheat on her with Monique, but this was a whole other dimension. This wasn't a relationship of equals—it involved a young woman who was eighteen years his junior and had less education and money.

Hannah knew she should open the chat but her fingers fumbled as if they didn't want to reveal the further awfulness she believed lurked in there. Her laptop pinged with a notification and she glanced at it. The folder on the USB stick had finally loaded rows of thumbnail-sized photos. They were too small to determine the contents, but the dominant colors were red and black.

She clicked on the first one and it filled her screen. It showed a dim room with a large cross on the wall and some other things that were out of focus. A woman in red latex that clung as tightly to her as a second skin lay prone on a bed, her head dangling off the edge, her body tied in ropes. Her face was covered in a matching red mask and her mouth was filled with a red ball, but her jet-black hair streaked with purple was eerily familiar. A man straddled her. He too was dressed in latex—black —which outlined every part of him in graphic detail—taut buttocks, muscle-toned thighs, broad chest and engorged genitalia. The only part of his body not covered was his head. Jamie's familiar grin leaped out of the photo and strangled Hannah.

She gasped as the image of Henry Fuseli's painting *The Nightmare* flared in her mind. One of Jamie's schoolfriends had sent a postcard of it and he'd put it on the fridge. They'd had a spirited discussion about it.

"It might be a famous painting, Jamie, but it's yet another example of a man hiding behind art to perpetrate violence against women."

"Poss, you've got it all wrong. It's a dream and the woman is in control."

The card sat on the fridge for a week and then Hannah had removed it and put it on Jamie's desk. She hadn't seen it since. Now she was looking at an interpretation of it, and Tameeka didn't look like she was in control—just young and vulnerable and desperate for money.

Hannah slammed the laptop down so hard she risked fracturing the screen. Her chest seized as tightly as if she was the one bound in rope and she struggled to breathe. This man was a stranger. She couldn't align any part of him with the person she'd lived with.

Yet Monique had hinted at this Jamie; had calmly implied that he had needs she'd accepted she couldn't meet. If Monique knew, then others did too. Who else had willfully kept Hannah in the dark?

Her mind lit up like the night sky on New Year's Eve. *He told Freya … you just didn't want to believe her.*

She grabbed her keys and slammed out the front door.

CHAPTER THIRTY-NINE

FREYA RESTED her head on Ryan's chest, listening to the rain pummeling the tin roof. The farmers would be happy—the autumn break had finally arrived. She was exhausted after a few big weeks. Her mother had insisted on staying in Perth and although Freya understood her mother's need to be close to Lexie, at the moment Vivian was only allowed to visit on the weekends. This left five days alone in Perth but depending on Freya as if she was just around the corner. That had meant connecting Vivian to a pharmacy on a bus route for her insulin and other medication needs. It also meant Freya was feeding Vivian's cat and watering her plants, and troubleshooting when Vivian needed things in Perth but had no clue where to source them. This had included finding a doctor for her when she'd had another heart-related dizzy spell, and talking her through downloading a rideshare app to her cell phone and adding payment details. After twenty-five minutes of sheer frustration Freya had been shocked to feel tears burning the backs of her eyes.

Ryan wasn't sympathetic. "She could catch the bus up on Fridays and home on Mondays."

His attitude had surprised Freya—he was always Mr. Caring.

"She's not exactly match fit. By the time she's recovered, she'll be getting back on the bus again."

"Meanwhile she's exhausting you."

"It's just short-term." But even as she said it she knew it would likely be a couple more months.

The first time Freya had visited Lexie, her sister had been bright-eyed and sparky. Too bright-eyed for comfort—she'd been exactly the same in the early days with Kane. It soon became apparent that Lexie had met someone at the rehabilitation facility. Part of Freya understood the attraction—the power of a shared experience—but even without any professional training in addiction therapy, she knew this kind of support was a double-edged sword. Lexie had talked too quickly, hugged too hard, hyped up Mia before forgetting her presence entirely as she told Freya all about Heath.

"He's had it tough. Much harder than me. He just needs love, you know?"

Freya didn't know if she wanted to cry or scream.

The aftershocks of the visit for Mia hadn't taken long to manifest. It was too hard for a young child to understand why she could visit Mummy but not stay with her, let alone make sense of why Lexie blew hot and cold. In the two weeks since the visit, Mia had clung to Freya like a limpet, and at night she was up and down asking for a glass of water, a toy—anything to check that Freya was still in the house.

Ryan's arm tightened around Freya now and she sank further into him. He'd taken Mia out on a long bike ride so Freya could open the store without needing to stick Mia in front of a screen in the back room. After the fresh air and exercise, Mia had fallen asleep early and, although Freya's job list was a mile long, she'd succumbed to Ryan's suggestion of a cuddle on the sofa.

Her leg jerked. Ryan laughed and stroked her hair. "Go to bed."

"Too comfy here."

She knew they needed to discuss next week—who was doing what and when—and draw up a schedule, but she didn't have the energy or the headspace for the required negotiations. With everything that was going on with Lexie and her mother, she was missing her friendship with Hannah more than ever. Earlier in the week she'd overheard Chrissie Lancefield telling Tiana Amberley that Hannah had started on IVF. She wanted to ask Ryan what he knew, but since her refusal to sign the affidavit, Ryan never mentioned Hannah.

You could have lied like everyone else.

But that had never been an option.

The long and loud ring of the old doorbell startled her, but it was the thumping on the front door that made her sit up.

"What the hell? If they wake Mia, I'll kill them."

Ryan was already on his feet and striding to the door as if anticipating an emergency.

As Freya rose from the sofa she heard him say, "Is everything okay?" and then Hannah strode in, her demeanor a mix of antagonism and despair. It took Freya straight back to the day Jamie died.

"You're the worst woman imaginable!" Hannah screamed. She turned to Ryan. "And you're just as two-faced. From the moment I arrived in town the pair of you have treated me like a mushroom, spinning stories to protect Jamie and keep me in the dark so I never worked out what the hell was going on under my nose!"

Adrenaline soaked Freya in sweat. When Jamie died, she'd thought his secret—her dilemma—had died with him. Then Hannah had wanted his baby and the threat had re-emerged, but she'd gotten through it without ever disclosing to Ryan or Hannah what else had happened during that unwanted conversation with Jamie. She'd lost Hannah's friendship in the process, but she'd protected her from the unpleasant truth as well as protecting Ryan and their relationship. So why the hell was it back again now, threatening to blow up her life?

Ryan was standing stock-still, his eyes wide. "Hannah, we've never hidden anything from you."

"Don't bullshit me," Hannah said.

"I'm not." He turned to Freya. "Frey?"

Her hand rose to her throat to loosen a button only to touch bare skin. "I'll go and make tea," she said.

"Stay here." Hannah's voice was now ominously calm. "I know you've both been keeping Jamie's secrets."

Ryan laughed. "He didn't have any secrets."

"Oh, he had secrets alright," Hannah spat. "Dirty little secrets that have been oozing out of the slime that was his life in seemingly random moments ever since he died. But today I discovered the truth. I hate him for what he did to me. I hate that I explained away so much of the unexplainable—like the Porsche—but I hate you more for enabling him."

"I did not enable him," Freya said firmly even though her conscience questioned her. "I told you he didn't want children and look what that did to us."

"But you were prepared to let me marry him knowing the things he was doing, his affair with Monique—"

"I didn't know he was back with Monique," she said firmly.

"*That's* what you're taking from this?" Hannah shrieked. "Not the fast cars, the swinging, the sex addiction and the fact he was using, likely abusing, young women to get his rocks off?"

Ryan's face drained of color. "Jesus."

"I'm sorry—" Freya tried.

"You don't get to be sorry."

"Freya." Ryan's voice, usually so calm and kind, was loaded with the sharpness of razor wire. "You don't seem particularly shocked about these allegations?"

"Of course she isn't," Hannah said.

"Freya, what the hell did you know?"

Survival mode kicked in, sliding over Freya's shock. She didn't want to have this conversation with Hannah in the room. She needed Ryan on his own.

"Hannah, can you give us a moment?"

"And give you two time to line up your stories? No way! I came here for the truth."

"Freya. Answer my question," Ryan said stonily.

She looked at their agonized faces and reminded herself that the only thing she'd done wrong was try to protect them. Except she had an ominous feeling it wouldn't be enough.

She blew out a breath. "If I'd known Jamie was back with Monique I would have told Hannah."

Ryan recognized her prevarication. "That doesn't tell us what you did know."

"I knew that when Jamie and Monique were together they occasionally used MDMA."

Hannah swore. "Of course he took ecstasy!"

"No, he didn't," Ryan said, visibly rallying. "That was Monique. Remember, I had to give her IV fluids once and Jamie was pretty pissed off with her."

"That's what he told you," Freya said, trying to lay the groundwork for the truth Ryan wouldn't want to hear let alone believe.

Ryan's face contorted as he tried to absorb the information. "No. He was the most straight-up-and-down guy I knew. If he'd been into stuff like that I would have known."

"Haven't you heard me?" Hannah interrupted. "The reason Jamie came back to Garringarup was to be closer to Monique. I was the smokescreen to preserve her Madonna-mother image and his upstanding citizen award! When he met me he'd already started seeing her again."

Freya caught Ryan's hands in hers. "I know this is hard. Up until Jamie split with Monique I thought he was straight-up-and-down too, but something happened."

"What?"

She took a breath as if it would help. "He came over one night when you were at work. He looked so gutted and miserable that I didn't think it was safe to let him leave. He poured out his heart about Monique and I listened. I gave him beer and tissues and sympathy, exactly as you would have done." She paused. She didn't want to remember specifics and she didn't want Ryan to hear them. "There was a moment when he made it abundantly clear that if I was interested in taking things further then he was too. Of course I told him no."

She saw the shock in Ryan's eyes—the betrayal and pain she'd tried to spare him. "Why didn't you tell me?"

"So many reasons."

"Like what?" His tone was belligerent.

"At first I was in shock. I was caught in a trap of asking myself 'Did he really just do that?' and shaking it off with 'No, not possible, he's Ryan's best mate'."

"And?" Ryan demanded.

She sighed. "In your eyes Jamie could do no wrong."

"That's not fair."

"Oh, come on, Ryan. Think about it. If I'd told you what happened you'd have been torn between struggling to believe that Jamie had broken the bro code and your need to support me. And if you had confronted him, he'd have denied it and implied I was jealous of your friendship. You would have found that easy to believe, because after he split with Monique he basically lived with us for months. I love you, Ryan, but I had the most to lose."

Ryan was rubbing his face so hard that Freya worried the skin might come off.

"But mostly I didn't tell you because Jamie begged me not to," she went on. "He said he'd never forgive himself if his one stupid mistake caused you and me any problems. I honestly believed his contrition—that he was in a dark place and it was only his grief over Monique that had made him act out of character."

"He was a hell of an actor," Hannah said bitterly. "He told us what we wanted to hear. He broke up with Monique over not wanting children, but he never let that slip. He let us believe she broke his heart and he milked every last bit of sympathy out of us that he could. He used it to bond us to him, to be on his side."

Hannah's words made sense, illuminating something about Jamie that Freya had never been able to articulate. "She's right, Ryan."

"And hitting on you is the real reason he went to Perth," Ryan said dully.

Freya nodded. "At the time my head believed his apology, but my gut churned whenever he was near. I told him if he didn't go to Perth, I'd tell you."

Ryan's hands fisted and he thumped them into the sofa cushions. When he looked up sadness ringed him. "God, Frey, you took a huge hit when he left. I was upset. Lydia convinced her friends not to buy from you and half the cricket club did the same."

She shrugged. "Most of them forgave me eventually. When he brought Hannah home I reassured myself I'd done the right thing. He was in a relationship and your friendship was safe."

"That's why you pushed him so hard to marry Hannah," Ryan said slowly, as if things were finally coming into focus.

Freya shifted her gaze to Hannah. "I truly believed he loved you. But I also thought that if he was married I could finally relax. I'm so sorry I was that stupid."

"Oh my God!" Hannah's voice was the high screech of a bow jagging on strings. "Are you saying he hit on you when we were engaged and you didn't tell me?"

Freya wrung her hands. "I tried to tell you. It was just before the tree fell on the marquee and you were worried Jamie was stressing about the wedding. I asked you if you really wanted to marry him."

"That's not telling me!"

"When did he do this?" Ryan ground out the words.

"The same night he told me he didn't want children."

"And yet you managed to tell me that and still not say he was a womanizing prick?" Hannah yelled.

"He died, Hannah! I thought he'd taken all those ugly truths with him. You and Ryan were distraught and I didn't want to add to your pain when it changed nothing. I was trying to protect you both. Protect myself. And, Hannah, if I'd told you, would you have believed me?'

Hannah's chest heaved and the battle in her head reflected clearly on her face. Seconds passed and eventually she said, "I would have hated you instead of hating him. Just like I hated you for telling me he didn't want kids." She went quiet. "Why was telling me that easier for you?"

A huff of sound shot out of Freya's mouth. "You think that was easy for me? I knew I had to break your heart because Jamie had lied to you, and the messenger always gets shot."

"Then why did you tell me?"

"Because as much as I detested Jamie—and it sounds like he was way more of a bastard than I thought—he still has rights. If we ignore those rights then we're as bad as he was."

Hannah suddenly pulled at her hair. "God, it's all such a mess. I don't know what or who to believe anymore."

"You're not alone there," Ryan said. "I hate what he did to you both."

"He did it to you too," Freya said. "He was too clever for any of us to stand a chance."

Mia's cry barreled under the closed door and Ryan stood. "I'll go."

When he left the room Freya asked Hannah, "What are you going to do now?"

"As in this minute? The next hour? The rest of my life? I have no fucking idea." Hannah hugged herself. "I'll have to face his parents eventually. Tell them about the house he bought for Monique."

Shock and anxiety walloped Freya. "Be careful. In their eyes, especially Lydia's, Jamie could do no wrong."

"Yeah, well, the evidence against that fable is stacking up pretty high."

"Do you want me to come with you?"

Hannah's gaze was rock hard. "And that would be useful how? Lydia detests you."

Freya followed Hannah to the door, wanting to hug her but uncertain if she would accept the touch. "I meant as moral support for you. I'm here if you need me."

Hannah turned, her face swimming with emotions—some hard, some soft, most jagged. "That's the thing, Freya. I don't know if I want or need anything from you ever again."

The reverberation of the slamming door crushed Freya's heart.

CHAPTER FORTY

HANNAH DIDN'T SLEEP, and at 5:00 she gave up. Pulling on boots and a fleece, she grabbed her keys and drove to Baile Na, desperate for a ride that would use all her concentration and leave no room for anything else.

Under the peach light of dawn she took the trail along the creek and let the wind steal her screams and sobs. When she returned to the stables she was exhausted, but her mind hadn't received the message—unwanted thoughts and images tumbled through it like debris in a windstorm.

She folded the saddle blanket. "Bastards!"

"Hannah?" Mac's voice rang through the stable. "Need a hand?"

She swore under her breath then called out brightly, "All good," before dropping her head onto Bullet's flank, breathing deeply to stall tears.

She heard footsteps ringing on the flagstones and knew Mac would appear any second. She stepped out and forced her lips upwards into what she hoped was a smile. Her face was so tight it threatened to crack.

"Hey, Mac. Hope you don't mind that I took you up on your offer of a ride any time."

"Glad you did." His gaze took in her outfit. Although the boots were regulation, her flannelette pajama pants were not.

She faked a laugh. "The dawn called and I didn't want to miss it. Isn't that what death teaches us? Live in the moment and all that."

He gave her a contemplative look as if he only half-agreed, but then he smiled.

Hannah caught a flash of something that took her straight back to the simmering moment between them at the graveyard. Straight back to the guilt she'd experienced at the unwelcome spin of attraction. The self-reproach that had accompanied her on every drive home from Baile Na because she'd been happy and Jamie couldn't share in it.

Fuck you, Jamie.

"You got time for breakfast?" Mac said.

"I've got all the time in the world."

Hannah sat at the table and watched Mac move around the kitchen poaching eggs, frying bacon and cooking toast. "No mimosas today?"

Surprise lifted his brows. "It's a work day and I'm out of orange juice."

"That's not a problem for me."

He hesitated, then opened a bottle of sparkling wine and poured her a glass. She downed it quickly. By the time he served the food, her head was spinning.

"I can make you a latte," he said.

"This works for now." Ignoring the concern in his eyes, she poured another glass.

Mac asked her about her plans for the day, but she steered the conversation firmly onto the farm and his day. While he talked about the autumn break she nodded, feigning interest, and kept drinking. The alcohol cast a warm and cozy glow around her, anaesthetizing the horrors of the previous day.

"Hannah?"

"Hmm?"

"What's going on?"

"Nothing."

He cocked a brow. "Yeah, nah. First you ask me about the autumn break when we both know you roll your eyes at weather chat. Now you're drinking that bottle like it's water and staring into space."

She had a sudden urge to find out if she was the only fool when it came to her dead fiancé. "What was Jamie like at school?"

Mac shifted uncomfortably in his chair. "Is this about the alumni thing? It's just—"

"No. And by the way, the trust idea is toast."

"Really?" He sounded relieved yet curious. "You seemed pretty passionate about it."

"Yeah, well, I changed my mind. Tell me what Jamie was like at school."

"He was in Dan's year so ..." Mac shoved a large portion of bacon and eggs into his mouth.

"That doesn't stop you having an opinion. You said you were in the same boarding house."

He took his time chewing and swallowing. "It was years ago, Hannah."

"So?"

He shrugged. "We all do stuff when we're young and stupid. Then we grow up, regret it and change for the better."

"Do we?" She laughed, the sound wild and unhinged.

Worry furrowed a deep line between Mac's eyes. "Something's happened, hasn't it?"

She shook her head, hating his perspicacity. "Just give me *your* opinion of young Jamie, not what you think I want to hear."

"You sure? You normally only want to hear good things about him."

She grimaced at the memory of shutting him down the time he'd told her that he and Jamie didn't always see eye to eye. "I need to know who he really was."

Mac's face was wary, as if he didn't fully believe her. "If you're sure ..."

She raised her glass to him. "Oh, I am."

"Jamie was like a ..." He clicked his fingers as if it would summon the word. "One of those African lizards that changes color."

"A chameleon?"

"Yeah, that's it. He was the person each group needed him to be. The teachers adored him because he was an academic kid who respected the school's traditions. Unlike me and Dan, he never rocked the boat. Whenever the teachers were about he hung out with the computer nerds, but there were plenty of times he'd get a weekend pass and party hard with the day kids. I'm not judging the partying—hell, we all did it—but when we got caught we took the carpeting and the detention. Not Jamie; he was Teflon. As much as we hated it, we couldn't help but be impressed by how he did it. For a while anyway, and then something ugly happened."

"What?"

"You don't want to hear about it."

You don't have to worry about that, poss.

We did it in a way that protected you, David and Will.

I know it's hard, Hannah, but bear with us.

Rage spiked, swift and hot. "It's not up to you to decide what I can and can't hear. I'm not a child."

"I'm aware. This is more me—I don't particularly enjoy talking about it." He drained his coffee. "There was an incident at a party involving a couple of girls. Three boys were expelled but not Jamie. He came out of it the hero—the bloke who defended the girls' honor and rescued them from badly behaved, misogynistic private-school boys."

The photos she'd seen on her computer roared back. Hannah drained her glass. "And you don't think he saved them?"

"Put it this way. He might not have been *as* involved as the others, but it's unlikely he was entirely innocent. But he let the others take the blame while he soaked up the glory."

Had the fallout from that high-school party been the start of a lifelong mode of behavior? Getting away with it must have been exhilarating in both its duplicity and relief. Was that the start of him taking sexual risks?

Hannah hauled her mind away from the thoughts so fast she gave herself whiplash. She didn't bloody care how it had started.

"He didn't change," she said, bitterness clinging to her words. "In fact, it got a whole lot worse. Turns out that motherfucker cheated on me in more ways than I imagined possible. I've been grieving a stranger."

Mac squeezed her hand. "I'm sorry. That's got to be—"

"Humiliating? Embarrassing? Excruciating? Like swimming in a pool of shame?"

"I was gonna say hard."

"Hah!" The need to move had her pushing back from the table. "I wish he was here so I could scream at him, punch him, slash his tires and throw his clothes onto the street. But he's dead, so the bastard's stolen that from me too!"

She was sobbing now and she didn't want to cry. She wanted to be strong. She wanted to rage and storm, but Mac and the dogs were looking at her with worry and care bright in their eyes.

"Hannah?"

She turned and sagged against him. He brought his arms up, his touch respectful and light, and patted her back as if she was an unexploded bomb.

It infuriated her. She didn't want to be pitied. She wanted to be seen. Had Jamie ever seen her or had she just been convenient to him? The gullible young woman who propped up his squeaky-clean image of a man to be admired by his community.

She thought about the photos on the USB stick and every part of her boiled. The few times she'd tried to spice up their sex life he'd used a particular look and words to make her feel just a little bit dirty, and the entire time he'd been off doing things that went far beyond healthy fantasy. Things that degraded women. Things that made her skin crawl.

She wanted to rid herself of every memory of Jamie—the role he'd created for her in his life, his lying words, his touch. The urge to evict him from both her body and her soul exploded in every cell. She wound her arms around Mac's neck, pulled his head down to hers and kissed him.

For a moment he stilled, then wound his hands through her hair and returned the kiss.

She pressed in, lining her body against his, soaking in his heat. Her palms longed to feel his skin against them, the muscular strength of his chest, the broadness of his body—the antithesis of—Her mind veered away as her fingers fumbled on the buttons of his shirt.

His lips lightened on hers and suddenly there was air between them.

His large hands gently covered hers. "Hannah? I'm not sure this is such a good idea. You're dealing with a lot and trying to make sense of something that makes no sense and—"

"You think I don't know all that?" She couldn't keep the shrillness out of her voice. "Of course I know it and I need to forget every single thing. I could drink myself unconscious or I could take something, but sex with you is the safer option. You're here, I'm here. It's nothing more complicated than getting out of my own head. And there've been moments between us, right? Like on that horse ride? The way you just kissed me? I thought—" She stepped back. Had she misread him? "But if you're uncomfortable, I'll ask Sam Dillinger."

Mac flinched and swore softly. "A vibrator would be safer."

But this was about so much more than an orgasm.

"Hannah, it's not that I don't want to ..."

She closed the slight gap. "That sounds hopeful."

"It's just ..." He ran his hand through his hair.

She didn't want to know what followed the "just', but she asked anyway. "What?"

"Call me old-fashioned—"

She flinched, her desire vanishing. "That was Jamie's line for treating me like a child."

His mouth twisted as if he was in pain. "Let me put it another way. I don't want to make things worse for you. I don't want you to regret it."

Exasperation surged. "I won't. All I'm after is a chance to forget awhile before I have to deal with my crappy life all over again. You're either in or you're out."

"So to speak," he deadpanned.

She laughed then and this time, instead of it filling her with rage, she experienced a tiny moment of joy. "Exactly."

He paced in a circle. "I know you don't want to be looked after, but hell—Sam Dillinger?"

"I can see this is a dilemma for you. Perhaps the solution is we play you rescuing a maiden in distress."

His heavy-lidded eyes gazed at her and the smolder of desire flared again. He stepped in close and the next minute she was upside down on his shoulder, courtesy of a dexterous fireman's lift.

"There be dragons," he said.

She grinned and slid her hands down his back, cupping his buttocks, loving how they tensed under her hands. "There are always dragons."

"Let's slay them together."

Hannah woke later to a warm but empty bed. She shielded her eyes against the mid-morning sun and took in the freshly painted Baltic pine boards that lined the walls of the old cottage. Unable to help herself, she grinned. Mac had given her exactly what she'd needed—great sex and a few hours respite from her life. Not to mention the momentary power of revenge—posthumous cheating on a complete and utter bastard. She refused to allow anyone to use her ever again!

Mac let you use him.

The thought hit like a sniper's bullet and shame flooded her. Did that make her as bad as Jamie?

No! She'd been upfront and honest with Mac and laid out the

ground rules. But was that enough to lessen an uncomfortable post-sex moment?

Hannah didn't have a vast amount of experience in that area but, unlike at university, she knew she shouldn't just sneak out, shoes in hand. Mac was polite. He'd insist on waving goodbye to her as she drove away.

God, what had she been thinking? She should have used Sam Dillinger. At least Mac lived far enough away from Garringarup that she wouldn't be running into him every day.

You've trashed your chance to ride Bullet again.

I'll borrow a horse from someone and ride in Garringarup.

The thought spilled light over her life. Did she even want to live in Garringarup anymore?

But she couldn't think about that now, so, she wrapped a sheet around herself, padded to the door and stuck her head into the hall. The only sounds she heard were the tick of a clock and the hum of the fridge.

She grabbed her clothes and scurried into the bathroom. When she emerged, she squared her shoulders, mentally ready to face him. She'd thank him and hit the road.

With a "hi" on her lips, she stepped into the kitchen. There was a cake container on the table with a note stuck to the top.

Help yourself to coffee and cake. Cream is in the fridge. Safe trip back to G'up. Mac

In the distance she heard the rumble of farm machinery. He'd taken her at her word that this was a one-time event.

Relief flowed freely until a jolt startled her. She realized she wanted to thank him.

CHAPTER FORTY-ONE

Freya wished all the thoughts in her head were dandelion seeds that she could blow into the air to be carried away by the wind. Instead, they were drilling down taproots and taking hold.

The needs of her mother, Mia and Lexie.

The slump in sales courtesy of the latest economic forecast.

Hannah's accusations and devastation.

Ryan's silence and despair.

The morning after Hannah's bombshells, Ryan had gone for an extremely long bike ride. When he returned he'd both stunned and reassured her with, "I've got an appointment in Perth on Monday to talk to the work counselor."

She wanted to say, "Finally!" but settled on, "I think that's a good idea."

He'd shrugged. "You don't open on Mondays so why don't you come with me?"

"To the counselor?"

"To visit your mum."

She'd thought the fact Ryan had made an appointment with a

counselor meant he was ready to talk about Jamie with her. Hell, *she* needed to talk about Jamie with him. She had an overwhelming urge to reassure him over and over that everything she'd done came from a place of love for him. But each time she tried to say it, he shut down the conversation with variations on "It's not about you, Freya," which didn't dispel her fears.

She'd called Lexie's caseworker and requested an out-of-hours visit for herself and Mia. The response—"we'll discuss it at the team meeting"—hadn't sounded positive, but she'd received permission for a thirty-minute visit at 3:00 during the tea-break between program sessions. Vivian had wanted to come too, but the counselor was adamant—only Freya and Mia.

The rehabilitation center was nestled in a large and attractive garden, which Freya assumed was a calm oasis for the residents who spent their days in individual and group sessions wrestling demons. As arranged, Lexie met them outside and they hugged. She smelled of cigarettes and felt far too thin.

In the shade of a sprawling gum, Freya encouraged Mia to sit on the wooden bench next to her mother and tell her the stories depicted in the drawings and paintings she'd made for her.

It didn't take long for Mia to work out that her mother's attention had wandered, so after eating the snack Freya had packed for her she ran off to roll on the patch of soft green lawn. Parks in Garringarup never ran to such luxury. Freya kept an eye on her niece and closed the physical gap between herself and her sister, feeling their emotional distance bulging between them. The sparkle that had radiated off Lexie during previous visits was absent.

"How are you?" Freya asked.

"Yeah."

"Are you feeling better? I mean, is the program helping?"

Lexie shrugged and rubbed at the cuticle on her thumbnail.

Freya tried not to think *I travelled two hours to see you and this is the best you can do?* Instead she revisited what she'd been told at the relatives' session she and Vivian had attended: mental health problems take time—*so much time*—to resolve. Ups and downs are a normal part of recovery.

She racked her mind for something to talk about. Since Lexie's admission, Freya had sent her a daily photo of Mia along with a brief text outlining what the little girl had been up to, so there was nothing new to impart. She refused to ask Lexie about Heath. Her sister's tendency to attach herself to dropkick men was legendary, so if her infatuation with him had already hit a wall that could only be a good thing. She had a few eye-roll-worthy stories about Ainsley at pre-school pick-up, but worried they would only shine a light on the fact that Lexie wasn't currently caring for Mia.

Lexie broke the silence. "Why are you even here?"

"In Perth?"

Lexie nodded.

"Ryan's finally decided to talk to someone about Jamie. He's with the counselor now."

"Oh yeah?"

"Yeah. To be honest, it's been a shit few days. Hannah discovered that Jamie was back with Monique and—" Freya stopped, wondering if it was her story to tell.

Lexie, who hadn't looked at her directly since she'd arrived, turned her head so sharply that Freya heard a click. "And what?"

This time it was Freya studying her hands. Although Hannah had worn the look of someone capable of stabbing that cheating lying bastard in the heart, did she plan on making Jamie's transgressions public? Even if she didn't, these things had a way of getting out. Still, despite Freya believing that Hannah had no reason to blame herself for Jamie's actions or to feel any shame, she knew that logic and reality were worlds apart.

"Nothing. It doesn't matter," she said.

"That's bullshit. You were going to tell me something so spit it out."

Freya sighed, knowing Lexie would badger her until she broke.

"Besides the thing with Monique, it looks like Jamie had this whole other secret life outside of Garringarup. Apparently he was into some pretty hardcore stuff in Perth."

Freya expected a wide-eyed look from her sister, an "Oh my God!" or a long blown-out "No way!"—the same stunned surprise that had walloped her and Ryan.

Lexie snorted. "You and Ryan only ever see what you want to see."

"What's that supposed to mean?"

Lexie pulled out a cigarette. "Exactly that."

Freya struggled to follow. "Are you saying that you knew about Jamie's secret life?"

"I knew he wasn't as upstanding as he wanted everyone to believe."

"How?"

"I ran into him once in a place where he didn't belong."

"Why didn't you say something?" The hypocritical words fell out of her mouth before she could stop them.

Lexie lit her cigarette, took a long drag and exhaled, watching the smoke curl upwards. "That's the thing about a secret life, Freya. You want it to stay secret. That, and Kane didn't want me to tell you because he knew you'd have a cow."

Freya didn't want to think about what Kane might have got Lexie tangled up in. Had that been the start of her downward spiral? Pure hatred for him poured through her.

"But you're safe? Now, I mean?" she said.

"Locked up in here with the other crazies? Oh, yeah, totally safe."

Freya held onto her sigh. "You're not crazy, Lexie."

"I know that." Lexie forcibly ground out her cigarette.

"You're in the right place. The counselors here are experienced and everyone's working towards your goal of coming home to Mia."

"Which will make your life easier."

The animosity in Lexie's words slapped her. "What? No. This is nothing to do with me and everything to do with you."

"You say that, but it's always been about you, Freya. Do you have any idea what it was like growing up as your sister?"

I know what it was like growing up as yours.

Freya thought about the years of Lexie's tantrums, her periods of school refusal, her risk-taking behavior as a teen and how their parents had aged prematurely from worry. How Freya, not wanting to add to their burden, had done everything that was expected of her and, as a result, had faded into the background, all achievements unnoticed. But it had been worth it, because eventually the wild child in Lexie had found peace in motherhood and Freya had relaxed. Then Kane had torpedoed it all and Freya was back to worrying about and supporting Lexie, who appeared to be blaming her for ... what? Being a responsible adult? She wanted to scream.

"Why don't you tell me what it was like?" she said through gritted teeth.

"God, you sound like group therapy. I am *so* sick of group therapy." Lexie lit another cigarette.

Freya shoved her hands under her thighs so she didn't slap her sister. "Sounds like it's the perfect forum to bitch about me."

Lexie laughed. "I did. Turns out you're not the only bossy big sister to call social services."

Freya refused to apologize for that.

Mia waved. Freya waited, but when Lexie failed to notice she waved back. Her niece returned to rolling. Cockatoos squawked and Freya thought how anyone passing would have considered it lovely that two women were sitting together in the autumn sunshine enjoying the antics of a four-year-old.

A bell rang and Lexie swore. "God, this place. We're treated like children. 'Get up now. You're on lunch prep. It's time for group. Have you done your reflections? No, you can't have day leave.' And Anna's 'How does that make you feel, Lexie?' is the worst."

"I thought you liked Anna? Last week you said she was kind."

"She's a controlling bitch."

Freya tried to stall the sinking feeling in her gut as her words from years past echoed through her—*but I thought you liked that subject/school/job/boss/boyfriend/girlfriend ...*

"I'm sorry you feel that way. Perhaps you can ask to change counselors?"

"They all suck. Heath says I'll get better faster somewhere else."

Panic whipped Freya so fast she trembled. "This program's the best. And even if we could get you in somewhere else, you won't get credit for the time you've been here. You'd have to start over."

Lexie huffed out a long stream of smoke. "I don't need a treatment program, I just need a rest. Hell, Kane's getting to do whatever the hell he wants—why can't I? And being on the coast will clear my head faster and restore my soul so much better than this place. It's all organized. Heath's picking me up in the morning and we're heading north."

No, no, no! "And Mia?" Freya couldn't keep the wobble out of her voice.

"That's the beauty of the plan. By the time we arrive in Broome, I'll be relaxed and ready to work again. There are heaps of jobs up there—I can work in reception at one of those swanky resorts. Being surrounded by happy tourists will be heaps better for me than sick people at the hospital. That was really dragging me down. And Heath's great with his hands. He'll get a job in maintenance easy, and he loves kids so it's win-win." Lexie smiled as if the plan was foolproof. "Three months tops, we'll be ready for Mia."

Freya's brain melted. Her sister was running away with a man she'd met in a drug and alcohol center. A man she'd only known for three weeks and no one in her family had met, yet she was suggesting he'd be great with Mia? Freya wanted to berate Lexie. Shake her. Curl up in a ball and sob.

She gripped the edge of the counter and silently chanted, *This is the addict talking, not Lexie. This is the delusional addict, not Lexie.*

It worked inasmuch as it reminded her not to yell words and sentiments she'd regret, but that was as useful as it got. Freya had no difficulty picturing what Lexie was imagining. The honeymoon road trip. Driving around the crazy limestone formations of the Pinnacles. Visiting the dazzling beaches along the Ningaloo coast where outback red dust collided with brilliant white sand and ran into a clear turquoise sea. The romance of Broome: standing on Cable Beach with Heath watching the sun drop swiftly beneath the horizon in a blazing ball of fire—nature's natural high.

But the relaxed lifestyle of the north hid the reality of a cost of living higher than down south, a shortage of affordable housing, the impermanence of hospitality work and Lexie's inability to stay in a job for longer than a few months. Combined with her alcohol problem, it was a disaster waiting to happen. She'd spiral fast 2000 kilometers away from her family.

"Lexie, please. Finish the program. These next few weeks are nothing compared to the rest of your life."

Lexie shook her head. "Heath's leaving tomorrow."

"If he really wants you to get better he'll wait for you."

"I can't ask him to do that. Perth's toxic for him."

Breathe, breathe, breathe. "But what if leaving rehab early is toxic for you? Mia—"

"It'll be no different for Mia. You're the one who involved child protection so she's with you until the review date. By then Heath and I will be ready."

"Lexie, there has to be another way."

Mia ran up and Lexie pulled her onto her lap. "You and Mummy are going to live by the sea."

Mia's eyes rounded. "Can we build sandcastles?"

"Yes, and eat ice-cream and swim with the fish."

Mia clapped. "Yay! Now?"

"Soon. I'll send you a postcard of the world's biggest fish. I have to go inside now so give Mummy a big hug goodbye."

"Lexie, please don't do this," Freya begged.

"I tried things your way. Now it's my turn."

Knowing that Lexie was an addict was no protection against the barb that pierced Freya's heart and lodged there, spiking her with every beat.

"Will you tell Mum?" she managed.

"I'll send her a postcard."

As Lexie walked away, Freya held Mia's hand and heard herself saying in an unrecognizably jolly voice, "Let's wave bye-bye to Mummy."

CHAPTER FORTY-TWO

When Lydia followed up three text messages with a phone call, Hannah knew she could no longer put off visiting the McMasters. She'd initially fobbed her off by saying she had a cold, but if she waited any longer Lydia would arrive with immune-boosting soup and see she wasn't sick. Well, not with a virus anyway.

Since Monique had connected all the inexplicable details about Jamie and revealed a picture of a stranger, all the anchors in Hannah's life had vanished. She was adrift like a rudderless boat. In some ways the shock and pain of it mirrored her experience when Jamie died, but if she'd thought her anger at the universe for stealing him from her was hot enough to blister paint, it had nothing on her volcanic rage at *him* that bruised her from the inside out.

Once she would have said bereavement was the worst thing to happen to her, but Jamie's eviscerating duplicity made it look like a paper cut. The question, *What did I ever do to you that would make you do this to me?* played over and over in her head, echoing back unanswered.

On Sunday, Hannah drove her car across the cattle guard that protected the homestead's garden from the ravages of hungry sheep and parked next to Ian's four-wheel drive. Her stomach cramped and she took a deep breath. *Just open the door.*

She was wrapping her fingers around the handle when her phone pinged.

Hi Han na h Ma c her e R U OK?

She stared at the run of letters and worked out the words. Mac. It was the first communication they'd shared since she'd left Baile Na. Considering how firm she'd been about one-night-only, and how he'd respected her wishes by not being in the house when she left, she was surprised yet grateful for the text.

With so many secrets and lies ringing her like planets, she didn't plan to add to them. She replied honestly: *I have no idea what OK even looks like*

It didn't take long for another text to arrive. *Wha t Jamie did wason hime Dint let it lessen u. Im here if u ned me*

Three wiggly dots appeared then more words tumbled onto the screen: *As a friend* Three more squiggly dots.

Not that sex was nt awesome TY A facepalm emoji followed.

Hannah laughed, entertained by his half-comprehensible texting and obvious discomfort, but touched by his thoughtfulness. She pictured his huge fingers struggling to fit on the phone's screen and his swearing as his best intentions dug him deeper into a hole he was desperate not to occupy.

She accepted responsibility for that. It seemed Mac wasn't a natural one-night-stand kind of bloke. Not that she could trust her gut on what type of person anyone was anymore. She sent a laughing face and an eggplant emoji, then switched off her phone.

As she walked towards the house she sent a silent volley of abuse Jamie's way. Facing his parents was the absolute frosting on the stinking, steaming turd he'd left behind. She doubted Lydia and Ian knew of their precious son's sexual proclivities. Not even Freya had known about them, and outside of Monique she was the only person to get even a hint that Jamie wasn't as respectable as he'd pretended to be.

I'm here if you need me. For a moment Hannah wished she hadn't held onto her injustice and rejected Freya's offer. But trusting people had suddenly got hard, especially when she had proof that they'd lied to her.

She withheld one truth to protect you.

Yeah? And look how well that turned out for me, her and Ryan. No one has the right to decide what I should and shouldn't know.

Mac hasn't lied to you.

How would I even know that? I said the same thing about Jamie.

Hannah smoothed down her skirt and straightened her shoulders, as if that was all it took to fortify her for a difficult conversation. Based on Freya's "be careful" warning and Declan's advice to nail down all the financial stuff, her plan was to withhold the truth about Jamie until the money was in her account, the house was in her name, and she was financially protected. Jamie owed her every damn cent.

She found Lydia and Ian on the back veranda, sitting in white cane chairs. Ozzie greeted them enthusiastically and the usual Sunday lunch traditions played out. Ian mixed her a Pimm's, generous with fruit, and Lydia pushed a plate of runny brie and homemade quince preserve across the table.

"You're very pale, darling," Lydia said, suddenly gripping Ian's forearm to prevent him from handing Hannah the drink. Hope suffused her face. "Does this mean you've started the hormones? Should you be drinking or eating soft cheese?"

The one light in the dark tunnel that Hannah had been stuck in since Jamie's death, the one dream that had kept her going for months, now turned her uterus to stone. "Not yet." She accepted the drink, needing the hit of alcohol.

Disappointment sagged Lydia's shoulders. "I'm sure it will happen soon."

"I think the stress of Jamie's estate not being settled is delaying my period," Hannah said.

Who's lying now?

It's not strictly a lie.

"I feel like I'm stuck in limbo and I hate it," she continued. "It's time you gave me all the details so I know exactly what's going on."

Lydia visibly startled. "Oh, darling, nothing's going on. We're not hiding anything from you. It's just you've got so much on your plate already we didn't want to add to it. Your job is to concentrate on getting pregnant."

"I'm sorry, Hannah." Worry lines deepened around Ian's mouth. "Winding up Jamie's business has taken longer than expected, and now Rowan's run into a snag with the river house. Turns out it was a company asset."

Hannah studied Ian, looking for signs he knew about Monique's name on the title, but he just looked weary. "How does that affect me?"

"I'm afraid there were more debts against the business than expected."

Hannah's heart lurched. "But the business wasn't in the red."

Ian shifted in his seat, clearly uncomfortable. "It was a surprise to discover that Jamie had drawn against it to pay substantial personal debts."

After days of careening down the mudslide of salacious revelations about Jamie, Hannah thought she'd reached a plateau. Now she felt the tremors that heralded another descent. Personal debts? She supposed driving fast cars with a lover and paying young women to use and abuse them didn't come cheap. *You total motherfucking asshole!*

"I've got substantial debts now too." Her voice rose as her control slipped. "Debts you both told me not to worry about."

Lydia took her hand. "Hannah, you're family. We'll look after you."

Would they though, when she broke their hearts about their son and their longed-for grandson? In this moment she didn't doubt the veracity of Lydia's words, just the future capacity to honor them.

"How much money's left?" she asked.

"About 8,000," Ian said matter-of-factly.

Hannah gripped the highball glass so tightly she was surprised it didn't shatter in her hand. She'd already spent more than that on legal fees, harvesting and freezing fees, counselling, upfront IVF costs, hormones she'd never use, food, fuel, living. Her mind reeled as the mud sucked at her, carrying her further away from the financial security she'd believed circled her life.

A clear thought penetrated her shock. There was still the schoolhouse. It was a heritage-listed home on Garringarup's second-best street. She could sell it, pay off her debts to the McMasters and have enough left for a generous deposit on a flat in Perth. The plummeting feeling steadied.

"When do I get the paperwork?" she asked.

"What paperwork's that?" Ian said.

"The title to the house."

The McMasters exchanged a look. Despite the autumn sunshine, a chill raced across Hannah's skin.

"Darling, the house belongs to the farm," Lydia said.

Through the roar of incredulity, Hannah heard her adding, "But of course you can continue to live there—although when the baby comes it's probably easier if you move to the farm. That way we can be the extra pairs of hands you'll need exactly when you need them."

The house belonged to the farm? *Of course it bloody does* a fatalistic voice chimed in the recesses of her mind. Agitation skittered along her gut.

"What about Jamie's investment in the farm? I'll get dividends from that, right?"

Ian pulled on his ear. "I'm sorry, love. Jamie borrowed money against the business to invest in the farm and we've had to refinance to accommodate that debt. To be honest, money's tight, but grain prices are high. God willing, the next crop will be a bumper."

Phrases roared in Hannah's head: *if it rains enough, if it doesn't rain too much, if there isn't a frost, if fuel and fertilizer costs don't rise, if Russia or China don't blockade.* If. If. If! Her last financial hope crumbled.

She shuddered. All she'd ever believed about Jamie had been smoke and mirrors. Had he ever told her the truth about anything? Had he loved her at all?

Did she *want* to have been loved by such a calculating, cheating and manipulative prick? No! But the thought that burrowed deep into her like a flesh-eating bug was: how had she lived with him, worked alongside him, and never known?

She'd said the same words to Jamie soon after she'd moved to Garringarup and had read an article about a woman who'd discovered her dead husband had another family living three streets away from his marital home.

Jamie had shaken his head as if the idea was so alien to him that he had no way of reconciling it. "Keeping a secret like that would be exhausting." Then he'd dropped a kiss onto the top of her head and added, "You don't have to worry. I only have enough energy to keep up with you."

They'd both laughed.

And yet here she was, exactly like that duped wife, but with the added sting of owing his parents money. How had she allowed this to happen to her? How had she failed to have even an inkling?

Love and trust. The two things she'd been raised to believe in had blinded her.

Then the words of Mac's text lit up in her mind. She would not let Jamie lessen her.

"Hannah, we know this is a shock." Lydia's eyes were filled with worry. "But it's all going to be okay. I mean, what sort of people would we be if we didn't take care of the mother of our grandchild? You're not on your own. There's nothing to worry about."

"I can't have Jamie's baby." The words fell from Hannah's mouth like stones.

"Of course you can. You're young and fit and healthy, and we'll help you out financially until you're back on your feet."

"That's not the reason." She looked at their confused faces and drew in a deep breath. "Jamie was in a long-term affair with Monique."

Lydia laughed. "Don't be ridiculous."

"I'm not. He didn't buy that house on the river for us, he bought it for him and Monique. Clever really, but that was Jamie. It's far enough away from the main road to be hidden, but conveniently located between here and her husband's farm so he could pop in on his way home from Perth each week."

"Hannah, dear, I know you've been under a lot of stress but you're not making sense. Ian, call Angus. She needs a sedative."

Hannah ignored Lydia and spoke directly to Ian, hoping he'd hear her. "Did you know about the river house before Jamie died?"

He sighed. "No. When I saw the purchase date I assumed you'd bought it together."

"The first time I knew about it was when you told me. And if Jamie didn't want to hide the purchase, why did he use a shell company to buy it? Monique told me that once Rowan digs down you'll find her name."

Ian groaned and drained his glass.

"You can't believe anything *that* woman says about Jamie!" Lydia scoffed.

"I know you want to believe that," Hannah said, "but the ultimate irony in all this mess is that Monique has no reason to lie. The day I drove to the river house, she was there. She told me things I didn't want to know, let alone hear, about her and Jamie. I fought them, but her hints that Jamie was hiding more than their affair threw light on the worrying things about him that I couldn't explain."

"What things?" Lydia said.

"The Porsche that had *nothing* to do with our wedding and everything to do with Monique. The young woman who came to the house wanting money claiming that Jamie was paying her beauty school fees. It turns out he was paying her to do things no woman should ever have to do. Then there's the BDSM club he joined, the—"

"How dare you say such outrageous things!" Lydia slammed her hand on the table and a cheese knife clattered onto the veranda boards.

Hannah understood her shock. "I'm sorry. I get that no one wants to hear their son had a sex addiction, but it's the truth."

Ian's complexion matched the white of his chair. "It may account for his debt."

"Don't you dare believe her!" Lydia screamed.

"Lyd," Ian said gently, "he spent over a $100,000 in a few months."

"On donations. On the wedding!"

"No," Hannah said firmly. "I paid most of the wedding bills and he was going to reimburse me when I knew the final figure."

"My son was *not* a sex addict," Lydia ground out, her face florid. "He wasn't any sort of addict. He was a kind and generous man who did so much for his community. He got an award for his charity work. Ian, tell her to stop this nonsense."

"Hannah, do you have any proof?" Ian asked.

Hannah pulled the USB stick she could barely stand to touch out of her handbag and laid it on the table. "There are photos. They're very confronting."

They all stared at the thumb drive. Neither Ian nor Lydia reached for it.

Lydia finally broke the silence. "You haven't told anyone else these awful lies, have you?"

Hannah was long past propping up a false idol. "Freya and Ryan know. I accused them of enabling him and that's when I discovered none of us knew him. Except perhaps Monique, and even then he hid things from her."

"You two-faced bitch!" Lydia screamed. "If you think you're getting anything of his now, think again."

Hannah pressed her nails into her palms, using the pain to steady herself. "I was engaged to him and the law says I inherit."

"And you owe us more than $8,000."

Cold fury ran through her. First Jamie screwed her over and now his mother.

"Money you told me I didn't need to worry about. Money you spent because you were hell-bent on keeping a part of Jamie alive. Well, I don't want his child and I sure as hell don't want his DNA anywhere near me."

Lydia stood so fast her chair fell. "Get out! I want you gone from here, from the house, from our lives. You have twenty-four hours to pack up and get out before we change the locks. And we'll be there watching you, so don't even think about taking anything you didn't bring into that house. And if you besmirch my son's name in this town or anywhere else we'll sue you until you beg to take it all back."

Hannah watched the spittle flying from Lydia's mouth and realized Freya was right—the messenger always got shot.

She was jobless, homeless and stony-broke, but unlike Lydia, she'd let go of the pretense that was Jamie. It felt like freedom.

CHAPTER FORTY-THREE

HANNAH WAS WEARING one of Mac's blue work shirts while she recovered their clothes, which had formed a Hansel and Gretel trail between the kitchen and his bedroom. All except her jeans, which seemed to have vanished. When she returned to the bedroom she saw that Mac was sitting on them.

She held out her hand. "They won't fit you."

"Stay." His tone was identical to the one he used with the dogs and his eyes immediately widened in horror. "Sorry. What I mean is there's no need to rush off."

After the meeting with Jamie's parents, she'd driven to Baile Na and let herself into the cottage saying, "I'm not here to talk." Mac had let her lead the play. Later, he'd fed her, then sat on the sofa with her and they'd watched Monty Python movies until she'd fallen asleep.

"I can't stay," she said.

"Why not? Daisy and Ozzie would be in seventh heaven." He shot her a smile. "So would I."

She tried tugging her jeans out from under his bulk. "You know why."

"I don't know why," he said, and this time there was no hint of flirting. "But I'd like to." He passed her the jeans. "I'll make coffee."

By the time Hannah had finished getting dressed her latte was on the kitchen table and the rising sun was casting pearly pink fingers across the sky. The bleating of sheep competed with the piercing squeaks of a large flock of green budgies and it occurred to her that the farming day had likely started half an hour earlier.

"I don't want to hold you up," she said, but it was more about her than him.

"There's nothing needs doing that can't wait." He leaned against the kitchen sink. "What happened yesterday that made you need to get out of your head again?"

She flinched, torn that she'd used him a second time but glad as well. "Sorry."

He shook his head. "I'm an adult too, Hannah. I can say no, but I didn't want to. I think it's fair to say we have different reasons for wanting to have sex with each other, but the outcome's pretty much the same. That moment when nothing exists but pure sensation."

She gave a weak smile. "Thanks for understanding."

His ears pinked and he glanced at his feet before meeting her gaze. "I really like you, Hannah, and I enjoy your company in and out of bed, but I also know you're not in a headspace to deal with a relationship. I should probably heed those warning signs instead of tumbling into bed with you. But all that aside, as a friend I'm worried about you."

She opened her mouth to tell him that he didn't need to worry and shut it. Apart from Declan, who did she currently have in her life who cared for her?

Freya. And that was all too complicated to touch right now.

She pulled out a chair and sat. "Yesterday I learned that the prick died broke, the McMasters own the house we were living in and I owe them money for legal fees and IVF consultations. As I'm no longer going to have their grandchild, and I told them things about their son no parent ever wants to hear, I'm soon to be homeless." She checked her watch. "In fact I should probably go and pack my clothes before they change the locks."

Mac stared at her open-mouthed.

She threw up her hands. "I know. In a previous life I obviously pissed off someone big and powerful."

"Surely the McMasters won't chase you for the money? It would cost almost as much to try."

She shrugged. "I want to pay them back so I'm shot of the association. Even if they weren't kicking me out, I'd move. I can't cope with Lydia's denial and I want to be far away from everything that reminds me of him."

"Does that mean you're going back to Perth?"

She fiddled with the edge of a placemat. "Maybe. But I need some money behind me first so I can afford the bond and four weeks rent."

Mac looked into his coffee as if it was a font of wisdom. "There's a vacant cottage on the farm. The one that will be Georgie's. You could stay there until you find your feet."

For a moment the idea of hiding from Garringarup pulled so strongly she opened her mouth to say yes. Instead, she said, "Thank you."

"You're welcome."

"But it's not a good idea, is it?"

"Probably not." He tilted his head. "Why exactly?"

She took in his sleep-rumpled hair, his golden day-old stubble, the kindness etched around his eyes and mouth—his complete lack of guile. She remembered his generosity in bed and his solicitousness of her afterwards.

"Because there's a risk I'll keep using you, and the last thing you deserve is to be caught up in my mess. I mean, you're lovely—or at least I'm pretty sure you are—but I got it so wrong with Jamie I don't trust myself to trust anyone anymore. That would kill anything with us before it even started."

He drained his coffee. "I get that everything you believed about McMaster's been turned on its head. I get you're reeling, but I think you were incredibly unlucky. Most people don't live secret lives, Hannah. Most of us are barely keeping up with the one we've got."

She hugged herself. "He said that to me, once."

Mac sighed. "Sorry."

"Not your fault."

"I meant it in a 'that sucks' way."

She nodded, not trusting herself to speak. More than anything she wanted to luxuriate in bed with Mac, but Jamie had used her and she refused to inflict that sort of pain on anyone. Unlike Jamie, she was checking her behavior.

Mac stared out the kitchen window. "You're probably right about us stopping having sex." He swung back to face her. "But if you need a friend, I'm here. I'm not going anywhere—I've got a farm to run."

Her throat tightened but she managed to say, "Thank you."

Mac put bread in the toaster and pulled spreads from the fridge. "What about living with your brother? Is that an option?"

"I love Dec but not Singapore."

"So what's your plan?"

"I don't have one. Any thoughts?"

He dumped plates and knives on the table along with the hot toast. "Do you have friends in Perth?"

She shook her head. "Not anymore. And when I moved to Garringarup, I put all my friendship eggs into one basket." Mac gave her a blank look. "Freya."

"I like her."

"I did too." She buttered her toast so hard the knife scraped china. "But Jamie damaged that."

"You don't have to let him. As much as you were hurt by her refusal to sign the affidavit, in a way she was looking out for you. She was trying her best."

She thought about what Freya had kept secret. "What if her best isn't good enough?"

He shrugged. "We're only human. When he died she was trying to protect you from unnecessary pain."

"And herself! She didn't want to tell Ryan either because she knew he might not believe her. It wasn't entirely altruistic."

"She tried to tell you before the wedding. And to be fair, there was a time you refused to hear a bad word against him. None of us are perfect, Hannah."

This truth stung and Freya's anguished face filled her mind. *It wasn't easy. God, nothing about this has been easy.*

She sighed as she thought about Lydia's vitriol and abuse. "The woman is always the last one to be believed. That's what I did to Freya."

"Any chance of the two of you patching things up?"

"She's been trying for months."

"Ah." Mac bit into his toast.

"What?"

"Just looking at the cold hard facts."

"Oh, yeah, and what are they?" She couldn't keep the snippiness from her tone.

"You have a brother in Singapore but you don't want to live there. You have no real connections in Perth. Well, there's Georgie, but she bolts back here as often as she can. In Garringarup, you have Freya who wants to support you if you choose to let her, as well as Ryan. And you've got me just down the road. Plus, you may be surprised who crosses sides in town once the story really gets out."

Mac's facts were uncompromising. If Hannah ran to a place where no one knew her, she'd be free of gossip and able to pretend that her time with Jamie had never existed. But she'd be alone. If she stayed in Garringarup, word would inevitably get out that she'd parted company with the McMasters and Chrissie Lancefield would never rest until she'd discovered the full story. If the McMasters fought Monique over the river house there would be no hiding it. Monique would go public without a care, because she had loved and accepted all the parts of Jamie in a way Hannah never could.

Go or stay? Both choices may sink her, but right now the decision was moot. She refused to go any further into debt by borrowing money, which meant that until she'd earned enough to leave Garringarup, she was stuck. She needed a job and she needed somewhere to live.

Her gut ached. "I need to talk to Freya."

"Good plan."

"Any chance I can take Bullet for a ride first so I can work out what to say?"

"Too easy."

"That's not what Wombat says." Mia jabbed at the page as if she could read the words.

Freya, whose concentration had been fixed on Lexie, jerked her mind back to her niece, wondering what she'd just said. "What does Wombat say?"

"Carrots!"

"Of course he does. Silly me."

Freya finished the book and tucked Mia in, dropping a kiss on her forehead. "Sleep tight."

"Now Ryan," Mia demanded.

Freya tried not to sigh. They'd been through this already. "He's at work, sweetie. He'll kiss you when he gets home."

"Sing the song."

Ryan always sang Mia a goodnight song that he'd made up, but that was his thing and Freya didn't know the words.

"Night-night, Mia, it's time to go to sleep," she sang. Mia's look of disdain matched that of a theater critic at a sub-par performance. "Tomorrow you and Ryan can teach it to me."

Freya switched on the nightlight and closed the door, knowing Mia would be up soon enough and she'd have to lie down with her until she fell asleep. The child psychologist had recommended not doing that straight up, but Freya didn't mind—she quite enjoyed the power nap.

She picked up her phone to call her mother for the nightly check-in now Vivian was back home.

The stress of Lexie's departure had played havoc with Vivian's heart and she'd spent two days in the hospital with arrhythmias and had undergone a cardioversion. With the EKG machine beeping and an IV in her arm, Vivian had said, "I sometimes wonder if it's my fault. Growing up with a diabetic mother wasn't always easy."

Freya refused to play that game—she'd been bruised by it too many times before. If she agreed with her mother—and she didn't—it would only upset Vivian. If she commented that she'd been the child hefted with the responsibility of looking after Vivian and she wasn't running away, she'd get a lecture on how Lexie had always found life more complex.

"It's not that simple, Mum," she'd said.

"Lexie was always a sensitive child. I sometimes think she never got over Doug dying. Maybe this vacation is just what she needs."

Freya had wanted to punch a hole in the wall. Instead she'd asked Vivian if she wanted anything from the gift shop.

Now her phone lit up in her hand as a text came in. *Hi. When is a good time for us to talk F2F?*

Freya blinked to clear her focus. The words stayed the same. She hadn't heard anything from Hannah since she'd stormed out, slamming the front door.

She replied immediately. *Now works if you can come to me. Ryan's out. Mia's in bed atm but no guarantees*

C U in 5

Freya appreciated that Hannah arrived quietly so as not to wake Mia. But once she was inside, everything that had happened—the regret, hatred, heartache, fractured trust and devastation—filled the room, choking them both.

"Would you like something to drink?" Freya offered.

"Tea."

"You sure? I've got wine, beer and cider."

"Just lately I've been self-medicating with wine and sex. I'm trying to cut back."

"Sex?" Freya squeaked in surprise.

Hannah's lips ghosted a smile. "Mac Downie. It was supposed to be revenge sex against Jamie, but all it did was make me realize what a lousy lover he was."

"Mac?"

"No. Jamie. He might have been exploring every kink and fetish with other people, but with me he was Mr. Missionary in the dark. Any time I suggested something different he made me feel both guilty and precious. It was like I couldn't be sullied by anything other than strictly vanilla sex."

"Maybe that was a fetish too," Freya said without thinking.

Hannah stared at her, realization crossing her face. "Oh my God! I never thought of that. I don't know if it makes me feel better or worse."

"Don't go there," Freya said quickly. "If Mac made you feel more *you*, focus on that."

"Freya!" Mia's cry rang out as it did every night, timed to the second.

"Can you make the tea, Hannah? I'll be back as soon as I can but it may take a while."

Fifteen minutes later and fighting sleep, Freya returned to find Hannah sitting on the sofa, dark shadows under her eyes and staring blankly into space.

"Sorry about that."

Hannah seemed to jerk back to the present. "No problem. When does Lexie get back from her vacation?"

Freya almost said, "Soon," but she was no longer tweaking the truth to save pain when that had backfired so violently on her. "She's not on vacation." She heard herself laugh. "Actually, she is now."

"And that makes about as much sense as ..." Hannah sighed. "I'm too tired for metaphors. Are you okay? You look kind of strung out."

The concern on Hannah's face undid Freya and she fought tears. Not even Ryan had asked her lately if she was okay. They were both too busy juggling work, Mia, her mother and trying to find her sister.

"Lexie's been in rehab in Perth. But she discharged herself and took off with a bloke she met in there. The plan was a road trip to Broome, but I've got no idea if she's arrived. She's not answering calls, texts or emails, and because she told us where she's going the police don't consider her a missing person."

"Oh God, that's ..." Hannah opened her hands as if she had no words.

"Terrifying, awful, sad, infuriating, devastating. Yeah, all of that. And really confusing for Mia."

"She's lucky to have you and Ryan."

Freya was sick of talking about herself. "Have you spoken to the McMasters?"

"Yeah."

"How did that go?"

"Oh, they loved me right up until I refused to incubate their grandchild and told them the truth about their son."

Freya's stomach dropped—she'd lived with Lydia's wrath for a long time. "What happened?"

"Lydia kicked me out of the house. Currently everything I own is in my car."

"She can't do that. It's your house!"

"Turns out Jamie didn't own the old schoolhouse; it belongs to the farm. I don't even have the right to demand his frozen sperm be dumped as I didn't pay the storage fee."

Freya struggled to take it all in. "That's ... It's so unfair."

"Fair isn't something I'm spending much time thinking about because it only does my head in." Hannah fiddled with a tear in her jeans. "I'm so angry at him, at Monique—"

"Me."

"Yeah." Hannah huffed out a breath. "Now that everything's come out, I realize Jamie put you in an impossible position too, just like he did to me. Part of me wishes you'd told me, and another part knows that if you had I wouldn't have believed you, and either way we probably would have ended up where we are."

"I'm sorry."

"I know. You've been trying to tell me that for a long time but the words seemed too easy." Hannah rubbed her face. "God, this is hard. I know I told you I didn't need you or want anything from you, but at the time I was angry and in shock."

Freya dared to hope. "And now?"

"Now, I need a job and somewhere cheap to live. But more than that, I need a friend."

The hollow ache inside Freya flattened out. "Oh, Hannah. I've missed you."

"Me too." Hannah laced her fingers. "I was so hell-bent on having a baby I didn't want to hear what you were saying, let alone believe it. It didn't help that I had Lydia in my ear. I feel like a puppet whose strings were pulled first by Jamie and then by his mother. The worst thing is I didn't even realize I had no control over my life."

Freya hugged her. "Don't be so hard on yourself. They used what you wanted most against you."

"Well, it stops now. I have to be in charge of my own life. I know I can't live here, but any suggestions?"

Freya's mind kicked into practicalities. "Lexie's place is empty and it would be a win-win. Your rent would cover her mortgage."

"Only if I get a job."

"There's a fulltime ward clerk job going at the hospital."

"I can't take Lexie's job!"

Freya grimaced. "Once she left rehab she lost her leave of absence so Natalie's hiring. It's not a perfect match for you, but—"

"It's a job for now."

"And Saturday mornings at Just Because are tricky now because of Mia, so if you want a 9:00 till 1:00 shift ...?"

"I'd love it." Hannah smiled for the first time. "Georgie has a fabulous fiber-art rabbit she may lend us. It would lift the Easter window display."

Freya barked out a tired laugh. "You noticed?" The Easter window display barely existed because she'd been busy trying to keep up with her life.

"Freya!" Mia's scream surged into the room like a bore tide.

"You've got a lot on," Hannah said. "Let me look after the displays. I can do them around any other jobs I get."

"Thank you."

As Freya stood to go to Mia, the pressure of the last weeks eased a tiny bit.

CHAPTER FORTY-FOUR

FREYA WELCOMED SATURDAY with open arms. It had been a long week juggling work and Mia without much help from Ryan, who'd been covering gaps in the roster due to an early flu season. Now, with Hannah working in Just Because, Freya planned to catch up on paperwork, but Ryan had other ideas.

"The spreadsheet can wait. A picnic is just what we need." He nuzzled her neck. "Come on, Frey. We've hardly seen each other."

The bills couldn't wait much longer, but she was softening as she always did when he kissed her. He hadn't snuggled into her like this in weeks and she could only hope it meant the counselling was helping. She murmured okay and pressed her lips to his, planning to really kiss him, when Mia hurled herself at their legs.

Ryan laughed and picked her up. "Ready for a picnic?"

Freya mentally slapped herself and adjusted her expectations. They could still have a bit of one-on-one time—Mia was pretty good at entertaining herself for half an hour.

On the drive they sang to the Wiggles, and when they pulled up at the lake Freya was surprised to see Sally and Barry's car in the parking lot.

Ryan grinned. "Fancy some waterskiing?"

The day rolled out and it wasn't that Freya didn't enjoy herself but she hardly saw Ryan. As far as Mia was concerned, Sally and Barry were strangers so the one-time Freya and Ryan attempted to get into the boat alone, her screams brought the sky down.

"We can't do it to her," Freya said. "Not until she gets to know your parents better."

The rest of the day was spent tag teaming as Mia lurched between wanting to be on the boat and wanting to be on the shore. By the time they got home it was dark and Mia had sacked out. It was nothing short of a miracle that she transferred from the car seat to her bed without waking up.

Ryan dropped onto the sofa beside Freya, his eyes lighting up at the open beer and the charcuterie board.

"I figured after a big barbecue lunch this was enough," she said.

He slung an arm around her and pulled her in. "Perfect. It was a great day."

"It's nice seeing you so relaxed."

He hadn't volunteered anything from the sessions he'd had with the counselor. Nor had he discussed his feelings around why Freya hadn't told him the real reason behind Jamie going to Perth or what had happened just prior to the wedding. She wasn't certain if this was because of the drama with Lexie, her mother's needs, Mia, their crazy work schedule, or if he was still angry with her. But now seemed a good time to ask.

"Is talking to Peter helping?"

Ryan's chest tensed underneath her. She sat up. His face was twisted, but whether in anger or bewilderment it was hard to tell. She kicked herself for raising the topic.

"It's hard," he said after a long silence. "I'm trained to look after people and I didn't notice my best mate was a fucking narcissist and a sex addict." His mouth sagged. "But mostly I hate that I didn't know enough to protect you. Peter's pointed out a few things and you were right. I did idolize Jamie. Maybe if I'd gone to boarding school or uni with him, I might have noticed stuff."

"He didn't want you to."

"That's what Peter said." Ryan was quiet awhile, staring down at their linked hands. "I hate that you didn't tell me."

Her throat tightened. "I'm sorry."

"Yeah." He made a soft huffing sound. "But now at least I understand why you didn't."

Her breath rushed out and relief filled the space. She dropped her head onto his shoulder. "Thank you."

He wrapped his arms around her and pressed a kiss into her hair. The hum of the house circled them and she lay listening to and feeling the regular lub-dub beat of his heart—a constant reassurance. A calm she hadn't experienced in weeks rolled over her like the comforting presence of a weighted blanket. Her eyes were fluttering closed when Ryan cleared his throat.

"But Jamie's not our problem, is he?" he said.

She looked at him through the fog of fatigue, uncertain where this was leading. "What do you mean?"

"Come on, Frey." He stroked her hair. "You know I want a baby."

The pool of comfort and relief she'd been soaking in drained away. Ryan hadn't mentioned babies since their chat in January and with everything they'd learned about Jamie she'd assumed it had reset their world to how it had been before the accident.

"I know when Jamie died you were grieving and you wanted to live his life for him and that's why you wanted to get married and have a baby," she said carefully. "But you don't have to do that anymore. Especially now we know his life was a lie."

Ryan shifted, forcing Freya to sit up. "I didn't want to live his life then and I sure as hell don't want to live it now, but him dying kickstarted things for me. It made me question what's important, what I want out of life. And I want a baby." He entwined his fingers with hers. "You asked for space and I've respected that. But it's time to talk about it again, especially now Mia's with us."

Dread clawed at her. "What's Mia got to do with it?"

He gave her a look that implied it was obvious. "You were worried we couldn't manage a kid, our careers, us. Mia's proved we can. We've been doing a great job for weeks."

So many thoughts crowded her brain that she didn't know which one to voice first. "We?" shot out, loud, uncensored and incredulous.

"Yeah." He smiled at her, love and adoration in his eyes. "We've always been a good team and we're acing this."

She stared at him. "Ryan, most of the first two weeks Mia was with us you weren't here."

He frowned. "That's not fair. She arrived unexpectedly and I couldn't back out of the conferences."

"Sorry, I know that." But the memories hadn't softened with time. "It's just those ten days were so awful and people so—I don't think I'll ever forget them."

Contrition crossed his face. "But it's been better since then, right? Now we're sharing everything."

Were they? "When you're here we do," she said carefully.

He sat up straighter, suddenly tense. "What does that mean?"

"Your job, the shiftwork, the callouts." Her hands opened. "You're gone a lot."

"That's nothing new."

She sighed, having anticipated his reaction. "I know it isn't. And before Mia, when you got caught up at work I missed you but I wasn't bothered by it. But now, especially when you're out at night and I'm here on my own trying to get Mia to sleep, I resent it. And I don't want to resent it. Or worse, I don't want to resent you, but there's been moments when I have."

His eyes widened. "When?"

"The night Lexie vanished. I called you at work but you were busy with a patient and you cut me off. And one part of me understands why, but the part that was worried about Lexie and Mia was furious. I can't fight the nature of your job, and I know you love it and you're great at it, but it means I'll be left holding the baby. It will put us under even more strain than we are now. I don't want to risk it. Risk us."

"I get parental leave," he said, instantly switching to fix-it mode. "And I've got long service. I could be home for months."

She knew many men wouldn't make this offer even if they had the entitlements, but what were months against years? But she didn't say it because he'd leap to the next solution. All the solutions in the world wouldn't change the fundamental problem—she didn't want a baby.

"We have Mia," she said. "Can't she be enough?"

"But Mia's not our child. She won't be with us forever."

"Neither would our kid. They grow up and leave home, Ryan."

"You know what I mean." Exasperation crept into his voice. "She's Lexie's daughter. Living with us is temporary."

Freya thought about her sister, who was yet to make contact weeks after checking herself out of the rehabilitation center. Nor had she kept her promise to send Mia a postcard. Even allowing for the slow mail delivery, enough time had passed for at least three or four to have arrived. Freya could no longer hide from the pattern of Lexie's adult life—passionately pursuing something before dropping it cold and moving on to a newer, shinier obsession. Only this time she wasn't walking away from a university course or jillarooing or every job she'd ever worked. She was walking away from her daughter.

Devastation swam through Freya and she tried not to let it sink her. "We both know Lexie hasn't even started dealing with her addiction. And if she does manage to stay dry, she still has to prove to child protection that she can cope with and care for Mia. Mia's going to be living with us for a long time, and if she does return to Lexie, we're always going to be her safe house."

Ryan was nodding. "I love Mia, Frey, I do, and I don't have a problem with any of that. I hope we can love her enough so she learns to trust in the world. But I want *our* child too. I want to be there right from the start and enjoy it all."

Fear spurted through Freya like a geyser. "I don't want to be responsible for another screwed-up human being."

Ryan didn't hide his not-this-again eye roll. "You won't be."

Why was he so confident?

"Children aren't stupid, Ryan. Even if you stepped out of your career to be the stay-at-home parent assuming all responsibility for our child, I'm still the mother. A child will demand my time, as they should and as they deserve to. But with Just Because and the family we've already got, I'm being pulled five ways. A baby will sink me. Worse than that, I can't hide resentment for twenty-three years."

Bafflement played across his face. "But you don't resent Mia, so you won't resent our child."

How could she make him understand the ominous sensation that bored into her with the intensity of a drill?

"Mia is here, Ryan. She exists. She's the innocent party in all of Lexie's and Kane's shit. We both know that as much as we love her and show her how important she is to us, she's going to crave their love more than ours. She'll blame herself for their abandonment of her and that's going to be rough. Hell, she's already having those moments even if she can't articulate them, and I'll move heaven and earth so she has a chance of knowing and trusting in unconditional love."

Right then Freya knew that every conversation they'd had about children, every time she'd sidestepped the issue out of uncertainty and fear, had been leading to this moment. As much as it terrified her, she could no longer avoid it, because giving Ryan what he wanted most meant losing herself.

"I don't want a baby, Ryan. I don't think I ever have. And I don't want to risk doing to a child what Lexie and Kane have done to Mia." She held up her hand. "And before you say I won't, you need to know that the whole time I was pregnant I was filled with dread and terrified about becoming a mother. The miscarriage was the best thing that could have happened."

The color drained from his face and he lurched off the sofa, shaking.

She reached out a hand to comfort him, but he refused to take it. "I love you so much. I love us."

His mouth tightened as if he struggled to believe her. "Then have our baby."

"As much as I want to do this for you—"

"For us, Freya. Us!"

She shook her head. "For you. I'm sorry, Ryan. Sorrier than I can say, but I can't have a child for you or I'll lose me."

The agony on his face ripped through her and regret threatened to drown her. There was a fleeting moment when her need to heal his hurt was so strong she almost said, "I'll have a baby." But the consequences of that decision roared back harder, faster, stronger, dwarfing his pain with her own. A baby was a life sentence for her and the adult it would grow to be.

His eyes pleaded with her. "So what are you saying? That this is the hill you'll sacrifice our relationship on?"

Sorrow almost made her double over. "Is it the hill you will?"

He spun around, as if movement would shed his pain. When he faced her again nothing had changed. "All I know is that I love you, Frey. I can't imagine not having you in my life."

She was fighting tears. "And I love you."

A hint of his smile—the one he only shone on her—touched his lips. "We agree on that. How do we make the rest work?"

"Can you love Mia and me without resenting us?"

He looked offended. "Of course I can!"

She kissed him in apology. "Sorry, that's the wrong question. I mean can you be content with just us? With living your dream of parenthood by being a dad to Mia?"

He rubbed his face. "I want to say yes, Freya, I really do ..."

She understood—she wanted to give him what he wanted too, but it was impossible. They sat firmly on opposing sides of an unbridgeable divide. Tears slid down her face and she wiped them on her sleeve.

"Until Jamie died, I honestly thought we were on the same page about children," she said, her voice shaky. "I should have checked in earlier. We should have talked about this sooner."

He scoffed. "You think back then it would have hurt any less? 'Cos

I can tell you now, it wouldn't. I've always imagined this house with kids running up and down the hall."

"But you would have been younger."

He jerked as if she'd struck him. "Jesus, Freya. What are you saying?"

Her heart was shredding. "There's no compromise here, Ryan. Only loss. If we stay together I'll be forever guilty that you're missing out. Your need to be a dad to your own biological kid will sit pulsing between us, sad, angry and devastating. It will slowly poison us."

"What if you change your mind in six months or next year?"

He was still in fix-it mode, grasping at straws and relying on her to find a solution.

"What if you change your mind?" she said.

He stilled for a moment as if the thought was new to him. "I don't know ..."

She saw it then—his absolute belief that he could talk her round. "I'm not going to change my mind, Ryan. Please stop hoping that I will."

He raked his hand through his hair, the action frantic and desperate. "I can't believe we've ended up here. How can we want such different things when we've always ... It makes no sense."

"I'm sorry." Her apology was rooted in every cell.

"For fuck's sake, Freya! Stop saying that."

She flinched—he'd never sworn at her. She lifted her watery gaze to his. "We're already making each other miserable."

He pulled her to him, his tears wetting her hair, her tears soaking his shirt. "I don't want to leave you."

"I don't want you to." Every beat of her heart pumped aching despair through her as she fought what she knew she had to offer him. "I love you, Ryan. I always have, but we've changed, or at least what we want in life has changed. You deserve to have what makes you happy and you can't find that with me. If you leave now, you've got a chance of meeting someone and making the family you deserve."

He was quiet for a long time and when he spoke, his voice was thick. "I love you, Freya. I want our kids. I can't even picture having them with anyone else."

She gazed up at him through a film of tears. She didn't have an answer for him, but she knew she couldn't ask him to stay and deny him his dream.

"How can you meet someone if you never leave?"

Misery scored his face. "So you honestly want us to break up?"

"No. I want you to stay. But if you do, it means you're giving up the chance to have the child you say you desperately want. Can you give up that dream without it destroying us?"

He made a wet, despairing sound and pulled away from her. "And what about Mia? I can't do this to her on top of everything else."

"Ryan," she said gently, "we'll make it work."

He looked utterly bereft. "How?"

She had no idea. "Love and respect? Surely they don't vanish just because we want different things?"

"Said no separating couple ever." But his momentary bitterness was replaced by regret. "I just wish nothing had to change."

"The accident changed everything."

He sighed and held her close, his arms gently cradling her against him. She breathed him in—his familiar scent of lingering sunshine, laundry powder and sunscreen—loving him, feeling his love pour through her. It had taken everything she had to offer him the chance to leave, but he deserved it. He was one of life's good and honorable men. But her offer wasn't entirely selfless. She hoped that by setting him free he'd find a way to stay. Find a way to be happy with her and Mia, and the wonderful life they shared.

She had no idea how long they stood there entwined, hearts beating in time, breaths synced. It was something they often did at the end of a long day—a time to connect, to be as one. A time that was just for them.

His arms tightened around her and peace flowed. With it came certainty. They would get through this. He would choose the life they had now. He would choose her and Mia.

As she raised her head to kiss him, she felt his breath deepen, his arms slacken and then his voice rumbled in her ear.

"I'm sorry, Frey."

Her heart shattered.

CHAPTER FORTY-FIVE

Freya sat in the nook off the kitchen on a chilly Saturday, sipping tea and checking her emails. Among the forest of advertising and junk, a new apiarist was inviting her to taste his infused honey—chili, espresso, salted and cacao—with a view to stocking it. Honey was a popular hamper item and a stand-alone gift and Freya didn't carry any infused honeys, so she replied, suggesting he drop into Just Because any Tuesday through Friday morning.

She automatically strained her ears for Mia, then checked herself—she was at Ryan's this weekend. After their life-defining conversation three months ago, everything had changed. He'd moved out and was now sharing Lexie's house with Hannah. He'd been true to his word about not abandoning Mia and, unless he was called out, she spent most Saturdays with him and slept over one night a week depending on his roster. At first Freya had worried Mia would be confused by their separation and by sleeping in her old house without her mother. She'd braced herself for more sleep issues, acting out and "where's Mummy?" questions, but they hadn't come.

The town was beside itself when, on top of the rumors about why

Hannah had fallen out so dramatically with the McMasters, people learned of Freya and Ryan's separation and the reason behind it.

"You better be one hundred percent sure you know what you want, because Ryan's living with Hannah," Chrissie Lancefield had said.

"They're *sharing* a house," Freya said equably.

Chrissie's brows rose. "And they both want babies, so proximity and all that. You'll only have yourself to blame if they get together. Just sayin' ..."

What Freya struggled to fathom was why her decision not to have children was taken as a personal insult by everyone who did have them. Why did it spark such moral outrage? If the tables were turned and Ryan was the one who didn't want a child, people would just accept his decision.

Tom Kroger had called Freya "a failure as a woman, completely unnatural, selfish and bitter."

"I wasn't aware my uterus carried social obligations," she'd said icily. "I'm contributing a hell of a lot more to the economy running Just Because than having a baby. And you know what, if I did have a baby, you and your kind would be first in line to judge my parenting skills while complaining about how hard it is to raise kids today. Oh, wait, you've already done that."

"It's probably a good thing you're not having kids," he said. "No child deserves what your sister did to hers."

It took monumental restraint not to punch him. Instead Freya pulled open the door with a jerk, setting the shop bell clanging. "Leave now."

"Happy to, as soon as you've rung up my gifts."

"I wouldn't take your money if you were the last man on earth. Get out and don't come back. You're officially banned."

Ryan's mother didn't come close to "doing a Lydia," but she was angry. "You're ruining his life. If you don't come to your senses soon you'll lose him to any number of women who'll have his baby in a heartbeat."

When Freya broke the news to Vivian, her mother said, "What if you wake up at forty and realize you've made a huge mistake?"

"I'm not going to do that."

"You can't know that!"

"Mum, I think I've known all my life. Well, at least since uni. When I listen to women like Hannah who talk about aching for a child, I can't even imagine what that feels like."

Vivian went quiet after that, and although they chatted as usual, she didn't broach the topic again. It was a relief to Freya, who had enough on her plate grieving her relationship with Ryan, learning how to live as a single woman, parenting Mia and running Just Because.

Three weeks later, Freya had walked in the door of Kitchener Street with a tired Mia to find Vivian in the kitchen with dinner ready to be served.

"Nana!" Mia had shrieked, excited to see her grandmother.

"Hello, chicken. Hang up your backpack and wash your hands. Then there's a surprise."

Freya had kissed her mother on the cheek. "Everything okay?"

"Everything's fine. I walked over for the exercise, and Henry's offered to pick me up after dinner so you don't have to drive me home."

"I don't mind."

"I know, but I'm here to help, not to add to your load."

Freya took in her mother's general demeanor—new clothes, styled hair, make-up, color in her cheeks. "You look good, Mum. Well, I mean."

Vivian smiled and poured two glasses of wine, pushing one towards Freya. "I am well. For the first time in months I have energy and my blood sugar is behaving itself. When I had that nasty turn after Lexie left and they zapped my heart, it did exactly what it was supposed to do. Now I have a lovely strong and regular beat. Unless anything changes, the cardiologist doesn't need to see me for another year."

"That's great!"

"It is, and now I'm back on my feet it's my turn to look after you."

"I don't need looking after, Mum."

Vivian looked unconvinced. "Support, help, looking after—let's not argue about the words. I don't know where Mia and I would be without you, and although Lexie ... Well, I'm sure she appreciates what you're doing."

The heat of familiar anger slammed into the wall of despair that was everything connected with the powerful hold addiction wielded over Lexie. "I'm doing it for Mia, Mum."

"I know and I'm both thankful and proud. What you're doing is the epitome of family and I want to be more involved. Perhaps I can pick Mia up early from day care a couple of times a week and bring her back here and cook dinner. Would that help?"

Freya wasn't sure if it was relief that the woman standing in front of her more resembled the dominant force her mother had always been, if it was Vivian's recognition of how much Freya's life had changed, or gratitude for the support, but tears stung the backs of her eyes.

She blinked rapidly and hugged her mother. "Thanks, Mum. That would be amazing."

Two months later, it *was* amazing how much difference her mother's help made to their week. Vivian took Mia to dance class on Tuesdays and Freya wasn't certain who enjoyed it more.

A whine came from the basket by her feet and Freya picked up Winston, their new puppy. Pekoe, the cat, was unimpressed by the silky-eared interloper, but the dog was an excellent distraction for Freya and Mia. Freya had always wanted a dog but Ryan hadn't been keen, so last week she and Mia had driven to the animal rescue center in Northam.

Hannah walked in through the back door, calling, "Hi, it's just me."

Freya checked the time. "Busy morning?"

"Yep and I'm starving." Hannah dropped her bag and the keys to Just Because on the table. "I thought you might feed me while we talk about Christmas in July?"

"Sounds fair." Freya rose and heated up some pea and ham soup.

"How was Ryan when he picked up Mia?" Hannah asked.

"Okay, why?"

As much as Freya was grateful for Hannah's friendship and support, she sometimes wished her friend wasn't sharing a house with Ryan because it brought him back into her life in ways that tried hard to undermine her decision.

Hannah grimaced. "He's been out of sorts ever since he heard about Winston."

"Getting a puppy is nothing like having a baby," Freya said tersely. She'd been batting away comments from the town that suggested otherwise each time she took Winston for a walk.

Hannah raised her hands. "I know. It's just I'm not sure he sees it that way."

"Is he dating anyone?" Freya asked, testing the intensity of the pain she hoped was fading. She only wished Ryan good things and if he truly wanted a chance of having a child of his own then he needed to date.

"Yes and no." Hannah pulled apart a piece of bread. "To be honest, I'm not sure he can imagine himself with anyone else. What if he changes his mind and decides he wants you more than a baby?"

In the early days, Freya had dreamed Ryan would do exactly that, but as the weeks had turned into months she knew it was most likely magical thinking. They faced an irreconcilable difference.

"I doubt he will," she said.

Hannah shrugged as if she didn't share Freya's conviction.

"But in the unlikely event that he did, I'd need to be one hundred percent sure he'd come to that conclusion from the right place, otherwise the risk would be too great."

"What do you mean?"

Although Freya was at peace with her decision about not having a child, she was only human. "Loneliness is a strong motivator."

Hannah shifted in her chair. "Lucky I have you to stop me from doing anything stupid then. So, Christmas in July?"

Freya let the veiled reference to Mac roll away untouched. She knew how hard Hannah was working to come out from under debt, throw off the long shadow of the McMasters and learn who she was and what she wanted in life. As Freya knew all too well, that didn't happen without heartache.

"I've loaded the winter bush Christmas banner onto the website and I'm pushing native flower wreaths and table runners," she said.

Hannah sat forward, her eyes lit with enthusiasm. "I could put the old pine table in the window and set it with that pretty bush green stoneware dinner setting. Then, underneath it I'll create a Christmas scene using some of Georgie's adorable bush animals. What did you think of the finger puppets she made to match Wombat Wally?"

A familiar spurt of excitement filled Freya—the one she got whenever she saw a good opportunity for Just Because. "Mia loves them. She refuses to go to sleep without wearing all of them, so if that's any indication of their appeal Georgie's onto a winner." Something about Hannah's wide smile made her say, "They were your idea, weren't they?"

"I might have suggested she make them, but she's the talent behind their utter cuteness."

"Well, you're on the money. I only stock a few books in the kids' section because they're not a big mover, but with the puppets as an add-on I sold more last week than in the previous two months. They'll sell well on the website too. Let's organize a meeting with Georgie to discuss how many sets she can commit to per month."

Freya remembered how she'd resented Hannah's ideas and display tweaks when she'd first worked in Just Because. Now she loved how they sparked her own ideas. Just Because was hers, and it always would be, but working with Hannah came with unexpected rewards that Freya appreciated.

It had taken time to find their way back into their friendship, but this new version was more mature, more equal. Both of them were living lives they'd never envisioned for themselves and that forged a strong bond as they leaned on and supported each other.

"I value everything you bring to Just Because," Freya told Hannah. "But more importantly, I value you. I couldn't do all that I do without you."

"Thank you." Hannah's cheeks pinked and then she laughed. "You're just softening me up to babysit, right?"

"Actually, I was hoping you'd come to Mia's concert. Most kids have at least six people in the audience and Ryan probably won't make it because of work. If you're there too, that makes three of us."

Hannah grinned. "Too easy!"

A week later, Freya sat in the Garringarup hall flanked by her mother and Hannah. Mia's excitement about the concert had been off the charts and Freya took her hat off to the dance and singing teachers who were backstage wrangling hyped-up children.

The world of children's concerts meant sitting through interminable performances by other people's children. Thankfully the junior children performed early in the program and Mia's class was the third number. A dozen kids ran onto the stage and haphazardly lined up. They were wearing black pants, yellow T-shirts and hats, and each had a large red-sequined V pinned to their chest.

"Oh my God, they're adorable," Hannah said.

"Thanks for sorting her costume, Mum," Freya said.

Vivian squeezed her hand. "I love a bit of glitter."

The music started and the four-year-olds lustily sang a slightly off-key version of "We're Happy Little Vegemites." Or most of them sang. One child wandered off, and another cried so was returned to her parents.

"Mia's a natural dancer," Vivian said proudly.

When one little boy twirled left instead of right and Mia grabbed him and turned him in the other direction, Freya lost her battle not to laugh.

"Shh!" Ainsley leaned forward, shooting Freya a killing look.

"Oops," Freya whispered. "I think the directionally challenged kid is her son."

Towards the end of the number a little girl sat down on the stage as if she'd had enough dancing, another took off her hat, and a little boy started bowing extravagantly before the song had finished. By the time the applause came, Freya was shaking from holding in her laughter.

She took in Mia's shining and happy face, her mother's love and Hannah's delight and savored it all. Her life might have jumped tracks, taking her on a journey to a destination she'd never anticipated, but she was surrounded by people who cared. And right now, that was enough.

CHAPTER FORTY-SIX

OZZIE BARKED in anticipation as Hannah strapped on her running shoes. They were running through the park and Hannah was instructing Ozzie to stay with her when she glimpsed Freya and Winston at obedience class. A bloke Hannah didn't recognize was talking to Freya, but she knew what the lean of his body and the tilt of his head meant. She'd bet her bottom dollar he was interested, but Freya's body language gave nothing away.

Life with Ryan at Lexie's place—they'd dubbed it the house of broken dreams—had settled into a mostly companiable pattern. Hannah had expected Ryan to be as furious with Freya as she'd been with Jamie when the extent of his betrayal had come out, and there were certainly times when Ryan chopped a lot of wood. But whether it was his honorable streak, or he was trying to respect Hannah and Freya's friendship, or something else entirely, he never badmouthed Freya to her and she appreciated it.

The nights Ryan was home she watched him half-heartedly swiping on Hinge as if he knew the only way to move forward was to meet someone, yet at the same time he was resisting it.

The other night he'd stomped through the door incandescent with rage. His mother had set him up with the daughter of one of her friends without telling him.

"Maybe you need to adjust to being single for a while before you start dating again," Hannah had suggested. "It's not like you have a fertility cliff."

He glared at her. "I don't want to be a first-time father at fifty, thanks very much."

"Great. You have thirteen years to meet someone."

He'd grunted, then gone outside and chopped more wood.

It broke Hannah's heart that her dear friends had found themselves at this impasse, and her first reaction had been shock and disbelief that Freya was prepared to risk the love of her life. But when Freya had swiped away tears while saying that contraception might have given her a choice about motherhood but that didn't make the choice easy, Hannah got a clear view of the dilemma Freya had wrestled with for months. She realized then how brave her friend was to stand up against everyone's expectations of her and do what she believed she needed to do to live life her way, even when it came with devastating consequences.

Did Hannah know herself that well?

She knew she wasn't burdened by the same freedom of choice as Freya. She wanted kids; she always had. Her issue was knowing what else she wanted in life alongside kids. Before she'd met Jamie she'd been aimless and so she'd invested in him and his business.

And look where that landed you.

She breathed through the complex anger and desolation that always rolled in when she let herself think about Jamie. It no longer flattened her though, and she took that as a sign of healing.

She'd spent every day of the last few months focused on reclaiming her life. Her job at the hospital was paying her bills and she'd already been promoted, but she was determined that, unlike her call-center job and the admin work she'd done for Jamie, the hospital job wasn't a long-term proposition. She was done spinning her wheels in jobs she endured rather than enjoyed, and she'd drawn up a budget with a target goal that gave the job an end date.

The saving grace was her time at Just Because. It flexed her sales and marketing skills and nurtured her creative side. For the first time in her adult life she'd glimpsed a career that would invigorate her.

Six kilometers later and panting hard, Hannah was back at the house. She dropped into a kitchen chair and sucked down water, watching as Ryan loaded a cooler with a delicious array of food.

"Who's the picnic for?" she asked as soon as she got her breath back. Maybe the woman in Northam he'd been chatting to on Hinge this week had agreed to meet.

"I'm taking Freya and Mia to the lookout."

"Is that a good idea?"

"My mother doesn't think so, but it's not up to her," he said curtly. "Or you."

"Okay." She raised her hands and backed out of the kitchen, heading to the shower.

Later, when she stepped out and was reaching for her towel, she heard the doorbell. "Ryan!" she yelled, hoping he was still home.

The doorbell pealed again.

Sighing, Hannah pulled on her light cotton dressing gown and headed to the door, dripping water as she went. The frosted glass made it difficult to see who was on the other side.

When she opened it, she unexpectedly came face to chest with Mac. Of course it was Mac—she was barely dressed. A wave of embarrassment rolled across her damp skin, which was ridiculous because he'd seen her naked. Twice.

She hadn't seen much of him since they'd decided to be friends. It wasn't that she was avoiding him per se. She'd been very adult and had used her open invitation to ride at Baile Na, but only when Georgie mentioned Mac was off the farm at sheep sales, on supply runs or at an ag conference in Perth. Okay, she was avoiding him. The 180-degree turn from friends with benefits to friends came with a combination of embarrassment, relief and regret that was too uncomfortable to face. But mostly she'd been busy working and supporting Freya and Ryan.

Mac texted at least once a week, although deciphering the messages required the skills of a codebreaker. He also called her every couple of weeks, but those conversations were stilted and brief. It made her wonder how they'd managed both easy and intensely difficult conversations in person. These days she talked to Georgie more often than to Mac, but here he was standing on her doorstep. His hands nervously fingered the brim of his hat, just as they had the first time they'd met.

"What are you doing here?" she said. She'd been shooting for breezy but it came out accusatory.

"Sorry. Georgie said I should have messaged, but me and texts ..." His mouth curved into his endearing shy smile. "Anyway ... you're looking good."

She rolled her eyes. "I'm dripping wet with sopping hair."

He grinned then, his eyes crinkling in sun-squint lines. "Like I said ..."

This time a different sort of heat rocked through her, making her even more aware of her naked and now tingling body under the light cotton. She tugged the sash tighter as if that was enough to stall her reaction and was casting around for something to say to change the subject when he spoke.

"I wondered if you wanted to go for a ride—a horse ride," he amended quickly, pointing to the horse trailer parked on the street.

"You've driven Bullet and Bix to me?" she asked incredulously.

"Is that okay?"

Without thinking, she threw her arms around his neck. "It's the nicest thing anyone's done for me in a long time."

He laughed but leaned away from her.

"Oh God, I'm making you all wet. Sorry."

This time his face was strained and he cleared his throat. "How about you put on your riding gear?"

• • •

They rode along a section of the rail trail before cutting down to the river to give the horses a drink. Hannah sat in the dust under the shade of a peppermint gum and watched the sun dance across the water, making the stones glitter orange and gold. She shocked herself by almost asking Mac if the recent rains were too early or just in time for wheat germination.

"I've missed this," she said as Bullet nuzzled her, hoping for an apple.

"Me too." But Mac's face clearly said he'd missed her.

She didn't know what to do with that so she stuck to horse-riding. "This sort of riding's tame compared to tearing across the paddocks."

"You know you're welcome at Baile Na any time."

"I know."

"But you don't come when I'm home."

She picked up a gum leaf and shredded it, trying to steady her agitation at being this close to Mac without touching him. Wondering why she'd agreed to being friends, but knowing it was the only sensible option.

"Texting's easier."

He groaned. "For some."

She laughed. "Safer then."

He gave her that smile—one that managed to combine shyness with a solid self-belief. "I'm a farmer, Hannah. I play the long game every day."

"Sex isn't the issue. We both know we're good at that."

He joined her in shredding leaves. "You talking about the trust thing?"

She nodded and he opened his phone and handed it to her.

"What?" she said.

"Look through it. Messages, emails, browser history, whatever you like."

She handed it straight back. "Jamie had five phones and they're the ones I know about. Showing me one isn't enough."

"Problem is, I don't own any others." He stared at the dirt for a bit. "Ask me anything. I'll happily tell you."

She remembered what he'd told her about Chelsea and his grief journey, but then Jamie's voice chimed in, telling his sob story about Monique's abandonment of him. *Lies, all lies.*

"You could tell me anything and I have no proof it's true," she said.

"Fact-check it with Mum and Dad."

Her heart wobbled at his generous offers, but then the protective voice in her head kicked in. "They can only tell me what they know about you. The McMasters were clueless about Jamie living three lives."

"True," Mac said thoughtfully. "But he also split his time between Perth and Garringarup, giving him plenty of unsupervised periods to play up. Whereas my numb ass hasn't left the tractor seat in days. I have, however, listened to current affairs and ag podcasts and two audiobooks."

"What were they?"

He named a current bestseller and *The Iliad.* "Mum studied classics at uni and she's been at me for ages to read it. I have to say, those Greeks tell a bloody good yarn."

"Ah, but is listening to a book really reading?" she teased.

"Definitely reading. But my point is, my mind might have left the farm but the rest of me hasn't." He gave a wry smile. "And I can tell you all the stuff Mum and Dad don't know about me and you can fact-check it with Dan."

"What about Georgie?"

"Nah. She was too young when I lost my virginity on an end-of-season footy trip, but Dan was there."

"Really? Your brother was there when you lost your virginity?" she deadpanned.

Mac's ears glowed red. "Not there there, but yeah. In Bali." He pressed his hands on his thighs, leaving red-dust prints on his pants. "I get that trust takes time and I can't rush it. All I'm trying to say is I'm happy to be an open book. Well, except for around birthdays and

Christmas. My limited experience tells me that women want presents to be a surprise and they get seriously ticked off if you tell them what it is and don't wrap it."

She laughed, then caught his look and sobered.

"When Chelsea died, I lost the life I'd dreamed about with her," he said quietly.

It wasn't the first time he'd mentioned his dreams with Chelsea, but this time something about the way he said the words made Hannah pay better attention.

"We'd been dating for a couple of years, her flying in and out of Baile Na, me on the farm daydreaming about our lives in five years' time—kids, farm, her still flying." He glanced at Hannah, regret deep in the brackets around his mouth, before turning back to stare at the river. "To be honest, I pictured her flying less than the punishing hours she was doing. At her funeral, a pilot mate of hers echoed what everyone else was saying about how bloody tragic it was, but then he said, 'Especially as she'd just been offered the Rex job out of Brisbane'."

Hannah hugged her knees as the implication sank in. "Brisbane's a very long way from here."

"Yeah. And she hadn't told me she'd gotten the job. She hadn't even told me she'd applied."

"Ouch."

"Ouch is the tame version. It left me with more questions than answers. Had she been planning on breaking up with me? Did she think we could make it work long-distance or was she going to suggest I give up the farm and follow her to Queensland? For a while, it drove me nuts that I couldn't ask her."

"I know all about that."

"I know you do." He sighed. "Thing is, Hannah, even if we could ask them why they did what they did, I'm not sure hearing their replies would help much. McMaster would flat out lie to you, and Chelsea—well, plan or no plan, my dream had already died with her."

"But don't you hate that she lied by omission?"

He shrugged. "Maybe she'd tried to tell me and I didn't want to hear. Maybe our dreams were different right from the start."

Hannah thought about Freya and Ryan and sadness rolled over her. Then the protective voice roared back. "Isn't that incredibly naive of you?"

"I don't think so." He shredded more leaves. "I know I'm further along the grief journey and my one unanswered question is nothing compared to what you've been through, but if I don't have trust then the only thing left is a long and lonely road. I've been living that one for long enough.' He turned to look at her again. "What I have learned is that even when two people love each other, relationships are never simple. They're complicated as hell."

"You won't get an argument from me."

"The other thing I've learned is you have to keep talking to each other about your hopes and dreams. What you want out of life—in one year, two years, five years—so you don't suddenly wake up one morning like Freya and Ryan and wonder how the hell you got there."

"Tell me your hopes and dreams then?" The question was supposed to be flippant—a mood lightener to stall her sadness about Freya and Ryan—but she realized she really wanted to know.

He ducked his head the way he did sometimes and then his mouth tweaked up in a sheepish smile. "Pretty much what every bloke on *Farmer Wants a Wife* says: love, a best friend, a family."

He suddenly looked serious. "The farm's the tricky thing for my partner's career. Me and the farm are a package deal; it means we can't relocate. Career-wise for her, there's not a lot of flexibility outside of what's on offer in the district. I get that's one-sided, but it is what it is, so not a lot of wriggle room."

"I guess it depends on her career. So much has changed since the pandemic that these days all sorts of careers work remotely."

"I hadn't thought of that."

"Maybe you should add 'willing to upgrade internet' to your Hinge profile."

Surprise crossed his face. "How do you know I have a dating profile?"

Her cheeks burned. Why the hell had she said that? "Um, I might have accidentally seen it when I was helping Ryan get his set up."

He laughed then, his entire body consumed by delight. "And my profile would have immediately popped up as a match for a heterosexual bloke seeking a woman to be the mother of his child."

Her embarrassment at letting the secret slip suddenly got tangled up with a warm buzz that he was happy. "You're enjoying this, aren't you?"

He nudged her gently with his shoulder. "Hell, yeah. It's an ego boost for sure."

"Dream on."

"Nah, dreaming got me into trouble last time."

He pulled her to her feet and helped her mount Bullet. As they headed back along the trail he said, "Where do you see yourself in five years?"

"You interviewing me?"

"Well, there's a vacant position in my life I'd love to fill."

"Still my beating heart."

"But seriously, Hannah. Last time we really talked you were in survival mode. But you're more than surviving now."

"Not sure a psychologist would agree."

"You have a place to live, a job and a budget. That sounds like responsible citizen territory to me."

Mac's words brought into focus yet another hard lesson Hannah had learned about herself. She'd always thought Jamie was supportive of her, but since she'd been forced to question everything about him she'd realized he'd deliberately moved her away from Perth so he'd become her entire world. With that came control. His constant "There's no rush to decide what you want to do" combined with "What would I do without you?" had kept her working for him. He'd never initiated a conversation asking her what she was interested in doing, and she'd wanted a child so badly that she'd delayed making a decision about her career, telling herself that she was an important part of their business when really she was just the bookkeeper.

"I've realized I'm good at selling things," she said.

"I thought you already knew that. My wallet knew it the first time we met."

She laughed. "I only sold you things you needed. But I don't mean sales on their own; I love styling things and matching people with products."

"Like finger puppets?"

"Georgie told you?"

"Sure. We talk about everything."

"She's really talented."

"She is. I'm not sure a fine arts major was such a great idea though. It's drained some of her joy. I hate she's given up painting."

Hannah thought about the large canvas hanging on Mac's wall and remembered Georgie's declaration that there was more wrong with it than there was right. How Hannah had disagreed.

"Would you consider selling her painting?"

"No!" The emphatic decision was immediately followed by, "Why? Do you think you could sell it?"

"Possibly. A chunk of change may be the thing that silences her tutor's negative comments." Ideas started popping. "Or I could use it to gauge interest and if there was enough, perhaps she may consider a limited print run."

"How would you gauge interest?"

She grinned at him. "How do you think?"

He grinned back. "I'll take a high-res photo of it tonight."

"We better talk to Georgie about it first," Hannah said, "but I reckon I can convince her."

They'd arrived back at the reserve and the horse trailer when she added, "I could gauge interest with some of your photos too if you like."

He stowed the saddles. "Photography's like my music. It's relaxation. A hobby."

"Doesn't mean it can't be a side hustle. Some of them are really good."

His blue eyes sparkled with pride and humility—a combination she now recognized as quintessentially Mac. "In that case, you better write up a business proposal and present it to Georgie and me."

She laughed then realized he was serious. Excitement bubbled in her gut. "Okay. But it may take a few weeks. I'll have to do some research on pricing, commission, what's hot at the moment, stuff like that. And discuss it with Freya to check there's no conflict of interest. She doesn't stock art so it's probably not an issue, but I don't want to undo everything we've spent months rebuilding."

"No hurry. Like I said, you always know where to find me."

With the horses loaded and the ramp secured, Mac jangled his keys. "I better get these two home. Thanks for the company, Hannah."

"Thanks for thinking of me. Do you want a coffee before heading back?"

"Sorry. I can't leave the horses."

"Oh, right. Of course." An unexpected stab of disappointment caught her under her ribs. "Maybe—"

Her phone rang and she pulled it out of her pocket—a video call. It took a moment for the pixels to focus and reveal Georgie's face.

"Hey, Hannah."

"Hi, Georgie. How are things?"

But Georgie was looking beyond her. "Is that our float?"

Before Hannah could reply Mac was leaning over her shoulder. "Hey, sis."

Georgie grinned at them. "Oh my God! You actually did it."

"Did what?" Hannah asked.

"I've been telling him for weeks to ask you out—"

"This isn't a date," Hannah and Mac said in unison.

Georgie laughed. "Aww, look how cute you both are, blushing and pretending you just want to be friends.'

A pained look crossed Mac's face. "Shut up, George."

"He's pretty shy, Hannah. If you ever want to advance beyond holding hands you may have to take the lead."

"She did that weeks ago," Mac said.

As Georgie squealed, Hannah spun around, spluttering indignation, but Mac's eyes danced with fun.

"I didn't think you'd want me to lie," he said.

"Surely you know the difference between what stays a secret and what doesn't?"

His teasing faded. "That's the thing, Hannah. Everyone has a different interpretation."

An odd feeling washed through her. She thought of all the secrets Jamie had kept. Freya's pleas for understanding that she'd only kept a secret to protect Hannah. How it made no difference if a secret was kept for good reasons or bad—it always inflicted damage and pain.

"Like I tried to say before," Mac continued, "after everything you've been through I think I need to be a totally open book so there's a chance you'll trust me."

She thought how tritely she'd dismissed his earlier offer to search his phone, to quiz his family, and realized he'd just actively demonstrated his intent. The voice in her head urging caution dropped a notch in volume and her heart flipped.

"You realize Georgie's going to tease you mercilessly that you didn't initiate things?" she said.

"No worries." He grinned. "I've got plenty of dirt on her."

"So, you're just FWB?" Georgie sounded disappointed. "I hoped you were dating."

"Not even FWB, mate," Mac said. "Just friends. Right, Hannah?"

"Hang on a sec, Georgie." Hannah muted then lowered her phone. "Should we try dating?" she asked cautiously.

Mac looked momentarily stunned, then happy, then wariness moved in. "The thing is, Hannah, I'm thirty-three and I'm ready to settle down. I really like you but I don't want to dick around. I'm all in for exclusive and committed dating with a view to a long future. I hear your hesitation and I respect it. But for me—and no pressure if you're not one hundred percent ready to date—I'd rather you wait until you are instead of jumping early and risking it all going to hell."

"So this is practical romance?" She heard the sarcasm in her voice and regretted it. All Mac had done was state what he wanted and at the same time acknowledge that he might be ahead of her. Her words had shot out on the back of bubbling panic, relief, fear and something that possibly resembled happiness.

And what did waiting mean? Did she care? Was it even a choice or was it masquerading as pressure?

"How long will you wait?" she asked.

He took his time considering his answer. "I reckon by this time next year you're gonna know for sure if you want to jump all in or if you don't. And if you don't, then I'll put real effort into Hinge."

A year? All thoughts of pressure drained away. She didn't want to cry—she really didn't—but a tear slipped out anyway.

She sucked in a fortifying breath. "You asked me about my five-year plan." He nodded. "You know I want to start a business, but I also want an equal partner, marriage and kids."

"How many kids?"

"Two and then assess. You?"

"I thought three, but that's probably because I grew up as one of three. I'm not welded to it. What I want most is to enjoy being a dad and not lose my marriage in the process."

This conversation was so far removed from any she'd shared with Jamie that it was unrecognizable. Even so she swallowed, thinking about what she needed to say next and wondering if it was the first hurdle they wouldn't clear.

"I understand that if we survive dating—"

"Survive?" His brows shot up. "What about enjoy?"

She was suddenly hot and uncomfortable. "Okay, poor choice of word. I've never had this sort of conversation before dating someone. I've always just fallen into it."

"Me too." He rocked back on his heels. "But I'm hoping there's something in this practical romance."

She cleared her throat. "What I'm trying to say is, if after dating for long enough so you know that I'm clean but not tidy and I get irritable when I'm hungry, and I've had enough time to discover your socks always fall just short of the laundry basket and you play the piano so loudly sometimes that I can't think, and those things haven't killed us, then commitment means me living at Baile Na. But, Mac, I can't promise you I'll ever be as excited about sheep and wheat and canola as you are."

He grinned, his eyes bright. "Wow, you actually know I grow canola. I may be in with a chance."

"I'm serious!"

"Fair enough." The twinkle faded. "I think the important thing is that we respect each other's careers. Besides, the farm has a way of getting under your skin." When she looked skeptical he added, "Keep riding out there with me and get to know her. That's enough for now."

Hannah's anxiety and panic receded enough to allow a new shoot of longing to push through. Embracing this process of being honest about what she wanted instead of assimilating into his life like she'd done with Jamie, she blurted, "I also want a best friend."

"Um ..." He looked a bit taken aback by her vehemence. "Between Georgie and Freya, you've got solid options. Why not both?"

"I meant you." And she realized she'd jumped right in. "Would you like to audition for the role?"

He rubbed the back of his neck, clearly bewildered. "What do you think I've been doing since I met you? What I've been trying to show you for months? Today."

She thought about his unintelligible texts and the weather-focused phone calls and tried not to laugh as joy rippled through her.

She stepped in close and wrapped her arms around his waist. "The thing is, you do it so much better in person."

He gazed down at her. "Even when I tell you to sit?"

She laughed. "You only do that when you're stressed."

"And you call me on it."

"I do." She rested her hand gently on his chest, over his heart. "I think you're one of the kindest and most modest blokes I've ever met. You've let me sob all over you and have sex with you. You've listened to me, but you've also called me on things when it was important. You've seen me at my absolute worst and, despite all of that, here you are again."

He tucked some hair behind her ear. "Don't make me a saint, Hannah. It's not all selflessness."

"I know. But even if you didn't fancy the hell out of me and we hadn't tumbled into bed, you would have been kind. I see that in the love and regard you have for your parents and the bond you have with Georgie. I even see it in the way you deal with the sheep."

He grinned. "My girls are pretty special."

"So here's my question. Will you go round with me and see where it leads?"

"In a circle by the sounds of it."

"I'm risking my heart and you're making fun of me?" But even the teasing was reassuring. She never wanted to be put on a pedestal again.

"My bad." Mac pulled her closer until his body heat merged with hers. "I would love to officially date you."

Last time she'd dated she'd been blinded by rose-colored glasses and giddy with dreams of a future filled with glitter and rainbows. This time she knew the road ahead would be a series of blind curves loaded with negotiation and compromise. But she also knew it was paved with shared hopes and respect, two things she'd never had before. It bolstered her battered trust and she stepped away from her past and into her future.

She rose on her toes, but he'd already dropped his head towards hers, meeting her halfway. She took it as a sign and kissed him.

ACKNOWLEDGMENTS

This novel was written on Wadawurrung and Eastern Maar land. I pay my respects to the First Nation Peoples of this land as custodians of learning, literacy, knowledge and story.

It takes a village to write a book, especially when I had the "brilliant" idea to set it in Western Australia after a terrific vacation there. It never occurred to me that this would cause me problems. My first hurdle came with the very different flora from Victoria so I joined the York Avon Valley Facebook gardening group. They kindly answered my questions such as "what flowers in August?" and "does this plant grow there?" Writing mate Rachael Johns was my go-to person for WA expressions such as "over east" and "bottle-o," and for details about the Wheatbelt.

Thank you Dr. Victoria Francis, forensic pathologist, for answering my questions about protocols for families visiting loved ones at the Victorian Institute of Forensic Medicine. I extrapolated it across to WA so any mistakes are mine. Thanks to Marilyn Townsend for talking me through the role of the radiographer in the process of conducting a pregnancy ultrasound, and to Jodie Townsend for putting me in contact with her.

Claire Dadd, a St John WA volunteer, kindly explained the management structure of the WA ambulance service and answered my many questions so I could accurately depict Ryan's job. Thank you! The information was pure gold.

Once again fellow author Penelope Janu explained some of the legalese I didn't understand as I read Western Australia's Human

Reproductive Technologies Act. She guided me through how applications are made to the Supreme Court and the laws around inheritance. I am so appreciative of her help. Gayle Narita took the time to answer all my questions about cataract surgery, from the cost to the post-op treatment; and Heather Frizzell of Merrylegs Art demonstrated how she makes her adorable fiber-art animals so I could describe Georgie's artwork.

During the write, I drew on my own personal IVF experiences and recalled the difficult ethical decisions we were required to make around frozen embryos knowing the law can always change and the impact that could have on ourselves and a child two decades on.

Many thanks to Rachael Donovan for believing in me and talking me off a ledge during the first draft of this novel that fought me every inch of the write. Thanks also to Nicola O'Shea and Annabel Blay for their wise counsel in what were very challenging structural edits, not helped along by a bad dose of the flu. We got there!

Thanks to Norma Blake for reading the North American version and checking for missed or incorrect quotation marks—it's the opposite of how we do it in Australia. This time we didn't change as much Aussie language so I would be interested if you found anything truly confusing. Team Lowe continues to support me in getting this book into your hands. Thanks to Barton for the amazing cover, all the banners, slideshows and website maintenance. Thanks to Sandon for always being happy to brainstorm book ideas and plot problems, and to Gabi for reading the books so enthusiastically. And last but not least, thanks to Norm for the meals, the laundry, being the driver on research trips and always being in my corner.

And a HUGE thanks to you, dear reader, for spending your precious time reading *The Accident*. The choice of books is enormous, and the book budget limited, so I appreciate it very much. I love meeting you on book tours, Facebook, Instagram, TikTok and email. Please stay in touch; your enthusiasm keeps me writing.

ABOUT THE AUTHOR

FIONA LOWE has been a midwife, a sexual health counsellor and a family support worker; an ideal career for an author who writes novels about family and relationships. She spent her early years in Papua New Guinea where, without television, reading was the entertainment and it set up a lifelong love of books.

Authentically Australian, her stories are often triggered by a secret or a mystery, and explore the themes of family, community and second chances. Described as gripping, thought-provoking, heart-warming and ultimately uplifting, Lowe's books have been praised for their emotional depth. She is the recipient of the prestigious USA RITA® award and two Australian RuBY awards. When she's not writing stories, she's a distracted wife, mother of two "ginger" sons, a volunteer in her community, guardian of eighty rose bushes, a slave to a cat, and is often found collapsed on the couch with wine. You can find her at her website, fionalowe.com, and on Facebook, TikTok, Instagram and Goodreads.

BOOK CLUB QUESTIONS

*Contraception allows women to control their fertility but does society? How much have women really gained in regard to choosing to be mothers or choosing to remain child-free? (You may want to look up former Australian Prime Minister Julia Gillard's misogyny speech.)

*Freya talks about the "burden of choice' around the decision of having a child. Does this choice make it easier or harder for women?

*The desire for a child can be so strong that some people will go to great lengths to have one. Discuss the rights of the child in regards to donor eggs and donor sperm.

*Anyone not intimate with assisted human reproduction may think of it as an easy solution to a problem, but like all technology it comes with its own sets of positives and negatives and the law is constantly struggling to catch up. Posthumous sperm retrieval remains contentious. In the novel, Freya was the only person to defend Jamie's rights. Why do you think other people chose to ignore them?

*Why is it that total strangers feel they can touch pregnant women's bellies without permission?

*Compared to fifty years ago, motherhood today comes with incredible societal expectations. Would you agree that society judges a woman's parenting far more harshly than a man's? If yes, why do you think this is?

*In society, women who choose to be childfree are frequently labelled as selfish and yet many are also caring for family members or others in the community, which is the antithesis of selfish. Why do you think this belief exists?

*Jamie's storyline was drawn from real life, such as true stories of people who have led secret lives for years, their spouses having no idea until after their deaths. How hard do you think it is to reconcile the person they knew with the secret life? Does it destroy the memory and the life they shared with them?

*Addiction is a disease that impacts on families in many difficult ways including relationships, finances and safety. In the novel, Lexie's illness changes Freya's life. Discuss the ways each family member may struggle with a loved-one's addiction.

*In marriage/lifelong partnerships you and your partner become one emotional unit, both receptive and responsive to the other. It can be easy to forget you are still an individual within and outside your relationship, so where does one draw the line between compromise and self-sacrifice?